Crochet Carnage

Copyright © 2025 by Patti Petrone Miller
All rights reserved.

No part of this publication may be reproduced, stored in a retrieval system, or transmitted in any form or by any means—electronic, mechanical, photocopying, recording, or otherwise—without the prior written permission of the author, except in the case of brief quotations embodied in reviews, articles, or scholarly analysis.

This is a work of fiction. Names, characters, places, and incidents are either the product of the author's imagination or used fictitiously. Any resemblance to actual persons, living or dead, events, or locales is entirely coincidental.

Publisher: AP Miller Productions
ISBN:
Cover Design by: TMT BOOK COVER DESIGNS

Printed in the United States of America

Patti Petrone Miller

Social Media Links
https://www.facebook.com/pattipetronemiller/
https://www.facebook.com/pattipetronemillerexecutiveproducer/
https://www.facebook.com/halloweenismyfavoriteholiday/
https://www.pinterest.com/pattipetmiller/
htps://www.threads.net/@pattipetronemiller
Website and Blog
https://pattipetronemillerexecutiveproducer.wordpress.com/2024/09/22/a-comprehensive-guide-to-crystals-history-magic-and-tinctures/

Crochet Carnage

Authors Book List

Accidental Vows
A Very Merry Krampus Christmas
A Devil's Bargain
The Devilf of London
Sin Takes A Holiday
Barking Up The Wrong Bakery, Thankgiving
Barking Up The Wrong Bakery, Christmas
Best Served Dead
Bewitching Charms
Christmas at Hollybrook Inn
Christmas on Peppermit Lane
Cabinet of Curiosities
Krampus
Hex and the City
Love in Stitches
Pies and Perps
Spectres and Souffles
Mamma Mia It's Murder
Once Upon A Christmas
The Fatman
The Frosted Felony
The Purr-fect Suspect
The Boogeyman
The Gingerdead Men
Vikings Enchantress
Welcome to Scarecrow Hollow
The Pendleton Witches
Christmas In Pine Haven
Love in the Stacks
Once Upon A Christmas
Frosted Felony
Truth or Dare
Before the Fire
Heart of the Beast
Savage Bloodline
The Secret Ingredient, Mad Batter Bakery Mysteries Prequel

Patti Petrone Miller

Drive By Pies, Mad Batter Bakery Mysteries book 1
Venom in Vanilla, The Sundae of Secrets Series
A Scoop of Murder
Blood Moon Justice
Hot Flashes and Homicide

Crochet Carnage

For all my puppies

Crochet Carnage

by Patti Petrone Miller

Crochet Carnage

Chapter 1
A Stitch in Time

Julie Sommers woke to the familiar weight of Tessa, her miniature dachshund, pressed against her side and the less subtle pressure of Hildi, her orange tabby, sprawled across her chest. She blinked against the early morning light filtering through the curtains of her bedroom window, momentarily disoriented until she remembered what day it was.

"First day of autumn," she murmured, gently relocating Hildi to a less suffocating position. The cat responded with an indignant meow before hopping off the bed altogether, tail swishing in mild protest.

Julie's second-floor apartment above Yarn Haven—her pride and joy—was snug but comfortable, with sloped ceilings and windows that offered a picturesque view of Meadowgrove's Main Street. The town was just beginning to stir beneath a canopy of maple trees whose leaves were hinting at the impending riot of orange and crimson that made this corner of New England famous.

Three years ago, she'd left behind a high-pressure marketing job in Boston, along with a fiancé who'd been more married to his corporate ambitions than interested in building a life with her. Some might have called her decision to purchase a struggling yarn shop in a small town impulsive, but Julie had never regretted it. Not once.

After a quick shower, she dressed in jeans, a hand-knit burgundy sweater (her own design), and comfortable flats. She secured her chestnut hair in a loose bun, with a few tendrils escaping to frame her face, applied minimal makeup, and headed to the small kitchen to start the coffee maker.

"Come on, Tessa. Breakfast, then work," she called, filling the dog's bowl with kibble and refreshing Hildi's water. She took her coffee and a toasted English muffin to the small dining table by the window, where a half-finished shawl in shades of amber and gold lay beside her sketchbook. The pattern was her own creation for the upcoming Harvest Festival—a design she hoped would showcase the locally sourced merino wool she'd been promoting in the shop.

Her phone buzzed with a text from Marilyn: *Meeting the museum committee at 9. Will stop by after with those vintage buttons we talked about.*

Julie smiled. Marilyn Green had been one of her first friends when she'd moved to Meadowgrove. The retired schoolteacher, with her silver-gray bob and penchant for sensible shoes, had initially seemed stern and intimidating, but Julie had quickly discovered the warmth and loyalty beneath that efficient exterior. Marilyn's organizational skills were legendary in town, as was her inability to fully embrace retirement. She served on half a dozen committees and taught knitting at the community center twice a week.

A glance at the clock told Julie it was time to head downstairs. She gave Tessa a final pat, knowing the dog would follow once she'd finished breakfast. Hildi, predictably, had already curled up in a patch of sunlight and wouldn't make her appearance in the shop until mid-afternoon.

The stairs from her apartment led directly to a small back room that served as both office and storage space for Yarn Haven. Julie breathed in the comforting scent of wool and lanolin as she switched on lights and made her way to the front of the shop. Large display windows framed the entrance, currently showcasing a fall-themed arrangement of yarns in russet, gold, and deep purple, alongside patterns and finished pieces. She'd learned early on that showing both the materials and completed projects helped customers envision possibilities.

Julie unlocked the front door, flipped the sign to "Open," and stepped outside for a moment to straighten the small chalkboard advertising the Thursday evening yarn group. The air held the crisp promise of autumn, and she took a deep breath, appreciating the contrast to the perpetual exhaust and hurry of her former city life.

Across the street, the historic Wilkins Building stood as it had for over a century—three stories of weathered redbrick with ornate cornices and arched windows. Once the town's first bank, it had housed various businesses over the years but had been vacant for the past eighteen months. Julie had heard rumors about a potential buyer, someone with plans for renovation, but nothing concrete.

Back inside, she adjusted a few displays, restocked a basket of discounted yarn ends, and checked the schedule for the day. Two regulars had booked time for her to help with tricky pattern sections, and she had a shipment of new bamboo needles arriving. Otherwise, it promised to be a quiet Monday, perfect for working on her Harvest Festival designs.

The shop's bell chimed just as she settled behind the counter with her coffee and sketchbook. Betsy Sullivan bustled in, her diminutive frame belying her status as the town's most prolific gossip.

"Julie, dear! I'm so glad you're open. I need another skein of that alpaca blend for Harold's scarf, and I have the most interesting news," she announced, her voice pitched with the excitement of fresh gossip.

"Good morning, Betsy. The alpaca's right over here." Julie led her to the appropriate shelf, already anticipating the inevitable sharing of town news. Betsy's husband was on the town council, which gave her access to information before it became public knowledge.

"Did you hear about the Wilkins Building?" Betsy asked, fingering the soft yarn. "It's finally been sold."

"Really? To whom?" Despite herself, Julie was curious. The building was a Meadowgrove landmark, and its location directly across from her shop meant any changes would affect her business environment.

"A woman named Victoria Thompson. Apparently, she's some sort of real estate developer from New York. Has big plans, from what Harold tells me." Betsy lowered her voice conspiratorially. "She's talking about a boutique hotel with a high-end restaurant on the ground floor."

Julie's eyebrows rose. "A hotel? In Meadowgrove? We barely get enough tourists for our existing bed and breakfasts, except during leaf season and the Harvest Festival."

Crochet Carnage

"That's exactly what I said! But this Victoria person thinks our little town is ready to become a 'destination.'" Betsy sniffed, clearly skeptical. "She's staying at The Pines Inn while she finalizes everything. Drove into town in one of those enormous black SUVs with tinted windows. Very New York."

As Betsy continued her commentary on the newcomer's designer clothes and "city manners," Julie rang up the alpaca yarn and half-listened, her mind already considering the implications of a boutique hotel. On one hand, more tourists could mean more customers for Yarn Haven. On the other, she valued the small-town character of Meadowgrove and worried about changes that might alter its charm.

The bell chimed again, and Julie looked up to see Rose Chen, the town librarian, slipping in quietly. Unlike Betsy, Rose was reserved, almost shy, though Julie had discovered a sharp wit beneath that calm exterior during their Thursday yarn group sessions.

"Morning, Rose," Julie called. "The new knitting magazines came in yesterday. I set aside the Japanese one you like."

Rose's face lit up with a small but genuine smile. "Thank you. Their cable techniques are always so innovative." She moved toward the magazine rack while Betsy, never one to lose an audience, shifted her attention to include the newcomer.

"Rose, have you heard about the Wilkins Building sale? I was just telling Julie..."

The morning continued in this pleasant rhythm—customers coming and going, conversations about patterns and town news, Tessa greeting favorites with gentle enthusiasm from her bed near the counter. Around eleven, the bell chimed again, and Julie looked up to see a woman she didn't recognize step hesitantly into the shop.

The stranger was striking—tall and slim, with expertly styled ash-blonde hair cut in an elegant bob. Her clothes screamed money without being flashy: camel-colored trousers, a cream silk blouse, and a cashmere wrap in a subtle herringbone pattern. Diamond studs glinted at her ears, and a slim gold watch circled her wrist.

"Welcome to Yarn Haven," Julie said warmly, setting aside the sock she'd been working on during a lull. "Can I help you find something?"

The woman's gaze swept the shop with the assessing look of someone accustomed to making quick judgments. "Perhaps. I'm Victoria

Thompson." She extended a manicured hand. "I've just purchased the Wilkins Building across the street."

So this was the mysterious developer. Julie shook the offered hand, noting the firm grip. "Julie Sommers. This is my shop."

"Yes, I gathered that." Victoria's smile didn't quite reach her eyes, which remained coolly appraising. "Charming place. Very... rustic."

Julie couldn't decide if that was a compliment or a subtle dig. "Thank you. We focus on quality yarns, with an emphasis on local and sustainable sources. Are you a knitter?"

"God, no." Victoria laughed lightly. "I don't have the patience. Or the time." She ran a fingertip over a display of hand-dyed merino. "I wanted to introduce myself, since we'll be neighbors soon. My plans for the Wilkins Building will bring a new level of sophistication to Meadowgrove. I think it will benefit all the local businesses. Well, the viable ones, at least."

There was something subtly dismissive in her tone that made Julie straighten her spine. "Yarn Haven has been 'viable' for over thirty years, Ms. Thompson. I've owned it for three, but it was a Meadowgrove institution long before that."

"Of course," Victoria said smoothly. "And I'm sure a quaint little shop like this adds to the town's charm. That's precisely the atmosphere my boutique hotel will capitalize on—authentic New England charm with world-class amenities."

Before Julie could respond to the backhanded compliment, Tessa emerged from behind the counter, her nails clicking on the hardwood floor as she approached the visitor. Victoria took a step back.

"It doesn't bite, does it?" she asked, eyeing the dachshund warily.

"*She* is very friendly," Julie said, unable to keep a note of frost from her voice. Anyone who referred to Tessa as "it" automatically lost points in her book. "This is Tessa."

Victoria made no move to pet the dog, instead adjusting her wrap and glancing at her watch. "Well, I should go. I have a meeting with Mayor Johnson about zoning permits. I just wanted to introduce myself and let you know that construction will begin next month. There may be some... disruption. Noise, dust, the usual. But the end result will be worth it."

"I appreciate the heads-up," Julie said neutrally. "Good luck with your project."

Crochet Carnage

With a nod and another coolly professional smile, Victoria swept out of the shop, leaving behind a subtle waft of expensive perfume and an air of disturbance, like ripples across a previously calm pond.

Julie absently scratched Tessa's ears, her thoughts troubled. Something about Victoria Thompson rubbed her the wrong way—perhaps the woman's faintly condescending attitude, or her obvious assumption that she was doing Meadowgrove a favor by gracing it with her presence.

The bell chimed again, this time heralding the arrival of Marilyn, punctual as always. Her salt-and-pepper bob was tucked neatly behind her ears, and she wore her standard uniform of pressed slacks, a button-down shirt, and comfortable loafers, along with the hand-knit cardigan Julie had given her for her sixty-fifth birthday last year.

"Was that Victoria Thompson I just saw leaving?" Marilyn asked without preamble, setting a small paper bag on the counter. "The vintage buttons, as promised."

"The one and only," Julie confirmed, opening the bag to examine the carved mother-of-pearl buttons. "These are perfect for the baby sweater sets, Marilyn. Thank you."

"Never mind the buttons. What did Ms. High-and-Mighty want?" Marilyn's no-nonsense tone made Julie smile. Her friend had a deeply ingrained suspicion of outsiders who arrived in Meadowgrove with grand plans and urban attitudes.

"Just introducing herself as our new neighbor. Apparently, the Wilkins Building is being transformed into a 'boutique hotel with world-class amenities.'" Julie couldn't help mimicking Victoria's precise diction.

Marilyn snorted. "That woman has been in town for all of three days and already thinks she knows what Meadowgrove needs. The historical society is in an uproar. The Wilkins Building is one of the oldest structures in town, and while it's not officially designated as a historic landmark, many think it should be."

"From what Betsy said, Victoria has the mayor on board."

"Linda Johnson would sell her grandmother if it meant more tax revenue," Marilyn said dismissively. "The council meeting Thursday night should be interesting. Several of us plan to speak about the importance of maintaining the town's historical character."

The shop door burst open before Julie could respond, and a whirlwind of color and energy entered in the form of Nelly Morrison. In contrast to Marilyn's neat appearance, Nelly was a riot of textures and hues. Her wild red curls were partially contained by a patterned headscarf, and she wore a flowing bohemian dress in peacock blue over purple leggings, with multiple beaded necklaces and dangling earrings completing the ensemble.

"Darlings! Am I interrupting?" Nelly's voice, warm and slightly husky, filled the shop. At fifty-two, she embodied the free-spirited artist stereotype, teaching yoga three mornings a week and selling her paintings and handcrafted jewelry at local fairs. She was also, improbably, one of Marilyn's closest friends, despite their opposing personalities.

"Just discussing our new neighbor," Julie said, nodding toward the Wilkins Building. "Have you met her yet?"

"Victoria Thompson? Oh yes." Nelly made a face, dropping her beaded bag onto a chair. "She came to my yoga class this morning, wearing designer exercise clothes and looking like she'd rather be getting a root canal. Left halfway through, claiming the 'energy wasn't right.' Pure nonsense—she just couldn't handle my intermediate poses."

Marilyn's lips twitched. "Not everyone appreciates your alternative approach to yoga, Nelly."

"Hmph. There's nothing 'alternative' about proper alignment and breath work," Nelly retorted, but her green eyes twinkled. She turned to Julie. "Any chance of tea? I'm parched after teaching back-to-back classes."

"Of course." Julie moved to the small kitchenette tucked behind the counter where she kept a kettle and assortment of teas for regular customers. "Green, herbal, or black?"

"Herbal, please. I've had enough caffeine for one day." Nelly settled onto a stool, absentmindedly stroking Tessa, who had trotted over to greet her. "So, this Victoria person. Word around town is that she's more than just a developer with her eye on the Wilkins Building. Apparently, she's looking at several properties."

"Including the old mill site," Marilyn confirmed. "The historical society is concerned. That property has been in limbo since the Wilson family trust dispute, but it's one of the few remaining examples of 19th-century industrial architecture in the county."

Julie returned with Nelly's tea and a refill of her own coffee. "It sounds like Ms. Thompson has big plans for our little town."

"Too big, if you ask me," Nelly said, blowing on her tea. "Meadowgrove doesn't need to become another overpriced weekend destination for Boston professionals. We already have enough vacation homes sitting empty most of the year."

The conversation was interrupted by the arrival of a young mother with a toddler in tow, looking for yarn for her first sweater project. Julie spent the next half hour helping her select an appropriate wool blend and explaining the pattern basics, while Marilyn entertained the child with a basket of soft yarn scraps kept specifically for that purpose.

After the customer left, promising to return for the Thursday yarn group, Marilyn checked her watch. "I need to run. Library board meeting at one, and I want to review the budget proposal beforehand."

"And I've got a commission to finish," Nelly added, draining her tea. "A family portrait for the Hendersons' anniversary. Conventional stuff, but it pays the bills."

"Before you both dash off," Julie said, "don't forget about Thursday. We're starting the charity knitting for the winter clothing drive. Hats and scarves for the homeless shelter in Burlington."

"I'll bring those donated alpaca skeins from my cousin's farm," Nelly promised.

"And I'll have the patterns copied and sorted," Marilyn added. "See you then, if not before."

As her friends departed, Julie turned her attention back to her shop duties, restocking shelves and helping the occasional customer. The afternoon passed quietly, punctuated only by Hildi's appearance around two, the cat sauntering in from the apartment stairs to claim her favorite perch on the window seat.

Around four, as Julie was updating the shop's social media page with photos of new yarn arrivals, the bell chimed again. She looked up to see Dr. Benjamin Walker, the town's most eligible bachelor according to Meadowgrove's contingent of matchmaking matrons.

At forty-two, Ben Walker was undeniably handsome in a quietly confident way, with dark hair beginning to silver at the temples and intelligent brown eyes behind classic tortoiseshell glasses. He'd taken over the town's medical practice five years ago when old Dr. Patterson retired, and had quickly earned the community's trust with his blend of modern medical knowledge and old-fashioned bedside manner.

"Dr. Walker," Julie greeted him with a smile. "What brings you to the realm of yarn today?"

"Ben, please," he reminded her, as he always did. "I'm looking for something for my mother's birthday. She's an avid knitter, as you know."

Julie did know. Margaret Walker, who lived in Burlington, was a skilled knitter who often sent her son to purchase supplies from Yarn Haven, despite having several shops closer to home. Julie suspected it was the widow's subtle attempt at matchmaking, but she didn't mind. Ben was always pleasant company.

"What did you have in mind?" she asked, coming around the counter.

"That's the problem. I'm out of ideas." He ran a hand through his hair in a gesture of mild frustration. "I've given her yarn for the past three birthdays. I thought maybe something different this time—knitting needles, or one of those kits you mentioned once?"

"We just got in some beautiful rosewood circular needles," Julie suggested, leading him to a display case. "Or there's this set of hand-carved cedar cable needles that are really special."

They spent a companionable fifteen minutes discussing options before Ben settled on a project kit for a lace shawl that included hand-dyed silk yarn and antique glass beads.

"She'll love this," he said with genuine appreciation as Julie wrapped it in tissue paper and placed it in one of the shop's distinctive bags, stamped with the Yarn Haven logo—a stylized ball of yarn with knitting needles.

"How are things at the clinic?" she asked as she processed his credit card. "Still busy?"

"Always." His smile had a tired edge. "Autumn brings the usual influx of seasonal allergies and early cold viruses. Plus, I'm short-staffed since Nurse Peterson retired last month."

"I heard you were looking for a replacement." Julie handed him the bag and receipt. "Any luck?"

"Not yet. Small-town medical practices aren't exactly drawing the top nursing graduates." He hesitated, then added, "Actually, I ran into your new neighbor this morning. Victoria Thompson came in for a tour of the clinic."

Julie's eyebrows rose. "She's interested in healthcare?"

"Apparently, her hotel plans include a 'wellness spa.' She wanted to discuss potential collaboration—her spa clients could be referred to my practice for actual medical needs, that sort of thing." He adjusted his glasses, a habit Julie had noticed when he was choosing his words carefully. "She's very... determined."

"That's one word for it," Julie replied dryly.

Ben's mouth quirked in a half-smile. "Not making friends with the locals, I take it?"

"Let's just say her vision for Meadowgrove seems to involve significant changes to its character."

"Progress isn't always bad," Ben noted, but his tone was thoughtful rather than challenging.

"True progress enhances what's already valuable about a place," Julie countered. "It doesn't replace it with a generic upscale experience you could find anywhere."

Ben nodded, considering this. "Fair point. Meadowgrove's charm is what brought me here from Boston, after all. Speaking of local character, will you be entering anything in the Harvest Festival craft competition this year?"

"A shawl design," Julie confirmed. "I'm using that local merino from the Johnston farm, dyed with natural materials. Very autumn-inspired."

"Sounds like a winner to me," he said warmly. "Though I'm hardly an expert."

Their conversation was interrupted by the ringing of Ben's phone. He checked the screen and grimaced. "Duty calls. Thanks for your help with the gift."

"Anytime. I'm sure your mother will love it."

After he left, Julie found herself smiling. There was something so genuine about Ben Walker, a quality increasingly rare in a world of carefully curated social media personas and superficial interactions. Not for the first time, she wondered if she should take Marilyn and Nelly's not-so-subtle hints and consider him as more than just a friendly customer.

The rest of the afternoon passed uneventfully. At six, Julie locked the shop door, fed Tessa and Hildi, and decided to treat herself to dinner at The Greenery, Meadowgrove's farm-to-table café run by her friend Sarah Lopez. The early evening was mild enough that she chose to walk the three blocks, enjoying the golden light as the sun began its descent behind the hills that cradled the town.

The Greenery occupied a converted Victorian house on Maple Street, its wraparound porch filled with small tables where diners could enjoy their meals in fair weather. Julie spotted Sarah behind the counter as she entered, her dark hair netted back as she prepared a coffee drink.

"Julie! Perfect timing—I saved you some of the butternut squash risotto," Sarah called, spotting her. "Counter or porch?"

"Porch, definitely. It's too beautiful to be inside." Julie settled at a small table with a view of the street, ordering the risotto and a glass of local white wine.

As she sipped her wine and watched the town's evening routines unfold—shopkeepers closing up, couples strolling, the occasional car heading toward the residential neighborhoods—Julie felt a deep contentment. This was why she'd left the city; these quiet moments of connection and community that grounded her in a way her previous life never had.

Her peaceful reflections were interrupted by the now-familiar sight of Victoria Thompson, walking briskly down the sidewalk opposite The Greenery. She was engaged in what appeared to be an intense phone conversation, her free hand gesturing emphatically.

"...don't care what they want. I've secured the permits, and the zoning board is on board. The historical society can complain all they want," Victoria's voice carried across the quiet street as she passed. "This town is a gold mine waiting to happen, and I intend to be the one who taps it."

Julie frowned, watching the developer disappear around the corner. There was something unsettlingly predatory about Victoria's attitude toward Meadowgrove, as if the town existed solely for her profit rather than as a living community with its own history and character.

Sarah appeared with the risotto, following Julie's gaze. "Ah, you've met our ambitious new neighbor, I see."

"Briefly. She came into the shop this morning." Julie turned her attention to the fragrant dish before her. "This looks amazing, Sarah."

"Local squash from the Millers' farm," Sarah said with justified pride, sliding into the chair opposite Julie. "So, what's your take on Ms. High-Powered Developer?"

Julie considered her response as she tasted the risotto. "I'm trying to keep an open mind. Change isn't inherently bad, and Meadowgrove could use some economic revitalization. But there's something about her approach that feels... off."

"Like she sees us as quaint local color for her real target audience of wealthy urbanites?" Sarah suggested.

"Exactly." Julie nodded. "As if we're props in her tourism brochure rather than an actual community."

"Well, she's definitely ruffled some feathers at the town council. My cousin works at the clerk's office and says the planning meeting yesterday got heated. Victoria wants to modify the Wilkins Building's façade, and the historical preservation committee is fighting it tooth and nail."

They chatted a while longer before Sarah was called back to the kitchen, leaving Julie to finish her meal and enjoy the deepening twilight. By the time she paid her bill and started home, the streetlights were coming on, casting pools of warm light along Main Street.

As she approached Yarn Haven, something caught her eye—a figure standing in the shadows across the street, seemingly studying her shop. The person was too far away and too obscured to identify clearly, but there was something in the posture that suggested intense interest rather than casual observation.

A chill that had nothing to do with the evening air ran up Julie's spine. She quickened her pace, fishing her keys from her purse. As she reached her shop door, she glanced back, but the figure was gone, leaving her to wonder if her imagination had been influenced by Victoria Thompson's disruptive presence in town.

Upstairs, Julie was greeted enthusiastically by Tessa and with dignified indifference by Hildi. She spent the evening working on her Harvest Festival shawl, the rhythmic motion of knitting soothing her earlier unease. By the time she prepared for bed, the incident outside the shop had receded to a minor blip in an otherwise pleasant day.

She couldn't have known that Victoria Thompson's arrival in Meadowgrove—and their brief encounter—would be the first stitch in a complex pattern of events that would transform the town and test Julie's courage in ways she never imagined.

The autumn wind picked up as night settled fully over Meadowgrove, rustling the trees along Main Street and carrying away the last warmth of the day. In the darkness across from Yarn Haven, a shadow moved briefly before disappearing into the night, leaving no trace of its presence or purpose.

Chapter 2
Tangled Threads

Thursday arrived with a crisp morning breeze that scattered fallen leaves across Main Street and carried the scent of woodsmoke from chimneys being put to use for the first time that season. Julie arrived at Yarn Haven early, eager to prepare for the evening's yarn group meeting. It was one of her favorite parts of owning the shop—hosting a diverse collection of crafters who'd become friends over shared projects and stories.

She hummed as she arranged chairs in a loose circle in the back room, placing the small electric kettle and tea supplies on a side table. Tessa followed at her heels, occasionally nudging Julie's calf as if offering supervision of the preparations.

"Yes, I know I forgot the cookie tray," Julie told the dachshund with a smile. "I'm getting to it."

The bell above the shop door jingled, and Julie glanced at her watch in surprise. It was only 8:30, half an hour before opening.

"Hello?" she called, stepping into the main area of the shop.

Marilyn stood just inside the door, looking uncharacteristically flustered. Her normally impeccable bob was slightly askew, and she clutched a folder of papers to her chest.

"Thank goodness you're already here," Marilyn said, making a beeline for Julie. "You won't believe what happened at the emergency town council meeting last night."

Julie raised an eyebrow. "Emergency meeting? I didn't hear about that."

"It wasn't publicly announced—technically just an 'executive session.'" Marilyn's voice dripped with disapproval. "But my neighbor Carl is on the council, and he called me first thing this morning, absolutely livid."

She laid the folder on the counter and extracted a document, spreading it flat for Julie to see. It appeared to be architectural renderings of the Wilkins Building, but with significant modifications. The classic brick façade was replaced with sleek glass and steel, and a modern rooftop addition extended the structure upward by at least one story.

"They approved this?" Julie asked, astonished. "What about the historical preservation regulations?"

"That's just it." Marilyn tapped a finger on another document—a legal-looking letter with the town seal. "Mayor Johnson pushed through a variance, claiming 'economic necessity.' Victoria Thompson had her architect and a so-called economic development expert present data suggesting her hotel would bring millions in revenue and dozens of jobs to Meadowgrove."

Julie studied the renderings with growing dismay. The proposed changes would completely alter the character of the building that had stood as a Meadowgrove landmark for over a century.

"This can't be legal," she murmured. "What about public comment periods? The historical society would never have approved this."

"That's why they did it in a closed session," Marilyn replied grimly. "By the time the historical society gets wind of it, the permits will be issued and construction started. Victoria Thompson clearly knows how to work the system."

A sharp knock on the shop's front door interrupted them. Nelly's wild red curls were visible through the glass, and Julie hurried to let her in.

"Have you heard?" Nelly demanded without preamble, brandishing her phone. "That woman is destroying a piece of Meadowgrove history, and our illustrious mayor is helping her do it!"

"Marilyn was just showing me," Julie confirmed, locking the door again. She wasn't officially open yet, and this conversation required privacy. "How did you find out?"

"George texted me," Nelly replied, referring to George Whitaker, a retired widower who had joined their yarn group last year. "His daughter works at the building inspector's office. They're expecting the final plans to be submitted today, with fast-tracked approval."

The three women gathered around the counter, examining the renderings with shared concern.

"We need to organize," Marilyn said decisively. "Get a petition started, call an emergency meeting of the historical society."

"Will that even help at this point?" Julie wondered. "If they've already approved the variance..."

"At minimum, we can demand a public hearing," Nelly insisted. "This affects the entire town, not just Victoria Thompson's profit margin."

They spent the next twenty minutes outlining a plan, with Marilyn agreeing to contact the historical society members and Nelly volunteering to create flyers for a town meeting. Julie promised to speak with other Main Street business owners who might share their concerns about the impact of radical changes to the town's historic character.

By the time Julie unlocked the shop for regular hours, she felt both troubled by the development news and heartened by her friends' immediate willingness to mobilize. This was what she valued about small-town life—people who cared deeply about their community and stepped up when it was threatened.

The morning passed busily. Word of Victoria's plans had begun to spread, and several customers mentioned the Wilkins Building renovations. Opinions were divided—some welcomed the potential economic boost a boutique hotel might bring, while others, particularly longtime residents, expressed dismay at the modern redesign.

Around lunchtime, the shop door opened to admit Dr. Walker, looking slightly harried in his white coat with a stethoscope still around his neck.

"Ben," Julie greeted him with surprise. "Aren't you usually at the clinic at this hour?"

"Emergency house call for old Mrs. Fenton," he explained. "Nothing serious—she fell but didn't break anything. I was passing by and thought I'd grab a sandwich from the deli, but then I saw you were open..." He trailed off, seeming slightly embarrassed by his impulsive visit.

Julie smiled, charmed by his awkwardness. "Well, I'm glad you stopped in. Have you heard about the Wilkins Building plans?"

His expression grew serious. "Just this morning. One of my patients is on the town council. To be honest, I'm concerned about the precedent it sets. If historical buildings can be modernized at will, Meadowgrove could lose the very character that makes it special."

"Exactly!" Julie exclaimed, pleased to find an ally. "Marilyn and Nelly and I are trying to organize some community response. There's talk of calling for a public hearing."

"Count me in," Ben said without hesitation. "The clinic has been in that building on Elm Street since 1922. I'd hate to see it or any of our historical structures compromised for short-term economic gain."

Their conversation was interrupted by the arrival of another customer, an elderly woman looking for yarn for her granddaughter's baby blanket. Ben took his leave with a promise to attend any community meeting they organized.

As Julie helped the woman select a soft, washable yarn in pale green, she found herself thinking about Ben's support. It was nice to know the respected town doctor was on their side. His opinion carried weight in Meadowgrove.

The afternoon grew increasingly busy as word spread about the evening's yarn group. In addition to the regulars, several curious newcomers had called to ask if they could attend. Julie always welcomed fresh faces, knowing that the group's friendly atmosphere often converted casual crafters into dedicated members.

By six o'clock, she had arranged a larger circle of chairs than usual and put out an assortment of cookies, cheese, and fruit on the back room table. Tessa, sensing the impending arrival of admirers, had positioned herself strategically near the refreshments, while Hildi had claimed a high shelf where she could observe the proceedings with feline detachment.

Rose Chen arrived first, punctual as always. The librarian's quiet demeanor concealed a dry wit that often caught new group members by surprise.

"I brought the book on traditional cable patterns you requested," Rose said, sliding a large volume from her tote bag. "And I heard about the Wilkins Building. The library board is quite concerned—we're hoping to expand into that block eventually."

Before Julie could respond, the bell chimed repeatedly as several members arrived at once: George Whitaker, tall and dignified with his silver hair and neatly trimmed beard; Betsy Sullivan, already talking animatedly about the latest town gossip; and the Peterson sisters, Eleanor and Irene, identical twins in their seventies who continued to dress alike despite being well past retirement age.

Marilyn and Nelly arrived together, Marilyn carrying a neatly organized folder of patterns for the charity knitting project, Nelly lugging a large cloth bag overflowing with donated yarn.

"The alpaca from my cousin," Nelly announced, upending the bag onto an empty table. "Enough for at least two dozen hats and scarves. Plus, I brought wine." She produced a bottle of local red from her voluminous purse.

The final arrivals included Sarah from The Greenery, who rarely had time to attend but had closed early specifically for the charity project; Frank Morelli, the high school woodshop teacher who had recently taken up knitting as therapy for his arthritis; and two newcomers—a young mother named Jessica with her teenage daughter, both eager to learn.

As Julie began to welcome everyone and explain the charity knitting project for the Burlington homeless shelter, the shop door chimed once more. To her surprise, Ben Walker stepped in, looking slightly abashed.

"Sorry I'm late," he said. "Clinic ran over. I know I'm not a regular, but I thought I might learn the basics tonight. For the charity project," he added, as if needing to justify his presence.

Julie felt an unexpected flutter of pleasure. "Of course! Everyone's welcome. We're just getting started."

As Marilyn efficiently distributed patterns appropriate to each person's skill level, Julie found herself watching Ben's interactions with the group. Despite being one of Meadowgrove's most prominent citizens, he displayed none of the self-importance that might have been expected. Instead, he listened attentively as Eleanor Peterson demonstrated the basic knit stitch, his forehead furrowed in concentration.

"Never thought I'd see the day," George murmured to Julie, nodding toward Ben. "Town doctor learning to knit. Times are changing."

"For the better, I'd say," Julie replied with a smile.

The conversation inevitably turned to Victoria Thompson and the Wilkins Building as the group settled into their projects.

"My Harold says the tax revenue alone would fund the new drainage system the town's been putting off for years," Betsy commented, her needles clicking rapidly as she worked.

"At what cost, though?" Frank countered. "My students did an architectural study of the Wilkins Building last semester. It's one of the finest examples of turn-of-the-century commercial architecture in the county."

"I heard they're planning to name the hotel restaurant after Victoria's grandmother," Rose added quietly. "Apparently, she has some historical connection to Meadowgrove, though Victoria hasn't elaborated on what that might be."

This nugget of information caught Julie's attention. "That's interesting. She never mentioned any personal connection to the town when she introduced herself."

"Maybe she's descended from one of the founding families," suggested Irene Peterson. "The Wilkins, the Johnsons, the Meadows—they all have living descendants scattered across the country."

"If she is, that makes her plans for the building even more puzzling," Marilyn remarked. "You'd think she'd want to preserve her own family's legacy."

The discussion continued as hands remained busy with needles and yarn. Julie noticed that Ben, while struggling with his stitches, was listening intently to every exchange. When Jessica, the young mother, mentioned that Victoria had visited the elementary school to discuss funding a new playground, his eyebrows rose slightly.

"She's certainly spreading her influence widely," he observed. "The clinic, the school, the town council—she's covered a lot of ground in just a few days."

"Laying the foundation for bigger plans, I suspect," Nelly said, her tone darkening. "The Wilkins Building is just the beginning. I've heard rumors she's interested in the old mill site and possibly the lakefront property that's been in the Sullivan family for generations."

Betsy looked up sharply at this. "Where did you hear that? Harold hasn't mentioned anything about lakefront inquiries."

Crochet Carnage

"My art student Emma works weekends at The Pines Inn where Victoria's staying," Nelly explained. "She overheard her on the phone discussing multiple Meadowgrove properties."

A thoughtful silence fell over the group as they processed this information. Julie found herself wondering about Victoria's true intentions. A single boutique hotel seemed an unusually small project for someone with her evident resources and ambition.

"Well, I for one am keeping an open mind," Frank eventually said. "Change isn't always bad. This town could use some fresh ideas."

"Fresh, yes. Destructive, no," Marilyn countered firmly.

The conversation shifted to other topics—the upcoming Harvest Festival, Rose's plans for the library's children's reading program, George's new woodworking project—but an undercurrent of concern about Victoria Thompson's plans remained palpable.

As the evening progressed, Julie found herself repeatedly drawn to Ben's corner of the room, offering assistance with his increasingly lopsided attempt at a basic scarf. His hands, so skilled in medical procedures, proved endearingly clumsy with knitting needles.

"I think I should stick to surgery," he joked after dropping stitches for the third time. "This requires a different kind of dexterity."

"You're being too hard on yourself," Julie encouraged, demonstrating the stitch again. "No one's an expert their first time."

"Some of us aren't experts our fiftieth time," George called out with good humor, holding up his own rather irregular work.

The warm camaraderie of the group was one of the things Julie valued most about these gatherings. People from different walks of life, spanning generations, found common ground in the simple act of creating something with their hands.

By nine o'clock, the official end time, most members had made significant progress on their charity projects. As people began packing up their supplies, the conversation returned to Victoria Thompson and the community response to her plans.

"We're calling a town meeting for next Tuesday," Marilyn announced. "Seven o'clock at the community center. We need as many people there as possible to show the council that their closed-door decisions won't go unchallenged."

"I'll spread the word at the clinic," Ben promised. "Many of my patients are longtime residents who care deeply about the town's character."

"And I'll put up notices at the café," Sarah added. "Maybe offer a discount to anyone who shows proof of attendance."

Julie felt a surge of pride in her community. This was Meadowgrove at its best—citizens coming together to protect what they valued, regardless of personal differences.

As the last of the yarn group members trickled out, Ben lingered, carefully wrapping his beginner's effort in tissue paper.

"I think my mother will get a good laugh out of this," he said, holding up the small, uneven piece. "She's been trying to teach me to knit since I was ten."

"It's actually quite good for a first attempt," Julie assured him, beginning to tidy the room. "You should bring her to the group sometime. We'd love to meet her."

"I'd like that," he said, then hesitated. "Julie, there's something I've been meaning to ask you. I know this is sudden, but would you consider —"

The shop door chimed, cutting off his words. Victoria Thompson stood in the entrance, her elegant figure silhouetted against the darkened street outside.

"I hope I'm not interrupting," she said, though her tone suggested she didn't particularly care if she was. "I saw the lights on and thought I'd stop by."

Ben straightened, his expression shifting to guarded politeness. "Ms. Thompson. I didn't realize you were interested in knitting."

"Dr. Walker." Victoria inclined her head slightly. "I'm interested in all aspects of Meadowgrove's... charm." The pause before the last word gave it an almost derisive quality. "Actually, I wanted to speak with Ms. Sommers about the upcoming community meeting I've been hearing about."

Julie exchanged a quick glance with Ben before responding. "We're organizing a town forum to discuss your plans for the Wilkins Building. Many residents feel the changes should have been presented for public input before approval."

Victoria's smile didn't reach her eyes. "I understand change can be uncomfortable for small communities. That's why I'd like to offer you an opportunity to hear my complete vision for the property. Perhaps over dinner tomorrow? I find that one-on-one conversations are often more productive than public forums where emotions can run high."

The invitation caught Julie off guard. She sensed a strategic move rather than a genuine desire for dialogue. "I appreciate the offer, but I think the community discussion is important. Transparency benefits everyone."

"Transparency. Of course." Victoria's tone cooled slightly. "Well, my invitation stands. Seven o'clock at Le Château, if you change your mind." She glanced around the shop, her gaze dismissive. "Charming place you have here. So... traditional. Good evening, Dr. Walker."

With that, she turned and left, the bell chiming sharply in her wake.

"Well," Ben said after a moment of stunned silence. "That was..."

"Calculating?" Julie suggested. "I get the feeling she's trying to divide and conquer—approach key community members individually rather than face united opposition."

"You're probably right." Ben ran a hand through his hair. "She invited me to discuss the 'wellness spa' concept again last week. When I expressed reservations about how it would integrate with local healthcare needs, she implied that my practice could benefit significantly from her clientele."

Julie raised an eyebrow. "Financial incentives for support?"

"Essentially. Very diplomatically phrased, of course." He shook his head. "I should get going. Early surgery tomorrow."

"What were you going to ask me?" Julie remembered. "Before we were interrupted?"

A flush of color touched his cheeks. "Oh, it was nothing important. Just... I wondered if you might want to have coffee sometime. To discuss the town meeting preparations," he added quickly.

Julie felt a small, pleasant warmth spread through her chest. "I'd like that. How about tomorrow afternoon? The shop is usually quiet around three."

"Three it is," he agreed, his smile brightening his tired eyes. "Good night, Julie."

After Ben left, Julie finished cleaning up, her mind replaying the evening's events. The yarn group's solidarity, Ben's unexpected participation, Victoria's calculated interruption—it all felt significant, though she couldn't yet see the pattern these threads would ultimately form.

By the time she locked up and headed upstairs with Tessa and Hildi, her thoughts had turned to practical matters. The town meeting would need flyers, perhaps a presentation of the original architectural significance of the Wilkins Building. She made mental notes as she prepared for bed, planning to discuss ideas with Marilyn and Nelly the next day.

Outside, the autumn night had grown chilly, a light frost beginning to form on windows and car windshields. Julie closed her curtains against the darkness, unaware that across the street, in the shadows of the Wilkins Building, a figure stood watching the lights of her apartment.

The next morning arrived with the hushed quality that follows a frost, the world seeming briefly crystallized and expectant. Julie woke early, her mind already buzzing with plans for the day. She dressed warmly in jeans and a chunky hand-knit sweater, pulling her hair into a casual ponytail.

Downstairs, she set about rearranging a front window display to showcase the charity knitting project, positioning partially completed hats and scarves alongside photos from last year's donation to the Burlington shelter. Tessa supervised from her bed near the counter, occasionally thumping her tail when Julie looked her way.

The bell chimed at precisely nine o'clock as Marilyn arrived, punctual as always, with a stack of freshly printed flyers for the town meeting.

"I stopped by the copy shop on my way," she explained, setting them on the counter. "What do you think?"

Julie examined the flyer, impressed by Marilyn's efficiency. "These are perfect. Clear, informative, not antagonistic. We want to encourage dialogue, not create deeper divisions."

"Exactly my thinking." Marilyn began sorting the flyers into distribution piles. "Nelly's taking the west side of town, I'll cover the east, and we thought you could handle Main Street since you know all the business owners."

As they finalized their distribution plan, the bell chimed again. Julie looked up, expecting another early customer, but instead found herself facing Derek Winters, Victoria Thompson's assistant. He was younger than Julie had expected, probably in his mid-twenties, with sandy hair and wire-rimmed glasses that gave him a scholarly appearance.

"Ms. Sommers?" he inquired, glancing between Julie and Marilyn. "I apologize for arriving before your official opening hours. Ms. Thompson sent me to deliver this."

He extended a cream-colored envelope with Julie's name written in elegant script.

"Thank you," Julie said, accepting it with a measure of caution. "You're Derek, right? Victoria's assistant?"

He nodded, pushing his glasses up nervously. "And nephew, actually. My mother is Victoria's sister."

This personal detail surprised Julie. Victoria had never mentioned family connections, and certainly not that her assistant was also her relative.

"You must know Meadowgrove well by now, helping your aunt with her projects," Marilyn observed, her tone conversational but her eyes sharp with interest.

"Not really," Derek admitted. "I only arrived last week, and most of my time has been spent in meetings or on conference calls." He hesitated, then added, "I heard about your community meeting. It sounds like a good idea—getting everyone's input."

The comment seemed genuine, and Julie noted with interest the subtle distinction between Derek's attitude and his aunt's dismissive approach.

"You'd be welcome to attend," she offered. "Tuesday at seven, at the community center."

"I'd like that, though I'm not sure my aunt would approve." His smile was wry. "I should get back. She has a full schedule of meetings today."

After he left, Julie opened the envelope. Inside was a formal invitation to dinner, along with a small, handwritten note: "I believe we could find common ground. Let's discuss how your shop might play a role in Meadowgrove's future. – V.T."

"Role in Meadowgrove's future?" Marilyn read over Julie's shoulder. "What does that mean?"

"I'm not sure," Julie replied slowly. "But it sounds like she's offering some sort of involvement in her plans."

"Or buying your support," Marilyn said bluntly. "Be careful, Julie. That woman strikes me as someone who believes everything and everyone has a price."

Julie nodded thoughtfully, tucking the invitation into her pocket. "I have no intention of being bought. But I am curious about what she has to say."

The morning proceeded with a steady stream of customers, many of whom took flyers for the town meeting. Around noon, Nelly burst in, her wild curls even more untamed than usual due to the brisk autumn wind.

"You won't believe what I just heard," she announced, shrugging off her multicolored shawl. "Victoria Thompson was seen meeting with the owners of the old mill property this morning. Emma's father works security there, and he said they were walking the grounds, discussing 'restoration potential.'"

Julie frowned. "The mill has been abandoned for decades. What could she possibly want with it?"

"That's just it," Nelly replied, lowering her voice conspiratorially. "According to local legend, there are historic artifacts hidden somewhere on the property—valuable items from Meadowgrove's founding days that disappeared during the mill's closure in the 1960s."

"Treasure hunting?" Marilyn scoffed. "That seems far-fetched, even for someone as ambitious as Victoria Thompson."

"Maybe, maybe not." Nelly shrugged. "But Emma also mentioned that Victoria has been asking questions about Meadowgrove's founding families—specifically the Wilkins family."

This caught Julie's attention. "Rose mentioned last night that Victoria was naming the hotel restaurant after her grandmother. Do you think she could be related to the original Wilkins family?"

"It would explain her interest in the building," Marilyn conceded. "Though not her willingness to modernize it beyond recognition."

The three friends continued to speculate as they distributed flyers and helped customers throughout the early afternoon. By two-thirty, the shop had quieted, and Julie found herself watching the clock, anticipating Ben's arrival for coffee.

"I'm heading to the library to research the Wilkins family history," Marilyn announced, gathering her things. "Rose said she'd help me access the historical archives. If Victoria has a connection to Meadowgrove's past, we should know about it."

"And I've got a yoga class to teach," Nelly added. "But I'll stop by later. I want to hear about your coffee date." She winked at Julie, who felt a blush rise to her cheeks.

"It's not a date," Julie protested. "We're discussing the town meeting."

"Of course you are," Nelly agreed with a knowing smile. "That's why you've checked your hair in the reflection of the window display three times in the past hour."

After her friends departed, Julie straightened the already-tidy shop and set up the electric kettle in the back room. She'd just laid out mugs and a plate of cookies when the bell chimed. Her heart gave a small, unexpected leap as she turned, expecting to see Ben.

Instead, Victoria Thompson stood in the doorway, impeccably dressed in a tailored pantsuit, her ash-blonde hair gleaming in the afternoon light.

"Ms. Sommers," she greeted Julie with cool professionalism. "I realize I'm early for our potential dinner meeting, but I thought we might speak privately first. I assume you received my invitation?"

Julie nodded, momentarily taken aback by the woman's presumption. "I did, thank you. But I haven't decided whether to accept."

Victoria's smile didn't reach her eyes. "That's why I'm here. I wanted to clarify the opportunity I'm offering you." She glanced around the shop with a calculating gaze. "Your business has...potential. With the right positioning, it could become a feature attraction for the tourists my hotel will bring to Meadowgrove."

"Feature attraction?" Julie repeated, not quite understanding.

"Yes. I'm envisioning a craft corridor—a series of artisanal shops that would complement the hotel's aesthetic. Your yarn shop, properly... enhanced... could be the centerpiece." Victoria moved further into the shop, running a manicured finger along a display of hand-dyed yarns. "We'd need to update the branding, of course. More sophisticated packaging, a refined shop design, perhaps a tagline emphasizing authentic New England craftsmanship for our urban clientele."

Julie felt a flicker of indignation. "Yarn Haven has been successful for over thirty years with its current 'branding.' Our customers appreciate authenticity, not marketing concepts."

"Current success and future potential are different matters," Victoria replied smoothly. "My plans for Meadowgrove will transform this quaint little town into a destination. Businesses will either evolve to meet the new market or be left behind."

The bell chimed again, and Julie looked up to see Ben Walker standing in the doorway, his expression shifting from pleasant anticipation to wary recognition as he spotted Victoria.

"Dr. Walker," Victoria acknowledged him without warmth. "How unexpected to find you here."

"Ms. Thompson." Ben nodded politely as he entered. "Julie and I had arranged to meet to discuss community matters."

"I see." Victoria's gaze flickered between them, shrewd and assessing. "Well, I won't intrude on your... community discussion. Ms. Sommers, do consider my offer. I believe we could be valuable allies in Meadowgrove's transformation."

With that, she swept out of the shop, leaving behind the lingering scent of expensive perfume and an atmosphere of unsettled tension.

"What was that about?" Ben asked once the door had closed.

Julie explained Victoria's unexpected visit and her proposition to "enhance" Yarn Haven as part of a curated shopping experience for hotel guests.

"She certainly doesn't waste time," Ben observed, accepting the mug of coffee Julie offered. "First the clinic, now your shop—she seems determined to reshape Meadowgrove entirely according to her vision."

"The question is, why here?" Julie mused, sinking into a chair opposite him. "There are dozens of picturesque New England towns. What makes Meadowgrove so special to her plans?"

Ben's expression grew thoughtful. "That's a very good question. Her focus on the Wilkins Building in particular seems significant."

They spent the next hour discussing strategies for the town meeting, sharing information they'd each gathered about Victoria's various proposals around town, and enjoying a comfortable rapport that occasionally ventured beyond their immediate concerns into more personal territory.

Julie learned that Ben had left a prestigious position at a Boston hospital to take over Dr. Patterson's practice, seeking a more balanced life after a health scare had prompted him to reevaluate his priorities. In turn, she shared stories of her transition from corporate marketing to small-town shopkeeper, and the unexpected joy she'd found in Meadowgrove's close-knit community.

As their conversation wound down, Ben hesitantly returned to the question he'd attempted to ask the previous evening.

"I was wondering if you might like to have dinner sometime," he said, his confident doctor's demeanor giving way to a more vulnerable sincerity. "Not to discuss town meetings or Victoria Thompson. Just... dinner."

Julie found herself smiling, a pleasant warmth spreading through her chest. "I'd like that very much."

"Saturday?" he suggested. "I could pick you up around seven?"

"Saturday sounds perfect."

After Ben left, promising to continue research into the Wilkins Building's historical significance, Julie went about the remainder of her afternoon with a lighter step. Despite the concerns about Victoria's plans, there was something undeniably pleasant about Ben's dinner invitation and the prospect it represented.

The shop grew busy again as people stopped in after work, many asking about the town meeting flyers they'd seen around Meadowgrove. Julie was encouraged by the response—it seemed the community was indeed concerned about preserving the town's character.

As closing time approached, she began her usual evening routine, straightening displays and tallying the day's sales. Tessa had long since retreated upstairs for her evening meal, and the shop was quiet save for the gentle tick of the old clock on the wall.

The sudden ringing of Julie's phone startled her. Marilyn's name flashed on the screen.

"Julie, you need to see this," Marilyn said without preamble when Julie answered. "I found something in the historical society archives about Victoria Thompson—or rather, about her family. Can you meet me and Nelly at The Greenery in fifteen minutes?"

"Of course," Julie agreed, intrigued by the urgency in Marilyn's typically composed voice. "I'm just closing up now."

After quickly finishing her closing tasks and locking the shop, Julie headed down Main Street toward The Greenery. The evening had grown chilly, and she pulled her scarf tighter around her neck as she walked, her mind buzzing with questions about Marilyn's discovery.

What connection could Victoria possibly have to Meadowgrove that would justify her intense interest in transforming it? And more importantly, how might that information help the community protect the town's historical integrity?

As Julie reached the café, she couldn't shake the feeling that the simple yarn shop owner she'd become in her quest for a quieter life was about to be pulled into something far more complex than community activism. There was a pattern forming—she just couldn't quite see its full design yet.

The warm lights of The Greenery beckoned as she quickened her pace, eager to unravel the mystery of Victoria Thompson's true intentions for their beloved town.

Chapter 3
Pattern of Suspicion

Julie pushed open the door to The Greenery, a bell similar to her own shop's chiming softly overhead. The café's warm lighting and soothing earth tones provided a stark contrast to the chilly evening outside. Sarah Lopez, spotting Julie from behind the counter, pointed toward a corner booth where Marilyn and Nelly were already seated, heads bent over what appeared to be old documents spread across the table.

"Julie!" Nelly waved, her collection of jangling bracelets catching the light. "You won't believe what Marilyn found."

Julie slid into the booth beside Nelly, grateful for the steaming mug of tea that Sarah delivered without being asked. "What's all this?"

Marilyn, looking more animated than Julie had seen her in months, carefully pushed forward a yellowed newspaper clipping protected in a clear plastic sleeve. "This is from the Meadowgrove Gazette, October 1965. I found it in the historical society archives while researching the Wilkins Building."

Julie leaned forward to examine the faded headline: "WILKINS HEIRESS FLEES TOWN AMID SCANDAL." Below was a grainy photograph of a young woman being escorted to a car, her face partially obscured by a hat, but her resemblance to Victoria Thompson was unmistakable.

"Margaret Wilkins," Marilyn explained, tapping the photograph. "The last of the original Wilkins family to live in Meadowgrove. She left town abruptly in 1965 after being accused of stealing historical artifacts that belonged to the town museum—items collectively known as the Meadowgrove Collection. The case was never proven, but the scandal was enough to drive her away."

"And you think Victoria Thompson is related to her?" Julie asked, studying the photograph more closely.

"Not just related," Nelly chimed in, unable to contain herself. "We think Victoria is Margaret Wilkins' granddaughter!"

Marilyn nodded. "I cross-referenced with what public records I could access. Margaret Wilkins married a man named Howard Thompson in New York in 1967. They had one daughter, Elizabeth, born in 1968. Elizabeth would be the right age to be Victoria's mother."

Julie sat back, processing this information. "So Victoria Thompson isn't just a random developer who happened to choose Meadowgrove. She has family ties here—and not just any family, but one of the founding families."

"Exactly," Marilyn confirmed. "And this might explain her intense interest in the Wilkins Building. It was originally built by her great-grandfather, Elias Wilkins, in 1897."

"But why not just say so?" Julie wondered. "Why hide her connection to Meadowgrove?"

Nelly glanced around before lowering her voice. "Because of the scandal. The Meadowgrove Collection was valued even back then at an enormous sum—it included gold ceremonial items from the town's founding, historical documents signed by notable early Americans, and jewelry that allegedly contained gems brought from Europe by the original settlers."

"None of which has ever been recovered," Marilyn added grimly. "The theft essentially ended the Wilkins family's standing in the community. After Margaret left, the remaining property was gradually sold off by distant relatives with no interest in the town."

Julie's mind raced with implications. "So Victoria returns to reclaim her family's position—and property—in Meadowgrove, but doesn't acknowledge her connection because she doesn't want people associating her with the scandal."

"Or," Nelly suggested with dramatic emphasis, "she knows where the artifacts are hidden and wants to recover them before anyone realizes who she really is."

Marilyn gave Nelly a reproving look. "We're getting ahead of ourselves with speculation. What matters is that Victoria Thompson has deliberately concealed her family connection to this town while buying up property and pushing for radical changes."

"It certainly adds another dimension to her interest in the Wilkins Building," Julie agreed. "She's not just a developer seeing an opportunity; she has personal history invested in that property."

Their conversation paused as Sarah approached with a plate of her signature apple spice muffins. "On the house," she said with a smile. "You three look like you're plotting a revolution over here."

"Just trying to understand our mysterious new neighbor," Julie replied, accepting a muffin gratefully. She hadn't realized how hungry she was.

After Sarah moved away, Marilyn produced another document—a map of downtown Meadowgrove from 1960. "Look at this," she said, pointing to several buildings highlighted in yellow. "These were all Wilkins family properties at one time. The Wilkins Building, of course, but also the old mill site, the lakefront property Nelly mentioned, and interestingly, the very building where Yarn Haven is now located."

Julie nearly choked on her muffin. "My shop? The Wilkins family owned it?"

"From 1903 until 1967, when it was sold after Margaret left town," Marilyn confirmed. "It was originally a Wilkins Mercantile branch, then housed various businesses before becoming a yarn shop in the 1980s."

"That might explain Victoria's specific interest in 'enhancing' your business," Nelly suggested. "She's systematically targeting former family properties."

Julie felt a chill that had nothing to do with the autumn evening. She recalled Victoria's calculating gaze as she'd surveyed Yarn Haven, her comments about the shop's "potential" taking on new significance. Was Victoria's ultimate goal to reclaim all of her family's former holdings in Meadowgrove?

"We should bring this information to the town meeting," Julie decided. "People have a right to know about Victoria's connection to Meadowgrove and the potential conflict of interest in her development plans."

"Agreed," Marilyn said firmly. "Transparency is essential, especially given the historical context."

Nelly was about to add something when the café door opened, bringing in a gust of cold air and the imposing figure of Sheriff Tom Harris. The sheriff, a tall man with salt-and-pepper hair and perpetually furrowed brows, paused just inside the entrance, his gaze sweeping the room until it landed on their booth.

With measured steps, he approached them. "Evening, ladies," he said, nodding to each in turn. "Mind if I join you for a moment?"

Without waiting for an invitation, he pulled up a chair from a nearby table and sat at the end of their booth. Despite having lived in Meadowgrove for over fifteen years, Sheriff Harris retained the aura of an outsider—professional, polite, but never quite one of them.

"What can we do for you, Sheriff?" Marilyn asked, subtly sliding the newspaper clipping beneath a menu.

"Just making my rounds," he replied, sharp eyes noting her movement but not commenting on it. "Heard there's been some community concern about the Wilkins Building renovation plans. Mayor Johnson mentioned you're organizing a town meeting."

"We are," Julie confirmed, meeting his gaze steadily. "Many residents feel the changes should have been subject to public discussion before approval."

The sheriff nodded slowly. "Can't argue with democratic process. Just make sure things stay civil. Last thing we need is division in the community."

"Our goal is constructive dialogue," Marilyn assured him, her former schoolteacher tone emerging. "We're simply advocating for transparency in decisions that affect Meadowgrove's character."

"Good to hear." Sheriff Harris rested his hands on his utility belt, a habitual gesture. "On another note, had a peculiar call today. Someone reported a break-in at the old mill property. Nothing taken that the caretaker could see, but evidence someone's been poking around inside recently."

Julie exchanged a quick glance with her friends. "The mill's been abandoned for years," she said carefully. "Who reported it?"

"That's the interesting part," the sheriff replied. "It was Victoria Thompson. Seems she had a tour scheduled with the property owners today and noticed signs of entry—footprints, a disturbed lock."

"Why would she care about trespassing at a property she doesn't own?" Nelly wondered aloud.

Sheriff Harris shrugged. "Said she's considering purchasing it and was concerned about security. Made quite a point of mentioning the historical value of the site."

This new information hung in the air between them. Julie felt a growing certainty that Victoria's interest in the mill was connected to Marilyn's discovery about her family history—and possibly to the long-missing Meadowgrove Collection.

"Well, if that's all, Sheriff," Marilyn said pointedly, "we were just finishing up here."

He studied them for a moment, his expression suggesting he knew they were withholding something. "All right then. You ladies have a good evening. And Ms. Sommers," he added, turning to Julie, "might want to check your shop's security system. Been a few reports of suspicious activity along Main Street after hours."

With that cryptic warning, he rose and departed, nodding to Sarah behind the counter on his way out.

"What was that about?" Nelly murmured once he was gone. "Is he warning you or threatening you?"

"Neither, I think," Julie replied thoughtfully. "Just letting me know he's paying attention." She turned to Marilyn. "What else do we know about the Meadowgrove Collection? If Victoria is looking for it, we should understand exactly what we're dealing with."

Marilyn extracted another document from her folder—a museum inventory sheet from 1964, the year before the theft. "The collection included twenty-three items of historical significance," she explained. "The most valuable were the Meadowgrove Charter, signed in 1794; a set of gold ceremonial items used by the town's founders; and what was called 'the Founder's Journal,' a handwritten account by Jonathan Meadow documenting the town's first decade."

"But why would Margaret Wilkins steal them?" Julie questioned. "Her family was already prominent and wealthy."

"According to town gossip at the time—which Rose's great-aunt recorded in considerable detail in her diary—Margaret believed the items rightfully belonged to the Wilkins family. Apparently, there was some dispute over who had actually donated them to the museum in the 1920s."

Nelly leaned forward eagerly. "So if Victoria believes her grandmother was innocent, or that the items belong to her family regardless, she might have returned to Meadowgrove specifically to find them!"

The pieces were beginning to fit together in Julie's mind. "And she needs access to properties like the Wilkins Building and the old mill to search for them. That would explain the rushed renovations and her interest in buying multiple historical properties."

They continued piecing together the puzzle until Sarah began turning chairs onto tables, a gentle hint that the café was closing. As they gathered their documents and prepared to leave, Julie felt a new sense of purpose. What had begun as concern about preserving Meadowgrove's architectural heritage had evolved into something far more complex—a historical mystery with Victoria Thompson at its center.

Outside, the temperature had dropped further, and a fine mist hung in the air, haloing the streetlights. Julie pulled her scarf tighter and bid her friends goodnight, promising to meet again the following day to prepare for the town meeting.

The walk back to Yarn Haven took only minutes, but Julie found herself unusually alert, the sheriff's warning about security echoing in her mind. Main Street was deserted at this hour, shops darkened and sidewalks empty. Only the Corner Pub at the far end showed signs of life, muted laughter and the glow of lights spilling onto the sidewalk.

As Julie approached her shop, fumbling in her purse for keys, she noticed something odd—a flicker of movement in the alley that ran behind the buildings on Main Street. She paused, peering into the darkness, but saw nothing further.

"Just nerves," she muttered to herself, unlocking the shop door and quickly stepping inside. She reset the alarm, double-checked the locks, and headed upstairs to her apartment, where Tessa greeted her with sleepy enthusiasm and Hildi surveyed her from the back of the sofa with typical feline indifference.

"You'll never guess what I learned tonight," Julie told Tessa as she knelt to scratch behind the dachshund's ears. She moved through her evening routine—changing into comfortable pajamas, making a cup of chamomile tea, checking her phone for messages—all while mentally reviewing the information Marilyn had discovered.

A text from Ben made her smile: *Hope your meeting went well. Looking forward to Saturday. Sleep well.*

She replied with a simple *Goodnight! Talk tomorrow* before settling on the sofa with her tea, Tessa curled beside her. The documents about Margaret Wilkins and the missing artifacts had stirred something in Julie—an investigative instinct she hadn't realized she possessed. The yarn shop owner in her wanted to protect Meadowgrove's small-town character from overdevelopment, but another part of her, perhaps the former marketing strategist accustomed to analyzing patterns and motivations, was intrigued by the puzzle Victoria Thompson presented.

Julie was about to head to bed when Tessa suddenly stiffened beside her, ears perked and head tilted toward the window. A low growl rumbled in the small dog's chest.

"What is it, girl?" Julie whispered, setting down her mug and moving cautiously to the window.

Pulling the curtain aside slightly, she peered down at the street below. A figure stood in the shadows across from Yarn Haven, positioned between two buildings, almost invisible except for the brief glow of what appeared to be a cigarette. The ember brightened as the person took a drag, illuminating just enough of their face for Julie to recognize Derek Winters, Victoria's nephew and assistant.

What was he doing watching her shop at nearly midnight?

Julie let the curtain fall back into place, her heart beating faster. She considered calling Sheriff Harris but hesitated. Derek wasn't actually doing anything illegal by standing on a public street, and she had no proof he was specifically watching her apartment.

Instead, she took out her phone and snapped a quick photo of Tessa, positioning herself so that the window was visible in the background. With apparent casualness, she uploaded it to Yarn Haven's social media page with the caption: "Late night crafting with my faithful companion. #YarnHavenLife #MidnightKnitting"

It was a calculated move—letting Derek know, if he was indeed watching for her, that she was awake and aware of street-level activity. Within minutes, the figure across the street moved away, disappearing around the corner toward where the Wilkins Building stood.

Julie released a breath she hadn't realized she was holding. She gave Tessa an extra treat for her vigilance, double-checked all the locks, and finally headed to bed, though sleep proved elusive. Her mind kept returning to the photograph of Margaret Wilkins fleeing town, to Victoria's hidden connection to Meadowgrove, to the missing historical artifacts.

There was a pattern here, and Julie was determined to decipher it—not just to protect her shop and town, but because once she pulled on this loose thread, she couldn't stop until she saw the entire design revealed.

The next morning dawned gray and drizzly, the kind of autumn day that drove customers into shops seeking warmth and comfort. Julie arrived downstairs earlier than usual, unable to shake a lingering unease from the previous night's observations. She moved through her opening routine with Tessa at her heels, oddly comforted by the small dog's presence.

The bell chimed at precisely nine o'clock as Marilyn arrived, her silver hair slightly damp from the mist, carrying a cardboard box labeled "TOWN MEETING" in her precise handwriting.

"I've prepared information packets," she announced, setting the box on the counter. "Historical data on the Wilkins Building, photographs of the original architecture, and summaries of relevant town preservation ordinances."

Julie smiled despite her fatigue. "You never do anything halfway, do you?"

"Not when it matters," Marilyn replied firmly. "And speaking of things that matter, I did some additional research after we parted last night." She extracted a folder from her tote bag. "I found property records for Victoria Thompson—or rather, for a shell corporation called Wilkins Heritage LLC. She's been systematically purchasing properties with historical connections to her family, not just in Meadowgrove but in three other New England towns."

"She's on some kind of mission," Julie murmured, examining the documents Marilyn spread before her. "But is it about reclaiming family heritage or finding those missing artifacts?"

"Perhaps both," Marilyn suggested. "The timing is interesting. Victoria began acquiring properties shortly after the death of her mother, Elizabeth, last year. I found the obituary." She produced a printout of a

New York Times death notice. "Elizabeth Thompson née Wilkins, aged 78, survived by her daughter Victoria and nephew Derek."

"So Derek is also related to the Wilkins family," Julie noted, remembering his vigil outside her shop the previous night. Should she mention it to Marilyn? Before she could decide, the shop door opened, bringing in Nelly along with a gust of damp air.

"Morning, crafters!" Nelly called cheerfully, shaking droplets from her plastic rain bonnet, a jarring neon green that somehow worked with her bohemian aesthetic. "Any new developments in our mystery?"

As Marilyn brought Nelly up to speed on her latest findings, Julie busied herself with preparing tea, half-listening while considering whether to share her midnight observation. She was saved from deciding when the bell chimed again, admitting a breathless Rose Chen, the librarian's typically calm demeanor visibly disrupted.

"You need to see this," Rose said without preamble, hurrying to the counter with a large archival book cradled in her arms. "I was cataloging donated materials from the Patterson estate this morning when I found this photograph album. It belonged to Dr. Patterson's father, who was apparently an amateur photographer in the 1960s."

She carefully opened the album to a marked page, revealing a black-and-white photograph of what appeared to be a social gathering at the old mill. A group of Meadowgrove's prominent citizens posed stiffly for the camera, dressed in formal attire from the mid-1960s.

"That's Margaret Wilkins," Marilyn identified, pointing to the young woman they'd seen in the newspaper clipping. "And next to her is Mayor Johnson's father, Charles Johnson. They were contemporaries."

"Yes, but look at the date and the caption," Rose urged, indicating the neat handwriting beneath the photograph: "Meadowgrove Historical Society Annual Dinner, October 12, 1965."

"That's the night before the artifacts were reported missing," Marilyn realized, her eyes widening.

"Exactly," Rose confirmed. "And according to Dr. Patterson's notes, there was an argument between Margaret Wilkins and Charles Johnson that evening. Something about rightful ownership of historical items."

Julie studied the photograph more closely, noting the body language—Margaret and Charles standing rigidly beside each other, neither quite looking at the camera, tension evident even across the decades.

"The Johnson and Wilkins families were both founding families of Meadowgrove," Marilyn explained, seeing Julie's questioning look. "They've had a rivalry going back generations, though most considered it ancient history by the 1960s. Or so everyone thought."

"Until the artifacts disappeared, and Margaret Wilkins was blamed," Julie concluded.

"And fled town, her reputation ruined," Nelly added dramatically. "Only to have her granddaughter return decades later to reclaim the family name—and perhaps the artifacts themselves!"

The bell chimed yet again, and Julie looked up to see Ben Walker entering, a paper bag from the bakery in hand. He paused, taking in the four women clustered around the counter with their heads bent over old documents.

"I brought muffins," he said, lifting the bag with a slightly bewildered smile. "But it seems I've interrupted an important meeting."

"Not at all," Julie assured him, grateful for both the muffins and his steadying presence. "We're just piecing together some local history related to Victoria Thompson. It turns out she has deeper connections to Meadowgrove than anyone realized."

As she explained what they'd discovered about Victoria's family ties and the missing artifacts, Ben listened attentively, occasionally asking perceptive questions that helped clarify their understanding.

"So if I'm following correctly," he summarized, "Victoria Thompson is actually Victoria Wilkins-Thompson, granddaughter of Margaret Wilkins who was accused of stealing valuable historical artifacts in 1965. She's returned to Meadowgrove under her married name, buying up properties connected to her family, possibly searching for the missing items or attempting to restore her family's position—or both."

"That's our working theory," Marilyn confirmed. "The question is, what do we do with this information?"

"Present it at the town meeting," Rose suggested. "People have a right to know who's behind these development plans and what her true motivations might be."

"But we need to be careful," Ben cautioned. "These are serious implications about someone's character and family history. We should stick to documented facts rather than speculation."

Julie nodded in agreement. "The focus should remain on transparent development processes and preservation of historical properties. Victoria's family connection is relevant context, but we don't want to turn this into a personal attack."

As they continued their discussion, Julie noticed Tessa had become unusually alert, her attention fixed on the shop's front window. Following the dog's gaze, Julie spotted Victoria Thompson herself, walking purposefully down the opposite side of Main Street toward the Wilkins Building. A moment later, Sheriff Harris appeared, coming from the same direction Victoria was heading, nodding to her as they passed.

"And there's another interesting connection," Julie murmured, nodding toward the window. "Victoria and Sheriff Harris."

The others turned to look, but both figures had already moved out of view.

"You think there's something between them?" Nelly asked, always ready to see intrigue.

"I don't know," Julie admitted. "But the sheriff seemed very interested in our discussion about Victoria last night at The Greenery. And he specifically warned me about security concerns."

The morning progressed with a steady stream of customers drawn in by the rainy weather, seeking the comfort of creative projects to match the cozy day. Julie's friends departed one by one—Marilyn to continue her research, Rose to return to the library, Nelly to teach her yoga class—leaving Ben as the last lingerer.

"I should get to the clinic," he said reluctantly, checking his watch. "But first, is everything all right? You seemed uneasy when you mentioned the sheriff's warning."

Julie hesitated, then decided to trust her instincts—and Ben. "Last night, after I got home from The Greenery, I noticed Victoria's nephew Derek watching my shop from across the street. It was around midnight, and he left as soon as he realized I'd spotted him."

Ben's expression darkened with concern. "That's unsettling. Have you told Sheriff Harris?"

"Not yet. It felt... insufficient, somehow. He wasn't doing anything technically wrong, just standing on a public street."

"Still, given what you've discovered about Victoria's family history and her interest in your building, it's concerning." Ben's professional demeanor shifted subtly, revealing a protective instinct that Julie found both touching and reassuring. "Promise me you'll be careful, and that you'll call if anything else happens that makes you uncomfortable."

"I promise," she agreed, touched by his concern.

After Ben left for the clinic, Julie found herself watching the street more carefully as she assisted customers and restocked displays. The drizzle had intensified to a steady rain, drumming against the shop windows and reducing visibility. Meadowgrove seemed wrapped in a misty cocoon, the world beyond Main Street fading into gray obscurity.

Around noon, the bell chimed, admitting a rain-soaked Derek Winters. He removed his fogged glasses, wiping them on his shirt before replacing them and blinking owlishly at Julie.

"Ms. Sommers," he began hesitantly. "I hope I'm not interrupting your work."

"Not at all," Julie replied, keeping her tone neutral while studying him with new awareness. After last night, she wasn't sure what to make of Victoria's nephew. "What can I help you with, Mr. Winters?"

"Derek, please." He approached the counter, seeming younger and more uncertain in daylight than the shadowy figure she'd glimpsed the previous night. "I wanted to apologize for my aunt's approach yesterday. She can be... intense about her vision for Meadowgrove."

Julie raised an eyebrow, surprised by this apparent breach of family loyalty. "That's one word for it."

Derek glanced around the shop, his expression suggesting genuine appreciation for its warm atmosphere. "This is a lovely place. I can see why it's been successful for so long."

"Thank you," Julie said, softening slightly. "Are you a knitter?"

"No, but my mother was," he replied, a flicker of sadness crossing his features. "She passed away last year. Aunt Victoria's sister," he added, confirming what they'd learned from Elizabeth Thompson's obituary.

"I'm sorry for your loss," Julie said sincerely.

Derek nodded in acknowledgment. "Actually, I came for a personal reason, not just to apologize for my aunt. I found something in her files that I thought might interest you." He reached into his messenger bag and withdrew a folder. "It's about your building—the history of Yarn Haven."

Julie accepted the folder with a mixture of curiosity and caution. Inside were photocopies of old deeds and what appeared to be architectural drawings of her shop building from the early 1900s.

"These are from my aunt's research into Wilkins family properties," Derek explained. "She's been collecting historical documentation for years—part of a personal project to record our family's contributions to various New England communities."

"Including Meadowgrove," Julie noted, studying the documents with interest. "This is fascinating. Thank you for sharing it."

Derek shifted uncomfortably. "There's something else you should know. My aunt isn't just interested in developing properties for profit. She's searching for items that belonged to our great-grandmother—heirlooms that were lost when she left Meadowgrove suddenly in the 1960s."

Julie kept her expression neutral, not revealing how much they'd already pieced together. "Lost items? What kind of heirlooms?"

"Family documents, mostly," Derek replied vaguely. "Letters, photographs, that sort of thing. Sentimental value more than monetary worth."

It was clearly a rehearsed line, and Julie didn't believe it for a moment. The missing Meadowgrove Collection was worth a small fortune, both historically and monetarily.

"And she thinks these items might be hidden in buildings like the Wilkins Building or my shop?" Julie prompted, watching his reaction carefully.

A flicker of surprise crossed Derek's face before he controlled it. "I... don't know exactly where she thinks they might be. She doesn't share all the details of her search with me."

"I see." Julie closed the folder, deciding to press a little further. "It's interesting that you mention this now, given that I saw you outside my shop quite late last night. Were you looking for these 'family documents' then?"

Derek flushed deeply, caught off guard by her direct approach. "I... That was... I was just walking back to The Pines Inn after meeting some locals at the Corner Pub. I stopped to answer a text message. I didn't realize you'd noticed me."

It was a plausible explanation, but Julie didn't quite believe it. Still, she decided not to push further. "Well, thank you for the historical information. It's always interesting to learn more about the building's past."

Visibly relieved to be off the hook, Derek nodded and backed toward the door. "I should get back. Aunt Victoria has meetings all afternoon. But if you have any questions about the documents, or if you happen to come across any old papers or items during renovations, please let me know."

After he left, Julie immediately took out her phone and texted Marilyn and Nelly: *Derek just confirmed V is searching for "family heirlooms" lost in the 60s. Claims they're just documents but seemed nervous when pressed.*

Nelly's response came instantly: *OMG! The Meadowgrove Collection! I knew it!*

Marilyn was more measured: *Interesting confirmation of our theory. Be careful—if she believes items are hidden in your building, you could be more involved than you realize.*

Julie set aside her phone as customers entered, but her mind continued working through the implications of Derek's visit. If Victoria believed valuable artifacts were hidden somewhere in Meadowgrove's historical buildings, including possibly Yarn Haven, it explained her aggressive pursuit of these properties and her rushed renovation plans.

The afternoon passed busily, the rain driving in steady customers seeking refuge and creative inspiration. By closing time, Julie was tired but satisfied with the day's sales and the progress they'd made in understanding Victoria's motivations.

As she completed her closing routine, checking the register and straightening displays, her phone buzzed with a text from Ben: *Still on for tomorrow night? I can pick you up at 7.*

She smiled, typing back: *Absolutely. Looking forward to it.*

His response came quickly: *Me too. Been a while since I had a reason to wear a tie.*

Julie chuckled, appreciating this glimpse of Ben's more playful side. Despite the mysteries and tensions swirling around Meadowgrove, the prospect of dinner with him remained a bright spot on her horizon.

After locking up, she headed upstairs with Tessa, looking forward to a quiet evening at home. She'd just settled on the sofa with a cup of tea and her current knitting project when her phone rang. The screen displayed Nelly's name.

"Julie! Turn on the local news, channel five, right now!" Nelly demanded without preamble, her voice pitched with excitement.

Reaching for the remote, Julie switched on the small television she rarely used, finding the channel just in time to see a serious-faced reporter standing in front of the old mill property, rain dripping from an umbrella held over her head.

"...where Sheriff Tom Harris confirmed that human remains were discovered this afternoon by workers conducting a preliminary site survey. The identity of the deceased has not been released, but sources close to the investigation suggest the remains may have been in the abandoned mill for decades..."

Julie felt a cold shock run through her. "Nelly, are they saying someone was buried in the mill?"

"That's what it sounds like!" Nelly confirmed, her voice tense with excitement. "And guess who was there when they found the body? Victoria Thompson! She was touring the property with the current owners when the discovery was made."

A chilling thought occurred to Julie. "Nelly, if someone died around the same time the artifacts disappeared..."

"Exactly!" Nelly exclaimed. "What if Margaret Wilkins wasn't the thief? What if she fled town because she knew something—or someone—dangerous was involved with the missing artifacts?"

"Let's not jump to conclusions," Julie cautioned, though her own mind was racing with similar speculations. "We don't know how long those remains have been there or who they belonged to."

"Maybe not yet," Nelly agreed reluctantly. "But I bet Victoria Thompson has some ideas. And I'm starting to think her return to Meadowgrove isn't just about reclaiming family properties or finding artifacts—it might be about clearing her grandmother's name."

After ending the call with Nelly, Julie sat in stunned contemplation, absently stroking Tessa's silky ears. The discovery of human remains at the mill added a disturbing dimension to the mystery surrounding Victoria Thompson and the missing Meadowgrove Collection. If there was a connection between the theft and whoever had died at the mill, the stakes of Victoria's quest—and potentially the danger—had just increased significantly.

The rain intensified, lashing against the windows like an urgent warning. In the darkened buildings across Main Street, including the Wilkins Building with its impending transformation, shadows seemed to deepen, as if the past itself was stirring after decades of dormancy.

Julie shivered, drawing Tessa closer. What had begun as concern about preserving Meadowgrove's architectural character had evolved into something far more complex—and possibly dangerous. The town meeting on Tuesday suddenly seemed insufficient to address the layers of mystery unfolding before them.

Her phone buzzed again with a text from Marilyn: *Sheriff just called an emergency meeting of the historical society for tomorrow morning. Says it relates to the mill discovery. Something about identifying artifacts found with the remains.*

Artifacts. The word seemed to pulse with significance. Julie responded quickly: *I'll be there. 9 am at the library?*

Yes, Marilyn confirmed. *And Julie—be careful. I have a feeling we've stumbled into something bigger than preservation politics.*

Julie gazed out at the rain-slicked street below, Meadowgrove transformed into a landscape of shadows and reflections. Somewhere in this familiar town she'd chosen as her sanctuary, long-buried secrets were surfacing—secrets someone might prefer to keep hidden, even now.

With a decisive click, she turned the deadbolt on her apartment door, an extra precaution she rarely took in peaceful Meadowgrove. Tonight, however, the comfortable certainties of small-town life seemed suddenly fragile, like delicate threads that could unravel with a single decisive pull.

Chapter 4
Casting On

The following morning dawned clear and crisp, the previous day's rain having washed the world clean. Julie woke earlier than usual, her sleep disturbed by dreams of hidden treasures and nameless threats. She dressed with care in a navy sweater dress of her own design, paired with comfortable flats—professional enough for the historical society meeting, yet practical for a full day at the shop afterward.

Downstairs, she placed the "Closed Until 11 AM" sign in the window, a rare occurrence that would surely spark curiosity among Meadowgrove's observant residents. Tessa seemed to sense Julie's unease, staying closer than usual as she completed her abbreviated morning routine.

"You can't come to the meeting, girl," Julie told the dachshund apologetically, filling her water bowl. "But I'll be back soon."

Outside, Main Street glistened in the morning sunlight, puddles reflecting the clear blue sky. Julie walked briskly toward the library, her mind organizing questions she hoped might be answered at the emergency meeting. Who were the remains found at the mill? How long had they been there? And most importantly, was there any connection to the missing Meadowgrove Collection?

The Meadowgrove Public Library occupied a graceful Victorian building at the end of Elm Street, its wide steps leading to imposing oak doors. Inside, the scent of old books and polished wood created an atmosphere of hushed reverence. Julie made her way to the conference room at the rear, where the historical society traditionally met.

Several people were already gathered, their murmured conversations creating a nervous undercurrent in the normally sedate space. Julie spotted Marilyn near the front, organizing papers with her characteristic efficiency. Nelly sat nearby, her wild curls particularly untamed this morning, suggesting she'd rushed out without her usual styling routine.

"Julie!" Nelly waved her over. "Have you heard anything new? The morning news had nothing beyond what we already knew."

"Nothing yet," Julie replied, sliding into a seat beside her friends. "Is Sheriff Harris here?"

"Not yet," Marilyn answered, checking her watch. "But several members of the town council have arrived, including Mayor Johnson."

Julie glanced toward the door where Linda Johnson stood conversing with two council members. The mayor, a petite woman in her sixties with an immaculately maintained blonde bob, projected an air of capable authority that had kept her in office for three terms. Despite Marilyn's disapproval of her development-friendly policies, even Julie had to admit the mayor managed Meadowgrove's limited resources with impressive skill.

"Any sign of Victoria Thompson?" Julie asked quietly.

"Not yet, though I'd be surprised if she isn't invited, given her connection to the mill property," Marilyn replied.

As if summoned by their conversation, Victoria entered the room, drawing all eyes with her commanding presence. Today she wore a tailored charcoal suit with a silk scarf at her throat, her ash-blonde hair swept into an elegant chignon. Derek followed a few steps behind, clutching a leather portfolio and looking distinctly uncomfortable under the collective gaze of Meadowgrove's most prominent citizens.

Victoria's eyes swept the room, momentarily pausing when she spotted Julie and her friends. A flicker of something—recognition? wariness?—crossed her face before she composed herself and nodded curtly in their direction.

"Well, that was chilly," Nelly murmured.

"I suspect she knows we've been asking questions," Marilyn whispered back. "Small towns have a way of circulating information."

Further speculation was cut short as Sheriff Harris entered, his tall figure commanding immediate attention. He moved to the front of the room with measured steps, his expression more solemn than usual.

"Thank you all for coming on such short notice," he began without preamble. "As many of you have heard, human remains were discovered yesterday at the old mill property during a preliminary site inspection. I've called this meeting because the circumstances suggest a connection to Meadowgrove's historical society."

A murmur rippled through the assembled group. Julie exchanged glances with Marilyn and Nelly, their shared thoughts evident: Was this about the missing artifacts?

"The remains appear to have been there for several decades," the sheriff continued. "Initial examination by the medical examiner suggests they date back to the 1960s."

Another, louder wave of whispers swept the room. Sheriff Harris raised a hand for silence.

"Along with the remains, we discovered a leather satchel containing what appears to be historical documents—specifically, pages that may have been removed from what you all would know as 'The Founder's Journal.'"

At this, the room erupted in exclamations. The Founder's Journal—one of the most valuable items in the missing Meadowgrove Collection—had been a handwritten account by Jonathan Meadow documenting the town's earliest days. Its disappearance in 1965 had been a significant loss to the town's historical record.

Julie watched Victoria's reaction carefully. The developer maintained an impressive composure, though Julie noticed her hands tightening slightly on the chair in front of her.

Sheriff Harris waited for the commotion to subside before continuing. "I've asked Dr. Eleanor Peterson from the university's history department to authenticate these documents. She'll be arriving this afternoon. In the meantime, I need your help identifying the remains."

He gestured to Deputy Sanchez, who distributed photocopies of what appeared to be a class ring and a partial identification card recovered with the body.

"The ID is too damaged to read clearly," the sheriff explained. "But the ring appears to be from Meadowgrove High School, class of 1958. We're hoping someone might recognize these items and help us identify who this person was."

The room fell silent as everyone examined the images. Julie studied the ring carefully—a simple design featuring the Meadowgrove High emblem of an oak tree. Nothing distinctive jumped out at her, but then, she hadn't grown up in Meadowgrove.

"Thomas Sullivan."

The voice came from the back of the room, where George Whitaker stood, his normally jovial face grave. "That ring belonged to Thomas Sullivan. I recognize the small nick on the band—he damaged it during baseball practice our senior year."

Mayor Johnson paled visibly. "Tommy Sullivan? But he left town to join the military in 1962. His family received letters from him for years afterward."

George shook his head slowly. "I always thought it strange that he never returned for visits. Tom loved Meadowgrove; he talked about coming back and taking over his father's business someday."

Sheriff Harris jotted notes while maintaining his professional demeanor. "Mr. Whitaker, are you certain of this identification?"

"As certain as I can be without seeing the actual ring," George confirmed. "Tom was my best friend in high school. We lost touch after he enlisted, but I'd recognize that ring anywhere."

"Sullivan," Marilyn whispered to Julie. "As in the lakefront property Nelly mentioned—the one Victoria was rumored to be interested in?"

Julie nodded slightly, the connections multiplying in her mind. The Sullivan family had been prominent in Meadowgrove for generations, owning valuable lakefront property that had remained undeveloped despite numerous offers over the years.

"If the remains are indeed Thomas Sullivan," Sheriff Harris continued, "we'll need to understand why he was in the mill around 1965, when his family believed he was serving overseas. And how his body ended up concealed there for nearly sixty years."

His gaze swept the room, lingering briefly on Victoria. "I'm treating this as a suspicious death and potential homicide investigation. I'll be conducting interviews with anyone who might have information about Mr. Sullivan or his connections to the mill property."

The meeting continued with logistical discussions about preserving potential evidence at the mill site and coordinating with the historical society to authenticate the recovered documents. Throughout, Julie observed Victoria, noting how the woman alternated between intense focus and careful detachment, as if consciously managing her reactions.

When the meeting finally adjourned, Julie found herself beside Mayor Johnson at the refreshment table. The mayor looked shaken, her usual poise diminished by the morning's revelations.

"Terrible business," Mayor Johnson murmured, her hand trembling slightly as she poured coffee. "Poor Tommy Sullivan. His sister Elaine still lives in the family home by the lake. She never married—devoted herself to preserving the property after their parents passed."

Julie saw an opportunity to gather information. "The Sullivan property is quite beautiful. I've admired it during summer walks around the lake."

"One of the few undeveloped lakefront parcels left," the mayor agreed. "Developers have been after it for years, but Elaine won't sell. Says it's her responsibility to future generations of Sullivans." She laughed softly, though without humor. "Though who those might be, I couldn't say. Tommy was the last male Sullivan, and with him gone..."

She trailed off, suddenly seeming to realize she'd been unusually forthcoming. "Well, Ms. Sommers, I should speak with Sheriff Harris about informing Elaine privately before this becomes public knowledge. Excuse me."

As the mayor moved away, Nelly appeared at Julie's elbow. "Did you see Victoria's face when they mentioned the Founder's Journal? For just a moment, she looked positively triumphant."

"I noticed," Julie confirmed. "If she's been searching for the missing artifacts, finding even parts of the journal would be significant—both personally and historically."

"But what's the connection to Thomas Sullivan?" Marilyn joined them, keeping her voice low. "And why would pages from the journal be with his body?"

Before they could speculate further, Sheriff Harris approached their small group. "Ms. Sommers, could I have a word?"

Julie nodded, following him to a quieter corner of the room while Marilyn and Nelly watched with poorly concealed curiosity.

"I understand you've been researching Victoria Thompson's family connections to Meadowgrove," the sheriff said without preamble.

Julie maintained a neutral expression. "The historical society has been reviewing records related to the Wilkins Building, yes. Ms. Thompson's family history came up during that research."

Sheriff Harris studied her for a moment, his experienced eyes missing nothing. "Ms. Sommers, I appreciate community interest in local history, but this is now an active death investigation. If you've discovered information that might be relevant to Thomas Sullivan's death or the missing artifacts, I need to know about it. Officially."

Julie considered her options. The sheriff's direct approach suggested he already knew much of what they'd uncovered. Withholding information would only create suspicion and potentially hinder the investigation.

"Victoria Thompson is Margaret Wilkins' granddaughter," she acknowledged. "We discovered that while researching the history of properties she's acquired or shown interest in. Given that her grandmother left town under a cloud of suspicion around the same time these artifacts disappeared—and apparently, around the time Thomas Sullivan died—it seemed worth noting."

Sheriff Harris nodded, unsurprised. "And her interest in your shop building?"

"It was once Wilkins property," Julie explained. "As was the Wilkins Building and the mill site. We think she's systematically acquiring or attempting to acquire properties with family connections."

"Possibly looking for the missing artifacts," the sheriff concluded. It wasn't a question.

"That would be speculation," Julie replied carefully.

A hint of amusement crossed the sheriff's face. "Very diplomatic, Ms. Sommers. But yes, that's our working theory as well. What's less clear is whether Victoria Thompson is merely trying to recover family heirlooms and clear her grandmother's name, or if she knows more about Thomas Sullivan's death than she's letting on."

This direct acknowledgment surprised Julie. "You suspect her involvement?"

"I suspect nothing and everyone until evidence indicates otherwise," Sheriff Harris replied with professional precision. "But I do find it interesting that human remains and missing artifacts surface shortly after Ms. Thompson's arrival in Meadowgrove." He lowered his voice further. "Between us, the renovation permits for the mill property were expedited last week at Ms. Thompson's request. She specifically asked to begin work in the area where the remains were found."

The implications of this were significant. "She knew where to look," Julie realized.

"So it appears." The sheriff straightened, resuming his more formal demeanor. "I'd appreciate it if you'd share any additional discoveries about the Wilkins or Sullivan families with my office directly. And Ms. Sommers? Be careful. Historical secrets sometimes have contemporary guardians."

With that cryptic warning, he nodded politely and moved away to speak with George Whitaker, leaving Julie with a growing sense that Meadowgrove's placid surface concealed dangerous currents.

She rejoined Marilyn and Nelly, who immediately demanded details of her conversation with the sheriff. As Julie relayed the key points, omitting the sheriff's final warning, they were interrupted by the approach of Derek Winters.

"Ms. Sommers," he began hesitantly, glancing over his shoulder to where Victoria was engaged in conversation with Mayor Johnson. "Could I speak with you privately for a moment?"

Intrigued, Julie agreed, following Derek to a quiet alcove near the library's reference section. He seemed even more nervous than usual, repeatedly pushing his glasses up his nose and checking to ensure Victoria remained distracted.

"I wanted to apologize again for last night," he began awkwardly. "I truly wasn't spying on your shop. It's just... my aunt has been acting strangely since we arrived in Meadowgrove, and I'm concerned about her obsession with certain properties."

Julie decided to be direct. "Including Yarn Haven?"

Derek nodded miserably. "She has files on every building that was once owned by the Wilkins family. Maps, architectural plans, renovation records—going back decades. She claims it's for proper historical restoration, but..."

"But you think she's looking for something specific," Julie finished for him.

"The Meadowgrove Collection," he confirmed in a near-whisper. "She's convinced her grandmother was innocent of the theft—that someone else took the artifacts and framed Margaret for it. She's been searching for proof for years, ever since her mother died and left her a letter from Margaret explaining that she fled town to protect herself."

This was significant new information. "Protect herself from what? Or whom?"

Derek glanced nervously toward Victoria again. "I don't know exactly. My aunt doesn't share everything with me, despite my position as her assistant. But I've overheard phone conversations... She believes someone powerful in Meadowgrove was behind both the theft and her grandmother's disgrace."

"Someone like Charles Johnson? The mayor's father?" Julie suggested, recalling the photograph Rose had shown them.

Derek's eyes widened in surprise. "How did you—" He cut himself off as Victoria looked in their direction, a sharp frown crossing her face. "I should go. But please be careful, Ms. Sommers. My aunt is determined to uncover the truth about what happened in 1965, regardless of who gets hurt in the process."

He hurried away, returning to Victoria's side with the subservient manner he usually displayed publicly. Julie watched their interaction thoughtfully, noting how Victoria's posture and expression communicated clear displeasure with her nephew's independent conversation.

When Julie returned to her friends, she shared Derek's warnings in hushed tones as they left the library together.

"So Victoria believes her grandmother was framed for the theft," Marilyn summarized as they walked along Elm Street. "And now Thomas Sullivan's body turns up with pages from the missing journal. The plot thickens."

"It's like something out of an Agatha Christie novel," Nelly declared, her artistic sensibilities clearly enjoying the drama despite its sobering implications. "A decades-old mystery, family secrets, a body hidden away all these years..."

"And a very real person who died," Julie reminded her gently. "Someone who was loved and missed, even if people thought he was simply living elsewhere."

They paused at the corner where they would separate—Marilyn heading to a historical society committee meeting, Nelly to her art studio, and Julie back to Yarn Haven.

"Be careful, both of you," Marilyn cautioned, her former teacher's protective instincts evident. "If there's a connection between Sullivan's death and the missing artifacts, someone in Meadowgrove has been keeping deadly secrets for a very long time."

"And might not appreciate our questions," Nelly added, for once without her customary dramatic flair.

Julie nodded, taking their concerns seriously. "I'll stick to public places and keep my doors locked. Besides, I have Tessa to warn me of trouble."

They parted with promises to check in later, each absorbed in their own thoughts about the morning's revelations. Julie walked briskly back to Yarn Haven, eager to reconnect with the comforting normalcy of her shop after the tension of the meeting.

As she turned onto Main Street, she noticed a sleek black car parked outside her shop—the same vehicle she'd seen Victoria driving. Her steps slowed as she approached, wondering what the developer wanted now.

Instead of Victoria, however, she found Ben Walker waiting by her door, a steaming take-out cup in each hand.

"I thought you might need coffee after that meeting," he said by way of greeting. "Heard it was quite the bombshell."

"News travels fast," Julie observed, unlocking the shop door with a grateful smile. "Thank you for this. It's been an intense morning."

Inside, Tessa greeted them enthusiastically, circling their legs and wagging her entire body until Julie knelt to properly acknowledge her. Ben watched the reunion with evident affection.

"She's a great companion," he commented. "Smart, too. Dogs have excellent instincts about people."

"She likes you," Julie noted as Tessa transferred her attention to Ben, accepting his gentle ear scratches with doggy approval.

"High praise indeed," he replied with a warm smile that crinkled the corners of his eyes. "So, human remains at the mill and missing historical artifacts. Meadowgrove's usually so peaceful that our biggest excitement is debating the harvest festival schedule."

Julie removed the "Closed" sign and flipped on the lights, creating the welcoming atmosphere her customers appreciated. "It's certainly disrupted our small-town routine. Even more so for the Sullivan family. I can't imagine learning that a relative you thought was living somewhere else has actually been... well, you know."

Ben nodded soberly. "I've already had a call from Elaine Sullivan's doctor. She's understandably devastated. Apparently, she received regular letters from her brother until the mid-1970s, when they suddenly stopped. The family assumed he'd settled somewhere and lost touch."

"Letters?" Julie frowned. "But if he died in the 1960s..."

"Exactly. Someone must have been writing those letters, pretending to be Thomas Sullivan." Ben set his coffee on the counter, his expression troubled. "It suggests a level of premeditation and ongoing deception that's disturbing. This wasn't just a moment of violence followed by panic and concealment. Someone deliberately maintained the fiction that Sullivan was alive for years afterward."

The implications sent a chill through Julie. "That's... methodical. And cruel."

"And potentially revealing," Ben added thoughtfully. "Those letters might contain clues—inconsistencies, details that the real Thomas wouldn't have included or known about."

"I wonder if Sheriff Harris has thought to look for them," Julie mused.

"I'm sure he has. Tom Harris is thorough, if nothing else." Ben checked his watch reluctantly. "I should get to the clinic. First patient in twenty minutes."

"Of course. Thank you again for the coffee." Julie walked him to the door, conscious of a comfortable ease between them despite the weight of the morning's events.

At the threshold, Ben turned back, his expression suddenly more serious. "About dinner tomorrow night... are you sure you still want to go? With everything happening, I'd understand if you wanted to postpone."

"Actually, I think I could use an evening away from Meadowgrove mysteries," Julie replied truthfully. "Something normal and pleasant to look forward to."

His smile returned, brighter than before. "I'm glad. Seven o'clock, then. Nothing too fancy—there's a nice Italian place in Burlington I thought you might enjoy."

"Sounds perfect."

After Ben left, the morning progressed with reassuring predictability. Customers came and went, seeking yarn for projects or advice on techniques. Julie guided a young mother through selecting yarn for her first baby blanket, helped an elderly gentleman find a pattern simple enough for his arthritic hands, and restocked the alpaca blend that had proven unexpectedly popular that season.

Yet beneath this normal routine, her mind continued processing the historical society meeting. The connections between Victoria Thompson, the missing artifacts, and now Thomas Sullivan's death formed a pattern that was beginning to take shape, though crucial elements remained unclear.

Around noon, the bell chimed, and Julie looked up to see Elaine Sullivan enter the shop. In her late seventies, Elaine was a Meadowgrove fixture—a dignified, private woman who lived alone in the Sullivan family home on the lake. Though not a knitter herself, she occasionally purchased handcrafted items as gifts.

Today, however, she appeared fragile and disoriented, her usual composure shattered by the morning's news. Julie immediately came around the counter, guiding her to a chair in the sitting area.

"Ms. Sullivan, I'm so sorry about your brother," Julie said gently, signaling to her only other customer that she'd be a few minutes.

"Thank you, dear." Elaine's voice wavered slightly. "Sheriff Harris came to tell me... It's such a shock. All these years, I thought Tommy was out there somewhere, living his life. To learn he never left Meadowgrove at all..."

Her eyes filled with tears that she blinked away with stern self-control. Julie offered her a tissue and a glass of water, respecting the older woman's need to maintain dignity even in grief.

"I don't mean to intrude on your workday," Elaine continued after composing herself. "But Sheriff Harris mentioned you were at the historical society meeting this morning. He thought you might... that is, he said you've been researching some of the town's history from that period."

Julie chose her words carefully. "The historical society has been reviewing records related to several properties from the 1960s, yes. Primarily because of Victoria Thompson's development interests."

"Victoria Thompson," Elaine repeated, a complex emotion crossing her face. "Or should I say Victoria Wilkins-Thompson? Oh yes," she added, seeing Julie's surprise, "I recognized her immediately, though she doesn't know it. She's the image of her grandmother Margaret—a woman I knew very well once."

This was unexpected. "You and Margaret Wilkins were friends?"

"More than that. Margaret was engaged to my brother Tommy before... before everything fell apart." Elaine reached into her handbag and withdrew a small photograph, creased and yellowed with age. It showed a young Thomas Sullivan with his arm around Margaret Wilkins, both smiling broadly at the camera.

Julie accepted the photo carefully, studying the young couple. Their happiness was evident, making the subsequent tragedies—Margaret's flight from town, Thomas's death—even more poignant.

"They were to be married in the spring of 1966," Elaine continued, her voice taking on the distant quality of someone revisiting long-buried memories. "Tommy had completed his military service and returned to Meadowgrove in late 1965. Only a few people knew he was back—he wanted to surprise the town by announcing his engagement to Margaret at the Harvest Festival."

Julie frowned, confused. "But I thought George Whitaker said Thomas left for the military in 1962 and never returned."

"That was the official story," Elaine confirmed. "Tommy requested it that way. He was working on something... something important. He needed people to believe he was still away."

"What was he working on?" Julie asked gently, sensing they were approaching crucial information.

Elaine hesitated, then seemed to make a decision. "I've kept silent for nearly sixty years, believing I was protecting Tommy's work. But with his body found... perhaps it's time for the truth." She straightened in her chair, her dignity reasserting itself. "My brother was investigating the disappearance of historical documents from the town archives—documents that suggested the original land grants in Meadowgrove were based on forged deeds."

Julie's breath caught. This was unexpected. "Forged deeds? Whose?"

"The Johnson family properties," Elaine replied, her voice barely above a whisper despite the empty shop. "According to what Tommy discovered, Charles Johnson's grandfather falsified records to claim land that rightfully belonged to other founding families, including portions of the Wilkins and Sullivan properties."

The implications were staggering. If true, it meant the Johnson family—including the current mayor—had built their prominence on fraudulent claims dating back generations.

"Tommy believed the proof was in the Founder's Journal," Elaine continued. "Specifically, in pages that detailed the original property boundaries. He was working with Margaret to access the journal through her family's connection to the historical society when it disappeared from the museum."

"And Margaret was blamed for the theft," Julie completed the thought. "But you believe..."

"I believe Charles Johnson discovered what Tommy was investigating and took the journal himself—along with other items to make it appear as a general theft rather than a targeted removal of specific documents. When Margaret was accused, Tommy tried to defend her, which must have led to a confrontation with Charles." Elaine's voice broke. "A confrontation my brother didn't survive."

Julie sat back, processing this new perspective on Meadowgrove's history. If Elaine's theory was correct, it painted a very different picture of the events of 1965—one where Margaret Wilkins was indeed innocent of theft, forced to flee a town that had unjustly accused her, while the true culprit not only went free but potentially committed murder to protect his family's secrets.

"Have you shared this theory with Sheriff Harris?" Julie asked.

Elaine shook her head. "Not yet. I wanted to... gather my thoughts first. And I wanted to ask if you've found anything in your research that might support Tommy's suspicions about the land grants."

"Nothing specific about land grants," Julie admitted. "But we did discover that Victoria Thompson has been systematically researching and acquiring properties with historical connections to her family. And according to her nephew, she believes her grandmother was framed for the theft."

"So she's come to clear Margaret's name," Elaine mused. "And perhaps to finish what my brother and her grandmother started—exposing the truth about the Johnson family's claims."

The bell chimed again as a customer entered, breaking the intensity of their conversation. Elaine rose, suddenly seeming tired.

"I've taken enough of your time, Ms. Sommers. Thank you for listening to an old woman's recollections." She carefully returned the photograph to her handbag. "I'll be speaking with Sheriff Harris this afternoon. Whatever happened to Tommy, he deserves justice—even after all these years."

Julie walked her to the door, struck by the woman's quiet strength. "Ms. Sullivan, if there's anything I can do to help, please let me know."

Elaine paused, studying Julie with shrewd eyes that belied her fragile appearance. "You remind me a bit of Margaret—determined, principled. She would have liked you." A shadow passed over her face. "Be careful, dear. Meadowgrove looks peaceful, but old secrets cast long shadows."

It was the second warning Julie had received that day, and she took it seriously. As Elaine departed and Julie turned to assist her waiting customer, she couldn't shake the feeling that merely by asking questions and seeking information, she had positioned herself at the intersection of powerful interests—some historical, some very much present.

The afternoon continued busy enough to keep her physically occupied, if not mentally distracted. Julie found herself watching the street outside with greater awareness, noting when Victoria's car passed by again, slowing slightly as it approached Yarn Haven before continuing toward the Wilkins Building.

Around four o'clock, her phone buzzed with a text from Marilyn: *Sheriff confirming identity of remains as Thomas Sullivan through dental records. Also found partial fingerprint on journal pages that doesn't match Sullivan. News will break publicly tomorrow. Town council calling emergency session tonight.*

Julie responded quickly: *Had visit from Elaine Sullivan. Says Thomas was engaged to Margaret Wilkins, investigating Johnson family land claims when he died. Will explain more later.*

She had just set down her phone when it rang—Ben calling from the clinic.

"I hate to do this," he began, genuine regret in his voice, "but I need to reschedule our dinner tomorrow. The medical examiner has asked me to consult on the Sullivan case, given my background in forensic medicine. We'll be conducting additional examinations tomorrow evening."

"Of course," Julie assured him, hiding her disappointment. "This is important. We can have dinner another time."

"I promise to make it up to you," Ben said warmly. "Perhaps Sunday instead? Assuming Meadowgrove's secrets don't uncover any more bodies between now and then."

His attempt at gallows humor made Julie smile despite everything. "Sunday works. And Ben? Please be careful. The more I learn about what happened in 1965, the more I suspect there are people who'd prefer these secrets stay buried."

"Always the cautious type," he replied lightly, though she detected a note of genuine concern beneath. "But I appreciate the warning. I'll check in tomorrow, let you know what we find—professionally speaking, of course."

After they hung up, Julie tried to refocus on work, but her encounter with Elaine Sullivan had shifted something fundamental in her understanding of Meadowgrove's past—and perhaps its present as well.

If Charles Johnson had indeed killed Thomas Sullivan to prevent the exposure of fraudulent land claims, and if those claims remained legally uncontested after sixty years of Johnson family prominence... what might the current generation of Johnsons do to protect that legacy?

The question lingered as Julie completed her closing routine, carefully locking the shop before heading upstairs with Tessa. She found herself double-checking the apartment locks, drawing the curtains fully closed, and keeping her phone closer than usual—small actions that acknowledged the subtle shift in her sense of security.

Outside, the streets of Meadowgrove grew quiet as evening settled in, the familiar rhythms of small-town life continuing despite the day's revelations. Lights came on in windows, people walked dogs along the sidewalks, cars occasionally passed heading home or to dinner engagements.

Yet beneath this peaceful surface, Julie sensed the town holding its collective breath—waiting to see what other secrets might emerge from the shadows of its past, and who might be implicated in their long concealment.

Chapter 5
Dropped Stitches

Julie woke with a start, momentarily disoriented until she recognized the familiar contours of her bedroom ceiling illuminated by the first hints of dawn. Beside her, Tessa snored softly, undisturbed by whatever had jolted Julie from sleep. Hildi was nowhere to be seen, likely already prowling the apartment in search of early breakfast.

It took a moment for Julie to identify what had awakened her—a vehicle door slamming on the street below, followed by the murmur of voices. She slipped out of bed and moved to the window, carefully drawing back the curtain just enough to peer outside.

A police cruiser was parked in front of Yarn Haven, its lights off but officially present. Sheriff Harris stood on the sidewalk conversing with Deputy Sanchez, both men scanning the surrounding buildings with professional vigilance. The scene was eerily reminiscent of crime shows Julie had watched, except this was happening on her doorstep in peaceful Meadowgrove.

She checked the time—5:47 a.m. Far too early for a casual visit. Something had happened.

Julie dressed quickly in jeans and a sweater, running a brush through her hair and splashing water on her face before heading downstairs. As she reached the shop level, she noticed the security system's green light blinking steadily—no breaches overnight. Still, an uneasy feeling persisted as she approached the front door.

Sheriff Harris turned at her appearance, his expression a careful mask of professional neutrality. "Ms. Sommers. Apologize for the early hour."

"Is something wrong?" Julie asked, unlocking the door to step outside into the crisp morning air.

"Potentially." The sheriff gestured toward the Wilkins Building across the street. "There was an incident overnight. Someone broke into the construction site. Security cameras caught them attempting to access the building's foundation area with specialized equipment."

Julie frowned. "Thieves looking for construction materials?"

"More like someone searching for something specific," Sheriff Harris replied. "They brought ground-penetrating radar equipment and seemed focused on the original cellar area. When the security guard approached, they fled, but not before firing a warning shot."

A chill ran through Julie that had nothing to do with the autumn morning. "Was anyone hurt?"

"Fortunately, no. But it escalates the situation considerably." The sheriff's gaze sharpened. "Ms. Sommers, given your shop's proximity and your... interest in the historical aspects of these properties, I wanted to personally advise caution. Whoever broke in was professional and potentially dangerous."

Deputy Sanchez nodded toward the shop. "We recommend reviewing your security procedures, ma'am. Maybe consider a temporary camera system."

Julie absorbed this advice, her mind connecting the break-in to their recent discoveries. "You think this is related to the artifacts? To Thomas Sullivan?"

Sheriff Harris glanced around before responding, his voice lowered. "In my experience, when a sixty-year-old body and missing historical items surface in a small town, followed immediately by an armed break-in at a connected property, coincidence isn't the most likely explanation."

"Has Victoria Thompson been informed?" Julie asked, recalling the developer's focused interest in the Wilkins Building.

"She's my next stop," the sheriff confirmed. "Though I'd appreciate your discretion regarding this conversation. Official statements will be released later today."

As if summoned by her name, Victoria's black car appeared at the end of the street, moving purposefully toward the Wilkins Building. The sheriff nodded to Julie.

"Remember what I said about caution, Ms. Sommers. And if you notice anything unusual, call the station immediately. Don't investigate yourself."

With that warning, he returned to the cruiser with Deputy Sanchez, driving the short distance to intercept Victoria as she parked.

Julie remained on her doorstep for a moment, watching as the sheriff approached Victoria. Even from this distance, she could see the developer's posture stiffen at whatever news Harris delivered. Victoria's gaze swept across the street, briefly locking with Julie's before returning to the sheriff with renewed intensity.

The encounter left Julie feeling exposed, as if merely witnessing these events had drawn her further into their orbit. She retreated into the shop, locking the door behind her and taking comfort in the familiar surroundings—shelves of colorful yarn, the comfortable seating area, Tessa's bed beside the counter, all bathed in the golden light of early morning.

She went through her opening routine mechanically, mind whirling with implications. Someone was searching the Wilkins Building's foundation—similar to Victoria's expedited excavations at the mill where Thomas Sullivan's body was found. Were they looking for more missing artifacts? Evidence related to Sullivan's death? Or something else entirely?

By the time Julie officially opened the shop at nine, she'd reached out to both Marilyn and Nelly, arranging to meet for lunch to share what she'd learned. She'd also called a security company to inquire about temporary cameras, taking Deputy Sanchez's advice seriously.

The morning passed in a blur of customers and routine tasks, Julie maintaining a professional demeanor despite her distraction. Around ten-thirty, the bell chimed, admitting Ben Walker. He looked tired but focused, nodding to a customer examining sock yarn before approaching the counter.

"I heard about the break-in," he said without preamble, voice low enough to avoid being overheard. "Sheriff Harris mentioned you might be concerned, given your location across from the Wilkins Building."

Julie appreciated his directness. "He stopped by this morning. Recommended security cameras."

"Good advice," Ben agreed. "I called because... well, this might be nothing, but yesterday after our call, I received a visit from Mayor Johnson at the clinic. She wanted to discuss 'community health initiatives,' but spent most of the time asking about my involvement with the Sullivan case and whether I'd found anything noteworthy during initial examinations."

Julie frowned. "That seems inappropriate."

"It was," Ben confirmed. "I kept my responses strictly professional, of course, but her interest struck me as unusual. When I mentioned working with the university's forensic anthropologist on dating the remains, she became particularly interested in whether we could precisely determine time of death."

"As if she wanted to know if it could be connected to a specific event—or person," Julie suggested.

"Exactly." Ben glanced around the shop, ensuring they weren't overheard. "Linda Johnson would have been quite young when Sullivan died—probably a teenager—but her father Charles was prominent in town then. If Elaine Sullivan's theory about land fraud is accurate..."

"Then Mayor Johnson might have personal reasons to be concerned about the investigation," Julie completed the thought. "Family legacy, possibly her own inheritance if the land claims were fraudulent."

Ben nodded grimly. "It's circumstantial, but worth noting. I just wanted you to be aware, especially after the break-in."

Julie felt a rush of warmth at his concern. "Thank you. I'm being careful, I promise."

"Good." His expression softened. "Still on for Sunday dinner?"

"Absolutely. A normal evening sounds perfect right now."

After Ben left for the clinic, Julie found herself watching the street outside with heightened awareness. The police presence had increased, with patrol cars passing regularly. Across at the Wilkins Building, workers had been sent home while crime scene technicians examined the break-in site.

Crochet Carnage

Victoria Thompson remained on the scene, her elegant figure distinctive even at a distance as she conversed with contractors and police alternately. Julie noticed she seemed to be directing particular attention to the foundation area, gesturing emphatically during one exchange with the construction foreman.

The bell chimed again, drawing Julie's attention back to the shop. Derek Winters entered, looking even more harried than usual, his sandy hair standing up as if he'd been repeatedly running his hands through it.

"Ms. Sommers," he began, then corrected himself. "Julie. I need to talk to you. Privately, if possible."

The urgency in his voice prompted Julie to guide him to the back room, asking her only customer—a regular who knew the shop well—to call if she needed assistance.

Once they were alone, Derek seemed to deflate slightly, sinking into a chair with uncharacteristic abandon. "Everything's falling apart," he murmured, removing his glasses to rub his eyes. "Aunt Victoria is obsessed with finding those artifacts, to the point of recklessness."

"The break-in last night," Julie prompted. "Was that her doing?"

Derek's head snapped up, alarm evident. "God, no! That's partly why I'm here. She's furious about it—someone else is searching for the same things she is, but they're willing to use violence."

This was a perspective Julie hadn't considered. Victoria might be driven and manipulative, but there was no evidence she was violent.

"Who else would be looking?" Julie wondered aloud.

"That's what I'm trying to figure out." Derek replaced his glasses, his demeanor shifting from panicked to determined. "Aunt Victoria believes it's someone connected to the original theft and Sullivan's death—someone who knows where the artifacts were hidden and wants to recover them before she exposes the truth about what happened in 1965."

Julie considered this. "The Johnson family has the most to lose if Victoria proves her grandmother was framed and uncovers evidence of fraudulent land claims."

"Yes, but would they resort to armed break-ins now, after keeping these secrets for sixty years?" Derek shook his head. "It seems desperate."

"Unless something has changed—like finding Sullivan's body and those journal pages," Julie pointed out. "If the missing artifacts contain proof of land fraud, and if that evidence has been hidden all this time, the discovery at the mill could have triggered a race to find the remaining items before the truth comes out."

Derek nodded slowly. "My aunt believes most of the collection is still hidden somewhere in Meadowgrove—specifically, in one of the properties originally owned by the Wilkins family. That's why she's been so intent on acquiring them."

"Including my shop?" Julie asked directly.

"Yes," Derek admitted. "Though she's recently shifted her focus to the Wilkins Building and the old mill. Something in her research indicated those are the most likely locations."

Julie remembered the sheriff's comment about Victoria's specific interest in the mill's excavation area. "She knew where to look for Sullivan's body, didn't she? That's why she expedited permits for that particular section of the mill."

Derek hesitated, clearly torn between loyalty to his aunt and growing concern about her methods. "She found references in her mother's papers—letters from Margaret describing a confrontation between Thomas Sullivan and Charles Johnson at the mill the night the artifacts disappeared. But Aunt Victoria didn't know about the body, I swear. She thought she might find more of the missing collection there."

"And instead found evidence of murder," Julie concluded. "No wonder she's escalated her timeline. She's not just clearing her grandmother's name anymore—she's potentially solving a homicide."

"While putting herself in danger," Derek added grimly. "Whoever broke into the Wilkins Building last night knows what they're looking for and is willing to fire warning shots. Next time might be worse."

Julie studied him, recognizing genuine fear beneath his agitation. "Derek, why are you telling me this? Why not go to Sheriff Harris?"

"Because Aunt Victoria doesn't trust the local authorities. She believes the power structures in Meadowgrove have protected the Johnson family for generations." He leaned forward earnestly. "But she respects you—your independence, your connection to the community without being part of its old guard. She mentioned it after your first meeting, though she'd never admit it to your face."

This was unexpected. "So what are you asking me to do?"

"Help me convince her to slow down, to work with proper authorities instead of conducting her own investigation," Derek pleaded. "After last night's break-in, I'm genuinely worried about her safety—and about what she might do next. She's talking about accessing the Wilkins Building herself tonight to search the foundation before the police finish processing the scene."

Julie frowned. "That would be interfering with an investigation—potentially destroying evidence."

"I know," Derek agreed miserably. "But she's convinced that whoever broke in last night will come back, and she's determined to find whatever they're looking for first."

Their conversation was interrupted by Julie's customer calling from the front of the shop. She excused herself briefly to assist with a purchase, returning to find Derek examining a photograph on her bulletin board—a snapshot of Yarn Haven from the 1930s when it was still a Wilkins Mercantile branch.

"Where did you get this?" he asked, an odd intensity in his voice.

"Town archives," Julie replied. "I was researching the building's history when I took over the shop."

Derek studied the image closely. "This architectural detail above the doorway—it's different from the current entrance."

Julie came to look over his shoulder. "Yes, the entrance was remodeled in the 1950s when it became a dress shop. The original doorway had an ornate pediment with the Wilkins family crest."

"And when the remodel happened, what became of the original stonework?" Derek asked, excitement creeping into his voice.

Julie considered the question. "I'm not sure. The basement storage area has some architectural elements from various renovations. I've never really explored it thoroughly—it's mostly used for seasonal inventory storage now."

Derek turned to her, eyes bright behind his glasses. "Aunt Victoria has been focusing on the Wilkins Building and the mill because they were the most prominent family properties, but what if that's wrong? What if Margaret and Thomas chose a less obvious hiding place for the artifacts—a building still in Wilkins hands but not as closely monitored?"

The implication was clear. "You think they might have hidden the Meadowgrove Collection here? In what is now my shop?"

"It would make strategic sense," Derek argued. "Hiding valuable items in plain sight, in a building still under family control but not one that would be immediately searched if suspicions arose."

Julie's mind raced with possibilities. She'd owned Yarn Haven for three years but had never thoroughly examined the older architectural elements in the basement. Like most shop owners, she used her limited time for customer-facing improvements rather than exploring forgotten storage areas.

"If there is something hidden here, we should tell Sheriff Harris," she said firmly. "This is now part of a potential homicide investigation."

"Of course," Derek agreed quickly. "But could we just take a preliminary look? If there's nothing suspicious, we haven't wasted the sheriff's time. If we do find something, we call him immediately."

Julie hesitated, torn between curiosity and caution. The sheriff had specifically warned her not to investigate on her own. Yet this was her building, and a quick look at the basement storage hardly constituted dangerous detective work.

"A quick look," she finally agreed. "And only during regular business hours, with customers present. I'm not taking unnecessary risks."

Derek nodded eagerly. "That's all I'm suggesting. When would be convenient?"

"I close at six," Julie said. "If you return around five-thirty, we can check the basement before I lock up. That gives us enough time but ensures we're not alone in the building after hours."

"Perfect. Thank you, Julie." Derek's relief was palpable. "And please don't mention this to Aunt Victoria yet. If we find nothing, it will just be another disappointment for her. If we find something significant, we'll involve Sheriff Harris immediately."

After Derek left, Julie returned to her regular duties, but her thoughts repeatedly drifted to the basement storage area and its potential secrets. Had she been living and working above hidden historical treasures all this time? The idea seemed fantastical, yet no more improbable than the other revelations of recent days.

At noon, Julie placed the "Back in 1 Hour" sign on the door and walked to The Greenery to meet Marilyn and Nelly. She found them already seated at their usual corner table, Nelly's wild curls particularly vibrant against her emerald tunic, Marilyn's silver bob neat as always above a sensible navy cardigan.

"There she is," Nelly called, waving enthusiastically. "Our friend at the center of Meadowgrove's biggest mystery in decades."

"Hardly," Julie demurred, sliding into her seat. "But I do have news."

Over lunch, she recounted both the early morning visit from Sheriff Harris and her later conversation with Derek, watching her friends' expressions shift from concern to fascination as she described the possible connection to her own building.

"It's not implausible," Marilyn acknowledged after careful consideration. "The shop was still Wilkins property in 1965 when the artifacts disappeared. If Margaret and Thomas were working together to expose the Johnson family's land fraud, they would have needed a secure hiding place for the evidence."

"And what better spot than a building right on Main Street, hiding in plain sight?" Nelly added, her artistic imagination clearly captured by the possibility. "This is absolutely riveting! When are we exploring the basement?"

"We aren't," Julie corrected firmly. "Derek is coming by at five-thirty, and we'll take a preliminary look. If anything seems suspicious, we call Sheriff Harris immediately."

"But you'll need witnesses," Nelly protested. "For safety and for verification if you find something."

"She has a point," Marilyn agreed, surprising Julie with her uncharacteristic endorsement of Nelly's enthusiasm. "If you discover important historical artifacts related to a potential homicide, having reliable witnesses would be prudent."

Julie sighed, recognizing the determined glint in both women's eyes. "Fine. You can both come at five-thirty. But this is a quick, careful examination of the basement—not an archaeological excavation or a treasure hunt. Derek seems genuinely concerned about Victoria's escalating behavior, and I don't want to contribute to the problem."

"Agreed," Marilyn said firmly, giving Nelly a pointed look. "Responsible adults examining architectural elements of historical interest. Nothing more."

Nelly rolled her eyes but nodded. "Yes, yes. Completely sensible and boring. Though if we do find a hidden chamber containing valuable artifacts connected to a sixty-year-old murder, I reserve the right to be appropriately excited."

Their conversation shifted to preparations for the upcoming town meeting, now further complicated by the Sullivan discovery and the break-in at the Wilkins Building. Julie found herself grateful for her friends' different perspectives—Marilyn's methodical approach and respect for proper procedures balanced by Nelly's intuitive insights and willingness to consider unconventional possibilities.

As they parted ways after lunch, Julie felt more centered than she had since waking to find police outside her shop. Whatever the basement exploration revealed—or didn't reveal—she wouldn't face it alone.

The afternoon passed steadily, with enough customers to keep Julie occupied without overwhelming her. She found herself studying the shop's interior with new awareness, noting architectural details she'd previously taken for granted—the height of the ceilings, the placement of support beams, the slightly uneven floorboards in the back corner that had always creaked underfoot.

Had Margaret Wilkins and Thomas Sullivan walked these same floors, planning where to hide evidence of historical fraud? Had they conversed in whispers as customers browsed, mapping out their strategy to expose the Johnson family's deception? The idea lent the familiar space an air of conspiracy and significance Julie had never considered before.

At five o'clock, her last customer departed with yarn for a grandchild's sweater, leaving Julie alone in the shop. She used the quiet time to tidy displays and prepare mentally for the basement exploration. The storage area was accessed through a door behind the counter, stone steps leading down to a space that ran the full length of the building but was divided by rough brick walls into several rooms of varying sizes.

Julie rarely ventured beyond the first room, which housed seasonal inventory and supplies. The deeper sections contained remnants of the building's previous incarnations—old display cases, forgotten signage, architectural elements removed during renovations. She'd always intended to sort through it properly but had never found the time amidst the demands of running the shop.

At precisely five-thirty, the bell chimed as Derek arrived, followed moments later by Marilyn and Nelly. Derek seemed surprised by the additional participants but recovered quickly, apparently relieved to have more support.

"I've been thinking about where to focus our attention," he said, setting his messenger bag on the counter. "Based on the photograph and the renovation date, we should look at architectural elements removed in the 1950s—particularly anything from the original entrance with the Wilkins crest."

"The oldest storage section is at the far end of the basement," Julie informed them, leading the way to the access door. "I don't go back there often—it's mostly remnants from before my time."

She flipped a switch at the top of the stairs, illuminating a bare bulb that cast more shadows than light on the stone steps. Tessa, picking up on the excitement, attempted to follow, but Julie gently redirected her to her bed.

"Sorry, girl. Too many hazards down there for small paws."

The four descended single file, Julie leading with her phone's flashlight augmenting the minimal lighting. The basement air was cool and slightly musty, carrying the scent of aged wood and stone that had stood for over a century.

They passed through the first storage room with its neatly organized bins of holiday-themed yarn and seasonal displays, then through a narrower doorway into a second chamber where previous owners had stored unused fixtures and furniture. Beyond this lay their destination—the deepest section of the basement, rarely visited and filled with the building's oldest remnants.

Julie swept her light across the space, revealing dusty shapes draped with cloths, stacked wooden crates, and leaning against one wall, the distinctive outline of the original doorway pediment bearing the Wilkins family crest—an oak tree with intertwined roots.

"There it is," Derek said softly, moving toward the stone piece. "Exactly as it appeared in the photograph."

Together they carefully examined the pediment, a substantial half-circle of carved limestone approximately four feet across. Derek ran his fingers along the detailed crest, his expression intent.

"These symbols had specific meaning to founding families," he explained. "The oak represented strength and longevity, while the roots symbolized deep connection to the land. For a family whose wealth came from property..."

"It would be particularly significant," Marilyn completed the thought. "And potentially ironic if used to conceal evidence of another family's land fraud."

Julie studied the pediment with fresh eyes, noting how the deeply carved design created numerous shadows and recesses. "Is there anything unusual about the carving? Any area that might conceal a small space?"

Derek examined it more closely, then shook his head. "It appears solid. But maybe it's not the pediment itself but where it was positioned..." He glanced around the basement. "Where exactly was the original entrance in relation to the current shop layout?"

"Directly above us," Julie realized. "The entrance was moved about ten feet to the right during renovations, but we're standing approximately where it would have been."

They all instinctively looked up, their lights revealing rough ceiling beams and exposed floor joists from the shop above.

"There," Nelly said suddenly, pointing to a section of the wall just behind where the pediment leaned. "That stonework looks different from the rest—more recent mortar."

She was right. A rectangular section of the foundation wall, approximately three feet wide and two feet high, showed subtle differences in the mortar between stones—slightly different coloration, a marginally different texture.

"Good eye," Marilyn commented, examining the section more closely. "This area has been opened and resealed at some point, though quite skillfully."

Derek ran his fingers along the edges of the suspicious area. "Could be a former coal chute or utility access that was sealed during renovations."

"Or a hiding place," Nelly suggested, her voice vibrating with excitement. "Created by someone who knew the building's structure and had time to work carefully."

Julie felt her heart rate accelerate. Could they actually be on the verge of discovering artifacts hidden for sixty years? She reminded herself to maintain perspective—this could easily be nothing more than an old utility access point, sealed during one of the building's many renovations.

"If someone did create a hidden compartment here," she said thoughtfully, "they would have needed a way to access it again. Some kind of mechanism or key."

Derek turned his attention back to the pediment, examining it with renewed focus. "The Wilkins crest might be more than decorative. These older architectural elements often incorporated practical features disguised as ornamentation."

He pressed various parts of the carved design experimentally, pausing when a small section of the intertwined roots shifted slightly under pressure. With more deliberate force, he pressed again, and they all heard a distinct click from within the wall.

"Did you hear that?" Nelly whispered, though they were alone in the basement.

Marilyn approached the wall section, running her fingers along the stones until she found a slight indentation. When she applied pressure, a portion of the wall moved inward an inch or two, revealing it was not solid stone but a cleverly disguised door.

"I think we should call Sheriff Harris now," Julie said, her voice steady despite her racing pulse. "This is beyond a casual exploration."

Derek nodded, though his gaze remained fixed on the partially revealed compartment. "You're right. This is potentially significant evidence."

Before anyone could move, however, a noise from upstairs froze them in place—the distinctive chime of the shop door opening, followed by footsteps on the wooden floor.

"Did you lock the front door?" Marilyn whispered to Julie.

"Yes," Julie confirmed, alarm rising. "And I placed the 'Closed' sign."

The footsteps moved purposefully across the shop above their heads, then paused.

"Tessa will bark if it's an intruder," Julie whispered. As if on cue, they heard the dachshund's distinctive warning growl, followed by sharper barking.

"We need to call 911," Marilyn stated firmly, already reaching for her phone.

Before she could dial, a voice called down the stairs. "I know you're down there. All of you. I suggest you come up immediately, without any sudden movements."

The voice was male, unfamiliar, and carried the unmistakable tone of someone accustomed to being obeyed. More disturbing was the implication that he knew exactly who was in the basement and what they might have discovered.

Derek's face had gone pale. "That's not my aunt," he whispered unnecessarily. "Someone followed me here."

"Options?" Nelly mouthed silently to Julie, gesturing to indicate there might be another exit.

Julie shook her head slightly. The basement's only exit was the stairs they'd descended—directly toward whoever had entered the shop.

"I'm coming up," she called, making a swift decision. "The others are just helping me with inventory. They're not involved in this."

"Admirable but futile," the voice replied. "All of you, please. I'm not a patient man, and your little dog seems quite agitated."

The mention of Tessa decided the matter for Julie. "Stay behind me," she instructed the others, moving toward the stairs with her phone discreetly in hand, hoping to dial 911 once she assessed the situation above.

As they ascended the narrow staircase single file, Julie's mind raced through possibilities. A thief? Someone connected to the break-in at the Wilkins Building? A Johnson family ally protecting old secrets?

Emerging into the shop, Julie found an answer she hadn't anticipated. Standing calmly beside the counter, one hand resting on a still-growling Tessa's head while the other held what was unmistakably a gun, was Edward Thompson—Victoria's ex-husband, who had made brief, unmemorable appearances in Meadowgrove over the previous weeks.

"Ms. Sommers," he acknowledged with a cold smile. "And friends. How fortunate to find you all together. Now, why don't you tell me what you've discovered in that quaint little basement of yours?"

Chapter 6
Weaving Clues

For a moment, the only sound in Yarn Haven was Tessa's continued growling, her small body tense beneath Edward Thompson's hand. Julie assessed their situation with growing alarm. The man she'd previously dismissed as Victoria's bland ex-husband now radiated a cold authority that transformed his unmemorable features into something more dangerous.

"Mr. Thompson," Julie acknowledged, keeping her voice steady despite her racing heart. "The shop is closed. I'm going to have to ask you to leave."

A thin smile crossed his face. "Admirable composure, Ms. Sommers. However, I think we both know this isn't a routine business encounter." His fingers tightened slightly on Tessa's collar, causing the dog to whimper. "Now, about that basement discovery..."

Behind Julie, she could feel Marilyn and Nelly shifting uneasily. Derek remained frozen, his face a mask of confusion and fear. Julie needed to gain control of the situation somehow, to create an opportunity for them to reach help.

"We were just examining old architectural elements," she said, gesturing vaguely. "The building has an interesting history."

"Indeed it does," Thompson agreed smoothly. "As do many properties in Meadowgrove. The Wilkins holdings in particular have... fascinating backgrounds." His gaze sharpened. "But let's not waste time with evasions. You found a concealed compartment in the foundation wall, did you not?"

The specific knowledge sent a chill through Julie. How could he possibly know about a hidden space they'd only discovered minutes ago? Unless...

"You're the one who broke into the Wilkins Building last night," she realized aloud. "With the ground-penetrating radar."

"A regrettable necessity," Thompson admitted without a trace of actual regret. "I had hoped to locate certain items without drawing attention, but time is becoming a factor. Especially now that Victoria's excavations have uncovered poor Thomas Sullivan."

Julie's mind raced. If Thompson was searching for the same artifacts as Victoria, but working independently, what was his connection to all this? And more urgently, how could she protect her friends from this armed intruder?

"I don't understand," Derek finally spoke, his voice strained. "You and Aunt Victoria divorced years ago. Why are you involved in her search for the Meadowgrove Collection?"

Thompson's smile widened, becoming more genuine yet somehow more disturbing. "Ah, young Derek. Always the loyal nephew, though your aunt hardly deserves such devotion. As for my involvement..." His expression hardened. "Let's just say I have a professional interest in recovering those artifacts—an interest that predates my strategic marriage to Victoria Wilkins."

The implications of this statement hung in the air. A strategic marriage? Professional interest? The pieces began to align in Julie's mind.

"You're not really Edward Thompson," she stated, the certainty growing as she spoke. "At least, that's not who you were when you married Victoria. You pursued her because of her connection to Margaret Wilkins and the missing artifacts."

"Very good, Ms. Sommers," he acknowledged with a slight nod. "Though the name is real enough—one of several I've used professionally over the years. Antiquities acquisition is my specialty, you see. Private collectors pay extraordinary sums for historically significant items with... complicated provenances."

"You're a thief," Marilyn said flatly, her schoolteacher voice cutting through the tension.

Thompson shrugged, unoffended. "A finder of lost treasures, I prefer. The Meadowgrove Collection has been technically lost for sixty years—no active claims, no current ownership records. Perfect for my purposes."

"Except the items rightfully belong to this town," Nelly interjected, her artistic sensibilities clearly offended by his mercenary attitude toward historical artifacts.

"Details," Thompson dismissed. "Now, since time is of the essence, I suggest we proceed to the basement where you'll show me exactly what you've found. After that, I'll be on my way, and this unpleasant encounter can become just another colorful anecdote about the dangers of amateur sleuthing."

Julie caught the subtle threat beneath his casual tone. Thompson had no intention of leaving witnesses who could identify him to authorities—not when he was so close to obtaining the valuable artifacts he'd pursued for years.

As if sensing her realization, Thompson's expression hardened. "Shall we?" He gestured toward the basement door with his free hand, the gun still firmly gripped in the other.

In that crucial moment, as Julie struggled to formulate a response that might buy them time, Tessa made a decision of her own. The little dachshund, perhaps sensing the tension or simply tired of being restrained by an unfamiliar hand, suddenly twisted and nipped at Thompson's fingers.

"Damn it!" he exclaimed, momentarily distracted as he pulled his hand away from the dog.

Julie seized the opportunity, lunging forward to snatch Tessa while simultaneously shouting, "Run! Get help!"

Chaos erupted in the small shop. Nelly bolted for the front door, her bohemian skirts swirling as she moved with unexpected speed. Marilyn, showing admirable presence of mind, grabbed a heavy wooden swift from a nearby display and swung it toward Thompson's gun hand.

The impact wasn't direct, but it was enough to throw off his aim as he raised the weapon. The gun discharged with a frighteningly loud crack, the bullet embedding itself in the ceiling as Derek tackled Thompson from the side, sending both men crashing into a display of merino wool.

"Julie, go!" Derek shouted, struggling to pin Thompson's gun arm. "Get Sheriff Harris!"

Instead of fleeing, Julie set Tessa down behind the counter and grabbed her phone, dialing 911 with shaking fingers as she moved to help Derek. Thompson was stronger than his bland appearance suggested, already gaining advantage in their struggle despite Marilyn's continued attacks with the wooden swift.

"Meadowgrove Emergency Services," a dispatcher's voice answered.

"Armed intruder at Yarn Haven on Main Street," Julie reported rapidly. "Shots fired. We need help immediately."

"Officers are being dispatched," the dispatcher assured her. "Can you safely leave the premises?"

Before Julie could answer, a sickening thud heralded Derek being thrown against the counter, his glasses shattering as he crumpled to the floor. Thompson rose, breathing heavily, his previously neat appearance disheveled but his grip on the gun once again secure.

"Enough!" he snarled, all pretense of civility gone. "No more games. To the basement, now, or I start shooting more permanently."

Julie dropped her phone, leaving the line open so the dispatcher could hear. "All right," she agreed, raising her hands placatingly while trying to position herself between Thompson and the unconscious Derek. "I'll show you what we found. Just please don't hurt anyone else."

Thompson gestured impatiently with the gun. "Move."

Marilyn caught Julie's eye, silently asking if they should comply or keep fighting. Julie gave a small nod—with Derek injured and Thompson armed, their best option was to cooperate until help arrived. Nelly had escaped; surely Sheriff Harris would be here soon.

They descended the basement stairs in tense silence, Thompson following close behind. Julie's mind raced, trying to formulate a plan. The basement offered few advantages—a confined space with only one exit, now blocked by an armed man.

"Where is it?" Thompson demanded as they reached the deepest section with the partially revealed compartment.

"Here," Julie indicated the wall section they'd discovered. "We had just found this hidden door when you arrived."

Thompson approached eagerly, momentarily lowering the gun as he examined the stonework. "Ingenious," he murmured. "Hidden in plain sight for sixty years."

Taking advantage of his distraction, Marilyn slowly reached for a heavy metal pipe leaning against a nearby crate. Julie caught the movement and deliberately continued talking to hold Thompson's attention.

"We think Margaret Wilkins and Thomas Sullivan created this hiding place," she explained, taking a small step to the side to block Thompson's peripheral vision of Marilyn. "They must have worked on it after hours, when the shop was closed."

"Of course they did," Thompson agreed, running his fingers along the edges of the hidden door. "Thomas was a skilled mason—worked construction between his military service stints. And Margaret had access to the building through her family connections. The perfect collaboration." He pressed experimentally on the door, which moved another inch. "How did you trigger the mechanism?"

"The pediment," Julie indicated the carved stonework. "There's a pressure point in the carved roots."

As Thompson turned to examine the pediment, Marilyn struck, swinging the pipe with all her strength toward his head. Whether through instinct or peripheral awareness, Thompson partially ducked, the pipe glancing off his shoulder instead of his skull. He staggered but maintained his footing, whirling to face Marilyn with rage contorting his features.

"You persistent old—" He raised the gun toward Marilyn, finger tightening on the trigger.

Julie reacted without conscious thought, grabbing the nearest object—a heavy ceramic mixing bowl left from when the building housed a bakery—and hurling it at Thompson's head. Her aim was true, the bowl connecting with a resonant crack that sent Thompson stumbling sideways, the gun firing harmlessly into a stack of crates.

Before he could recover, the basement was suddenly filled with shouting voices and the beam of powerful flashlights as Sheriff Harris and two deputies descended the stairs at a run, weapons drawn.

"Police! Drop the weapon!" Harris commanded, his service pistol trained on Thompson.

For a moment, it seemed Thompson might attempt something desperate, his eyes darting between the officers and the hidden compartment. Then, with the calculating precision that likely characterized his professional endeavors, he carefully placed the gun on the floor and raised his hands.

"This is a misunderstanding," he began smoothly, slipping back into his affable persona. "I was merely—"

"Save it," Sheriff Harris interrupted, nodding to Deputy Sanchez to secure the weapon while he handcuffed Thompson. "We heard plenty over Ms. Sommers' open phone line. Edward Thompson—if that's even your real name—you're under arrest for multiple felonies, including armed assault, unlawful imprisonment, and discharge of a firearm within city limits. More charges pending, I'm certain."

As Thompson was led away, still protesting his innocence, Julie sagged against the wall, the adrenaline that had sustained her throughout the confrontation beginning to ebb. Marilyn moved to her side, the older woman's hand trembling slightly as she patted Julie's shoulder.

"Are you all right?" Marilyn asked, her voice steadier than her hands.

"I think so," Julie managed. "Derek's hurt upstairs. And Nelly—"

"Is fine," Sheriff Harris assured her, holstering his weapon. "She flagged down a patrol car on Main Street—that's how we got here so quickly. Paramedics are attending to Mr. Winters upstairs. Now, would either of you like to explain exactly what Thompson was so interested in down here?"

Julie took a steadying breath and indicated the concealed compartment. "We believe this may contain items from the missing Meadowgrove Collection—historical artifacts stolen in 1965 when Margaret Wilkins left town."

Sheriff Harris examined the partially opened door with professional interest. "And how exactly did you come to find this hidden compartment in your basement?"

Julie explained Derek's theory about Yarn Haven being a potential hiding place due to its status as a less obvious Wilkins property, along with their discovery of the renovation changes and modified stonework. As she spoke, paramedics descended the stairs, coming to check on the two women despite their assurances that they were physically unharmed.

"Well," Sheriff Harris said when she'd finished, "I'd say this officially moves from interesting historical research to active evidence in two investigations—the theft of the Meadowgrove Collection and Thomas

Sullivan's homicide. I'm going to need to secure this basement as a crime scene until we can properly document and examine that compartment."

"Of course," Julie agreed readily. "Whatever you need."

"Does this mean we don't get to see what's inside?" Marilyn asked, voicing the question Julie hadn't quite dared to ask.

Sheriff Harris considered the two women thoughtfully. "Technically, I should clear everyone out and wait for the crime scene unit. However," he continued, his expression softening slightly, "given your direct involvement in this discovery and Ms. Sommers' status as property owner, I can allow you to be present when we open it—under my direct supervision, of course."

Julie and Marilyn exchanged glances of surprised gratitude. After the terror of their confrontation with Thompson, the opportunity to see the investigation through to this crucial revelation felt like necessary closure.

"Thank you, Sheriff," Julie said sincerely.

Harris nodded, then turned to the hidden compartment. "Now, how exactly does this mechanism work?"

With careful guidance from Julie, the sheriff located the pressure point in the carved pediment. The hidden door swung open further, revealing a space approximately two feet square carved into the foundation wall. Inside, illuminated by the officers' flashlights, sat a dusty leather satchel.

Sheriff Harris donned gloves before carefully removing the satchel and placing it on a nearby workbench. With methodical precision, he opened the aged leather flap to reveal the contents.

"Well, I'll be damned," he murmured, carefully extracting a leather-bound volume stamped with gold lettering: "The Founder's Journal."

Julie felt her breath catch. The journal—complete, not just the few pages found with Thomas Sullivan's remains—was the centerpiece of the missing Meadowgrove Collection, a firsthand account of the town's earliest days written by Jonathan Meadow himself.

"Is that really it?" Marilyn whispered, academic excitement momentarily overshadowing the trauma of their recent experience.

"Appears to be," Sheriff Harris confirmed, gently opening the cover to reveal the distinctive handwriting of Meadowgrove's founder. "And there's more."

One by one, he removed the remaining contents: a small wooden box containing what appeared to be the ceremonial gold seal of Meadowgrove, several folded documents with official-looking wax seals, and at the bottom, a sealed envelope addressed simply "To be opened in the event of my death - Thomas Sullivan."

This last item drew everyone's attention. Sheriff Harris held it up to the light, studying the aged but intact seal. "This could be crucial evidence," he noted. "Sullivan clearly anticipated the possibility of violence."

"What happens now?" Julie asked, her gaze lingering on the envelope that might finally explain the tragic events of 1965.

"Now we secure the evidence and continue the investigation properly," Sheriff Harris replied. "I'll need formal statements from both of you, as well as Mr. Winters and Ms. Morrison. And Ms. Sommers, I'm afraid your shop will need to remain closed tomorrow while we process the scene."

Julie nodded in understanding. After what they'd just experienced, a day's lost business seemed trivial. "What about Victoria Thompson? Does she know her ex-husband was trying to steal the artifacts?"

"We'll be questioning her, of course," the sheriff assured her. "Though based on what we heard over your phone line, it sounds like Thompson's interest in the artifacts predated and possibly motivated their relationship. She may be a victim of his deception as much as anyone."

This perspective gave Julie pause. She'd been so focused on Victoria as a potential antagonist that she hadn't considered the woman might have been manipulated by Thompson's hidden agenda. If he had married her specifically to gain access to family information about the missing artifacts, then divorced her when she proved less useful than expected...

Their conversation was interrupted by a deputy calling down from the top of the stairs. "Sheriff? Ms. Thompson is here. Says she needs to speak with you urgently."

Harris sighed, unsurprised. "News travels fast in Meadowgrove. Tell her I'll be up shortly." He turned back to Julie and Marilyn. "Ladies, I suggest you come upstairs as well. The paramedics should check you both more thoroughly, and I imagine Ms. Morrison is anxious to see you're unharmed."

They ascended the stairs to find Yarn Haven transformed into an impromptu command center. Deputies and paramedics moved purposefully through the space, while Derek sat on a chair near the counter, holding an ice pack to his forehead as a paramedic examined his pupils. Nelly paced near the window, her usual exuberance contained as worry etched her features.

"Julie!" she exclaimed, rushing forward as they emerged from the basement. "When I heard the gunshot after I left... I thought..." Uncharacteristically, words failed her as she embraced her friend.

"We're okay," Julie assured her, returning the hug before being guided to a chair by an insistent paramedic. "Thanks to your quick action getting help."

As the paramedic checked her vital signs, Julie glanced toward the shop entrance where Victoria Thompson stood in tense conversation with Deputy Sanchez, clearly being prevented from entering fully. Even from a distance, Julie could see the woman's uncharacteristic discomposure—her carefully maintained appearance slightly disheveled, her expression cycling between anger and what appeared to be genuine concern.

Sheriff Harris approached Victoria, their conversation too quiet for Julie to overhear. Whatever he said caused Victoria's composure to crack further, her hand flying to her mouth in evident shock as she stared past him toward where Thompson was being secured in a patrol car outside.

After a moment, Victoria's gaze shifted, scanning the shop until it landed on Julie. There was something new in that look—a vulnerability Julie hadn't seen before, quickly masked but unmistakable in the moment it appeared.

As the paramedic finished examining her, declaring her physically sound but warning about potential delayed shock reactions, Julie found herself crossing the shop toward Victoria and Sheriff Harris. Some impulse she couldn't quite name propelled her forward, perhaps the need to understand all aspects of the situation that had nearly cost her and her friends their lives.

"Ms. Thompson," she acknowledged as she approached.

Victoria straightened, reassembling her dignified facade. "Ms. Sommers. I understand my... Edward... threatened you and your friends. I assure you, I had no knowledge of his actions."

The careful phrasing struck Julie as significant. Not "my ex-husband" but simply "Edward," as if she was already distancing herself from their former relationship.

"He was looking for the Meadowgrove Collection," Julie stated rather than asked. "The same artifacts you've been searching for."

Something flickered in Victoria's eyes—recognition, perhaps, that pretense was pointless at this stage. "Yes. Though our motivations were quite different." She hesitated, then added with evident reluctance, "I came to Meadowgrove to clear my grandmother's name. Edward, it seems, came for profit."

"Using your research and family connections," Sheriff Harris noted, his tone neutral but his implication clear.

Victoria's jaw tightened. "A fact I'm still processing, Sheriff. It appears our entire relationship was predicated on his interest in the Meadowgrove Collection. A calculating deception spanning years."

Despite everything, Julie felt a flicker of sympathy. Whatever Victoria's flaws—her arrogance, her manipulative tactics, her dismissive attitude toward Meadowgrove's character—discovering her marriage had been a strategic ploy must be devastating.

"We found them," Julie said simply. "The artifacts. They were hidden in my basement all along."

Victoria's eyes widened, years of searching crystalized in her expression. "The journal? It's intact?"

"And other items," Julie confirmed. "Including a sealed letter from Thomas Sullivan."

At this, Victoria grew very still. "Thomas Sullivan left a letter?"

"Addressed to be opened in the event of his death," Sheriff Harris elaborated. "Which suggests he anticipated the possibility."

"My grandmother always maintained he was murdered," Victoria said quietly. "She believed Charles Johnson killed him to prevent exposure of the land fraud they'd discovered. That's why she fled—not because she was guilty of theft, but because she feared she'd be next."

The pieces were aligning, forming a coherent narrative out of decades of suspicion and speculation. Margaret Wilkins and Thomas Sullivan, engaged to be married, had discovered evidence of the Johnson family's fraudulent land claims in the town records. They secured the proof—including the Founder's Journal with its original property boundaries—in a hidden compartment in a Wilkins-owned building. But before they could present their findings publicly, something went terribly wrong.

"Charles Johnson confronted Thomas at the mill," Julie continued the thought aloud. "There was a struggle, Thomas was killed, and his body concealed. Margaret, fearing for her life and knowing she'd be blamed for the missing artifacts, fled town. And Charles Johnson maintained the fiction that Thomas had simply moved away, even sending fake letters to his family for years."

"A theory consistent with the evidence we've gathered," Sheriff Harris acknowledged. "Though we'll need to examine Sullivan's letter and complete forensic analysis before drawing final conclusions."

"What happens now?" Victoria asked, unconsciously echoing Julie's earlier question.

"A thorough investigation," the sheriff replied firmly. "Into both historical events and current ones, including your ex-husband's activities and the break-in at the Wilkins Building." He fixed Victoria with a pointed look. "I'll need your full cooperation, Ms. Thompson. Complete transparency about your research, your activities in Meadowgrove, and any information Edward may have shared with you."

Victoria nodded, surprisingly acquiescent. "Of course. Though I suspect I was as deceived by Edward as anyone."

Their conversation was interrupted by Deputy Sanchez approaching with urgency. "Sheriff, the suspect is requesting to speak with you. Says he has information about another party involved in the Sullivan case."

Harris frowned. "Another party? Not Charles Johnson?"

"No, sir. He specifically mentioned a current resident of Meadowgrove who he claims has been working to prevent the recovery of the artifacts. Someone with 'significant investment' in maintaining the historical narrative."

This new wrinkle drew everyone's attention. If Thompson was telling the truth, it suggested the conspiracy surrounding Thomas Sullivan's death and the missing artifacts extended beyond Charles Johnson—and continued into the present day.

"I need to address this," Sheriff Harris decided. "Ms. Sommers, I'd like you and your friends to remain here until we've completed preliminary statements. Deputy Collins will stay with you." He turned to

Victoria. "Ms. Thompson, please wait in my office at the station. I'll have further questions for you shortly."

As the sheriff departed, Julie returned to her friends, finding Derek now standing with Marilyn and Nelly, the three of them conversing quietly.

"How's your head?" she asked Derek, noting the bruise forming above his eye.

"I'll live," he replied ruefully. "Though I think I need new glasses. I'm sorry about all this, Julie. I never imagined Edward would follow me here—or that he was involved in the first place."

"None of us could have anticipated this," Julie assured him. "What matters is that we're all safe, and the artifacts have been found."

"And what artifacts they are!" Nelly enthused, some of her natural exuberance returning. "Did you see that journal? And the gold seal? Absolutely extraordinary that they've been hidden in your basement all these years, Julie."

"It's certainly going to change the historical narrative of Meadowgrove," Marilyn added thoughtfully. "Especially if Sullivan's letter confirms what we suspect about the Johnson family's land claims."

Julie glanced toward the front of the shop where Victoria stood in conversation with a deputy, preparing to leave for the sheriff's station. The developer caught her looking and held her gaze briefly, an unspoken communication passing between them—not friendship, certainly, but perhaps a mutual recognition of how their separate paths had converged around this decades-old mystery.

As Victoria departed, Ben Walker rushed in, his expression frantic until he spotted Julie among her friends. He crossed to her immediately, professional demeanor forgotten as he took her hands in his.

"I heard what happened," he said, his voice rough with emotion. "Are you all right? When they said there had been shots fired at Yarn Haven..."

"I'm okay," Julie assured him, suddenly aware of her friends' poorly concealed interest in this interaction. "We all are, thanks to quick thinking and quicker help."

Ben's relief was palpable. "When I think about what could have happened..." He stopped himself, visibly pulling his emotions under control. "The sheriff called me to examine Derek, but I see the paramedics have already checked everyone."

"Doctor's prerogative to verify," Derek suggested with a faint smile, sensing the personal undercurrent and tactfully creating an opportunity for Ben to regain his professional footing.

As Ben briefly examined Derek's injuries, pronouncing him concussed but not seriously, Julie found herself appreciating the doctor's genuine concern. Their postponed dinner suddenly seemed insignificant compared to the connection evident in his worried rush to her side.

"I understand you'll need to stay for statements," Ben said as he finished with Derek. "But afterward, you shouldn't be alone after an experience like this. Would you... that is, could I perhaps stay with you tonight? On the sofa," he added hastily, a flush coloring his cheeks. "Just to ensure you're truly all right."

Despite the trauma of the evening, or perhaps because of it, Julie felt a smile forming. "I'd appreciate that," she replied simply. "Thank you, Ben."

As deputies began taking formal statements from each of them, recording the events that had led to the discovery of the hidden compartment and the subsequent confrontation with Edward Thompson, Julie found herself marveling at how thoroughly her quiet life had been upended in just a few days.

What had begun as concern about historic preservation had evolved into a complex web of murder, theft, deception, and long-buried secrets that connected Meadowgrove's past to its present in unexpected ways. And somewhere within that web, she'd found not only danger but also deeper connections to her friends, to Ben, and perhaps even to Meadowgrove itself—the community she'd chosen as her sanctuary now bound to her through shared history and resilience.

Outside, night had fallen completely, transforming the shop windows into mirrors that reflected the activity within—deputies, paramedics, friends gathered in the aftermath of danger, supporting each other as statements were given and experiences processed. Beyond that reflection lay Meadowgrove itself, a town whose placid surface had concealed decades of secrets now bubbling to the surface, promising changes and revelations Julie could only begin to imagine.

Tomorrow would bring investigations, explanations, and likely more surprises as Thomas Sullivan's letter was examined and the full extent of the historical deception unraveled. But for tonight, surrounded by friends and with Ben's steadying presence beside her, Julie found herself focused on the immediate reality of safety after danger, connection after isolation, and truth emerging from long shadows.

The mystery wasn't fully solved—Thompson's mention of another involved party suggested more revelations to come—but a crucial threshold had been crossed. Whatever happened next, Julie knew that Meadowgrove would never be quite the same quiet town she'd moved to three years ago. And perhaps, she reflected as Ben's hand found hers during a quiet moment between statements, that wasn't entirely a bad thing.

Chapter 7
Knit One, Purl Two

Morning arrived with the soft persistence of autumn sunlight filtering through Julie's bedroom curtains. For a moment, drifting in the hazy space between sleep and wakefulness, she could almost believe the previous day's events had been a particularly vivid dream. Then the soreness in her muscles and the faint bruise forming on her wrist where Thompson had grabbed her confirmed the harsh reality.

She sat up slowly, Tessa stirring beside her with a sleepy stretch. The familiar weight of the dachshund and the sounds of someone moving quietly in the kitchen brought a rush of memories—Ben staying overnight as promised, sleeping on her sofa despite her protests that she would be fine alone.

Julie pulled on her robe and padded to the bathroom, catching sight of her reflection with mild surprise. Despite everything, she looked remarkably normal—perhaps a bit paler than usual, with shadows beneath her eyes, but otherwise unchanged. Somehow, she'd expected the previous day's trauma to have left a more visible mark.

When she emerged, she found Ben in her small kitchen, hair slightly rumpled but otherwise looking surprisingly fresh in the same clothes from yesterday. He glanced up from the coffee maker he'd managed to operate successfully, offering a warm smile that did more to settle her nerves than she would have expected.

"Good morning," he said, his voice gentle. "How are you feeling?"

"Like I lived through an armed confrontation in my own shop," Julie replied with surprising lightness. "But also strangely okay. Is that normal?"

Ben nodded, pouring coffee into two mugs. "Completely normal. Adrenaline and shock create a buffer initially. The emotional processing often comes later." He handed her a mug. "Just be patient with yourself if you experience delayed reactions—anxiety, sleep disturbances, heightened startle responses. All common after trauma."

Julie accepted the coffee gratefully. "Well, that's something to look forward to."

His smile turned apologetic. "Sorry. Doctor mode. What I meant to say was: you were incredibly brave yesterday. All of you were."

"Not brave. Just... reactive." Julie took a sip of coffee, appreciating its warmth and normalcy. "I didn't have time to be properly terrified until afterward."

They settled at her small dining table, the morning sun casting golden rectangles across the surface. Tessa placed herself strategically between them, hopeful for breakfast scraps, while Hildi observed from a windowsill, tail twitching with feline judgment.

"Sheriff Harris called while you were still asleep," Ben mentioned, his tone careful. "They've processed the scene downstairs and are releasing your shop back to you this morning. Though he said to tell you they've removed the hidden compartment contents for evidence processing."

Julie nodded, unsurprised. "Did he say anything about Thompson? Or the letter from Thomas Sullivan?"

"Only that Thompson remains in custody and has been increasingly cooperative, apparently hoping to negotiate leniency." Ben hesitated before adding, "And regarding Sullivan's letter—they're waiting to open it until they can assemble key stakeholders. Sheriff Harris asked if you would be available to come to the station at eleven."

"Me?" Julie blinked in surprise. "Why would they want me there?"

"You found the artifacts, Julie. And according to Sheriff Harris, you've become central to understanding the connections between past and present events in Meadowgrove." Ben's expression grew more serious. "Also, there's the matter of Thompson's claim about another person still involved in covering up what happened in 1965. Harris thinks your perspective might be valuable."

The reminder of Thompson's ominous statement sent a chill through her despite the warm kitchen. Someone still in Meadowgrove had a vested interest in keeping the truth buried—someone who might not appreciate Julie's role in uncovering these long-hidden secrets.

"Of course I'll be there," she decided. Whatever dangers might still exist, she was too deeply invested now to step back. Besides, she wanted—needed—to know what Thomas Sullivan had written in that final letter.

After breakfast, Ben reluctantly left for the clinic, extracting a promise from Julie to call if she needed anything. She appreciated his concern without finding it stifling—a balance she hadn't often experienced in previous relationships.

Alone with her thoughts, Julie showered and dressed, choosing a deep green sweater that had always given her confidence. She needed to check on the shop, assess any damage from yesterday's confrontation, and prepare to meet Sheriff Harris later.

Downstairs, Yarn Haven looked remarkably normal aside from the police tape across the basement door and several empty spaces where items had been bagged as evidence—including the wooden swift Marilyn had wielded so effectively and the ceramic bowl Julie had thrown at Thompson. The merino display had been tidied, though some skeins still showed evidence of being crushed during the struggle.

Julie moved through the space methodically, straightening, cleaning, and restoring order where possible. The physical activity helped settle her mind, giving her hands something productive to do while her thoughts circled around the discoveries and revelations of the past week.

The shop's bell chimed at precisely ten o'clock, and Julie looked up to find Marilyn in the doorway, impeccably dressed as always despite yesterday's ordeal.

"I thought you might appreciate some company," the former teacher said, her brisk tone belying the concern in her eyes. "And perhaps a decent cup of tea. I brought that Earl Grey you like."

Before Julie could respond, the bell chimed again as Nelly swept in, her wild curls confined today by a patterned headscarf, arms laden with a bakery box.

"Trauma requires carbohydrates," she announced without preamble. "I brought cinnamon rolls—the ones with extra icing from Henderson's Bakery."

Julie felt a rush of affection for her friends, their predictable responses to crisis—Marilyn's practical efficiency, Nelly's nurturing exuberance—providing a much-needed sense of normalcy.

"You two are exactly what I needed this morning," she admitted, gesturing them toward the sitting area. "The shop's closed today anyway, so we might as well make it a proper gathering."

As Marilyn prepared tea and Nelly arranged pastries on plates, Julie updated them on Ben's overnight stay (earning a knowing wink from Nelly) and the upcoming meeting at the sheriff's station.

"We're coming with you," Marilyn declared without room for argument. "We were all involved in finding those artifacts, and we all faced Thompson together."

"Besides," Nelly added, licking icing from her finger, "I'm dying to know what Sullivan wrote in that letter. Sixty-year-old evidence from beyond the grave! It's like something from a movie."

Julie didn't bother protesting—she wanted her friends' support, and their different perspectives might prove valuable if Thompson's claim about another conspirator was true.

"Have either of you heard from Derek?" she asked, suddenly realizing his absence from their impromptu gathering.

"He called this morning," Marilyn confirmed. "Concussion symptoms kept him up most of the night, but he's stable. Doctor Walker arranged for monitoring at the clinic rather than sending him to the Burlington hospital."

"And Victoria?" Julie's curiosity about the developer had shifted since yesterday's revelations.

Nelly leaned forward eagerly. "According to Sarah at The Greenery, Victoria checked out of The Pines Inn last night after her interview with Sheriff Harris. Rumor has it she's moved temporarily into the Johnson Lake House—you know, that rental property on the north shore? Apparently, she doesn't feel safe at the inn anymore."

"Can you blame her?" Marilyn mused. "Finding out your ex-husband married you solely to access family information about missing artifacts? I'd be looking over my shoulder as well."

Julie considered this new information thoughtfully. Victoria's relocation made a certain sense—removing herself from public scrutiny while maintaining proximity to the unfolding investigation. But something about the specific choice of the Johnson Lake House niggled at Julie's mind, a connection she couldn't quite grasp.

Their conversation continued, analyzing yesterday's events and speculating about Sullivan's letter, until it was time to head to the sheriff's station. Julie locked the shop, leaving Tessa upstairs with extra treats and a promise to return soon.

Meadowgrove's small police station occupied a tidy brick building near the town hall. As Julie and her friends approached, they noticed several vehicles already parked outside—Sheriff Harris's cruiser, Mayor Johnson's silver Lexus, and a county vehicle with government plates.

Inside, Deputy Sanchez greeted them with professional courtesy, escorting them to a conference room rather than an interview space. The distinction wasn't lost on Julie—this was a collaborative meeting rather than an interrogation.

The room already contained several people: Sheriff Harris standing near a whiteboard covered with notes and timelines; Mayor Johnson seated stiffly at the table, her usual poise undercut by evident tension; Elaine Sullivan, looking frail but determined; and to Julie's surprise, Victoria Thompson, positioned as far from the mayor as the table allowed.

"Ms. Sommers, Ms. Green, Ms. Morrison," Sheriff Harris acknowledged them. "Thank you for coming. We're waiting on one more participant—ah, there he is."

The door opened to admit Ben, now in his professional attire of button-down shirt and tie beneath a sport coat. He nodded to Julie with a small smile before taking a seat beside Elaine Sullivan, his medical credentials apparently placing him in a supportive role for the elderly woman.

"Now that everyone is here," Sheriff Harris began once they were all seated, "I want to clarify the purpose of this gathering. This is not an official deposition or formal statement-taking. Rather, it's an attempt to align our understanding of connected events spanning six decades of Meadowgrove history, with specific relevance to two cases: the theft of the Meadowgrove Collection in 1965 and the death of Thomas Sullivan during the same period."

He gestured to the items arranged carefully on the table's center: the Founder's Journal, now in a protective archival sleeve; the small wooden box containing the ceremonial seal; several folded documents; and most prominently, the sealed envelope addressed in Thomas Sullivan's handwriting.

"Ms. Sullivan has authorized us to open her brother's letter in this setting," Sheriff Harris continued. "As his only living relative, that decision rests with her. Before we proceed, however, I want to clarify some facts that have emerged from our investigation and Mr. Thompson's subsequent statements."

The sheriff turned to the whiteboard, where a timeline had been constructed showing key events from 1965 forward.

"Based on evidence now available, we can establish the following sequence: In early 1965, Thomas Sullivan returned to Meadowgrove after military service, his presence known only to select individuals including his sister and his fiancée, Margaret Wilkins. During this period, they discovered discrepancies in historical land grant documents suggesting the Johnson family had falsified records decades earlier to claim properties rightfully belonging to other founding families."

Mayor Johnson stiffened visibly but remained silent, her expression carefully neutral as Sheriff Harris continued.

"Sullivan and Wilkins removed the Founder's Journal and related documents from the town archives to protect this evidence, concealing it in a hidden compartment in what is now Yarn Haven. Shortly afterward, Sullivan disappeared, and Margaret Wilkins fled town under suspicion of stealing the historical artifacts."

He tapped a specific date on the whiteboard—October 15, 1965. "Thomas Sullivan's remains, found last week at the old mill site, have now been conclusively dated to this period through forensic analysis. Dr. Walker has confirmed cause of death as blunt force trauma to the skull, consistent with the industrial mallet found near the remains."

Elaine Sullivan closed her eyes briefly at this confirmation, grief evident in her posture despite the decades that had passed since her brother's death.

"Now," Sheriff Harris said, his tone shifting slightly, "we come to Mr. Thompson's claims about ongoing concealment efforts. In exchange for consideration in his own case, Thompson has provided information suggesting that Charles Johnson was not alone in his actions in 1965—

and that his co-conspirator has continued to preserve the deception into the present day."

The tension in the room thickened perceptibly, every gaze darting briefly to Mayor Johnson, who sat rigidly in her chair, knuckles white where her hands clasped on the table before her.

"According to Thompson," Sheriff Harris continued, "this individual contacted him approximately five years ago, offering information about the artifacts' potential location in exchange for a percentage of their black market value if recovered. This person feared Victoria Thompson's research was getting too close to the truth and wanted the artifacts removed from Meadowgrove permanently."

Victoria's eyes narrowed at this revelation, her focus intensifying on the sheriff's words.

"Thompson claims this individual provided detailed historical information unavailable in public records—information that helped him target his search once he gained access to Victoria's more extensive research through their marriage." Sheriff Harris paused deliberately. "He identified this person as Elaine Sullivan."

A collective gasp filled the room, all eyes swinging to the elderly woman who sat calmly, seemingly unsurprised by the accusation.

"That's preposterous," Marilyn exclaimed, ever loyal to Meadowgrove's respected citizens. "Ms. Sullivan lost her brother to this conspiracy. Why would she protect his killers?"

"I believe," Sheriff Harris said carefully, "that Thomas's letter may provide clarity on this matter. Ms. Sullivan, with your permission?"

Elaine nodded, her aged hands steady in her lap. "Please proceed, Sheriff. It's time for the full truth, whatever it may be."

With careful precision, Sheriff Harris donned gloves before picking up the sealed envelope. The room fell silent as he gently broke the wax seal and extracted several folded pages covered in neat, masculine handwriting. He cleared his throat and began to read:

"October 14, 1965 To whom it may concern,

If you are reading this, I must assume that something has happened to prevent me from presenting my findings publicly as intended. I, Thomas Andrew Sullivan, being of sound mind, hereby set forth the truth regarding land claims in Meadowgrove and my investigation thereof.

Through careful examination of original documents in the town archives, I have confirmed that in 1897, Harold Johnson, grandfather of current council president Charles Johnson, falsified deed records to claim approximately 200 acres of lakefront property rightfully belonging to the Wilkins, Sullivan, and Meadow families. This fraud was concealed through the selective destruction of original survey maps and the substitution of altered documents during a period when Harold served as town clerk.

The evidence supporting this conclusion is contained in the Founder's Journal and accompanying survey maps, which I have removed from the archives for safekeeping. My fiancée, Margaret Wilkins, has assisted in this investigation despite the personal cost to her family's relationship with the Johnsons.

Tomorrow I intend to confront Charles Johnson with this evidence and request that he voluntarily correct the historical record and initiate the legal process of returning misappropriated lands to their rightful heirs. I have no desire to destroy the Johnson family's reputation unnecessarily, only to restore justice after generations of deception.

If I have disappeared or met with misfortune after this confrontation, I ask that this evidence be presented to county authorities rather than town officials, as the Johnson influence in Meadowgrove may prevent proper investigation.

With one significant exception—my sister, Elaine Sullivan, must not be included in any investigation or revelation that follows. Despite our blood relationship, Elaine has formed a secret attachment to Charles Johnson spanning many years. Her loyalty to him supersedes all other bonds, including family. Indeed, it was through Elaine that Charles learned of my investigation, though she believed he would address the matter legally rather than through confrontation.

I have hidden this letter and the historical artifacts without Elaine's knowledge for this reason. Margaret alone knows their location and will retrieve them should something happen to me.

To Margaret, if you are reading this: I release you from any obligation to me or to this cause. Take the evidence or don't, seek justice or find peace elsewhere—my only wish is for your safety and happiness.

To whoever else may read these words in some distant future: judge not too harshly those caught in webs of loyalty and love. Even Elaine's misplaced devotion comes from a heart that loved too deeply, if unwisely.

With hope for eventual justice, Thomas A. Sullivan"

Crochet Carnage

Sheriff Harris finished reading, the room so silent that the shuffling of the pages seemed thunderous as he returned the letter to the table. All eyes turned to Elaine Sullivan, whose composure had finally cracked, tears streaming silently down her lined face.

"Is it true?" Mayor Johnson asked, breaking the silence, her voice barely above a whisper. "You and my father?"

Elaine straightened, wiping her tears with a lace-edged handkerchief. "Charles and I loved each other from childhood," she confirmed. "But your grandparents would never have accepted a Sullivan bride for their only son—not after the land disputes between our families. We kept our relationship secret for decades."

"And you betrayed your own brother to protect him," Victoria stated, not a question but a confirmation.

"I told Charles about Tommy's investigation, yes." Elaine's voice strengthened with a surprising note of defiance. "But I never, never imagined he would respond with violence. When Tommy disappeared and those dreadful accusations against Margaret emerged, I suspected what must have happened, but I couldn't bring myself to believe Charles would kill my brother."

"So you maintained the fiction," Sheriff Harris concluded. "Accepting the letters someone wrote pretending to be Thomas, never questioning the official story that he had moved away."

"The deception was easier than the truth," Elaine admitted. "And after Charles died in 1989, there seemed no purpose in exposing it all—only pain for his family and shame for the town."

"Until Victoria started searching for the artifacts," Julie realized aloud. "That's when you contacted Thompson—to remove the evidence before it could be found."

Elaine nodded slowly. "When I learned Victoria was Margaret's granddaughter, researching the Wilkins properties and the missing artifacts, I panicked. The idea of Linda having to face her father's crimes..." She looked at the mayor with genuine anguish. "I only wanted to protect you from that pain, my dear. You were like the child Charles and I could never openly have."

Mayor Johnson's expression was unreadable, decades of political training keeping her emotions masked even as her world realigned around these revelations.

"Did you know?" Sheriff Harris asked her directly. "About your father's actions or Elaine's involvement?"

"No." The mayor's response was immediate and firm. "I knew my father and Elaine were close—she was always present in our home, like an aunt. But their relationship? My grandfather's land fraud? My father's involvement in Thomas Sullivan's death? No." She took a steadying breath. "Though perhaps I should have questioned more, especially as an adult. The Johnson properties were always... well, extensive for a family that began as simple merchants."

"And the letters?" Julie asked, turning to Elaine. "The ones Thomas's family received for years after his death?"

"Charles wrote those," Elaine confirmed quietly. "He had always been able to imitate Tommy's handwriting—a game from their school days. Each one broke my heart anew, but I helped mail them from different locations during trips we took. A terrible deception that grew harder to maintain as years passed."

Sheriff Harris nodded thoughtfully, adding notes to his timeline. "Mr. Thompson claims you provided him with historical information about the Wilkins properties—details that helped him narrow his search."

"Yes," Elaine admitted. "I knew the buildings Margaret's family had owned. I didn't know where specifically they had hidden the artifacts, but I knew it would be somewhere with Wilkins connections." Her gaze shifted to Julie. "I should have considered your shop more carefully. It makes perfect sense in retrospect—an innocent-seeming location still under family control in 1965."

The revelations hung in the air like dust motes in the conference room's fluorescent lighting, decades of secrets now exposed to clinical examination. Julie found herself studying each face around the table, noting the complex emotions at play—Victoria's vindication, Mayor Johnson's controlled shock, Elaine's mix of relief and lingering grief.

"What happens now?" Marilyn finally asked, addressing the question on everyone's mind.

Sheriff Harris sighed, closing his notebook. "That's complicated. The statute of limitations has expired on the theft of the artifacts, which were technically recovered rather than stolen anyway. As for Thomas Sullivan's death..." He glanced at Elaine. "Charles Johnson is deceased and beyond earthly justice. Ms. Sullivan's involvement after the fact would typically warrant obstruction charges, but given the time elapsed and her age..."

"I'm not interested in pursuing charges against Elaine," Mayor Johnson stated, surprising everyone. "Whatever her involvement, she's suffered enough, living with these secrets for sixty years." She turned to face the elderly woman directly. "I won't pretend I'm not... shaken by these revelations about my father and grandfather. But vindictive prosecution won't change the past."

"What about the land claims?" Victoria asked, her voice carrying the professional precision Julie had first found so off-putting, but which now seemed merely efficient. "If the Johnson properties were fraudulently obtained, there are inheritance implications spanning generations."

Mayor Johnson nodded grimly. "Yes, there are. And I assure you, Ms. Thompson, I'll be consulting with county legal authorities about the proper resolution. Whatever the cost to my family's legacy, Meadowgrove deserves honest accounting of its history."

This declaration, delivered with evident sincerity, shifted something in the room's atmosphere—a collective exhalation as the confrontation everyone had anticipated failed to materialize, replaced instead by a measured commitment to rectification.

"The Founder's Journal and accompanying documents will be properly examined by historical experts," Sheriff Harris confirmed. "Once their authenticity is verified, the legal process regarding property claims can proceed appropriately."

As the meeting continued with discussion of next steps and formal statements, Julie found her attention drawn again and again to the artifacts on the table—particularly the journal, its aged leather cover embodying the physical connection between past and present. These items had cost Thomas Sullivan his life, Margaret Wilkins her home and reputation, and had shaped the trajectory of Meadowgrove for generations. Their recovery wouldn't erase those consequences, but perhaps it could begin to heal the fractures their absence had created.

When the meeting finally concluded, people departed in pairs and small groups, the natural human instinct to process overwhelming information through shared conversation. Mayor Johnson left with Elaine Sullivan, their body language suggesting a difficult but necessary discussion to come. Victoria Thompson exited alone, pausing briefly to meet Julie's gaze with a complex look that conveyed something like reluctant respect before continuing on her way.

Julie, Marilyn, and Nelly lingered on the station steps, the autumn sunlight a welcome contrast to the fluorescent lighting and weighty revelations inside.

"Well," Nelly said finally, breaking their thoughtful silence. "I don't think any of us saw that particular twist coming. Elaine Sullivan and Charles Johnson—star-crossed lovers turned conspirators."

"It explains her lifelong devotion to the Sullivan property," Marilyn noted. "Not just family legacy but a monument to forbidden love and terrible secrets."

Julie nodded, considering the human complexities beneath the factual timeline Sheriff Harris had constructed. "Thomas was right, in his letter—about not judging too harshly. Everyone involved was caught in circumstances beyond their complete control, making choices that seemed necessary in the moment, even when those choices led to tragedy."

"Very philosophical," Ben's voice came from behind them, his approach unnoticed during their conversation. "And unusually merciful, given that those choices led to an armed confrontation in your shop yesterday."

"Yesterday seems far away," Julie admitted, smiling as he joined their group. "Today's revelations have shifted my perspective on everything—even Thompson's actions seem less personally menacing and more...pathetically mercenary."

"Speaking of Thompson," Ben said, "I passed Sheriff Harris on my way out. He mentioned they've located two other museums that reported thefts matching Thompson's modus operandi—getting close to female staff or family members connected to specific collections, then disappearing along with valuable artifacts once he'd gained access."

"So Victoria wasn't his first target," Marilyn concluded, shaking her head. "What a detestable pattern."

"At least he'll face consequences for this attempt," Julie said. "And the artifacts have been recovered."

They began walking back toward Main Street together, the conversation gradually lightening as they processed the morning's discoveries. Nelly declared her intention to create an art series based on the Meadowgrove scandal, already envisioning dramatic paintings of clandestine meetings and hidden compartments. Marilyn, ever practical, wondered how the historical society would manage the inevitable tourist interest once the story became public.

Ben walked beside Julie, their hands occasionally brushing with a companionable ease that felt both new and familiar. "Still up for dinner Sunday?" he asked quietly while the others debated the artistic merits of Nelly's proposed series.

"Absolutely," Julie confirmed. "Though after everything that's happened, it feels like we've already moved well beyond first-date territory."

His smile crinkled the corners of his eyes. "True. Facing armed antiquities thieves together does tend to accelerate a relationship."

As they reached Main Street, Julie paused to look across at Yarn Haven, its familiar façade unchanged despite the momentous discoveries within its walls. Soon she would reopen, welcome customers, resume the rhythms of small-town business ownership—but with a new appreciation for the layers of history beneath Meadowgrove's tranquil surface, and her own unexpected place in that continuing narrative.

"What will you do about Victoria's development plans now?" Ben asked, following her gaze to the Wilkins Building across from her shop. "Given everything that's happened, do you think she'll still pursue the hotel project?"

Julie considered the question thoughtfully. "I'm not sure. The historic preservation arguments have certainly gained weight with these discoveries. But more importantly, I think Victoria herself has changed through this process. Finding out her grandmother was telling the truth all along, being deceived by her ex-husband..." She shrugged. "Those experiences transform perspectives."

As if conjured by their conversation, Victoria Thompson appeared at the corner, emerging from the bank and pausing when she spotted their group. After a moment's hesitation, she approached, her usual confident stride slightly subdued.

"Ms. Sommers," she acknowledged, then included the others with a nod. "I wanted to thank you for your role in uncovering the truth about my grandmother. After six decades of family disgrace, vindication matters —even if it comes too late for Margaret to witness."

The sincerity in her voice surprised Julie, who had grown accustomed to Victoria's more calculated interactions. "I'm glad the truth has finally emerged," she replied. "For Margaret's sake, and for Thomas Sullivan's."

"Yes." Victoria's gaze drifted toward the Wilkins Building. "In light of these revelations, I've decided to modify my development plans. The Wilkins Building will still be renovated, but as a historical museum rather than a hotel—focusing specifically on Meadowgrove's founding families and the artifacts we've recovered."

This announcement drew sounds of approval from Marilyn and Nelly, while Julie studied Victoria with new understanding. "That seems appropriate. A way to honor both sides of your heritage."

"Precisely." Victoria's professional demeanor reasserted itself. "The economic benefits to Meadowgrove will be comparable, though differently structured. I've already discussed preliminary concepts with the historical society via email."

Julie smiled slightly, recognizing that despite her evolved perspective, Victoria remained fundamentally herself—driven, efficient, focused on results. "I look forward to seeing the plans," she said genuinely. "And to having the Meadowgrove Collection properly displayed where everyone can appreciate its significance."

With brief farewells, Victoria continued on her way, her purposeful stride suggesting that while the past week had transformed many things, her essential nature remained intact—perhaps tempered by experience, but not fundamentally altered.

"Well," Nelly declared as they watched her go, "if anyone had told me last week that I'd be approving of Victoria Thompson's plans for Meadowgrove, I'd have questioned their sanity. Life certainly takes unexpected turns."

"Indeed it does," Marilyn agreed sagely. "Though in my experience, most mysteries have logical explanations once all the facts are known."

Ben chuckled. "The teacher's perspective. Always seeking order in chaos."

"And finding it," Marilyn insisted with dignity. "Though I admit, this particular mystery had more twists than most."

As they continued their walk toward The Greenery for a well-deserved lunch, Julie found herself reflecting on the journey from her initial concerns about historic preservation to uncovering decades-old secrets that had shaped Meadowgrove's development. Like a complex knitting pattern, the individual stitches had seemed random or misplaced when viewed too closely, only revealing their purpose and design when seen as part of the larger work.

And her own place in that pattern had shifted too, her connections to the town and its people deepening through shared discovery and danger. What had begun as a simple desire for a quieter life away from corporate pressures had evolved into something far richer—a true belonging that encompassed not just present-day Meadowgrove but its complex history as well.

As Ben's hand found hers more deliberately, his fingers intertwining with her own, Julie sensed another pattern beginning to take shape—this one personal rather than historical, but no less significant for its newness. Life in small towns might appear tranquil on the surface, but beneath that calm exterior, human connections continued to form and evolve, creating designs as intricate and beautiful as any she might craft with yarn and needles.

Meadowgrove had yielded its secrets reluctantly, but in doing so had woven Julie more tightly into its fabric, creating bonds that would endure long after the sensation of yesterday's danger had faded into memory.

Chapter 8
Binding Off

Two days after the dramatic revelations at the sheriff's station, Julie stood behind the counter of Yarn Haven, carefully arranging a new display of locally sourced alpaca yarn. The shop had officially reopened that morning, and though customer traffic remained light—partly due to lingering police tape and partly to Meadowgrove's instinctive need to process recent events before resuming normal activities—she found comfort in the familiar routines.

The bell above the door chimed, admitting George Whitaker, his silver hair neatly combed and a newspaper tucked under his arm. Despite not being a knitter himself, George had become a regular visitor since joining the Thursday yarn group last year, often stopping by on his morning walk for what he called "maintaining community connections"—and what Julie suspected was simple loneliness since his wife's passing.

"Morning, Julie," he greeted her, his normally jovial expression subdued. "Thought I'd see how you're doing after all the excitement."

"I'm fine, George, thank you," Julie assured him, genuinely touched by his concern. "How about you? This must have brought back difficult memories, learning what really happened to your friend Thomas."

George nodded solemnly, settling into one of the chairs in the sitting area. "Sixty years is a long time, but some friendships stay with you. I've been thinking about Tommy a lot these past few days—remembering how he was before he left for the service, always so principled. Even as teenagers, he couldn't abide unfairness."

Julie joined him, sensing he needed to talk. Tessa emerged from her bed near the counter to place her head on George's knee in silent canine sympathy.

"You know, the strangest part is that I should have questioned those letters more," George continued, absently stroking Tessa's silky ears. "Something about them always felt... off. The Tommy I knew would never have stayed away for decades without visiting, especially after his parents passed. But I suppose we believe what's easier to accept."

"That's human nature," Julie offered gently. "Elaine believed the same fiction, even knowing the truth deep down. Sometimes the comfortable story is easier than confronting painful realities."

George sighed, then seemed to make a deliberate effort to lighten his mood. "Well, it's all coming out now, isn't it? Front page news." He unfolded the Meadowgrove Gazette on the small table between them, revealing the headline: "HISTORICAL ARTIFACTS RECOVERED: DECADES-OLD MYSTERY SOLVED."

The article outlined the basic facts that Sheriff Harris had released to the public—the recovery of the Meadowgrove Collection, the identification of Thomas Sullivan's remains, and the revelation that Charles Johnson had been responsible for Sullivan's death following a dispute over historical land claims. Notably absent was any mention of Elaine Sullivan's role in the subsequent cover-up, a kindness Julie suspected came from Mayor Johnson's influence.

"The town's buzzing like a disturbed beehive," George commented. "Historical society's already fielding calls from state newspapers, and there's talk of a PBS documentary. Quite the commotion for our little Meadowgrove."

"How's Mayor Johnson handling the attention?" Julie asked, curious about the political fallout.

"With surprising grace, all things considered. Called an emergency town council session last night, laid everything out plainly—her father's actions, the fraudulent land claims, her commitment to rectification." George shook his head with grudging admiration. "Must've taken real backbone, facing a room full of people with that kind of family revelation. She's announced she won't run for another term, though."

This news didn't surprise Julie, though she felt a twinge of sympathy for the mayor despite their previous policy disagreements. Learning that your family legacy was built partially on fraud would shake anyone's foundations.

"And Victoria Thompson's museum plans?" she inquired, remembering the developer's unexpected pivot.

"Moving forward faster than anyone expected. Historical society's practically falling over themselves with excitement." George's mouth quirked in a half-smile. "Amazing how quickly opinions change when donations and prestigious projects are involved. Same folks who were ready to run her out of town with pitchforks last week are now singing her praises."

Their conversation was interrupted by the shop door opening again, bringing a welcome surprise—Derek Winters, looking somewhat improved though still sporting an impressive bruise above his eye and new, slightly too-large glasses.

"Derek! How are you feeling?" Julie rose to greet him.

"Better, thanks," he replied with a sheepish smile. "Dr. Walker says I'm officially cleared from concussion watch, though these temporary glasses make everything look slightly off-kilter."

George stood, offering his hand. "Don't believe we've been properly introduced. George Whitaker. Heard you took quite a hit defending our Julie here."

Derek's cheeks colored slightly at the implied heroism. "Just reacted without thinking, honestly. Wish I'd been more effective."

"Sometimes showing up is bravery enough," George responded kindly. "Well, I should continue my constitutional. Julie, we'll see you Thursday for yarn group?"

"Absolutely," she confirmed. "We're still focusing on the charity project for the Burlington shelter."

After George departed with a friendly wave, Derek approached the counter, his expression turning more serious. "I actually came by for two reasons. First, to thank you properly for everything you did. If you hadn't kept your wits about you when Edward... well, things could have ended very differently."

"It was a team effort," Julie demurred, uncomfortable with singular credit. "How's your aunt handling everything? It can't be easy, learning your ex-husband essentially married you to access family information."

Derek sighed, removing his ill-fitting glasses to rub the bridge of his nose. "Surprisingly well, actually. Aunt Victoria has always been... resilient. She's channeling everything into the museum project now. Which brings me to my second reason for stopping by."

He reached into his messenger bag, extracting a formal-looking folder embossed with 'Wilkins Heritage Foundation' in elegant script. "The preliminary museum prospectus. Aunt Victoria wanted you to have the first copy, before the public presentation next week."

Julie accepted the folder with surprise. "Me? Why?"

"Her exact words were, 'Ms. Sommers deserves to see the project first, given her central role in recovering the artifacts.'" Derek's smile turned slightly mischievous. "Which, coming from Aunt Victoria, is practically effusive praise."

Julie opened the folder, revealing professionally designed renderings of the reimagined Wilkins Building. The exterior maintained its historical integrity while subtle updates enhanced its accessibility and structural stability. Inside, modern museum spaces showcased Meadowgrove's history, with a special gallery dedicated to the recovered artifacts and the story of their sixty-year disappearance.

"This is beautiful," Julie acknowledged, genuinely impressed by the thoughtful design. "The perfect balance between preservation and progress."

"She's hoping you'll attend the presentation next Tuesday," Derek added. "Your endorsement would mean a lot, especially to the historical society members who might still harbor doubts about her intentions."

Julie considered the request, recognizing its strategic nature while also appreciating the olive branch it represented. "Of course I'll come. The project deserves support."

"Great. I'll let her know." Derek seemed relieved, then hesitated before continuing. "There's something else. Aunt Victoria has decided to sell the other properties she acquired in Meadowgrove—including the old mill site and some residential parcels. With the revelations about the Johnson family's fraudulent land claims, she feels it's appropriate to allow the legal process to determine proper ownership before any development proceeds."

"That's... unexpectedly principled," Julie observed.

Derek nodded. "The whole experience has shifted her perspective, I think. Not fundamentally changing who she is, but perhaps reconnecting her with values that got overshadowed by ambition." He glanced around the shop thoughtfully. "Which reminds me—what happens to your hidden compartment now? Is it permanently sealed as a crime scene?"

"Sheriff Harris's team removed the stonework for evidence processing, then returned it yesterday," Julie explained. "They documented everything thoroughly, then helped restore the wall. It's technically still part of an active investigation, but they understood the practical need to use my basement for business purposes."

"Are you keeping the compartment accessible? It's quite the historical feature."

"Actually, yes. The historical society has already asked about including Yarn Haven on a walking tour once everything settles down." Julie smiled wryly. "Apparently, being the site of a sixty-year-old mystery's resolution makes for good tourism."

Their conversation continued in this companionable vein until more customers arrived, seeking both yarn and firsthand accounts of the dramatic events. Derek tactfully departed, promising to keep Julie updated on the museum preparations.

Throughout the day, a steady stream of visitors filtered through the shop—some genuine customers, others barely disguising their curiosity about the site where historical artifacts had been hidden for six decades. Julie handled their questions with patient good humor, recognizing that Meadowgrove's processing of recent revelations included a natural desire to connect physically with the locations involved.

By closing time, she felt simultaneously exhausted and satisfied. Community interest would eventually normalize, but for now, she represented a tangible link to events that had reshaped local understanding of Meadowgrove's past.

After locking up, she climbed the stairs to her apartment, greeted enthusiastically by Tessa and with typical feline restraint by Hildi. She had just changed into comfortable clothes when her phone chimed with a text from Ben: *Still on for dinner tomorrow? I can pick you up at 6:30.*

Julie smiled, typing back: *Absolutely. Looking forward to it.*

His response came quickly: *Me too. Tablecloth establishment, so I'll dust off my good blazer. Rest well.*

The brief exchange left her with a pleasant warmth that persisted as she prepared a simple dinner and settled on the sofa with her knitting. The pattern—a complex cable design she'd been developing for weeks—

suddenly seemed to flow more naturally under her fingers, as if recent events had somehow aligned her creative instincts.

A knock at her door startled her from this peaceful state. Cautious after recent events, she checked the security peephole, surprised to see Elaine Sullivan standing in the hallway, looking frail but determined.

"Ms. Sullivan," Julie greeted her, opening the door. "This is unexpected."

"I apologize for the intrusion, dear," Elaine said, her voice carrying the slight quaver of advanced age. "I hoped we might speak privately. May I come in?"

Julie hesitated only briefly before stepping aside. Despite Elaine's confessed role in the historical deception, she presented no physical threat, and Julie's natural compassion wouldn't allow her to turn away someone so elderly without at least hearing what she had to say.

"Of course. Please, sit down. Can I offer you tea?"

"That would be lovely, thank you."

As Julie prepared tea, she observed Elaine surreptitiously. The older woman seemed diminished somehow, the dignity that had characterized her for decades now undercut by revealed secrets and public exposure. Yet there remained a core of composure in her posture, a resistance to complete surrender to circumstances.

"I expect you're wondering why I've come," Elaine began once they were settled with steaming mugs. "The truth is, I owe you an apology—not just for my role in concealing what happened to Tommy, but for the danger you and your friends faced because of my arrangement with Edward Thompson."

"You couldn't have anticipated he would resort to armed confrontation," Julie offered generously.

Elaine's smile held little humor. "Perhaps not specifically, but I knew he operated outside legal boundaries. That willful blindness doesn't absolve me of responsibility for the consequences." She sipped her tea, gathering thoughts. "When you reach my age, Ms. Sommers, you accumulate many regrets—paths not taken, words not spoken, truths not faced. Most remain private burdens. Few are exposed to public scrutiny."

Julie remained silent, sensing Elaine needed to speak without interruption.

"I loved Charles Johnson for sixty-three years," Elaine continued, her voice strengthening. "Through impossible circumstances, social boundaries, family expectations—and yes, even through the knowledge that he was responsible for my brother's death. That's the most unforgivable part, isn't it? That I could continue loving someone who committed such an act."

"Love isn't rational," Julie replied carefully. "Especially when it's been part of your life for so long."

"No, it isn't. Though perhaps it should be." Elaine set down her cup with a decisive click. "But I didn't come to seek understanding or forgiveness. I came because I wanted you to have something."

She reached into her handbag, extracting a small velvet box that she placed on the coffee table between them. "This belonged to Tommy. He was going to give it to Margaret Wilkins when they announced their engagement at the Harvest Festival in 1965."

Julie hesitated before gently opening the box to reveal a delicate ring—a modest diamond flanked by smaller sapphires in an antique setting.

"It's beautiful," she murmured, touched by the tangible connection to a romance cut tragically short six decades earlier.

"Charles returned it to me after... after what happened," Elaine explained. "He claimed he found it among Tommy's things at the mill, but I suspect he took it from Tommy's body, perhaps intending to eliminate evidence of the engagement. I've kept it all these years, unable to part with it but unwilling to wear it. A talisman of sorts, representing all that was lost."

"Why give it to me?" Julie asked, genuinely perplexed.

"Because you found the truth Tommy died protecting," Elaine said simply. "And because I understand from Sheriff Harris that Victoria Thompson is Margaret's granddaughter. Perhaps you might consider passing it to her—a small restoration of what her grandmother lost, if she would accept it."

The request startled Julie. "Are you sure? This is a family heirloom—"

"I have no children, Ms. Sommers. No direct heirs to whom such items would naturally pass. And every time I look at it, I'm reminded of my most grievous betrayal." Elaine's voice remained steady despite the emotion evident in her eyes. "Please. Consider it a small atonement."

Before Julie could formulate a response, Elaine rose with surprising agility for her age. "I won't impose on your evening further. Thank you for the tea, and for listening to an old woman's confessions."

Julie walked her to the door, conflicted about accepting such a significant item but recognizing the importance of the gesture to Elaine. "I'll give it careful thought," she promised. "And speak with Victoria when the moment seems right."

After Elaine departed, Julie returned to the velvet box, studying the ring with its poignant history. The small diamond caught the lamplight, refracting it into momentary rainbows across her coffee table. Such a ordinary object, yet laden with extraordinary significance—like so many elements of Meadowgrove she'd previously overlooked.

The following morning dawned bright and clear, perfect autumn weather for Yarn Haven's Thursday extended hours. Julie had just finished arranging a window display highlighting regional fiber artists when Marilyn arrived promptly at opening time, a stack of file folders tucked under her arm.

"The historical society voted unanimously to create a special exhibition about the Meadowgrove Collection and its recovery," she announced without preamble, setting the folders on the counter. "I'm heading the research committee, naturally, and wondered if you'd be willing to contribute a firsthand account of finding the hidden compartment."

"Of course," Julie agreed, unsurprised by Marilyn's characteristic efficiency in organizing historical documentation. "Though Derek deserves most of the credit for making the connection to the architectural changes."

"Already on my list to interview," Marilyn assured her. "Along with Sheriff Harris, Dr. Walker for the forensic perspective, and Victoria Thompson regarding her grandmother's experience." She hesitated before adding, "We've decided, as a society, not to delve too deeply into Elaine Sullivan's role. Some histories are perhaps better left... contextualized rather than emphasized."

Julie nodded, understanding the instinct to protect an elderly community member despite historical accuracy. "I think that's appropriate. Elaine's suffering her own private reckonings."

"Indeed. The mayor visited her yesterday—spent several hours there, according to my neighbor who lives across the street." Marilyn's tone suggested both disapproval of neighborhood surveillance and appreciation for the resulting information. "Quite remarkable, considering the circumstances."

"Perhaps they're finding common ground in shared disillusionment," Julie suggested. "Both had idealized versions of Charles Johnson shattered by these revelations."

Before Marilyn could respond, the shop door opened to admit several customers—a mother with a teenage daughter interested in learning to knit, and an older gentleman seeking a birthday gift for his wife. Julie greeted them warmly while Marilyn discreetly transferred her files to the back room, slipping out with a whispered promise to return for yarn group that evening.

The day passed in steady rhythm, the shop busier than usual with both regular customers and curiosity-seekers. Julie handled the latter with patient good humor, understanding that Meadowgrove needed time to integrate recent revelations into its collective identity.

Around lunchtime, Sarah from The Greenery delivered a sandwich and coffee, refusing payment with a friendly wave. "On the house for Meadowgrove's resident historical detective," she insisted. "Besides, I've made a killing this week with all the out-of-town reporters stopping in. Consider it profit-sharing."

As afternoon mellowed toward evening, Julie prepared for the yarn group meeting, setting out refreshments and arranging chairs in a welcoming circle. The regular members began arriving promptly at six—Rose from the library, the Peterson sisters, George Whitaker, and several others, each bringing not only their projects but excited commentary on recent events.

"I heard the county historical association is sending experts next week to authenticate the Founder's Journal," Rose informed them as she settled with her intricate lace project. "They're particularly interested in the original property boundaries documented there."

"Good thing too," Irene Peterson declared, her needles clicking rhythmically. "If the Johnson claims were fraudulent, there could be dozens of affected properties. My sister and I have been reviewing our family documents—our great-grandfather sold land to Harold Johnson in 1901 that might have been improperly acquired in the first place."

The conversation continued in this vein, blending historical speculation with progress reports on charity knitting projects. Nelly arrived in her typical whirlwind fashion, ten minutes late but bearing cider donuts from the orchard outside town. Marilyn followed shortly after, her precise movements contrasting with Nelly's exuberant disarray.

Julie observed the group with quiet satisfaction, appreciating how the yarn circle had evolved into something beyond a simple crafting gathering—a community forum where Meadowgrove processed events collective and individually, wisdom and perspectives flowing alongside knitting techniques and pattern advice.

A gentle knock on the shop door drew her attention. Through the glass, she spotted Ben, raising his hand in greeting but remaining outside, clearly not wanting to intrude on the group. Julie excused herself momentarily to speak with him.

"I was passing by and thought I'd say hello," he explained with an apologetic smile. "Didn't realize yarn group was meeting."

"We're just getting started," Julie said. "Would you like to join us? Your beginner scarf could use some attention."

Ben chuckled, shaking his head. "Maybe next week. I have evening rounds at the clinic, just taking a coffee break. Still on for tomorrow night?"

"Absolutely. Looking forward to it."

Their easy exchange was interrupted by Marilyn calling from inside: "Julie, Nelly's about to demonstrate that cable technique you were asking about."

"Duty calls," Julie said with a smile. "See you tomorrow."

Ben's expression warmed. "I'll be counting the hours."

As she returned to the group, Julie felt the weight of curious gazes and knowing smiles. "Not a word," she warned good-naturedly, resuming her seat in the circle.

"Wouldn't dream of commenting," Nelly assured her with exaggerated innocence. "Though I will note that Dr. Walker looked particularly handsome today. That blue shirt really brings out his eyes."

The group's laughter dispelled any remaining tension, conversations returning to a comfortable blend of crafting advice, local updates, and thoughtful processing of Meadowgrove's evolving historical narrative.

As darkness fell outside, casting the shop's warm lighting into greater contrast, Julie found herself observing the circle with fresh perspective. These people—some friends, some acquaintances, all connected through shared interest and community belonging—represented the true heart of Meadowgrove. Beyond historical revelations and real estate developments, beyond decades-old secrets and present-day consequences, this continuity of human connection provided the foundation that sustained small towns through changing circumstances.

The yarn group continued until nine, disbanding with promises to return the following week and genuine appreciation for the normalcy the gathering represented amid recent upheavals. Julie cleaned up afterward, storing leftover refreshments and returning furniture to its usual arrangement with Tessa supervising from her bed near the counter.

When the shop was finally restored to order, she locked up and headed upstairs, physically tired but mentally stimulated by the day's interactions. Tomorrow brought her dinner with Ben—a bright point of anticipation in an already improving situation.

As she prepared for bed, Julie's gaze fell on the small velvet box containing Thomas Sullivan's engagement ring, still sitting on her coffee table where Elaine had left it. The physical embodiment of a love story interrupted decades ago, now entrusted to her safekeeping until she could determine its proper destination.

She thought of Victoria Thompson, whose grandmother had never received this token of Thomas's commitment. Would she want this tangible connection to Margaret's past? Or would it represent unwelcome complications in her carefully constructed life?

Julie closed the box gently, deciding that question could wait for another day. For now, it was enough to know that long-buried truths had finally emerged into the light, allowing healing to begin—for individuals and for Meadowgrove itself.

Outside her window, Main Street lay quiet under the autumn moon, the Wilkins Building's stately outline visible across the way. Soon it would transform into a museum celebrating local history, including the dramatic events of recent days. Julie's shop, with its hidden compartment and connection to the recovered artifacts, would become part of that narrative—a place where past and present had converged in unexpected ways.

As she drifted toward sleep, Julie reflected that this was perhaps the true meaning of community—not just shared geography but shared stories, connecting people across time through common experiences and collective memory. Meadowgrove's history had been partially rewritten by recent discoveries, but its essence remained unchanged—a tapestry of interconnected lives, each contributing unique threads to a design larger than any individual.

Her own thread had become more integrally woven into that tapestry than she could have imagined when she first arrived three years ago, seeking simplicity and finding instead complex connections that enriched her life beyond measure. Like the intricate patterns she created with yarn and needles, these relationships formed something both beautiful and durable—a fabric strong enough to withstand even the revelation of long-hidden secrets.

With that comforting thought, Julie fell asleep to the familiar sounds of her apartment—Tessa's gentle snoring from the foot of the bed, Hildi's occasional soft movements along the hallway, the distant church clock marking the quarter hour. Tomorrow would bring new developments in Meadowgrove's ongoing story, but for tonight, this peaceful interlude provided necessary rest and perspective before the next chapter began.

Chapter 9
A Stitch Out of Place

Friday evening arrived with the particular golden quality of autumn light that transformed Meadowgrove's modest buildings into something almost enchanted. Julie stood before her bedroom mirror, critically assessing her appearance. She'd chosen a deep burgundy dress that complemented her chestnut hair, simple yet elegant enough for what Ben had described as a "tablecloth establishment."

It felt oddly momentous—her first official date with Ben, though they'd shared meals before and had certainly been through enough together already to bypass many of the usual early relationship uncertainties. Still, anticipation fluttered in her stomach as she applied a touch of lipstick and fastened small pearl earrings that had been her grandmother's.

Tessa watched from the bed, head tilted in canine curiosity at her owner's unusual preparations. Hildi, less interested, remained curled on the windowsill, occasionally opening one eye to track Julie's movements.

"What do you think?" Julie asked Tessa, who responded with an enthusiastic tail wag that seemed to indicate approval. "I'll take that as a yes."

A knock at the door sent a fresh wave of nerves through her, which she firmly suppressed as she crossed the apartment to answer. Ben stood in the hallway, looking handsomely unfamiliar in charcoal gray slacks and a navy blazer, the blue dress shirt he'd worn earlier replaced by a crisp white one.

"Hi," he said, his confident doctor's demeanor momentarily giving way to a more endearing awkwardness. "You look beautiful."

"Thank you," Julie replied, feeling a light flush warm her cheeks. "You clean up pretty well yourself."

As she gathered her purse and coat, Ben knelt to greet Tessa, who had trotted over to investigate this dressed-up version of her friend. "Don't worry, I'll have her home at a reasonable hour," he assured the dachshund solemnly, earning a laugh from Julie.

"She's actually more concerned about her evening snack than my curfew," Julie noted, setting out an extra treat for Tessa and making sure Hildi's water bowl was filled. "There. Everyone's taken care of."

They descended the stairs and exited through the shop, Julie pausing to set the security system—a habit that felt more significant since Thompson's break-in. Outside, Ben's car waited, a practical sedan that somehow suited him perfectly—reliable, understated, but with an underlying quality that revealed itself on closer inspection.

"I made reservations at Bella Vista," Ben mentioned as they drove through Meadowgrove's quiet streets. "It's about twenty minutes outside town—Italian place overlooking Lake Champlain. Seemed like a good place to have an actual conversation without running into half of Meadowgrove."

"Sounds perfect," Julie agreed, appreciating his thoughtfulness. After the past week of community scrutiny and constant discussion of recent events, the prospect of a meal away from curious eyes and inevitable questions was deeply appealing.

The restaurant proved to be everything Ben had described—elegant without pretension, housed in a restored Victorian with large windows offering spectacular views of the lake and distant Adirondacks. Their table near the windows caught the last of the sunset, the water's surface transformed into hammered gold beneath the fading light.

"This is lovely," Julie said as they settled in, accepting the menu from a discreet server. "How did you find it?"

"Professional recommendation, actually," Ben admitted. "One of my patients owns it—Sophia Marconi. She's been trying to get me to visit since I moved here, claiming proper Italian food has medicinal properties."

"A theory I'm very willing to test," Julie replied with a smile. "Especially after this week."

They ordered wine, and as they studied the menus, Julie found herself relaxing into the moment, the constant tension of recent days finally beginning to ease. Ben seemed similarly unburdened, his usual thoughtful demeanor softening into something more playful.

"So," he began once they'd ordered, "I propose a rule for this evening—no discussion of missing artifacts, historical land fraud, or anything related to Edward Thompson. Just regular first date conversation."

"Agreed," Julie said, lifting her wine glass in a mock toast. "Though that does eliminate about ninety percent of what Meadowgrove has been talking about this week."

"All the more reason," Ben insisted. "I'd rather hear about Julie Sommers than Meadowgrove's historical scandals."

The directness of his statement caught her slightly off guard, but pleasantly so. "What would you like to know?"

"Everything," he said simply. "But let's start with how a corporate marketing executive decided to become a small-town yarn shop owner. That's quite a transition."

Julie considered how to encapsulate that significant life change. "The short version is that I burned out. The long version involves seventy-hour work weeks, a broken engagement to a man who was married to his career, and the realization that I was designing marketing campaigns for products I didn't believe in." She sipped her wine reflectively. "My grandmother taught me to knit when I was eight. It was always my stress relief, my creative outlet. When I inherited some money after she passed away, it coincided with seeing Yarn Haven listed for sale online. I visited on a whim, fell in love with Meadowgrove, and made an offer two days later."

"That's remarkably decisive," Ben observed. "Most people contemplate major life changes for months or years."

"I'd already done the contemplating," Julie explained. "I just hadn't found the right alternative. When Meadowgrove appeared, it felt... right. Like recognizing something you didn't know you were looking for."

Ben nodded, understanding in his eyes. "I had a similar experience leaving Boston. The prestige of a major hospital position looked impressive on paper, but the reality was crushing. After my minor heart scare—just a warning sign, but enough to make me reevaluate—I started looking for something different. When Dr. Patterson contacted me about taking over his practice..." He gestured expressively. "Like you said, it felt right."

Their conversation flowed easily as their meals arrived—handmade pasta for Julie, seafood risotto for Ben. They discovered shared preferences for historical fiction and hiking, divergent opinions on jazz versus classical music, and a mutual appreciation for the quiet rhythms of small-town life despite their urban backgrounds.

"Did you ever regret it?" Ben asked as they shared a tiramisu. "Leaving your old life behind?"

Julie considered the question honestly. "There were moments—usually at tax time when I was knee-deep in small business paperwork, or during slow winters when I worried about making payroll. But no, not really regret. More like occasional nostalgia for certain aspects—the resources of a large company, the energy of a city. But the trade-offs have been more than worth it."

"I feel the same," Ben agreed. "Though I occasionally miss access to advanced medical technology, the opportunity to know my patients as people rather than case numbers more than compensates."

As they finished their coffee, Ben hesitated before asking, "Would you like to take a short walk? There's a lakeside path with lights. The evening's mild enough."

The prospect of extending their evening appealed to Julie. "I'd love that."

They strolled along the illuminated pathway, close enough that their hands occasionally brushed, creating a pleasant anticipation until Ben finally took her hand in his. The simple contact felt both monumental and completely natural, like the completion of a circuit long prepared but only now connected.

"This has been wonderful," Julie said softly as they paused at a viewing point overlooking the lake, now a vast darkness with distant lights from the New York shore reflected on the water's surface.

"It has," Ben agreed, turning to face her. The path lighting created gentle shadows across his features, emphasizing the warmth in his eyes.

"I've wanted to ask you to dinner since about a week after I moved to Meadowgrove and first visited your shop. Three years of working up the courage."

Julie raised an eyebrow, surprised. "Three years? I had no idea."

"I'm methodical," he admitted with a self-deprecating smile. "And cautious. Moving to Meadowgrove was such a significant change, I wanted to establish myself professionally before pursuing anything personal. Then it just became habit—stopping by the shop, enjoying our conversations, telling myself there was always time." His expression grew more serious. "Until Thompson broke in with a gun, and suddenly the concept of 'always time' seemed dangerously naive."

The reminder of their recent brush with danger created a momentary shadow, but Julie understood the sentiment behind it. "Sometimes we need a push to act on what matters."

"Exactly." Ben's hand gently touched her cheek, a question in his eyes that Julie answered by closing the distance between them. Their kiss was gentle at first, a careful exploration that deepened as Julie's arms slipped around his neck. When they finally separated, both were smiling.

"Definitely worth the three-year wait," Ben murmured, tucking a strand of hair behind her ear.

Their drive back to Meadowgrove seemed simultaneously too short and comfortably unhurried, their conversation punctuated by comfortable silences that required no filling. As they approached the town limits, however, Julie noticed Ben frowning slightly at his rearview mirror.

"Is something wrong?" she asked.

"Probably nothing," he replied, though his tone suggested otherwise. "That car behind us has been following since we left the restaurant. Could be coincidence—there's only one main road back to Meadowgrove."

Julie turned slightly, glimpsing headlights at a consistent distance behind them. "Maybe they're heading to town too."

"Maybe." Ben didn't sound convinced. After a moment's consideration, he made a decision. "Let's find out."

At the next intersection, he signaled right, then took the turn deliberately slowly. The car behind them hesitated briefly at the corner before also turning right.

"That's... concerning," Julie acknowledged, memories of Thompson's threats about someone else in Meadowgrove being involved surfacing despite her efforts to enjoy the evening.

"Let me try something else." Ben took another turn, this time into a residential neighborhood, then another, essentially heading back toward the main road through a circuitous route. The headlights continued to follow, maintaining the same careful distance.

"Definitely following us," Ben confirmed, his doctor's calm now tinged with protectiveness. "I'm calling Sheriff Harris."

He activated his car's bluetooth system, and the sheriff answered on the third ring, his voice slightly gruff with evening interruption. "Dr. Walker. Everything all right?"

"Not entirely," Ben replied. "I'm driving back to Meadowgrove with Julie Sommers, and we've picked up a tail—vehicle following us through multiple deliberate detours. Given recent events, I thought it warranted a call."

"Current location?" Sheriff Harris asked, all business now.

"Approaching Meadowgrove on Route 7, about five minutes out."

"Continue normally into town," the sheriff instructed. "Head toward the station. I'll have deputies positioned to intercept once you're in town limits. Don't attempt to confront or evade."

Ben confirmed understanding before ending the call, his hand reaching across to squeeze Julie's briefly. "Try not to worry. Probably just an overzealous reporter hoping for an exclusive on the Meadowgrove artifacts. They've been circling all week."

"Right," Julie agreed, though the tension in her shoulders belied her casual tone. "Just a journalist with questionable ethics."

They continued toward Meadowgrove, the following headlights maintaining their position. As they entered town, Ben drove directly toward the police station as instructed, turning onto Main Street where Deputy Sanchez's cruiser was visibly positioned near the town square.

The following vehicle suddenly accelerated, pulling into the opposing lane to pass them before speeding away down a side street—but not before Julie caught a glimpse of a familiar silver Lexus.

"That was Mayor Johnson's car," she said, stunned by the recognition.

Ben frowned, clearly having seen the same thing. "Are you certain?"

"Positive. I've seen it parked outside the town hall dozens of times."

They pulled up beside Deputy Sanchez, who approached their window. "The vehicle turned off on Elm Street," Ben informed him. "Silver Lexus sedan. Looked like Mayor Johnson's car."

The deputy's expression registered surprise before smoothing into professional neutrality. "We'll check it out. Please continue to the station as planned to file a report."

Twenty minutes later, they sat in Sheriff Harris's office, having recounted the evening's concerning conclusion. The sheriff listened carefully, making notes while maintaining an impressively neutral expression.

"Deputy Sanchez confirmed it was indeed the mayor's vehicle," he finally said. "We've requested she come in to explain, but her housekeeper reports she's not at home."

"Could someone have taken her car?" Julie suggested, finding it difficult to imagine Linda Johnson personally following them.

"Possible," Sheriff Harris acknowledged. "Though the mayor lives alone and is generally the only one with access to her vehicle." He closed his notebook decisively. "We'll continue looking into this. In the meantime, I'd advise extra caution for both of you. Thompson's claim about another involved party clearly warrants continued investigation."

After providing formal statements, they departed the station, the pleasant mood of their dinner date thoroughly displaced by this troubling development. Ben insisted on walking Julie to her door, his earlier relaxed demeanor now replaced by vigilant awareness of their surroundings.

"I'd feel better if you stayed at my place tonight," he admitted as they reached Yarn Haven. "But I understand if that seems too forward after one official date."

Julie smiled despite the tension. "Normally it might, but nothing about our relationship has followed conventional timing. Let me pack an overnight bag—and Tessa's things. She'd never forgive me for an impromptu sleepover without her."

Fifteen minutes later, they were headed to Ben's home on the outskirts of town—a modest Craftsman bungalow set back from the road with a generous yard bordered by woodland. Inside, the space reflected its owner's personality: comfortable without being fussy, bookshelves filled with medical texts alongside historical fiction, walls adorned with local landscape photography.

"Guest room is through there," Ben indicated a hallway off the living room. "Bathroom's adjacent. Make yourself at home while I check the perimeter."

Julie settled Tessa with her travel bed and favorite toy, then unpacked her minimal overnight essentials in the guest room. The space was clearly used more as a home office than for visitors, with a desk in one corner covered in medical journals and a comfortable reading chair beside a well-stocked bookshelf.

She was examining the book titles when Ben returned, having secured doors and windows. "All clear," he reported. "Would you like some tea? I find it helps after... unexpected developments."

"That sounds perfect," Julie agreed, following him to the kitchen.

As Ben prepared the tea, he seemed to be weighing his words carefully. "I'm sorry about how the evening ended," he finally said. "Not exactly the conclusion I'd envisioned for our first date."

"The first part was wonderful," Julie assured him, leaning against the counter beside him. "And the unexpected developments aren't your fault."

"Still," he persisted, "most women don't expect police reports and potential stalking situations when they agree to dinner."

"I'm not most women," Julie pointed out. "And Meadowgrove isn't exactly demonstrating typical small-town tranquility lately."

This observation earned a smile from Ben as he handed her a steaming mug. "True on both counts."

They moved to the living room, settling on the comfortable sofa with Tessa immediately claiming a spot between them. The dog's presence lightened the mood, her uncomplicated contentment at finding herself in new surroundings with two of her favorite humans a reminder that life continued alongside mystery and concern.

"What do you think it means?" Julie asked after a companionable silence. "Mayor Johnson following us?"

Ben considered the question thoughtfully. "It's puzzling. She seemed genuinely shocked by the revelations about her father, and her willingness to pursue legal rectification of the land fraud appeared sincere. Following us doesn't align with that response."

"Unless she's concerned about what else might emerge," Julie suggested. "Thompson mentioned another party still involved in covering up what happened in 1965. What if there are aspects of her father's actions she does know about—things not yet revealed in Thomas Sullivan's letter or the recovered artifacts?"

"Possible," Ben acknowledged. "Though it's equally possible someone else had access to her car. We should be careful about assumptions until Sheriff Harris completes his investigation."

Julie nodded, appreciating his measured perspective. Despite the concerning end to their evening, she found comfort in Ben's presence—his careful consideration of possibilities without jumping to conclusions, his balance of vigilance and calm reassurance.

"Thank you," she said suddenly, earning a questioning look. "For dinner, for handling the situation so well, for... all of it."

Ben's expression softened as he reached across Tessa to take her hand. "You're very welcome. Though I should be thanking you for agreeing to a second date after all this."

"Is that what this is?" Julie teased, gesturing to their surroundings. "A second date?"

"Improvised emergency sleepover," Ben clarified with a smile. "Second date will involve significantly fewer police reports and suspicious vehicles, I promise."

Their light banter continued as they finished their tea, the tension of the evening gradually dissipating into comfortable conversation. Eventually, exhaustion from the emotional roller coaster of recent days caught up with Julie, and Ben walked her to the guest room with a gentlemanly goodnight kiss at the door.

Alone in the unfamiliar room, Julie reflected on the evening's stark contrasts—the perfect dinner and lakeside walk shattered by the discovery of being followed, leading to this unexpected sleepover in Ben's home. Yet despite the concerning circumstances, she found herself smiling as she prepared for bed, Tessa already settled contentedly in her travel bed.

Tomorrow would bring more developments, more questions about Mayor Johnson's behavior, more pieces to fit into the complex puzzle of Meadowgrove's past and present. But tonight had also confirmed something important—her connection with Ben was real and deepening, weathering unexpected complications with mutual support rather than strain.

Crochet Carnage

As she drifted toward sleep, Julie's last coherent thought was that relationships, like well-crafted knitting patterns, revealed their true quality not during easy, straightforward sections but in how they handled unexpected complications and necessary adjustments. By that measure, tonight's unplanned detour had demonstrated promising resilience for whatever might come next.

Chapter 10
Crossing Threads

The morning light filtering through unfamiliar curtains momentarily disoriented Julie as she woke. It took several seconds to remember she was in Ben's guest room, with Tessa still contentedly snoring in her travel bed nearby. The events of the previous evening came rushing back—their wonderful dinner, the disturbing discovery of being followed, and the shocking revelation that it had been Mayor Johnson's car.

She checked her phone to find several messages waiting: one from Marilyn asking if she was free to discuss historical society business, another from Nelly with multiple exclamation points about "juicy gossip" at The Greenery, and a third, more surprising one from Derek Winters inquiring if she'd be attending Victoria's presentation on Tuesday.

Before she could respond to any of them, a gentle knock sounded at the door.

"Coffee's ready when you are," Ben called softly. "No rush."

Julie smiled at his consideration. "I'll be out in a few minutes," she replied, already moving to freshen up.

When she emerged into the kitchen, dressed in the casual clothes she'd packed for the morning, she found Ben at the stove, expertly flipping pancakes while juggling his phone against his shoulder.

"Yes, Sheriff, I understand," he was saying. "We'll be there at ten. Thanks for the update." He ended the call and turned to Julie. "Good morning. Hope you slept well despite everything."

"Surprisingly well," she admitted, accepting the mug of coffee he offered. "Though I'm curious about that call."

Ben flipped the last pancake onto a waiting plate. "Sheriff Harris wants to see us at the station this morning. Apparently Mayor Johnson came in voluntarily at dawn to explain her behavior last night."

"Really?" Julie's eyebrows rose in surprise. "That's... unexpected."

"Agreed," Ben said, placing breakfast on the table. "Though this whole situation has been one unexpected development after another."

They settled into a companionable breakfast, Ben explaining that he'd already taken Tessa outside for a morning constitutional, earning Julie's appreciative thanks. There was an easy domesticity to the scene that might have seemed premature given the official newness of their relationship, but somehow felt natural after all they'd shared.

"So," Ben began as they cleared the dishes together, "besides our meeting with Sheriff Harris, what's on your agenda today?"

"The shop's open until three, so I should get back soon," Julie replied. "Though the curious visitor traffic has actually been good for business—people coming to see the historical hiding place and leaving with yarn."

Ben smiled. "Silver linings. Want me to drop you back at Yarn Haven after the station?"

"That would be perfect, thank you."

They arrived at the sheriff's station precisely at ten, finding Sheriff Harris waiting in his office with a file open before him and a serious expression. To Julie's surprise, Deputy Sanchez was also present, positioned near the door with a professional neutrality that suggested importance.

"Dr. Walker, Ms. Sommers," the sheriff greeted them. "Thank you for coming in. As I mentioned on the phone, Mayor Johnson has provided a statement regarding last night's incident. I thought you should hear it directly."

He gestured for them to sit, then leaned forward with his fingers steepled. "According to the mayor, she was not driving her vehicle last night. She claims it was taken without her knowledge by Elaine Sullivan."

Julie blinked in surprise. "Elaine? But she's nearly eighty years old."

"And still a licensed driver," Sheriff Harris noted. "The mayor states that Ms. Sullivan had access to her spare keys due to their longtime family connection, and apparently borrowed the vehicle without permission while the mayor was attending a budget meeting."

Ben frowned. "That seems... convenient. And odd. Why would Elaine Sullivan follow us?"

"That's where things get interesting," Sheriff Harris continued, flipping a page in his file. "Mayor Johnson claims that after the revelations about her father and the land fraud, Elaine has become increasingly anxious about what additional information might surface. According to the mayor, Elaine has developed a particular fixation on you, Ms. Sommers, as the person who discovered the hidden artifacts."

"But that doesn't make sense," Julie protested. "Elaine came to my apartment two days ago to give me Thomas's engagement ring for Victoria. She seemed reflective, remorseful even—not threatening or fixated."

Sheriff Harris nodded thoughtfully. "I've noted that inconsistency. We're attempting to locate Ms. Sullivan for confirmation, but she's not answering her phone or door. The Sullivan lake house appears empty."

"Could the mayor be covering for her own actions?" Ben suggested carefully.

"It's being considered," the sheriff acknowledged, his noncommittal tone suggesting professional caution rather than dismissal. "We're checking traffic cameras and pursuing other verification methods."

Deputy Sanchez cleared his throat. "There is another development you should be aware of, Sheriff."

At Harris's nod, the deputy continued, "The county assessor's office called this morning. They've begun reviewing the documentation from the Founder's Journal regarding the disputed Johnson land claims. Preliminary findings suggest the fraudulent deeds affect approximately 320 acres of prime lakefront property—including the entirety of what's now the mayor's residence and the Sullivan family home."

This revelation hung in the air with palpable weight. If the Johnson family's most valuable property holdings were proven to be fraudulently obtained, the financial and social implications for the mayor would be devastating—regardless of her personal innocence in the original fraud.

"That certainly establishes motive," Ben observed quietly. "For monitoring anyone who might uncover additional evidence."

Sheriff Harris sighed, looking uncharacteristically tired. "It does. Though it complicates rather than simplifies our situation. Mayor Johnson has been cooperative throughout this investigation and seemingly transparent about addressing her family's historical wrongdoing. This behavior represents a significant deviation."

"Or perhaps reveals her true position," Julie suggested. "Public cooperation while privately monitoring those involved for potential threats to her interests."

The sheriff closed his file decisively. "We'll continue investigating both possibilities. In the meantime, I'd advise continued caution for both of you. Report any unusual observations or encounters immediately."

They provided additional details from the previous night's incident before being released, walking out into the bright autumn morning with more questions than answers.

"Well, that was informative if not conclusive," Ben commented as they headed toward his car. "What do you think?"

Julie considered carefully. "I'm having trouble reconciling the Elaine Sullivan who visited my apartment with someone who would follow us in a borrowed car. She seemed genuinely remorseful about her role in concealing her brother's death, almost relieved that the truth was finally out."

"People are complicated," Ben noted. "Trauma and guilt can manifest in unpredictable ways, especially when combined with advanced age and decades of secrecy."

"True," Julie acknowledged. "But something about the mayor's explanation feels too convenient."

They continued discussing possibilities as Ben drove her back to Yarn Haven, agreeing to remain vigilant while avoiding paranoia. When they arrived at the shop, Ben insisted on checking the premises before leaving, his medical calm undercut by genuine concern.

"Call me if anything seems off," he instructed as he finally prepared to leave. "Anything at all."

"I will," Julie promised, touched by his protectiveness without finding it stifling. "And thank you for everything—dinner, emergency lodging, pancakes."

His smile softened the worry lines around his eyes. "My pleasure. Despite the complications, it was still the best first date I've had in years."

After he departed for the clinic, Julie opened the shop, greeted by the familiar comfort of colorful yarns and the routine of beginning a business day. She responded to her waiting messages, arranging to meet Marilyn at lunch to discuss historical society matters and promising Nelly details about her date "minus certain security concerns" when they next met.

The morning passed steadily, with enough customers to keep Julie occupied without overwhelming her. Around eleven, the bell chimed to admit Derek Winters, looking marginally better than during his last visit though still sporting temporary glasses.

"Just checking if you received my message," he explained, adjusting the frames that clearly didn't fit quite right. "Aunt Victoria is quite keen on having you attend Tuesday's presentation."

"I did, and I'll be there," Julie confirmed, studying him curiously. "How is she? I haven't seen her since the meeting at the sheriff's station."

Derek's expression turned thoughtful. "Changed, I'd say. Not fundamentally different—still driven and efficient—but more... reflective. Finding vindication for her grandmother while simultaneously learning her marriage was a calculated deception has been a lot to process."

"I can imagine," Julie said, though in truth she found Victoria's particular combination of experiences difficult to fully comprehend. "The museum plans look impressive."

"They're occupying most of her energy now. She's channeling everything into making the Wilkins Building a proper historical showcase." Derek hesitated before adding, "She also mentioned wanting to speak with you privately at some point. Something about 'adjusted perspectives' and 'community integration.' Coming from Aunt Victoria, that's practically an admission of having misjudged you."

Julie smiled slightly at this assessment. "Tell her I'm open to conversation whenever she's ready."

After Derek left, promising to relay her message, Julie found herself contemplating how thoroughly her initial impressions of Victoria Thompson had been revised by subsequent revelations. The woman she'd first met—coldly ambitious, dismissive of Meadowgrove's character, focused exclusively on profit—had revealed unexpected complexities:

loyalty to family legacy, resilience in the face of betrayal, and an evolving appreciation for historical preservation beyond commercial advantage.

This reflection was interrupted by the arrival of Marilyn at noon, precisely on schedule, carrying a tote bag bulging with what appeared to be file folders and books.

"The historical society has been inundated with research requests," she announced without preamble, setting her burden on the counter. "Everything from academic historians to film producers. We're establishing protocols for managing access to the artifacts once they're officially authenticated."

Julie smiled at her friend's characteristic efficiency. "And they've put you in charge of organization, naturally."

"Joint committee leadership with Professor Harper from the university," Marilyn clarified, though her tone suggested the arrangement was more nominal than practical. "But that's not why I wanted to speak with you specifically."

She extracted a folder labeled "Sullivan-Wilkins Documentation" and opened it to reveal photocopies of old letters. "These were donated by Elaine Sullivan yesterday. Correspondence between Thomas and Margaret from 1964-65, during their investigation of the land fraud. I thought you might find them particularly interesting given recent developments."

Julie examined the copies with careful hands, struck by the tangible connection to the couple whose interrupted love story had indirectly led to so many current circumstances. Thomas's handwriting was neat and decisive, Margaret's more flowing but equally clear. Their letters discussed not only their investigation but their plans for the future —a small house by the lake, children named after favorite relatives, dreams of creating a legal practice together once Margaret completed her education.

"It's heartbreaking," Julie murmured, reading Thomas's description of the home he hoped to build for them. "All these plans, dissolved by Charles Johnson's desperate attempt to protect his family's fraudulent claims."

"Indeed," Marilyn agreed somberly. "But there's something specific I wanted you to see." She turned pages until reaching a letter dated October 12, 1965—just two days before Thomas's death. "This passage here."

Julie read the indicated section aloud: "*Margaret, we must consider the possibility that C.J. is not working alone in this. Today I observed E.S. removing documents from the town archives—the same property maps we had been examining yesterday. When questioned, she claimed it was routine historical society business, but her manner was furtive. I hate to consider what this might mean, but we must be realistic about potential complications.*"

She looked up at Marilyn with widening eyes. "E.S.—Elaine Sullivan. Thomas suspected his sister's involvement before his confrontation with Charles Johnson."

"Exactly." Marilyn's expression was grave. "And this creates a significantly different context for evaluating current events, including Mayor Johnson's claim about Elaine borrowing her car to follow you and Dr. Walker last night."

Julie sat back, processing this new information. "If Thomas was right about Elaine's deeper involvement in 1965, it suggests her recent displays of remorse might be... incomplete at best."

"Or tactical," Marilyn suggested with characteristic directness. "Sheriff Harris should see these letters immediately. They provide important historical context for present behavior."

Julie nodded in agreement, a chill settling over her previous sympathy for Elaine Sullivan. The elderly woman's visit to her apartment, her gift of Thomas's engagement ring—were these genuine attempts at atonement, or carefully calculated efforts to influence Julie's perception while monitoring her activities?

"I'll close early and go with you to the sheriff," Julie decided. "This connection seems too important to delay."

After placing the "Closed for Lunch" sign in the window, they headed directly to the sheriff's station, the copied letters secured in Marilyn's meticulous organization. Sheriff Harris received them promptly, his expression growing increasingly serious as they explained their discovery.

"This corroborates another development," he informed them after examining the relevant passages. "We've located Elaine Sullivan—at Mayor Johnson's residence. She apparently spent the night there after supposedly borrowing the car, though neither woman mentioned this during their separate statements this morning."

"That seems significantly misleading," Marilyn observed with characteristic understatement.

"Indeed." The sheriff's tone remained professional, but a muscle tightened in his jaw. "We're bringing both women in for additional questioning. The timing of these letters is extremely helpful, Ms. Green. The historical society has my thanks."

They provided formal statements about the letters before departing, the autumn sunshine outside the station creating a jarring contrast to the dark historical secrets being untangled within.

"I should get back to the shop," Julie said as they reached Main Street. "But thank you for bringing these to my attention."

"Knowledge is often our best protection," Marilyn replied with the quiet wisdom of her teaching years. "Especially when dealing with deceptions maintained for decades."

After Marilyn departed for the library, Julie returned to Yarn Haven, her mind whirling with implications. If Elaine's involvement in the events of 1965 was deeper than she'd admitted—if she had actively assisted Charles Johnson rather than merely failing to report her suspicions—it cast her current behavior in a much more concerning light.

The afternoon passed slowly, customer interactions providing welcome distraction from troubling thoughts. Julie found herself glancing more frequently at her phone, half-expecting updates from Sheriff Harris or concerned messages from Ben. Instead, at three o'clock, as she was preparing to close for the day, the shop door opened to admit Victoria Thompson herself.

The developer looked as impeccably put together as always, but subtle changes registered in Julie's observation—less rigid posture, a hint of uncertainty beneath the professional demeanor, clothing that while still elegant seemed less aggressively formal than her previous corporate armor.

"Ms. Sommers," Victoria greeted her with a slight nod. "I hope I'm not interrupting your day."

"Not at all," Julie replied, gesturing toward the sitting area. "I was about to close anyway. Would you like tea?"

The offer seemed to momentarily disarm Victoria, who hesitated before nodding. "That would be... pleasant. Thank you."

As Julie prepared tea, she watched Victoria surreptitiously from the small kitchenette. The woman moved through the shop with measured steps, examining displays with what appeared to be genuine interest rather than the clinical assessment of her first visit. When Tessa emerged from her bed to investigate, Victoria actually knelt to greet the dachshund, offering her hand for inspection with unexpected gentleness.

"She's very sweet," Victoria commented as Julie returned with two mugs. "I had a terrier as a child. Frederick. Dreadfully spoiled by my mother."

This glimpse of personal history—volunteered rather than extracted—represented a significant shift from their previous interactions. Julie accepted it as the olive branch it seemed intended to be.

"Tessa rules the shop with benevolent authority," she replied with a smile. "Customers often come to see her rather than me."

A hint of answering humor touched Victoria's eyes before she straightened, returning to her more businesslike demeanor. "Derek mentioned you'll be attending the presentation on Tuesday. I appreciate that, especially given our... complicated history."

"The museum is a wonderful concept," Julie said sincerely. "Exactly the kind of development Meadowgrove needs—honoring history while creating something new."

Victoria nodded, her gaze dropping to her tea. "I've come to realize that preservation and progress aren't necessarily opposing forces. They can be complementary when approached with appropriate respect."

Coming from the woman who had initially dismissed Yarn Haven as "quaint" and "rustic," this philosophical adjustment represented significant evolution. Julie acknowledged it with a simple nod, allowing Victoria space to continue.

"There's another matter I wanted to discuss," Victoria said after a moment. "Derek mentioned that Elaine Sullivan gave you something—Thomas's engagement ring intended for my grandmother."

Julie blinked in surprise. "Yes, she did. I've been considering the best time to approach you about it. It seemed like a sensitive matter."

"It is," Victoria acknowledged, her composure wavering slightly. "But I'd like to see it, if you're willing. It represents a connection to my grandmother I never expected to have."

"Of course." Julie rose and went to her apartment stairs, retrieving the velvet box from where she'd secured it in a drawer. Returning, she handed it to Victoria without comment, respecting the emotional significance of the moment.

Victoria opened the box carefully, studying the ring with an expression Julie couldn't quite interpret—something between wistfulness and analytical assessment, personal connection and historical appreciation.

"Grandmother never married after leaving Meadowgrove," Victoria said softly, still looking at the ring. "Never spoke of Thomas to my mother except once, near the end of her life, when she said there had been someone once who believed in justice enough to die for it." She closed the box with gentle precision. "I didn't understand what she meant until now."

"Would you like to keep it?" Julie offered. "Elaine specifically wanted you to have it, as Margaret's granddaughter."

Victoria considered this, then shook her head slightly. "Not yet. I think... I think it should be part of the museum exhibit initially. A tangible representation of what was lost beyond mere artifacts. After that..." She met Julie's gaze directly. "After that, perhaps. When I've earned it."

This unexpected humility rendered Julie momentarily speechless. The Victoria Thompson she'd first met would never have questioned her entitlement to any object or opportunity.

"That seems appropriate," she managed after a moment. "I'll keep it safe until then."

Victoria nodded, then shifted to a more practical tone. "There's something else you should know. The sheriff contacted me an hour ago with questions about Elaine Sullivan's recent activities. Apparently she and Mayor Johnson have been less than forthcoming about their interactions following the revelation of the artifacts."

"I know," Julie confirmed. "Marilyn discovered letters suggesting Elaine's involvement in 1965 was more significant than she's admitted. And last night, someone in Mayor Johnson's car followed Ben and me after dinner. The mayor claims it was Elaine who took her car without permission."

Victoria's eyebrows rose slightly. "That's... concerning. Derek mentioned you'd experienced some security issues, but not specifics." She frowned thoughtfully. "It makes sense, though. If the disputed land claims affect the most valuable Johnson properties, Linda would have powerful motivation to monitor anyone who might uncover additional evidence."

"That's what we thought," Julie agreed. "Though it's still surprising to see such duplicity from someone who publicly committed to transparency and rectification."

"People with inherited privilege often believe in justice until it costs them personally," Victoria observed with unexpected insight. "Then principles become negotiable."

Their conversation was interrupted by Julie's phone chiming with a text message. She glanced at it, then felt her heart rate accelerate.

"Everything all right?" Victoria inquired, noticing her expression.

"It's from Ben," Julie replied, reading the message again to ensure she hadn't misunderstood. "Sheriff Harris just called him. They've issued arrest warrants for both Mayor Johnson and Elaine Sullivan—obstruction of justice and tampering with evidence. Apparently they've been systematically removing documents from both the town archives and the Sullivan family records that provide additional details about the land fraud."

Victoria absorbed this information with a slight nod, as if it confirmed a private theory. "And now they've disappeared, I assume?"

"Yes," Julie confirmed, reading further. "Neither woman is at their homes, and Mayor Johnson's car was found abandoned at the bus station in Burlington."

"They won't have taken public transportation," Victoria said with certainty. "Too easily traced. They'll be heading for the lake."

Julie looked up sharply. "What makes you say that?"

"It's what I would do in their position," Victoria explained, her business acumen shifting to strategic assessment. "The Sullivan property has private boat access. From there, they could reach New York state within an hour, then continue to Canada if necessary."

The precision of this analysis suggested Victoria had considered such contingencies herself at some point, a reminder that beneath her evolving perspective remained a calculating mind accustomed to evaluating all possible scenarios.

"We should tell Sheriff Harris," Julie decided, already dialing.

As she relayed Victoria's theory to the sheriff, who immediately dispatched deputies to the Sullivan lake house, Julie found herself in the surreal position of standing in her yarn shop collaborating with Victoria Thompson—the woman she'd initially perceived as Meadowgrove's greatest threat—to help apprehend the town's respected mayor and a longtime resident.

The weaving together of unlikely alliances, the crossing of threads that had once seemed destined to remain separate—it created a pattern more complex and ultimately more compelling than Julie could have imagined when she first encountered Victoria Thompson just over a week ago.

As she ended the call with Sheriff Harris's thanks ringing in her ears, she turned to find Victoria studying her with something like respectful appreciation.

"You've handled this entire situation with remarkable composure, Ms. Sommers," Victoria observed. "Meadowgrove is fortunate to have you."

Coming from Victoria Thompson, this represented high praise indeed. Julie accepted it with a simple nod, recognizing that while they might never be close friends, they had achieved something perhaps more valuable—mutual respect forged through adversity and evolving understanding.

"Thank you for your insight about the lake," Julie responded. "It may make all the difference."

Outside Yarn Haven's windows, Main Street continued its normal late-afternoon rhythms, residents and visitors moving between shops, autumn leaves occasionally dancing across sidewalks in the gentle breeze. Yet beneath this tranquil surface, Meadowgrove's foundations were shifting—historical truths emerging, present deceptions unraveling, and new connections forming among unlikely allies.

Julie found herself curious about what the next chapter might bring, both for the town she'd chosen as home and for her own unexpected place within its unfolding story.

Chapter 11
Picking Up Loose Ends

"Absolutely not." Sheriff Harris's tone left no room for argument as he stood in Yarn Haven's back room, arms crossed over his chest. "This is now an active pursuit of fugitives who may be desperate. Civilians cannot be involved."

Julie had expected this response, but Victoria Thompson seemed less willing to accept it.

"Sheriff, I understand your position," Victoria countered with the practiced negotiation skills of a career developer. "But Ms. Sommers and I are simply offering information, not requesting to join your deputies. My familiarity with waterfront properties and Ms. Sommers's knowledge of local people could prove valuable in a situation requiring discretion."

The sheriff's expression remained unmoved. "I appreciate the offer, but this isn't a committee project. If Mayor Johnson and Elaine Sullivan have indeed fled to the lake house with stolen documents, apprehending them requires trained personnel following established protocols."

The conversation had developed rapidly after Julie's call to the sheriff about Victoria's lake house theory. Harris had arrived at Yarn Haven within ten minutes, accompanied by Deputy Sanchez, to take their formal statements before proceeding with the operation to apprehend the fugitives.

Julie, recognizing the futility of further argument, tried a different approach. "What about Ben—Dr. Walker? He called to say he's heading to the station. Would his medical expertise be useful if Elaine experiences health issues during arrest? She is nearly eighty."

This practical consideration seemed to register with Sheriff Harris, who paused thoughtfully. "That's actually a reasonable contingency to address. I'll have Deputy Collins contact Dr. Walker to accompany the medical response team staging nearby." He checked his watch. "I need to join the operation. Please remain available by phone in case we need additional information, but do not—I repeat, do not—approach the Sullivan property under any circumstances."

After extracting firm promises from both women, the sheriff departed with Deputy Sanchez, leaving Julie and Victoria alone in the increasingly dim shop as afternoon shadows lengthened.

"Well," Julie said after a moment, "that went about as expected."

Victoria's mouth quirked in what might have been amusement. "Law enforcement officers dislike civilian involvement. Understandable, if occasionally inefficient." She studied Julie with new assessment. "You seem remarkably calm about all this."

"Trust me, I'm processing internally," Julie assured her, moving to turn on additional lights as darkness gathered. "One week ago, my biggest concern was whether to order more alpaca for winter projects. Now I'm discussing fugitive apprehension strategies while the mayor and a longtime resident flee with stolen historical documents. Calm is a survival mechanism at this point."

This earned a genuine smile from Victoria—the first Julie had witnessed from the usually composed developer. "Adaptability is an underrated quality," she observed. "Though I suspect your transition from corporate marketing to small-town shopkeeper provided excellent training."

Before Julie could respond, her phone chimed with a text from Ben: *At staging area with medical team near Sullivan property. Sheriff's operation moving forward cautiously. Will update when possible.*

She showed the message to Victoria, who nodded thoughtfully. "Good. At least we have a connection to what's happening."

"Would you like more tea while we wait?" Julie offered, suddenly aware of the surreal quality of hosting Victoria Thompson for an impromptu stakeout-by-proxy in her yarn shop.

"That would be welcome, thank you."

As Julie prepared fresh tea, she found herself curious about Victoria's evolution from adversary to unexpected ally. "May I ask you something personal?" she ventured, returning with steaming mugs.

Victoria accepted hers with a nod. "You may ask. I reserve the right not to answer."

"Fair enough," Julie acknowledged. "When you first arrived in Meadowgrove, was clearing your grandmother's name your primary motivation? Or did that emerge more fully after the discoveries about your ex-husband?"

Victoria considered the question with evident care, her usual rapid responses temporarily suspended in favor of reflection. "Initially, I approached Meadowgrove as a business opportunity with a personal component," she finally said. "The Wilkins family connection provided convenient leverage and local knowledge, but profit remained the dominant motivation." She sipped her tea before continuing. "Learning about Edward's deception forced me to reevaluate not just our relationship, but my own priorities. When one foundation crumbles, you naturally examine others more critically."

This unexpectedly philosophical response revealed depths to Victoria that Julie hadn't previously recognized. "And what did you find when you examined those foundations?"

"That I'd constructed an identity predominantly around achievement and acquisition," Victoria replied with surprising candor. "Proving my worth through professional success while simultaneously validating my grandmother's innocence through recovering what was stolen from her." Her expression grew more introspective. "When Edward's betrayal exposed how thoroughly I'd been manipulated—used for access to family information rather than valued for myself—it prompted uncomfortable questions about what truly matters."

"And the museum project emerged from that questioning?" Julie suggested.

"Partly," Victoria acknowledged. "Also from recognizing that Meadowgrove isn't merely a development opportunity but a community with genuine historical value. Preservation and profit needn't be mutually exclusive."

Their conversation was interrupted by Julie's phone ringing—Ben calling rather than texting, which immediately heightened her attention.

"Everything all right?" she answered, putting the call on speaker for Victoria's benefit.

"Complicated situation," Ben replied, his voice slightly hushed. "The Sullivan lake house was empty when deputies arrived, but showed signs of recent occupancy—food still warm in the kitchen, boat missing from the dock. They've initiated water search patterns, but visibility is decreasing with sunset."

"Were the documents there?" Victoria asked, leaning toward the phone.

"Partially," Ben confirmed. "Several folders of town archives scattered in what appeared to be hasty sorting. Sheriff Harris thinks they were interrupted mid-process and took the most crucial documents with them."

Julie exchanged a concerned glance with Victoria. "Any indication where they might be heading?"

"The lake has numerous secluded coves and private docks," Ben explained. "Sheriff's marine unit is coordinating with New York authorities for cross-jurisdictional search, but it's challenging territory, especially as darkness falls."

"What about tracking Elaine's phone?" Julie suggested.

"Found abandoned at the lake house," Ben replied. "Mayor Johnson's was similarly discarded at the bus station—classic misdirection. These women have clearly planned this contingency."

After promising to update them with any developments, Ben ended the call, leaving Julie and Victoria to process this latest information in thoughtful silence.

"They won't risk crossing to New York immediately," Victoria said finally, her analytical mind clearly mapping strategic options. "Too obvious, and marine patrols would be concentrated near the state line. They'll seek temporary shelter at an unoccupied seasonal property, then attempt crossing when surveillance decreases."

Julie considered this assessment. "There are dozens of vacation homes along that shoreline, many empty after summer."

"Precisely." Victoria set down her mug decisively. "Which is why local knowledge would be valuable to law enforcement, despite Sheriff Harris's resistance to civilian involvement."

Before Julie could respond, the shop door opened with its familiar chime, admitting Marilyn and Nelly in a unified front that suggested prior coordination.

"We heard about the arrest warrants," Nelly announced without preamble, her bohemian skirts swirling as she entered. "The entire town's buzzing. Is it true they fled by boat?"

"Word travels impossibly fast," Julie observed, bringing additional mugs for her friends while explaining the current situation.

Marilyn listened with characteristic intense focus, her organizational mind visibly processing each detail. "The Sullivan boat is a distinctive vintage Chris-Craft," she noted when Julie finished. "Wooden hull, deep blue with brass fittings—easily identifiable even at a distance."

"But not at night," Nelly pointed out practically. "And they'd know that."

"They'll need shelter," Victoria reiterated. "Somewhere with limited access and observation."

"The old boathouse at Willow Point," Marilyn suggested after a moment's consideration. "It's been unused since the Gregory family sold their property for subdivision, but the development stalled with permit issues. The boathouse is structurally sound but officially vacant—perfect temporary hiding place with water access."

Victoria raised an eyebrow, clearly impressed by Marilyn's detailed knowledge of local properties. "That's exactly the kind of specific information law enforcement needs. Where exactly is this boathouse?"

As Marilyn described the location, Julie texted Ben with this potential lead, receiving a prompt response: *Forwarding to Sheriff Harris immediately. Stay where you are.*

The emphasis on their non-involvement was clear, but Julie found herself increasingly restless as darkness fully claimed the October evening. The thought of Mayor Johnson and Elaine Sullivan escaping with documents that might contain crucial evidence about Thomas Sullivan's death and the Johnson family's fraudulent land claims created a sense of impending injustice that was difficult to ignore.

"We should be doing something," Nelly voiced the collective sentiment, pacing energetically between displays of autumn-colored yarns. "Not just sitting here drinking tea while history potentially disappears into the night."

"Sheriff Harris was quite explicit about civilian non-involvement," Julie reminded her, though her own inclination aligned with Nelly's frustration.

"Because he doesn't recognize our collective resources," Victoria observed unexpectedly. "Between Ms. Green's historical knowledge, Ms. Morrison's familiarity with local geography from her painting expeditions, your community connections, and my strategic planning experience, we represent a formidable analytical team."

This assessment, delivered with Victoria's characteristic precision, created a shifting dynamic in the room—four women with diverse skills united by common purpose rather than divided by different perspectives.

"What exactly are you suggesting?" Marilyn asked, her usual cautious approach tempered by evident interest.

Victoria leaned forward, her business presentation posture emerging naturally. "Not physical pursuit or confrontation—that remains law enforcement territory. But we can construct contingency scenarios based on our collective knowledge, anticipating potential movements if the boathouse lead proves unsuccessful."

"A strategy session," Julie clarified, finding the concept both reasonable and potentially useful. "Generating intelligence rather than attempting direct intervention."

"Precisely," Victoria confirmed with an approving nod. "Sheriff Harris rejected our assistance because he envisioned physical involvement. This is entirely different—leveraging intellectual resources to support official efforts."

The distinction seemed to satisfy Marilyn's concern for proper procedure, while the active problem-solving component appealed to Nelly's more impulsive nature. Julie found herself once again struck by the unlikely alliance forming in her shop—Victoria Thompson, Marilyn Green, and Nelly Morrison, three women who could scarcely be more different in personality and approach, now collaboratively addressing a community crisis.

"We'll need a map," Marilyn declared practically, transitioning from skepticism to organization with characteristic efficiency.

Within minutes, they had transformed the yarn shop's sitting area into an impromptu strategy center, with lake charts from Marilyn's historical society resources spread across the table, Nelly's artistic sketches of shoreline features adding detail to official maps, and Victoria's analytical notes creating a methodical framework for their discussion.

Julie contributed local knowledge gathered from three years of community conversations—which property owners were away, which docks were maintained year-round, which coves provided natural shelter from observation. As they worked, she texted relevant insights to Ben, who confirmed each message was conveyed to the sheriff's team.

"They're actively investigating the boathouse lead," he reported in a brief call around seven o'clock. "Marine patrols have been repositioned based on your shoreline analysis. Sheriff Harris sends grudging appreciation while maintaining his position on physical non-involvement."

This acknowledgment of their contribution, however reluctant, energized the group's efforts. They continued refining potential scenarios, considering factors like Elaine's age and physical limitations, weather conditions affecting water travel, and the logistics of transporting document boxes while maintaining boat control.

"The fundamental question," Victoria observed during a thoughtful pause, "is whether their primary objective is escape with the documents or document destruction. Different goals demand different strategies."

"Destruction could be accomplished more simply at the lake house," Marilyn pointed out. "The fact that they fled with the materials suggests preservation is the priority."

"Or they hadn't finished sorting what to destroy and what to keep," Nelly countered. "Maybe certain documents protect them while others incriminate."

Julie considered these possibilities, remembering Elaine's complex involvement with Charles Johnson and their decades-long deception. "They've maintained this secret for sixty years," she noted. "That level of commitment suggests they'll prioritize protecting the information over their own convenience or safety."

As their strategy session continued into the evening, Julie maintained regular text communication with Ben, each exchange reflecting the increasingly focused nature of the search operation guided partially by their insights. Around nine o'clock, his messages gained new urgency: *Possible sighting near Willow Point. Marine units converging. Will update soon.*

The following forty minutes passed with excruciating slowness, their conversation reduced to sporadic observations as attention remained fixed on Julie's silent phone. When it finally rang, all four women startled visibly.

"We have them," Ben announced without preamble. "Your boathouse lead was correct. Sheriff's team found the Sullivan boat concealed inside, with both women and multiple document boxes. They're being transported to shore now."

A collective exhalation of tension filled the yarn shop, the culmination of hours of focused strategy and accumulated concern.

"Any resistance?" Victoria asked practically.

"Verbal only," Ben assured them. "Elaine appears physically exhausted but stable. Mayor Johnson is..." he hesitated, seemingly searching for the appropriate description, "remarkably composed given the circumstances."

After promising to call with additional details once the suspects were processed at the station, Ben ended the call, leaving the unlikely strategy team to absorb their unexpected success.

"Well," Nelly declared, breaking the momentary silence, "I believe this calls for something stronger than tea." She produced a flask from her voluminous bag with theatrical flourish. "Homemade blackberry brandy. Medicinal purposes only, of course."

Even Marilyn accepted a small measure in her teacup, the unusual circumstances apparently justifying deviation from her typical abstention. Victoria, after a moment's consideration of the unconventional offering, similarly accepted with a gracious nod.

"To unexpected alliances," Julie proposed, raising her cup in a toast that acknowledged the remarkable collaboration that had developed in her shop that evening.

"And to justice, however delayed," Victoria added, her expression reflecting the personal significance of these events for her family legacy.

As they sipped Nelly's surprisingly excellent brandy, Ben called again with additional information. "The documents they attempted to remove appear to include detailed financial records showing how proceeds from fraudulently obtained properties were laundered through various town improvement projects over decades. Sheriff Harris believes these records will provide crucial evidence for the county's investigation into the land fraud."

"And Thomas Sullivan's death?" Julie asked, the historical murder remaining a central concern despite more recent developments.

"There's a journal," Ben confirmed. "Apparently maintained by Charles Johnson and continued by Elaine after his death. Initial review suggests it contains explicit details about the confrontation that led to Sullivan's death, including Elaine's role in helping conceal the body and maintain the fiction of his departure."

This confirmation of Elaine's deeper involvement silenced the room momentarily, the weight of sixty years of deception settling around them like dust from a disturbed archive.

"When will they be formally charged?" Victoria asked, the practical question breaking the contemplative pause.

"Processing now, arraignment tomorrow," Ben replied. "Sheriff Harris asked me to convey his official thanks for your analytical assistance, though he maintains his position that the actual apprehension should have remained entirely with law enforcement."

After the call ended, the four women began gathering maps and notes, the impromptu strategy center returning to its usual identity as a yarn shop sitting area. The transition seemed symbolic of Meadowgrove itself—layers of unexpected complexity revealed beneath familiar surfaces, then reintegrated into the community's ongoing life with new understanding.

"I should go," Victoria announced, checking her watch. "Derek will be concerned about my extended absence."

"As will my cats," Marilyn agreed, her organizational efficiency extending to the neat stacking of historical society materials.

"And I have a late yoga class to teach," Nelly added, reclaiming her flask with a wink. "Relaxation techniques seem particularly appropriate tonight."

As they prepared to depart, Julie was struck by the unlikely bond that had formed through their collaborative effort—not friendship exactly, particularly regarding Victoria, but a mutual respect forged through shared purpose and complementary contributions.

"Thank you all," she said simply. "For everything tonight."

Victoria paused at the door, her characteristic composure softened by what appeared to be genuine appreciation. "Your shop has proven remarkably central to Meadowgrove's recent dramas, Ms. Sommers. Not what one typically expects from a yarn retailer."

"I've found expectations rarely align with reality in the most interesting circumstances," Julie replied with a smile. "Especially in small towns."

After her unexpected allies departed, Julie locked the shop and headed upstairs with Tessa, who had observed the evening's activities with sleepy confusion from her bed. The dachshund seemed relieved to resume normal evening routines—dinner, brief outdoor visit, then settling on the sofa beside Julie with a contented sigh.

When Ben called again around eleven, his voice carried the weariness of an intensely demanding day. "Everything's secured for the night. Mayor Johnson and Elaine Sullivan are in custody, documents are being cataloged and secured as evidence, and I'm finally heading home."

"You sound exhausted," Julie observed sympathetically.

"Long day," he agreed. "Though ending better than it might have, thanks to your impromptu strategy team. Sheriff Harris is still processing that particular development."

Julie smiled at the mental image of the sheriff attempting to reconcile his insistence on excluding civilians with the undeniable assistance their analysis had provided. "Sometimes unexpected combinations produce remarkable results."

"Speaking of unexpected combinations," Ben continued, his tone lightening, "our dinner date seems to have developed unusual complications. Perhaps we should try again with additional security measures? Armed guards, secure location, advanced surveillance..."

His teasing suggestion made Julie laugh, the tension of the day finally releasing. "Or maybe just dinner at my place tomorrow night? I make a decent risotto, and Tessa provides excellent security."

"Perfect," Ben agreed warmly. "Though I insist on bringing dessert and a background check for all ingredients."

After ending the call with plans confirmed for the following evening, Julie found herself contemplating the remarkable sequence of events that had transformed her perception of Meadowgrove over just nine days. What had begun as concern about historic preservation had evolved into murder investigation, artifact recovery, decades-old conspiracy exposure, and now the arrest of the town's mayor and a respected elderly resident.

Through it all, her own place within the community had shifted—deepening connections with friends like Marilyn and Nelly, developing a promising relationship with Ben, and even establishing unexpected respect with formerly antagonistic Victoria. The yarn shop itself had transcended its commercial purpose to become a gathering place for truth-seeking and community action, an identity Julie found surprisingly satisfying.

Outside, Meadowgrove settled into nighttime quiet, streets empty of traffic, buildings darkened except for occasional porch lights and the Corner Pub's neon sign. The peaceful scene belied the dramatic developments unfolding behind closed doors at the sheriff's station, where sixty years of deception were being methodically documented and prepared for legal proceedings.

Tomorrow would bring new developments—arraignments, public announcements, community reactions to the shocking arrests. Julie would open her shop as usual, welcome customers, assist with projects, and maintain the reassuring rhythms of small business ownership that provided ballast during turbulent times.

And in the evening, Ben would arrive for a proper dinner without interruption or pursuit, a small normal moment carved from extraordinary circumstances. As she prepared for bed, Julie found herself looking forward to that normalcy almost as much as she anticipated learning what the seized documents would reveal about Meadowgrove's long-buried secrets.

Tessa had already claimed her spot on the bed, circular nest created from careful turning before settling with a contented sigh. Julie joined her, mind still processing the day's events but body surrendering to accumulated fatigue.

Her last conscious thought before sleep claimed her was that communities, like well-crafted garments, revealed their true quality not in how they appeared during ordinary circumstances but in how they maintained essential structure while adapting to unexpected challenges. By that measure, Meadowgrove—despite its flaws and hidden secrets—demonstrated remarkable resilience. As did, perhaps, Julia Sommers herself.

Chapter 12

Binding Off

Julie stood in the center of her destroyed shop, heart hammering in her chest as she surveyed the damage. Balls of yarn—her beautiful, carefully curated collection—lay strewn across the floor like fallen soldiers. Circular needles had been snapped in half, their cables curling like wounded snakes. Pattern books were ripped, pages scattered. But worst of all was the message spray-painted in ugly red letters across the pristine white wall behind the register: "LEAVE THE PAST BURIED."

She hugged herself, fighting the urge to cry. The shop had been her fresh start, her new beginning after leaving behind twenty years of corporate law in Boston. It represented everything she'd wanted her new life in Lakeside to be—creative, peaceful, community-focused. Now someone had violated that sanctuary.

Sheriff Harris moved around the space, taking photos with a digital camera that looked at least ten years old. He hadn't said much since arriving fifteen minutes ago, just asked her to stand back and let him document the scene.

"Any idea who might have done this?" he finally asked, not looking up from his camera.

"If I knew, I wouldn't need you here," Julie replied, immediately regretting her tone. "Sorry. I'm just... upset."

Harris lowered the camera and fixed her with a steady gaze. "I understand. But sometimes people have suspicions they don't want to voice. Or maybe someone's been hanging around, watching the place."

Julie shook her head. "Nothing like that." She paused, considering. "Though I suppose it could be related to Victoria's murder."

At the mention of Victoria's name, something shifted in Harris's expression. "And why would you think that?"

"Because I've been asking questions," Julie admitted. "And someone clearly doesn't like it."

"Questions," Harris repeated flatly. "About the murder."

"Yes."

"The murder I'm investigating."

Julie lifted her chin. "The murder you're supposedly investigating. It's been three weeks, Sheriff. Have you made any progress at all?"

Harris slipped his camera into its case with deliberate care. "Ms. Chen, I understand you were some hotshot lawyer in Boston, but this isn't a courtroom, and I'm not on trial. I'm doing my job. Maybe you should stick to knitting and let me do mine."

"I would, if I saw any evidence that you were actually doing it."

Harris's jaw tightened. "You know what I think? I think you're bored. Small-town life not exciting enough for you? Needed to play amateur detective to feel important again?"

The accusation stung because there was a grain of truth in it. Julie had been feeling adrift in Lakeside, unsure of her place. The investigation had given her purpose. But that didn't mean her concerns weren't valid.

"What I need is to feel safe in my own town," she replied evenly. "Victoria was my friend, and someone killed her. Now someone's trashed my shop and left a threatening message. If those two things aren't connected, it's one hell of a coincidence."

Harris stepped closer, lowering his voice. "Here's what I know, Ms. Chen. I know you've been all over town asking about Victoria's finances. I know you took her assistant Derek out for coffee to pump him for information. I know you and your knitting club friends have been poking around Victoria's lake house. So yeah, I'd say there's a connection, but maybe not the one you're thinking."

Julie felt a chill run through her. He'd been tracking her movements. "Are you suggesting I brought this on myself?"

"I'm suggesting that whoever trashed your shop is warning you to back off. And as the sheriff of this town, I'm strongly advising you to take that warning seriously."

"Or what?" Julie challenged.

"Or next time it might not just be your yarn getting cut." Harris headed for the door. "I'll have a deputy drive by regularly for the next few days. In the meantime, get a cleaning crew in here and call your insurance. And Ms. Chen? Stay out of my investigation."

After he left, Julie sank onto a stool behind the counter, hands trembling slightly. She pulled out her phone and sent a group text to the Purls of Wisdom: *Emergency meeting. My shop. Now.*

Marilyn arrived first, gasping when she saw the destruction. "Oh, Julie! This is awful!" She picked her way through the yarn carnage to give Julie a hug. "Who would do such a thing?"

"Someone who doesn't want me investigating Victoria's murder," Julie replied grimly.

Nelly bustled in next, her usual bohemian outfit replaced with paint-splattered overalls. "Holy hell," she breathed, taking in the scene. "This is some serious intimidation tactics."

Eleanor arrived last, impeccably dressed despite the early hour. Her perfectly made-up face couldn't hide her shock. "My dear, how dreadful." She surveyed the damage with a frown. "The sheriff has been here?"

"He has," Julie confirmed. "And he made it clear he thinks I brought this on myself by asking questions about Victoria."

"That's victim-blaming nonsense," Nelly scoffed.

"It is," Julie agreed. "But he's also right that someone wants us to back off."

Eleanor's eyes narrowed as she read the spray-painted message. "Leave the past buried... Interesting choice of words."

"What are you thinking?" Julie asked.

"That whatever Victoria was involved in, it's something old. Something from the past that someone doesn't want resurfacing." Eleanor turned to Julie. "Have you called Craig yet?"

Julie shook her head. She'd been avoiding thinking about Craig Thornton, even though he'd been nothing but kind since Victoria's death. The attraction she felt toward him was complicated by his connection to Victoria—and by the fact that she still couldn't rule him out as a suspect.

"I should," she acknowledged. "But first, I need to tell you what I found at the historical society yesterday."

She quickly explained about the old newspaper articles documenting the drowning of William Jenkins thirty years ago at the exact spot where Victoria's body had been found.

"That can't be a coincidence," Marilyn said. "Do you think Victoria knew something about Jenkins's death?"

"I don't know. But I think we need to find out more about him and what happened back then." Julie turned to Marilyn. "Any luck tracking down Derek?"

Marilyn brightened. "Yes, actually! That's why I'm late. I was on the phone with an old colleague from the school district. Derek's mother teaches third grade in Millersville, the next county over. Donna Peterson. I have her number."

"Excellent," Julie said. "What about Victoria's finances, Eleanor? Did your banking contact come through?"

Eleanor nodded. "Victoria made a large cash withdrawal three days before she died. Fifty thousand dollars."

Julie whistled softly. "That's a lot of cash. Any idea what it was for?"

"No, but I'm having dinner with Jonathan tonight," Eleanor said, naming the bank manager who'd been pursuing her for months. "I plan to be very curious about it."

"And I've got something too," Nelly added. "I'm working on a mural at the community center this week, and guess who's on the maintenance staff there? Ray Jenkins."

"William Jenkins's son?" Julie clarified.

"The very same. I struck up a conversation yesterday. He's not exactly chatty, but he did mention that his father's death 'never sat right' with him. Said there were 'unanswered questions.'"

Julie felt a surge of excitement despite the chaos surrounding them. "This is all connecting somehow. We just need to figure out how." She paused, considering their next steps. "Marilyn, can you call Derek's mother today? See if she'll talk to us about him and Victoria?"

"Already scheduled for lunch," Marilyn said proudly.

"Perfect. Nelly, try to get Ray Jenkins talking more about his father. Eleanor, see what you can charm out of Jonathan tonight." Julie stood up. "I'll get this place cleaned up and then pay Craig a visit. If

Victoria confided in anyone about whatever she was mixed up in, it would have been him."

"What about the sheriff's warning?" Marilyn asked anxiously.

Julie looked at the threatening message one more time. "Whoever did this wanted to scare us off. I say we show them it had the opposite effect."

Cleaning up the shop took most of the morning. Julie salvaged what she could of the yarn and supplies, making neat piles of what could be reused and what had to be discarded. The insurance adjuster came and went, assuring her that the damage would be covered. By two o'clock, the red spray paint had been mostly removed from the wall, though a faint pink shadow remained.

Julie was just closing up to head to Craig's when her phone rang. It was Marilyn.

"You're not going to believe what I found out," Marilyn said without preamble.

"Try me."

"Derek isn't just Victoria's assistant—he's her nephew!"

Julie blinked in surprise. "Her nephew? She never mentioned any family."

"According to his mother, Victoria and her sister—Derek's mother—had a falling out years ago. Derek was sent to work for Victoria about six months ago as a condition of his trust fund. The family wanted someone to keep an eye on Victoria's spending."

"Why?"

"That's where it gets interesting. Victoria's family has serious money—old timber industry fortune. But Victoria was the only one with access to the main trust until she turned sixty-five, which would have been next year. After that, the money would be distributed among all the family members."

Julie's mind raced with the implications. "So Victoria dying before her sixty-fifth birthday means..."

"The family gets access to the money now," Marilyn confirmed.

"Did Derek's mother know about the fifty thousand in cash Victoria withdrew?"

"No, and she seemed genuinely shocked when I mentioned it. But she did say that Derek called her in a panic the day before Victoria died, saying he needed to come home immediately. He showed up at her house that night, grabbed some clothes, and took off again. She hasn't seen him since, though he texts occasionally to let her know he's safe."

"He's in hiding," Julie murmured. "But from what?"

"Or who," Marilyn added. "I got the sense his mother knows more than she's saying."

"Great work, Marilyn. This changes everything." Julie locked the shop door behind her. "I'm heading to Craig's now. I'll call you after."

Craig's house was a modest Craftsman bungalow on the edge of town, surrounded by towering pines. Julie pulled into the driveway, noting the impeccably maintained garden. As a landscape architect, Craig clearly brought his work home with him.

He answered the door on the second knock, surprise registering on his face. "Julie. Is everything okay?"

"Not really," she admitted. "Can I come in?"

He stepped aside, ushering her into a living room that was both orderly and comfortable, with well-worn leather furniture and built-in bookshelves. A fire crackled in the stone fireplace despite the mild spring day.

"I heard about your shop," he said as he gestured for her to sit. "Sheriff Harris called me this morning."

"Did he?" Julie wasn't sure what to make of that.

"He seemed to think I might know why someone would target you." Craig sat across from her, his expression troubled. "He mentioned you've been investigating Victoria's death."

Julie decided honesty was her best approach. "I have been. And I think I've uncovered some things that might be relevant."

She told him everything—the connection to William Jenkins's drowning, Victoria's family money, Derek's true identity, the cash withdrawal. Craig listened without interrupting, his face increasingly grave.

"What I don't understand," Julie concluded, "is why Victoria never mentioned any of this to you. You were close, weren't you?"

Craig sighed heavily. "We were. But Victoria was intensely private about certain aspects of her life, especially her family and finances." He rubbed his jaw, looking suddenly tired. "The truth is, our relationship was complicated."

"In what way?"

"We'd known each other for years—met through work when her company hired my firm for a project. We dated briefly, but it didn't work out. Remained friends, though. Then about a year ago, she called out of the blue, said she was moving to Lakeside and wanted my help finding property."

"She moved here because of you?" This was news to Julie.

"Not exactly. She said she'd been looking for a place to retire, and knowing I was here made the decision easier." He paused. "But I always sensed there was more to it. Victoria didn't do anything without multiple reasons."

"Did she ever mention William Jenkins to you?"

Craig's brow furrowed. "No, never. But the name sounds vaguely familiar."

"He drowned in the lake thirty years ago. In the exact same spot where Victoria was found."

Craig went still. "That can't be a coincidence."

"That's what I thought."

"Have you told Sheriff Harris about this?"

Julie made a face. "Harris thinks I should mind my own business. Actually, he more than implied that my 'poking around' is what led to my shop being vandalized."

Craig leaned forward. "Julie, what if he's right? Not about it being your fault—it's absolutely not—but about the danger. Whoever did this to your shop is serious. If they're willing to destroy property, who knows what else they might do?"

"I can't just drop it," Julie insisted. "Victoria was murdered, Craig. Someone put stones in her pockets and pushed her into that lake to die. Don't you want to know who did that to her?"

"Of course I do. But not at the cost of putting you in danger." His expression softened. "I care about you, Julie. I don't want to see you hurt."

The sincerity in his eyes made her heart flutter uncomfortably. "I care about you too. That's why I need to know—is there anything else about Victoria you haven't told me? Anything that might help make sense of all this?"

Craig hesitated, clearly wrestling with something. Finally, he stood up. "There is one thing. Follow me."

He led her to his study, a small room lined with drafting tables and architectural drawings. From a desk drawer, he pulled out a sealed envelope. "Victoria gave me this about a week before she died. She made me promise not to open it unless something happened to her."

"And you haven't opened it?" Julie asked, eyeing the envelope.

"I was going to. After the funeral. But then the sheriff came asking questions about my relationship with Victoria, and I got nervous. What if it contained something that made me look guilty?"

Julie understood his concern. "But you're showing it to me now."

"Because I trust you," he said simply. "And because you're right—we need to know the truth."

He handed her the envelope. Her name was written on the front in Victoria's elegant handwriting.

"She addressed it to you," Julie said, confused.

Craig nodded. "She told me that if anything happened to her, I should give it to 'someone who would know what to do with it.' When I asked who, she said I'd know when the time came." He gave Julie a rueful smile. "I think she meant you."

With trembling fingers, Julie broke the seal and pulled out a single sheet of paper and a small key. The note was brief:

The truth about William is in the blue cabin, lockbox under the floorboards beneath the bed. This key opens it. Be careful who you trust.

Julie looked up at Craig. "Do you know what blue cabin she's talking about?"

"I think so. There's an old fishing cabin on the north shore of the lake. Victoria bought it quietly through an LLC last year. I helped her with the paperwork, but she never told me what she wanted it for."

"We need to go there," Julie said, already standing.

Craig hesitated. "Shouldn't we call the sheriff?"

"And tell him what? That we have a mysterious key and a cryptic note? He already thinks I'm interfering. No, we need to see what's in that lockbox first."

Craig looked conflicted but finally nodded. "Alright. But we go together, and we're careful."

The blue cabin was aptly named—its weathered boards painted a faded navy that blended with the deepening afternoon shadows. It sat back from the lake, partially hidden by a stand of birch trees, looking like it had been there for decades.

"Victoria bought this place a year ago?" Julie asked as Craig parked his truck on the overgrown drive.

"Yes, though from the looks of it, she didn't do much with it."

They approached cautiously. The cabin door was secured with a padlock, but Craig produced a key from his pocket. "Master key," he explained. "I have one for all of Victoria's properties."

Inside, the cabin was spare but tidy. A small kitchenette occupied one wall, a sitting area with a woodstove another. A queen-sized bed took up most of the remaining space, covered with a simple blue quilt.

"Under the floorboards beneath the bed," Julie murmured, moving toward it.

Together, they pushed the heavy bed frame to one side, revealing wide pine floorboards. Julie got down on her hands and knees, running her fingers along the seams between boards.

"Here," she said, feeling a slight give in one board. "This one's loose."

With Craig's help, she pried up the board, revealing a metal lockbox nestled in the space below. Julie's heart pounded as she inserted Victoria's key. It turned with a satisfying click.

Inside the box were several items: a stack of old photographs, newspaper clippings yellowed with age, a small notebook, and a USB drive.

Julie picked up the top photograph. It showed a group of young people on a dock, arms around each other, lake water sparkling behind them. She turned it over. Written on the back was: *Lake weekend, August 1994. Will, Vic, Marcus, Elaine, Peter.*

"That's Victoria," Craig said, pointing to a young woman with long dark hair and a confident smile.

"Then this must be William Jenkins," Julie said, indicating the young man with his arm around Victoria.

They went through the photos quickly. Many featured the same core group in various settings—a bonfire on the beach, a boat on the lake, a cabin that might have been this very one in its earlier days. William Jenkins appeared in most of them, often beside Victoria.

"They were friends," Julie said. "Maybe more than friends?"

"Look at this," Craig said, holding up a newspaper clipping. It was the same article Julie had found at the historical society about Jenkins's drowning, but this copy had handwritten notes in the margins: *No accident. Ask P about the boat. M knows what happened.*

Julie felt a chill. "Victoria thought his death wasn't an accident."

She picked up the notebook next. Flipping through it, she found entries in Victoria's handwriting, dated over the past year. It appeared to be a record of her investigation into Jenkins's death—notes from conversations, theories, questions.

The final entry, dated just three days before her murder, read: *Confronted P today. He admits being on the boat but says M pushed Will overboard during the argument. Says it was an accident, they all panicked. Paid M to leave town and keep quiet. Buying his silence again now is costing him 50K. Meeting him tomorrow with the money. Will record the confession.*

Craig and Julie looked at each other, the implication sinking in.

"She was blackmailing someone," Craig said quietly.

"No," Julie corrected. "She was gathering evidence. Victoria was a lawyer. She wanted proof of what happened to William Jenkins."

"And someone killed her to keep her quiet," Craig finished.

"But who? Who are P and M?" Julie rifled through the remaining contents of the box. "Maybe the answers are on this." She held up the USB drive.

"We can check it on my laptop in the truck," Craig offered.

They carefully repacked everything except the USB drive into the lockbox and returned it to its hiding place. After pushing the bed back into position, they headed outside.

The sudden crack of a gunshot froze them in their tracks.

"Get down!" Craig yelled, pulling Julie behind the cabin wall as another shot splintered the wood where they'd been standing.

"Who's there?" a gruff voice shouted from the trees. "I know someone's in there! This is private property!"

Julie's heart hammered against her ribs. "What do we do?" she whispered.

Craig peered carefully around the corner. "I can't see them, but they're coming closer." He turned to Julie, his expression grave. "You need to run for the truck. I'll distract them."

"No way. I'm not leaving you."

"Julie, you have the USB drive. That's the evidence. You need to get it somewhere safe."

Another shot rang out, closer this time.

"Last chance to come out peacefully!" the voice called. "Sheriff's department!"

Julie and Craig exchanged alarmed looks. "That's not Harris," Julie said. "I know his voice."

"Could be a deputy," Craig suggested, though he looked uncertain.

"Or someone pretending to be a cop." Julie clutched the USB drive tightly. "If we both make a break for it..."

"Too risky." Craig shook his head. "I know these woods. There's a hiking trail about fifty yards behind us that leads back to the main road. You go that way while I create a diversion. Meet me at Eleanor's house in an hour."

Julie wanted to argue but knew he was right. She was the one carrying the evidence that might solve both Victoria's murder and William Jenkins's death three decades earlier.

"Be careful," she whispered, squeezing his hand.

"You too."

Julie slipped around to the back of the cabin while Craig moved toward the front. She heard him call out, "This is private property! I'm the caretaker! Who's there?"

She didn't wait to hear the response. As soon as the attention was diverted, she darted into the trees, running as fast as she could through the underbrush toward where Craig had indicated the trail would be.

Behind her, she heard shouting, then the sound of breaking glass. She forced herself not to look back, not to think about what might be happening to Craig. She had to get the USB drive to safety. It was their only hard evidence.

As she ran, clutching the small device that might hold the answers to everything, Julie couldn't shake the feeling that she was being followed. The forest seemed to close in around her, shadows deepening as the sun began its descent toward the horizon.

She reached the hiking trail and increased her pace, feet flying over the packed dirt path. Her lungs burned, but fear kept her moving forward. All she could think about was reaching Eleanor's house, about getting somewhere safe where they could examine the contents of the USB drive.

Because somewhere on that drive was the identity of a murderer—possibly two. Someone who had killed thirty years ago and was still killing to keep their secret buried.

And Julie was carrying the proof in her pocket.

The sun had fully set by the time Julie reached the edge of town, gasping for breath, a stitch burning in her side. She'd seen no further signs of pursuit since leaving the woods, but anxiety still churned in her stomach. Where was Craig? Had he gotten away safely?

As she approached Eleanor's elegant Victorian home on Maple Street, she spotted a familiar truck parked out front. Relief flooded through her. Craig had made it. He was safe.

Eleanor answered the door before Julie even knocked, concern etched on her face. "Thank goodness," she exhaled, pulling Julie inside and quickly securing the door behind her. "Craig arrived twenty minutes ago. He's in the study with the others."

"The others?" Julie questioned as Eleanor led her through the house.

"I called an emergency meeting of the Purls of Wisdom," Eleanor explained. "After what Craig told us, I thought we all needed to hear this."

In Eleanor's wood-paneled study, Julie found Craig, Marilyn, and Nelly gathered around a laptop computer. Craig jumped up when she entered, embracing her tightly.

"You made it," he murmured into her hair. "I was so worried."

Julie returned the embrace, surprising herself with how natural it felt. "What happened after I left?"

"Our mystery shooter turned out to be Ray Jenkins," Craig explained, stepping back. "William's son. He's been keeping an eye on the cabin ever since Victoria bought it. Said he figured she was connected to his father's death somehow."

"Is he here?" Julie asked.

Craig shook his head. "Once I explained who we were and what we'd found, he agreed to give us a head start before he calls the sheriff. Said he's wanted answers about his dad's death for thirty years and doesn't trust the local authorities to deliver justice."

Julie pulled the USB drive from her pocket. "Then let's not waste time. This might have everything we need."

Craig took the drive and inserted it into Eleanor's laptop. A single video file appeared on the screen.

"It's dated three days before Victoria died," Craig noted, clicking to open it.

The video began playing, showing Victoria sitting in what appeared to be a restaurant booth. She looked directly at the camera, speaking in a low, clear voice.

"My name is Victoria Winters. The date is April 12th. I'm meeting with Peter Hargrove to discuss the death of William Jenkins on August 24, 1994."

The camera shifted slightly as Victoria placed it on the table, partially concealed but with a clear view of the booth across from her. Moments later, an older man with silver hair and an expensive suit slid into the seat.

Julie gasped. "That's Peter Hargrove. The mayor."

On screen, Victoria spoke calmly. "Thank you for meeting me, Peter. I assume you brought what we discussed?"

Hargrove placed an envelope on the table. "Fifty thousand, as agreed. Now can we put this behind us?"

"That depends," Victoria replied. "I want the full truth about what happened to Will that night. No more lies."

Hargrove glanced around nervously before leaning in. "I told you. It was Marcus. We were all drinking on my father's boat. Will and Marcus got into an argument about you, of all things. It got physical. Marcus pushed him, Will lost his balance and went overboard. We tried to find him, but it was dark..."

"And then you covered it up," Victoria finished. "Paid Marcus to disappear and filed a false report saying Will had been swimming alone."

"We were scared! My father was running for state senate. Marcus was on scholarship. We had futures to protect."

"And Will didn't?" Victoria's voice was ice.

"It was an accident," Hargrove insisted. "A terrible accident compounded by terrible decisions. We were just kids."

"Kids who let my boyfriend drown and then let his family believe he was reckless enough to swim drunk at night."

Hargrove's expression hardened. "Why are you doing this now, Vic? It's been thirty years. Marcus is long gone. I've paid for my sins every day since."

"Not enough," Victoria replied. "Will's son deserves to know the truth. His family deserves closure."

"And what do you deserve?" Hargrove asked coldly. "Does blackmail make you feel better about running away after it happened? You didn't stick around to ask any questions then."

"I'm asking them now," Victoria said. "And this isn't blackmail. It's justice."

"What are you going to do with this recording?"

Victoria gathered the envelope. "That depends on you, Peter. I want a full public confession and a proper memorial for Will. You're the mayor now—make it happen."

The video ended abruptly.

For a long moment, no one in Eleanor's study spoke.

"The mayor," Julie finally said. "The mayor killed Victoria."

"Maybe not personally," Craig noted. "He mentioned this Marcus person was directly responsible for William's death."

"But Marcus left town years ago," Nelly pointed out. "Who's to say Hargrove didn't handle this latest 'problem' himself?"

Marilyn, who had been quiet throughout, suddenly spoke up. "The sheriff. We need to take this to Sheriff Harris."

"You think he'll arrest the mayor based on this?" Julie asked skeptically.

"He has to," Eleanor said firmly. "This is evidence of conspiracy and coverup in William's death, and it establishes clear motive for Victoria's murder."

Julie nodded slowly. "We should also find Derek. He must have known something was wrong after Victoria met with Hargrove. That's why he ran."

"One thing at a time," Craig suggested. "First, the sheriff."

As if on cue, the study door burst open. Sheriff Harris stood there, Ray Jenkins slightly behind him.

"Sorry," Ray said to the startled group. "I couldn't wait. Not after thirty years."

Harris surveyed the room, his gaze landing on the laptop still displaying the paused video. "I understand you folks have some evidence you'd like to share with me."

Julie stood to face him. "We do. Evidence that Mayor Hargrove was involved in the coverup of William Jenkins's death in 1994, and potentially in Victoria Winters's murder three weeks ago."

Harris's expression remained unreadable. "That's a serious accusation against a public official."

"We have proof," Julie said, gesturing to the laptop. "Victoria recorded everything."

The sheriff stepped forward, looking at the screen. "Then I suggest you play it for me from the beginning." He looked around at the assembled Purls of Wisdom. "All of you have some explaining to do about interfering in a police investigation, but right now, I need to hear what you've found."

As Craig restarted the video, Julie felt a strange sense of completion. In knitting terms, they were binding off—securing the final stitches of a complex pattern that had begun decades ago with a young man's death and continued through to Victoria's murder. The mysteries were unraveling, threads connecting in ways none of them could have anticipated when they'd started pulling at them.

Whatever happened next—whether Harris took their evidence seriously, whether Hargrove faced justice, whether they ever found Marcus—Julie knew one thing for certain: sometimes the most important patterns were the ones hidden beneath the surface, waiting for someone persistent enough to bring them into the light.

Chapter 13
Wrong Side of the Pattern

Julie woke to the sound of rain pattering against her bedroom window. A perfect backdrop for the Harvest Festival's opening day, she thought wryly. She checked her phone—5:45 AM. Too early to get up, but too late to fall back asleep. Her mind was already racing with a mental checklist for the day ahead.

The Yarn Haven needed to look its best. This wasn't just any weekend; the annual Meadowgrove Harvest Festival brought tourists from all over the region, and for local businesses, it could make or break their quarterly earnings. Julie had spent the past two weeks preparing a special display featuring yarns sourced exclusively from farms within a thirty-mile radius of town. Each skein had been labeled with the name of the farm and a brief story about the animals it came from—the alpacas at Henderson's, the heritage-breed sheep at Willowbrook, even some angora from Maggie Thorne's small rabbitry.

Julie rolled out of bed and padded to the kitchen, where she made herself a strong cup of coffee. Through the window above the sink, she could see the town square, where festival tents had been erected yesterday afternoon. Even in the dim pre-dawn light and through the rain, she could make out workers scurrying about, making final preparations. The forecast promised clearing skies by mid-morning.

Her phone buzzed with a text from Eliza: "Still on for setup at 7? Bringing you that cinnamon roll you love."

Julie smiled. Eliza had been uncharacteristically supportive since their conversation at the cabin. Their friendship had been strained for months, but lately, it felt like they were finding their way back to solid ground. Julie texted back a thumbs-up emoji and a "See you then!"

By the time Julie showered and dressed, the rain had slowed to a drizzle. She selected a hand-knit sweater in autumn colors—her own design, featuring a leaf motif that started at the hem and wound its way up to the shoulders. It was one of her best pieces, and more than one customer had asked for the pattern. Today, she was her own best advertisement.

When Julie arrived at The Yarn Haven at 6:45, she was surprised to find the lights already on. Through the window, she could see Eliza arranging a display of locally dyed yarns, steam rising from a coffee cup at her elbow.

"You're early," Julie said as she unlocked the door.

Eliza turned and smiled. "Couldn't sleep. Too excited about the festival, I guess." She gestured to a paper bag on the counter. "Cinnamon roll, as promised. And an extra cup of coffee."

"You're a lifesaver," Julie said, hanging up her raincoat and dropping her bag behind the counter. "I was up early too. Something about festival days always makes me jittery."

"Good jittery or bad jittery?" Eliza asked, studying Julie's face.

Julie considered the question. "Both? I love the energy, but after what happened at Victoria's cabin... I can't shake the feeling that things are coming to a head somehow."

Eliza's expression darkened. "Have you found anything else in the journal?"

"Not yet. I've been so busy getting ready for today that I haven't had time to dive back into it." Julie took a bite of the cinnamon roll, the sweet, spicy flavor momentarily distracting her from her worries. "But I did notice something odd. Some pages toward the back seem to have been torn out."

"That could be nothing," Eliza said carefully. "Old journals fall apart."

"Maybe," Julie conceded. "But these weren't crumbling with age. The edges were clean, like someone deliberately removed them." She wiped her fingers on a napkin and began arranging skeins in the window display. "Anyway, I'll get back to it after the festival. Today's about making sales and promoting local fiber arts."

"Speaking of which," Eliza said, "we should finish this display. I've got the farm map almost ready." She indicated a large cork board where she'd been pinning a map of the county, with colorful pins marking each farm that had contributed to their local yarn collection.

For the next hour, the two women worked in companionable silence, arranging displays, adjusting lighting, and triple-checking that every price tag was in place. Just before eight, Julie flipped the "Closed" sign to "Open" and unlocked the front door.

"Ready for the onslaught?" she asked Eliza with a grin.

"As I'll ever be," Eliza replied, straightening her shirt. "Let the games begin."

The morning passed in a blur of customers, demonstrations, and sales. By eleven, the rain had stopped completely, and sunlight streamed through the front windows, making the colorful yarns glow. Julie had just finished ringing up a substantial sale—a woman from Burlington had purchased enough locally sourced wool for an entire sweater—when the bell above the door jingled and Edward Thompson walked in.

He wore a tweed jacket with leather patches at the elbows and carried a stylish umbrella, though it was now unnecessary. His silver hair was neatly combed, and his eyes, behind wire-rimmed glasses, scanned the shop with interest.

"Ms. Morgan," he said, approaching the counter with a warm smile. "Your shop looks wonderful. The festival seems to be bringing you good business."

"Mr. Thompson," Julie said, surprised to see him again so soon after their encounter at the library. "Yes, it's been busy. Are you enjoying the festival?"

"Very much," he replied. "It's charming—exactly the sort of community event that makes small towns like Meadowgrove special." He glanced around. "I see you've put together quite a display of local products."

"That's our focus this weekend," Julie confirmed. "Everything you see on this wall comes from within thirty miles of here. We've even mapped the farms." She gestured to Eliza's completed map.

Thompson approached it, studying it with unusual intensity. "Fascinating. Some of these farms must have histories dating back generations."

"Many do," Julie said. "The agricultural tradition in this valley is deep."

"And you've developed an interest in that history, I understand," Thompson said, turning back to her. His tone was casual, but something in the way he watched her made Julie uneasy.

"I've always been interested in local history," she replied carefully. "It helps me feel connected to the place."

"Indeed." Thompson nodded. "I was speaking with Diane at the historical society yesterday. She mentioned you've been researching some of Meadowgrove's older families."

Julie couldn't tell if this was a question or a statement. "Just following some threads," she said vaguely.

"She mentioned the Wilkins journal in particular," Thompson continued, his eyes never leaving her face. "A fascinating primary source, I understand."

The bell jingled again as more customers entered, but Julie barely registered them. "Yes, it's been... illuminating," she said. "How do you know about it?"

"Oh, I make it my business to know about significant historical documents," Thompson said with a dismissive wave of his hand. "Especially those pertaining to this region. The Wilkins family was quite influential in their day."

"They were," Julie agreed, watching Thompson carefully. "Though not everyone remembers them now."

"History has a way of being forgotten when it's convenient," Thompson said. His voice had taken on an edge that hadn't been there before. "Or selectively remembered."

Before Julie could respond, Eliza appeared at her side. "Julie, we need more of the Henderson alpaca in the window display. Do we have any more in the back?"

"I'll check," Julie said, grateful for the interruption. "Excuse me, Mr. Thompson."

In the storeroom, Julie took a moment to collect herself. There was something unsettling about Thompson's interest in her research. She retrieved several skeins of the soft alpaca yarn and was about to head back to the sales floor when her phone vibrated in her pocket. A text from Eliza: "Everything OK? You looked spooked."

Julie quickly typed back: "Tell you later. Thompson asking about Wilkins journal."

When she returned to the main shop area, Thompson was examining a display of hand-carved wooden buttons.

"These are exquisite," he said as she approached. "Local artisan?"

"Yes, Tom Blackwood makes them. He has a woodworking studio just outside town."

Thompson selected a set of buttons carved to look like oak leaves. "I'll take these," he said. "A souvenir of my visit to your lovely town."

As Julie rang up his purchase, Thompson leaned slightly over the counter. "I hope you'll be careful with that journal, Ms. Morgan," he said quietly. "Old documents can be... delicate. And sometimes the stories they tell are better left in the past."

The hair on the back of Julie's neck stood up. "What do you mean by that?"

Thompson smiled, but it didn't reach his eyes. "Just friendly advice from one history enthusiast to another. Some paths of inquiry lead to unexpected places."

He took his neatly wrapped package, nodded politely, and left the shop. Julie watched him go, a chill running down her spine despite the warm sweater she wore.

"What was that about?" Eliza asked, appearing at her elbow.

"I'm not sure," Julie said slowly. "But I think I just got warned off."

For the rest of the morning, Julie did her best to focus on customers and sales, but Thompson's words kept replaying in her mind. By one o'clock, the initial rush had slowed, and when Eliza offered to watch the shop for an hour, Julie gratefully accepted.

"I need some fresh air," she said. "And maybe some festival food. Can I bring you back something?"

"One of those apple cider donuts from the Peterson farm stand," Eliza said. "And take your time. It's going to pick up again later."

Outside, the festival was in full swing. The town square had been transformed into a marketplace of tents and booths, with local farmers, craftspeople, and food vendors offering their wares. The air was filled with the scents of kettle corn, barbecue, and cinnamon, and a local bluegrass band played on a small stage near the gazebo.

Julie wandered through the crowded pathways, stopping occasionally to greet neighbors or examine handcrafted items. She bought herself a pulled pork sandwich and found a spot on a bench to eat it, watching the festival-goers stream past. Families with children, elderly couples, teenagers in groups—the whole community seemed to be out enjoying the beautiful fall day.

As Julie finished her sandwich, she had the distinct feeling of being watched. She scanned the crowd but saw no one paying particular attention to her. Still, the sensation persisted. She stood and began walking, meandering between booths as if browsing, but actually trying to determine if anyone was following her.

At a tent selling handmade soaps, Julie pretended to examine a display while surreptitiously glancing behind her. There—a tall man in a dark jacket seemed to turn away quickly when she looked in his direction. She moved to another booth, and moments later, saw the same man, now pretending to be interested in artisanal honey.

Heart pounding, Julie picked up her pace, weaving through the crowd. When she glanced back again, the man was definitely following, no longer bothering to hide it. She couldn't make out his face clearly—he wore a baseball cap pulled low—but his purposeful stride told her all she needed to know.

Julie cut through a food court area, dodging between lines of people waiting at various trucks and stands. The man followed. She turned down a row of craft tents, walking faster now. When she emerged back onto the main pathway, she broke into a jog, ignoring the curious glances from festival attendees.

Ahead, she spotted a large tent with "Johnson for Mayor" emblazoned on its side. Without thinking too much about it, Julie ducked inside, hoping to lose her pursuer in yet another crowded space.

The campaign tent was surprisingly quiet compared to the bustling festival outside. A few volunteers staffed a table of campaign materials—buttons, yard signs, pamphlets—and a couple of visitors browsed the offerings. At the back of the tent, partly screened by a display board covered with photos of Mayor Johnson at community events, two people were engaged in a heated discussion.

Julie recognized Mayor Carolyn Johnson's voice immediately, though she couldn't see her from where she stood.

"We cannot afford another setback," the mayor was saying, her voice low but intense. "The timeline is already tight."

"I'm doing everything I can," a man responded. Julie recognized Thomas Drake, the mayor's campaign manager and longtime advisor. "But these things take time, and with the scrutiny we're under—"

"I don't want excuses, Thomas. Victoria's money was supposed to solve everything. Now she's dead, and we're left scrambling."

Julie froze. Victoria's money? What did the mayor have to do with Victoria Winters?

"Lower your voice," Drake hissed. "This isn't the place."

"Then where is the place?" Johnson snapped. "You keep telling me to wait, but the election is five weeks away, and if we don't secure that land deal—"

"Excuse me," a volunteer said, approaching Julie. "Can I help you with something? Would you like a campaign button?"

Before Julie could answer, Mayor Johnson stepped around the display board, her campaign smile already in place. It faltered briefly when she saw Julie.

"Ms. Morgan," she said, quickly recovering. "How nice to see you. Enjoying the festival?"

"Yes, Mayor Johnson," Julie replied, trying to sound casual. "Just taking a break from the shop. It's been busy."

"I'm glad to hear it. The festival is so important for our local businesses." The mayor's smile remained fixed, but her eyes were calculating. "Were you looking for information about my platform? Thomas, why don't you give Ms. Morgan one of our packets."

Drake appeared beside the mayor, a folder in his outstretched hand. "All the information about Mayor Johnson's vision for Meadowgrove's future," he said smoothly.

Julie accepted the folder automatically. "Thank you," she said. "I should probably get back to my shop."

"Of course," the mayor said. "Please let us know if you have any questions about our plans for downtown development. Small businesses like yours are at the heart of our economic strategy."

Julie nodded and backed toward the tent entrance. She peered outside cautiously, scanning the crowd for the man who had been following her, but didn't see him. Taking a deep breath, she stepped back into the festival throng and made her way quickly toward The Yarn Haven.

Back at the shop, Julie found Eliza helping a customer select yarns for a complex color-work project. She waited until the customer had paid and left before pulling Eliza into the storeroom.

"What happened?" Eliza asked, alarmed by Julie's expression. "You look like you've seen a ghost."

"Someone was following me at the festival," Julie said, keeping her voice low. "And then I overheard the mayor and Thomas Drake arguing about Victoria's money."

"What? Are you sure?"

"Positive. The mayor said, and I quote, 'Victoria's money was supposed to solve everything. Now she's dead, and we're left scrambling.'"

Eliza's eyes widened. "That's... incriminating."

"It gets weirder," Julie continued. "They were talking about a land deal of some kind, and how the election is only five weeks away. Eliza, what if Victoria's death is connected to local politics somehow?"

"That seems like a stretch," Eliza said, but she looked troubled. "Though I guess anything's possible in this town." She hesitated. "And you're sure someone was following you?"

"Absolutely. Tall guy, dark jacket, baseball cap. Very persistent until I lost him in the mayor's tent."

"Should we call Sheriff Miller?"

Julie considered this. "And tell him what? That someone might have followed me and I overheard a vague conversation? He already thinks I'm overreacting about everything."

"Still," Eliza insisted, "if you felt threatened—"

"I'll be fine," Julie said, though she wasn't entirely convinced. "Let's just focus on the shop for now. We've got customers waiting."

The rest of the afternoon passed without incident. As dusk fell, the festival lights came on in the town square, and the evening crowd began to arrive. Sales remained steady until closing time at eight.

"What a day," Eliza sighed as they counted the till. "But worth it. We made more today than we did all last week."

"And tomorrow should be just as good," Julie said, trying to sound enthusiastic despite her lingering unease. "The parade is in the morning, which always brings people downtown."

They finished closing procedures, and Julie insisted on walking Eliza to her car, still wary after her experience earlier.

"Text me when you get home," Eliza said as she unlocked her car door. "And Julie... be careful, okay? All this weirdness—Thompson, the person following you, what you overheard—it can't be coincidence."

"I know," Julie admitted. "I'm starting to think everything is connected somehow. Victoria's death, the journal, whatever the mayor's involved in... but I can't see the pattern yet."

"Sometimes it's safer not to see the pattern," Eliza said quietly. "Goodnight, Julie."

Julie watched her friend drive away, then walked the three blocks to her apartment building. The streets were still busy with festival-goers, which was reassuring. She checked over her shoulder frequently, but saw no sign of the man who had followed her earlier.

As she approached her building, Julie noticed something propped against her apartment door—a manila envelope. Her name was written on it in block letters. Heart pounding, she looked around, but the hallway was empty. She picked up the envelope and quickly unlocked her door, locking it again behind her before turning on the lights.

Julie set the envelope on her kitchen counter and stared at it for a long moment. Finally, curiosity overcame caution, and she carefully opened it.

Inside were several yellowed newspaper clippings, photocopied from old issues of the Meadowgrove Gazette. The headlines leapt out at her:

"MEADOWGROVE COLLECTION STOLEN: PRICELESS ARTIFACTS MISSING" "MUSEUM CURATOR QUESTIONED IN THEFT INVESTIGATION" "SEARCH FOR MEADOWGROVE TREASURES CONTINUES"

The dates on the clippings were from 1965. Julie read them quickly, learning that a collection of historical artifacts—diaries, letters, maps, and several pieces of jewelry belonging to the town's founding families—had been stolen from the Meadowgrove Historical Society. The investigation had apparently focused on the curator, a man named Harrison Wilkins, though no charges were ever filed.

Crochet Carnage

Harrison Wilkins. The same family name as the journal's author.

Beneath the clippings was a handwritten note on plain white paper: "History repeats itself. Stop digging."

Julie sank into a chair, her mind racing. This wasn't just about Victoria's death anymore. Whatever secret lay buried in Meadowgrove's past, multiple people were determined to keep it hidden—and they knew she was getting close to uncovering it.

She pulled out her phone to call Eliza, then hesitated. What if Eliza was right? What if it was safer not to see the pattern? But as Julie looked again at the newspaper clippings and the ominous note, she knew it was too late for that. She was already on the wrong side of the pattern, and there was no going back.

Chapter 14

Increasing Tension

Julie woke before her alarm, the morning light filtering through her curtains. She'd slept poorly, the newspaper clippings and threatening note from last night haunting her dreams. The Meadowgrove Collection—stolen artifacts from the town's founding families—and the accusation against Harrison Wilkins, presumably a relative of the journal's author. The connection couldn't be coincidental.

After a quick shower, she made coffee and spread the clippings across her kitchen table, reading them more carefully. The articles were sparse on details about what exactly constituted the "priceless artifacts," referring only to "historical items of significant cultural value to Meadowgrove." Harrison Wilkins had been the curator at the time, but according to the final article, dated three weeks after the theft, police had found insufficient evidence to charge him.

Julie's phone buzzed with a text from Eliza: "How are you feeling about today's event? Need me there early?"

The charity knitting circle. With everything else happening, Julie had almost forgotten. For the festival's second day, she had organized a community knitting event in the town square to make winter hats and scarves for the local homeless shelter. It had seemed like a good idea

Crochet Carnage

months ago when she'd proposed it to the festival committee—a way to showcase fiber arts while giving back to the community.

"Yes please," she texted back. "8 AM setup. Bringing coffee and trying not to panic."

Julie gathered the newspaper clippings and tucked them into her messenger bag along with the Wilkins journal. She wasn't letting either out of her sight now. Before heading out, she hesitated, then snapped photos of each clipping and the threatening note, sending them to Eliza with a brief explanation of where she'd found them.

Eliza's response came immediately: "This is serious. Should we call the sheriff?"

"Let's talk at the shop," Julie replied, not wanting to make that decision via text.

The morning was crisp and clear, perfect fall weather for the festival's second day. As Julie walked the few blocks to The Yarn Haven, she couldn't shake the feeling of being watched. She checked over her shoulder several times but saw no one suspicious. Still, after yesterday's experience, she wasn't taking chances.

Eliza was already waiting when Julie arrived, two large coffee cups in hand.

"You look terrible," Eliza said bluntly as she handed Julie a cup. "Did you sleep at all?"

"Not much," Julie admitted, unlocking the shop. "I kept thinking about those newspaper clippings and what they might mean."

"I've been thinking about that too," Eliza said, following Julie inside. "The Wilkins journal, the stolen collection—it feels like we're being drawn into something that started decades ago."

Julie nodded, setting her bag behind the counter. "And somehow Victoria Winters was involved. The mayor said 'Victoria's money was supposed to solve everything.' What if that's connected to whatever was stolen in 1965?"

"But how?" Eliza asked. "Victoria would have been a child then, if she was even born."

"I don't know yet," Julie admitted. "But it can't be coincidence that all this is happening now." She took a steadying sip of coffee. "Come on, we need to load the van for the knitting circle. We can talk while we work."

They spent the next half hour gathering supplies: folding chairs, portable tables, baskets of yarn in various weights and colors, knitting needles and crochet hooks for beginners, pattern handouts, and a banner announcing "Knit for a Cause: Meadowgrove Cares."

As they loaded the last of the supplies into Julie's aging Subaru, Eliza brought up the sheriff again. "I really think you should tell Sheriff Harris about the note and the clippings. Someone is threatening you, Julie."

Julie sighed, closing the hatchback. "Maybe you're right. But what if he dismisses it like he did when I tried to tell him about the journal? He already thinks I'm overreacting about Victoria's death."

"This is different," Eliza insisted. "This is a direct threat against you. If nothing else, it creates a record if anything else happens."

Julie reluctantly agreed, and they drove the short distance to the town square, where the festival was already coming to life for its second day. They found their designated area—a grassy spot near the gazebo, sheltered by ancient maple trees now resplendent in autumn colors.

With Eliza's help, Julie set up a circle of chairs with small tables between them for participants to rest their supplies. By the time they finished, a line of volunteers had already begun to gather, eager knitters and crocheters ready to contribute to the cause.

"I'll go open the shop," Eliza said. "Text me if you need anything, and please, talk to the sheriff when you get a chance."

Julie promised she would and turned her attention to organizing the volunteers. The event started smoothly, with about twenty people taking seats in the circle. Julie demonstrated some basic stitches for the beginners and distributed yarn and needles. Soon the group was chatting happily as their projects took shape.

Around mid-morning, Julie noticed Sheriff Harris making his way through the festival crowd. He wasn't in uniform, instead wearing jeans and a flannel shirt, but the way people naturally made space for him marked him as an authority figure.

When he spotted Julie, he changed course, heading directly for the knitting circle. Julie excused herself from the elderly woman she'd been helping and met the sheriff at the edge of the group.

"Morning, Ms. Morgan," Harris said, his expression serious. "Quite an event you've put together here."

"Sheriff Harris," Julie acknowledged. "It's for a good cause."

"Community service is admirable," he agreed. "Can we talk privately for a moment?"

Julie led him away from the circle, to a quiet spot beneath one of the maples. "Is this about Victoria Winters? Have you found something new?"

Harris shook his head. "This is about you, Ms. Morgan. I've been hearing some concerning things."

Julie tensed. "What do you mean?"

"Word gets around in a small town," Harris said. "I understand you've been asking questions about Victoria Winters, digging into old town histories, making connections that might be better left unmade."

"Is it a crime to be interested in local history?" Julie asked defensively.

"No," Harris conceded. "But it becomes my concern when that interest might be putting you in danger." His eyes narrowed slightly. "Has anyone approached you? Made any threats?"

Julie hesitated, thinking of the note left at her door and the man who had followed her yesterday. This was her opening to tell the sheriff exactly what Eliza had advised, but something in his demeanor made her cautious.

"Why do you ask?" she countered.

"Because," Harris said, lowering his voice, "Victoria Winters didn't just fall down those stairs. Her death is now officially a homicide investigation, though we're keeping that quiet for now."

Julie felt her heart skip. "I knew it," she breathed. "I knew something wasn't right about her accident."

"Which brings me back to my concern," Harris continued. "If you're poking around in things connected to her death, you could be putting yourself at risk. Whatever you think you're investigating, I strongly suggest you leave it to the professionals."

"But I found something—" Julie began, then stopped herself. She still wasn't sure if she could trust Harris. What if he was somehow involved? "I mean, I've heard rumors about Victoria being involved in some kind of land deal with the mayor."

Harris's expression didn't change, but Julie noticed a slight tensing of his jaw. "What kind of land deal?"

"I'm not sure of the details," Julie said carefully. "Just something I overheard."

"Well, if you hear anything else, I expect you to come directly to me," Harris said firmly. "And in the meantime, watch your back. Whoever killed Victoria might not appreciate amateur sleuthing."

With that warning, he nodded curtly and walked away, leaving Julie with a chill despite the warm morning sun.

The knitting circle continued until early afternoon, producing an impressive pile of hats, scarves, and mittens for the shelter. Julie thanked the volunteers, packed up the leftover supplies, and loaded them back into her car. The threatening note and Sheriff Harris's warning weighed heavily on her mind as she drove the few blocks back to The Yarn Haven.

After unloading the supplies at the shop and checking in with Eliza, who reported another busy day of sales, Julie decided to head home for a quick lunch before returning for the afternoon shift. She was exhausted, both physically and emotionally, and needed a moment of quiet to process everything that had happened.

As she approached her car, Julie noticed a dark stain on the pavement beneath it. Frowning, she crouched down to look and saw a puddle of fluid. Not being particularly mechanically inclined, she wasn't sure what it was, but it didn't look normal. She popped the hood and stared at the engine, not entirely sure what she was looking for.

"Car trouble?"

Julie startled and turned to find Dr. David Walker standing a few feet away, a concerned expression on his face.

"I'm not sure," she admitted. "There's some kind of fluid leaking."

Walker approached and peered under the hood. "Mind if I take a look? I'm no mechanic, but I know the basics."

Julie stepped back, allowing him space. Walker examined the engine carefully, then got down on one knee to look underneath the car. When he straightened, his expression was grave.

"Your brake line has been cut," he said quietly. "Not completely severed, but enough that it would fail when you needed it most. Probably on your drive home."

Julie felt the blood drain from her face. "Cut? You mean... deliberately?"

Walker nodded grimly. "This wasn't an accident. Someone wanted to harm you, Ms. Morgan."

"Julie," she corrected automatically, her mind racing. "I need to call a tow truck."

"And the sheriff," Walker added firmly. "This is attempted murder."

Julie thought of her conversation with Sheriff Harris just hours ago and felt a wave of uncertainty. "I'm not sure—"

"This isn't negotiable," Walker interrupted. "Someone just tried to kill you." He pulled out his phone. "I'll call both. And I insist on driving you home afterward. It's not safe for you to be alone right now."

Too shaken to argue, Julie nodded. While Walker made the calls, she texted Eliza to let her know what had happened and that she wouldn't be back for the afternoon shift. Eliza's response was immediate and panicked: "OMG!!! Are you OK? I'll close the shop and come right over!"

Julie assured her that wasn't necessary, that Dr. Walker was helping her, and promised to call later with more details.

The sheriff arrived before the tow truck, his expression darkening when he saw the cut brake line. He took photos and asked several questions about who might have had access to the car and whether Julie had noticed anyone suspicious.

"I warned you just hours ago," Harris said, shaking his head. "And already someone's made a move against you."

"I parked the car here this morning around eight," Julie told him. "It was in plain view of the festival the whole time, but with so many people around..." She trailed off, realizing that anyone could have tampered with her car amid the crowd and confusion.

Harris took her statement, promised to increase patrols around her apartment, and advised her again—more forcefully this time—to stop investigating Victoria's death. When the tow truck arrived to take her car to the local repair shop, Harris left as well, leaving Julie standing on the sidewalk with Dr. Walker.

"I meant what I said about driving you home," Walker said gently. "My car's just around the corner."

Julie hesitated, then nodded. She was still processing the fact that someone had deliberately sabotaged her car—had tried to kill her. The danger that Sheriff Harris had warned her about was real, and much closer than she'd realized.

Walker's car was a sensible mid-sized sedan, neat and well-maintained. As they drove the short distance to Julie's apartment, silence hung between them until Walker finally spoke.

"I owe you an apology," he said, keeping his eyes on the road. "When we spoke before about Victoria Winters, I wasn't entirely forthcoming."

Julie turned to look at him, surprised by this admission. "What do you mean?"

Walker sighed. "Victoria and I had a complicated relationship. Not romantic," he added quickly, seeing Julie's expression. "But... complicated nonetheless."

He pulled up in front of Julie's apartment building but made no move to get out of the car. Instead, he turned off the engine and turned to face her.

"Victoria Winters was blackmailing me," he said simply.

Julie stared at him. "Blackmailing you? But why?"

Walker ran a hand through his silver hair, suddenly looking older than his years. "My medical clinic has been struggling financially for some time. Meadowgrove isn't a wealthy community, and I've never been good at turning away patients who can't pay. Over the years, it's added up."

"That's hardly something to be blackmailed over," Julie said. "It's commendable."

"The commendable part, yes," Walker agreed with a wry smile. "The less commendable part was how I tried to solve the problem. I made some... creative adjustments to insurance claims. Nothing that hurt patients, but definitely in a gray area legally."

"And Victoria found out," Julie guessed.

Walker nodded. "She approached me about six months ago. Said she had evidence of my 'billing irregularities' and would be happy to keep it to herself—if I supported her development plans for Meadowgrove."

"The resort project," Julie said, pieces falling into place. "She needed the town council's approval."

"And I sit on the town council," Walker confirmed. "She needed my vote, along with Mayor Johnson's backing. Victoria offered to solve my money problems in exchange for my support. A generous donation to the clinic, all above board, if I voted her way."

"Did you agree?" Julie asked.

"I was considering it," Walker admitted. "Not ideal, but it would have allowed me to keep the clinic open, to keep helping people. Then she died, and..." He shrugged. "Now I'm back to square one with the clinic's finances, but at least I'm not being coerced anymore."

Julie studied his face, seeing the genuine worry and fatigue there. This confession explained his evasiveness when they'd first discussed Victoria, but it also raised new questions.

"Why are you telling me this now?" she asked.

"Because secrets are dangerous in this town," Walker said quietly. "And after what happened to your car—" He broke off, shaking his head. "I don't know what you've stumbled into, Julie, but it's clearly bigger than Victoria's little blackmail scheme. And I wanted you to know that you can trust me. That despite my... ethical lapse with the clinic billing, I'm not your enemy here."

Julie wasn't sure how to respond. Walker's confession seemed genuine, but trust was in short supply these days.

"Thank you for your honesty," she said finally. "And for saving me from driving a car with cut brake lines."

Walker nodded. "Be careful, Julie. Whoever did this is serious, and they're clearly worried about what you might discover." He hesitated, then added, "If you need anything—a safe place to stay, someone to talk to—please call me."

He handed her a business card with his personal cell number written on the back, then insisted on walking her to her apartment door and checking inside before leaving. As the sound of his footsteps faded down the hallway, Julie locked and bolted her door, leaning against it as the events of the day caught up with her.

Her phone rang—Eliza calling for an update. Julie answered, grateful for her friend's concern, and explained what had happened with the car and Dr. Walker's surprising confession.

"So Victoria was blackmailing people," Eliza said, sounding troubled. "I wonder who else was on her list."

"The mayor, maybe?" Julie suggested. "Remember what she said about 'Victoria's money was supposed to solve everything'?"

"Maybe," Eliza agreed. "Listen, I'm still at the shop, but I've been doing some digging while things were slow. Marilyn came by earlier—she's been helping at the historical society booth at the festival—and I mentioned the newspaper clippings you found."

Julie tensed. "What did she say?"

"She knew about the theft right away. Apparently, it's somewhat infamous in local history circles. But here's the interesting part—Marilyn said there were rumors at the time that the Johnson family was actually behind the theft, not Harrison Wilkins."

"The Johnson family? As in Mayor Johnson's family?"

"Exactly," Eliza confirmed. "According to Marilyn, the Johnsons and the Wilkins families had been rivals for generations. Both were founding families of Meadowgrove, but the Wilkins family was more prominent in the historical record because they kept better documentation. The Meadowgrove Collection primarily featured Wilkins family artifacts, which allegedly didn't sit well with the Johnsons."

"So the theory is that the Johnsons stole the collection out of jealousy?" Julie asked skeptically.

"Or to rewrite history," Eliza suggested. "Marilyn said that without those artifacts, much of the Wilkins family's contribution to founding the town was eventually forgotten. Over time, the Johnson family narrative became more dominant in local lore."

Julie thought about the journal she'd been reading, with its accounts of early Meadowgrove that differed from the official history she'd learned growing up.

"And Marilyn says this rivalry has been simmering for decades? Even now?"

"Apparently," Eliza said. "Mayor Johnson's great-grandfather was the main suspect after Harrison Wilkins was cleared, but nothing was ever proven. The collection was never recovered."

"And now Mayor Johnson is involved in some land deal with Victoria Winters," Julie mused. "I wonder if that's connected somehow."

"It's a small town with long memories," Eliza said. "Marilyn thinks the rivalry never really ended. She's going to bring over some other historical society records tonight, things that might shed light on the connection."

After they hung up, Julie sat in her living room, turning over everything she'd learned. Victoria blackmailing Dr. Walker. The generations-old feud between the Johnsons and the Wilkins families. The missing Meadowgrove Collection. The mayor's mysterious land deal. And someone who was desperate enough to cut her brake lines to stop her from connecting these dots.

Crochet Carnage

The pattern was becoming clearer, but the full picture remained just out of reach. One thing was certain—she was getting closer to the truth, and someone in Meadowgrove was willing to kill to keep it hidden.

Julie pulled out the Wilkins journal, determined to finish reading it before Marilyn arrived with the additional records. Perhaps the final entries would provide the missing piece, the connection that would make sense of it all. As she opened to where she'd left off, she couldn't shake the feeling that time was running out—not just for solving the mystery of Victoria's death, but for her own safety as well.

Chapter 15
Blocking the Design

Julie paced the length of her apartment, phone pressed to her ear. "Are you sure about this, Eliza?"

"No, I'm not sure about anything at this point," Eliza replied, her voice tight with worry. "But someone cut your brake lines, Julie. You can't just sit around waiting for them to try again."

"I know, but setting a trap? It seems extreme." Julie stopped at her window, staring out at the autumn evening. Dusk had fallen over Meadowgrove, and the festival lights twinkled in the town square a few blocks away.

"More extreme than attempted murder?" Eliza countered. "Look, we know someone's desperate to stop you from digging into all this. The threatening note, the brake lines—they're escalating. If we don't do something proactive, I'm afraid of what might happen next."

Julie sighed. Eliza had a point. "So what exactly are you suggesting?"

"A simple plan. You announce you're leaving town for a few days —family emergency or something. Make it public. Post it on the shop's social media, tell a few gossipy customers. Word will spread."

"And then?"

"And then we stake out the shop overnight. Whoever's after you might see it as an opportunity to search for the journal or whatever else they think you've found."

Julie considered the idea. It was risky, but sitting around waiting for another attack seemed worse. "We should involve the sheriff," she said reluctantly.

"After what you told me about your conversation with him today? I'm not so sure. He might be involved somehow."

"That's a serious accusation, Eliza."

"I know. But in a town this small, with secrets this old, can we really be sure who to trust? Sheriff Harris has been here his whole life. His family goes back generations in Meadowgrove."

Julie rubbed her temples, feeling a headache coming on. "Who would we have with us, then?"

"I was thinking Marilyn from the historical society. She clearly knows more about town history than she initially let on. And maybe Nelly—she's tough and practical, and she genuinely seems to care about you."

"Nelly?" Julie was surprised. Her elderly neighbor had shown concern since Victoria's death, but involving her in a potentially dangerous stakeout seemed irresponsible.

"Don't underestimate her," Eliza said. "She was telling me the other day that she used to work security at the state university back in the eighties. The woman knows how to handle herself."

Julie shook her head, amazed at how little she knew about the people in her own building. "Okay, let's say I agree to this. How soon are we talking?"

"Tomorrow night. We'll use tonight to spread the word that you're leaving town early tomorrow morning."

"That's... very soon."

"The sooner the better. I don't like how fast things are escalating."

After hanging up, Julie sat at her kitchen table, mulling over the plan. It was impulsive, potentially dangerous, and possibly misguided. But what was the alternative? Waiting for another attack? Leaving town for real, abandoning the business she'd worked so hard to build?

She opened her laptop and drafted a quick post for The Yarn Haven's social media accounts: "Due to a family emergency, the shop will be closed for a few days starting tomorrow. Thank you for your understanding during this difficult time."

After publishing it, she sent text messages to Marilyn and Nelly, asking if they could meet tonight. Both responded quickly in the affirmative, seeming concerned by the urgency in her message. An hour later, all three women were seated in Julie's living room, listening as she explained the situation and Eliza's proposed plan.

"I've suspected for years that the Johnson family was behind the theft," Marilyn said when Julie finished. The older woman's eyes gleamed with interest. "But there was never any proof. If Victoria Winters found something connecting them to the Meadowgrove Collection..."

"That might explain why someone's so desperate to stop Julie's investigation," Nelly added, her weathered face serious. "Old secrets, powerful families. It's a dangerous combination."

"So you both think the plan could work?" Julie asked.

"It's risky," Nelly admitted. "But I'm in. Been too long since I've had a proper adventure."

Marilyn nodded in agreement. "I want to know the truth about the Meadowgrove Collection as much as you want to know what happened to Victoria. Count me in."

The following day passed in a blur of careful preparation. Julie packed a suitcase and made sure she was seen leaving her apartment building with it, telling neighbors she'd be gone for a few days. She drove her newly-repaired car (the mechanic had replaced the entire brake system) to The Yarn Haven, made a show of closing up the shop early, and then slipped out the back with her suitcase still inside.

Eliza picked her up a block away and drove her back to the neighborhood, where she spent the day hiding in Nelly's apartment. As evening approached, the four women gathered to finalize their plan.

"We enter the shop after dark using Julie's keys," Eliza explained. "Two of us take the front room, two in the back office. We wait."

"And if someone does show up?" Marilyn asked nervously.

"We call the sheriff," Julie said firmly. "No confrontations. We just want to identify whoever's behind this."

"Agreed," Nelly said, patting her large handbag. "Though I'm bringing protection just in case."

Julie eyed the bag warily. "Please tell me that's not a gun, Nelly."

The older woman snorted. "Nothing so dramatic. Just pepper spray and a taser. Like I said, I used to work security."

At eleven that night, with the festival long closed and the town quiet, they made their way to The Yarn Haven. Julie unlocked the back door, and they slipped inside, locking it behind them. The shop was dark except for the dim security light near the register and whatever moonlight filtered through the front windows.

They positioned themselves as planned: Julie and Marilyn in the back office, Eliza and Nelly in the main shop floor. Then they settled in to wait, speaking only in whispers.

The hours crawled by. Midnight came and went. Julie was beginning to think the plan had failed—that perhaps whoever was targeting her hadn't taken the bait—when, at nearly two in the morning, they heard a soft scraping sound at the back door.

Julie and Marilyn exchanged alarmed glances. The noise came again—someone was definitely at the door, trying to pick the lock. Julie's heart hammered in her chest as she quietly texted Eliza: "Someone at back door."

The reply was immediate: "We hear it. Stay hidden."

The scraping continued for several minutes, punctuated by muffled curses. Whoever was trying to break in wasn't particularly skilled. Finally, there was a faint click, and the door eased open. A figure slipped inside, dressed in dark clothing, face obscured by a hood.

The intruder moved cautiously through the storeroom, using a small flashlight to navigate. Julie and Marilyn crouched behind a large shelving unit, barely daring to breathe. The figure moved past them toward the office, apparently unaware of their presence.

Once inside the office, the intruder began searching through drawers and cabinets, movements growing increasingly frantic. Julie could hear papers being shuffled, drawers opening and closing.

She caught Marilyn's eye and nodded. They'd seen enough to confirm that someone was indeed searching her shop. Time to end this.

Julie pressed the light switch, flooding the office with sudden brightness. The intruder spun around, momentarily blinded, and Julie got her first clear look at the face.

"Derek?" she gasped.

Victoria's assistant—and alleged nephew—stared back at her, eyes wide with panic. He looked terrible—unshaven, dark circles under his eyes, clothes rumpled as if he'd been sleeping in them.

"How—" he began, then lunged for the door.

But Eliza and Nelly had heard Julie's exclamation and blocked his escape. Nelly already had her taser out, pointed squarely at Derek's chest.

"I wouldn't, young man," the elderly woman said calmly. "Sit down and explain yourself."

Derek's shoulders slumped in defeat. He collapsed into Julie's office chair, burying his face in his hands. "You don't understand," he said, voice muffled. "I'm not trying to hurt anyone. I'm trying to stay alive."

"By breaking into my shop?" Julie demanded. "After someone cut my brake lines yesterday?"

Derek's head snapped up. "That wasn't me! I would never—" He broke off, looking genuinely horrified. "Oh god, they're trying to kill you too."

"Who's 'they'?" Eliza asked, moving closer but keeping Nelly and her taser between herself and Derek.

"I don't know exactly," Derek said miserably. "But it's connected to why Victoria really came to Meadowgrove."

Julie exchanged glances with the others. "We're listening."

Derek took a deep, shuddering breath. "Victoria didn't just come here for property development. That was true, but it wasn't the whole truth. She came looking for the Meadowgrove Collection."

Marilyn gasped softly. "The stolen artifacts? But that was decades ago."

"Fifty-eight years," Derek confirmed. "Victoria became obsessed with finding them after she discovered a connection to her own family history." He looked at Julie. "That's why we were so interested in the Wilkins Building. Victoria believed the collection was hidden somewhere inside it."

"Wait," Julie said, trying to process this. "How did Victoria even know about the collection?"

"Her grandmother was from Meadowgrove originally," Derek explained. "She moved away in the late sixties, but she kept newspaper clippings about the theft. Victoria found them after her grandmother died last year."

"And she thought she could just come back and find artifacts that have been missing for nearly six decades?" Eliza asked skeptically.

"She had more than just clippings," Derek said. "She had evidence—papers that suggested the Johnson family was behind the theft. Specifically, Mayor Johnson's grandmother."

A heavy silence fell over the room as they absorbed this information.

"What kind of evidence?" Marilyn finally asked.

"Letters, mainly. Correspondence between Victoria's grandmother and someone in Meadowgrove who claimed to know what really happened. But the most damning was a journal entry Victoria found in the attic of the cabin—hidden in the wall during some previous renovation." Derek rubbed his face tiredly. "It was written by Martha Johnson—the current mayor's grandmother—basically admitting to orchestrating the theft to 'restore balance to Meadowgrove's history.'"

"Where is this evidence now?" Julie asked.

"Most of it was in Victoria's personal safe in the cabin. I don't know if it survived the break-in that happened after her death."

"Break-in?" Julie frowned. "What break-in?"

Derek looked surprised. "You didn't know? The day after Victoria died, someone broke into the cabin and tore it apart. I was there—I'd gone back to collect some of Victoria's things—and I barely got out before they saw me. I've been hiding ever since."

"Why didn't you go to the sheriff?" Nelly asked.

Derek laughed bitterly. "With what I know about who might be involved? I didn't know who I could trust."

"So you came back to search my shop because...?" Julie prompted.

"Victoria kept notes on everyone in town she thought might help or hinder her search. Your name was in them. She thought the journal you found might contain clues about the collection's location." Derek looked embarrassed. "I was desperate. I've been hiding for days, running out of money and options. I thought if I could find the collection myself, I could use it as leverage to ensure my safety."

Before anyone could respond, they heard a noise from outside—a car door closing, then footsteps approaching the back of the shop.

Derek went pale. "Someone's coming," he whispered, panic evident in his voice. "They must have followed me."

"We need to call the sheriff," Julie said, reaching for her phone.

"No!" Derek lurched to his feet. "You don't understand. It's not safe. I have to get out of here." Before anyone could stop him, he bolted toward the office window, yanking it open. "Find Victoria's evidence. It's the only way to end this."

"Derek, wait!" Julie called, but he was already climbing through the window. In his haste, he knocked over a stack of files, and something fell from his pocket—a smartphone.

"His phone," Eliza said, quickly retrieving it.

The footsteps outside had stopped. They waited in tense silence, but whoever had approached seemed to have gone. After several minutes, Nelly cautiously checked the back door and reported that there was no one there.

"Maybe they saw the lights and got spooked," Marilyn suggested.

Julie nodded absently, her attention on Derek's phone. Thankfully, it wasn't password protected. "He must have been using it as a flashlight," she murmured, opening the photo gallery.

What she found made her breath catch. "Look at these," she said, showing the others. The gallery contained dozens of photos of documents—letters, journal entries, old photographs, all apparently taken hurriedly and in poor lighting.

"He must have photographed the contents of Victoria's safe before he fled the cabin," Eliza said, peering over Julie's shoulder.

They scrolled through the images, most too blurry or poorly lit to read clearly. But one stood out—a recent letter on official stationery from the Office of the Mayor, signed by Carolyn Johnson herself.

"'In light of your claims regarding certain historical artifacts,'" Julie read aloud, "'I believe we could come to a mutually beneficial arrangement. Meet me at the agreed location to discuss terms. I'm prepared to make a deal that satisfies both our interests.'"

"A deal about the artifacts," Marilyn breathed. "This proves the Johnson family was involved in the theft."

"It proves the mayor was willing to negotiate about them," Julie corrected. "Not quite the same thing, but still significant." She continued scrolling through the photos, stopping at another that showed what appeared to be a hand-drawn map. "What's this?"

The map showed what looked like the interior layout of a building, with an X marked in one corner and some handwritten notes that were too small to read clearly in the photo.

"Could be the location of the collection," Eliza suggested. "But which building?"

"The Wilkins Building," Julie said suddenly. "Derek said Victoria believed the artifacts were hidden there. That's why she was so interested in purchasing it, despite its poor condition."

"But why would stolen artifacts connected to the Johnson family be hidden in the Wilkins Building?" Nelly asked, frowning.

"Because no one would look for them there," Marilyn said slowly, as if piecing together a puzzle. "If the Johnson family stole them to erase the Wilkins family from history, hiding them in plain sight, in the very building named for their rivals, would be the ultimate irony."

"And the perfect hiding place," Julie agreed. "The building has been in disrepair for decades. Parts of it have been closed off completely."

They spent the next hour examining every photo on Derek's phone, but many were too blurry to yield much information. The letter from Mayor Johnson was the clearest evidence, followed by several pages that appeared to be from a personal journal—presumably the one Derek had mentioned finding hidden in the cabin wall—but the handwriting was small and difficult to read in the photos.

"We need to go to the cabin," Julie said finally. "See if any of this evidence is still there, despite the break-in Derek mentioned."

"And if it's not?" Eliza asked.

"Then we go to the Wilkins Building," Julie said firmly. "If the collection is hidden there, we need to find it before someone else does."

"Or before someone decides we're too close to the truth and tries something worse than cutting your brake lines," Nelly added grimly.

Julie nodded, a chill running down her spine. "We should leave here. It's not safe to stay in one place too long, especially after Derek's visit. We can regroup at my apartment in the morning."

They left The Yarn Haven as quietly as they'd entered, making sure to lock up properly. The streets of Meadowgrove were deserted at that late hour, the festival infrastructure sitting silent and empty in the town square. As they passed the mayor's campaign tent, Julie couldn't help but wonder how many generations of secrets the Johnson family had been protecting—and what lengths they might go to keep those secrets buried.

Back at her apartment, Julie downloaded the photos from Derek's phone to her laptop for safekeeping, then wrapped the phone in a cloth and hid it at the bottom of her knitting basket. If Derek didn't return for it, it might become their most valuable piece of evidence.

After Eliza, Marilyn, and Nelly left, promising to return early the next morning, Julie sat alone at her kitchen table, surrounded by the pieces of a decades-old puzzle that had somehow become entangled with her present. The Wilkins journal. The threatening note. Derek's revelations. The photos on his phone.

Someone had been willing to kill Victoria Winters over the Meadowgrove Collection. Someone had tampered with Julie's car, presumably with similar intent. The stakes were clearly higher than she'd initially realized.

Julie pulled out the Wilkins journal and opened it to the section where pages had been torn out. If those missing pages contained information about the collection or its location, they might be the key to everything.

She traced the ragged edge where the pages had been removed, wondering who had taken them and why. Then her finger caught on something—a tiny corner of paper still trapped in the binding. Using a pair of tweezers from her sewing kit, Julie carefully extracted it.

It was just a fragment, barely larger than a postage stamp, but it contained part of a sentence in the same handwriting as the rest of the journal: "...hidden where only those who understand patterns will find it."

Patterns. The word resonated with Julie in a way she couldn't immediately explain. Then it clicked—she was a fiber artist, someone who worked with patterns every day. The Wilkins family had been prominent in the textile industry during Meadowgrove's early days. What if the clue to finding the collection had to do with textile patterns or designs?

Julie felt a surge of excitement. She might have an advantage that Victoria Winters, for all her resources and determination, had lacked—an understanding of patterns, both literal and figurative.

As dawn began to break over Meadowgrove, Julie finally allowed herself to rest, but her dreams were filled with hidden treasures, unraveling designs, and the growing certainty that she was closer than ever to uncovering the truth—if she could stay alive long enough to find it.

Chapter 16
Cabling Complications

The final day of the Harvest Festival dawned bright and clear, perfect weather for the parade and craft competition that would mark the event's climax. Julie had barely slept, her mind racing with everything they'd learned from Derek the night before. The Meadowgrove Collection, Victoria's true purpose in town, Mayor Johnson's involvement—it was almost too much to process.

She rolled out of bed and went straight to her knitting basket, fishing out Derek's phone from its hiding place. The device remained silent overnight—no calls or texts. Either Derek hadn't noticed its absence yet, or he was too afraid to attempt contact.

Julie's own phone buzzed with a text from Eliza: "Everyone still meeting at your place at 9?"

"Yes," Julie typed back. "Bring coffee if you can."

She showered quickly and laid out her festival outfit—a dress in autumn colors topped with her entry for the craft competition: a complex cable-knit shawl she'd been working on for months. The design featured an intricate pattern of intertwining cables that formed a subtle tree motif, the branches spreading across the shoulders. She'd used locally sourced wool in three complementary shades of blue, the color deepening toward the edges like twilight falling over the mountains.

Under normal circumstances, Julie would have been nervous about entering her work in the competition. Today, it felt like a necessary distraction, a way to maintain her cover story of being primarily concerned with the festival rather than investigating decades-old thefts and recent murders.

Her doorbell rang precisely at nine. Marilyn arrived first, followed closely by Nelly and then Eliza, who came bearing a tray of coffees and a bag of pastries from the bakery on Main Street.

"I figured we could all use the fuel," Eliza said, setting everything on the kitchen counter. "It was a late night."

"And possibly another one ahead," Julie agreed, distributing the coffees. "We need to decide our next move."

They gathered around Julie's small dining table, where she had already set up her laptop with the photos from Derek's phone.

"I've been thinking about what Derek said," Marilyn began, warming her hands around her coffee cup. "About Victoria believing the collection was hidden in the Wilkins Building. It makes a certain kind of sense—hiding stolen artifacts in a building owned by the family they were stolen from."

"A form of poetic injustice," Nelly agreed. "But the building's been through multiple renovations and ownership changes since the sixties. How could the collection remain hidden all this time?"

"Maybe it's somewhere not easily accessible," Julie suggested. "A sealed room, a hidden compartment. Old buildings like that often have secrets."

"Or maybe it's not there anymore," Eliza pointed out. "Derek said Victoria was searching for it, not that she'd found it."

Julie nodded, swiping through the photos on her laptop until she found the one showing the hand-drawn map. "This is our best lead. I'm almost certain it's the Wilkins Building, but the image quality is too poor to make out the details or notes."

"We should go there," Marilyn said firmly. "Tonight, after the festival ends. See for ourselves."

"Break into a construction site?" Eliza looked alarmed. "That's trespassing, possibly breaking and entering."

"Do you have a better suggestion?" Nelly asked. "We can't exactly ask the mayor for permission to search for stolen artifacts that her grandmother may have hidden."

"What about the sheriff?" Eliza tried again.

Julie shook her head. "Not until we have concrete evidence. Right now, all we have are theories and some blurry photos of documents we can barely read."

"And someone tried to kill you yesterday," Eliza reminded her. "This isn't a game, Julie."

"I know that," Julie said quietly. "Which is why we need answers, not just speculation." She turned to Nelly. "You mentioned your husband George worked security. Do you think he might have advice on how to... investigate a site like the Wilkins Building without being caught?"

Nelly's eyes gleamed with unexpected excitement. "He might. And he might even want to join us. He's been complaining for years that retirement is too boring."

"No," Julie said firmly. "The fewer people involved, the better. Just ask him about the building's likely security measures and how to avoid them."

"I still don't like this," Eliza muttered.

"Neither do I," Julie admitted. "But I like the alternative even less."

They spent another hour discussing logistics and reviewing what they knew, then agreed to meet back at Julie's apartment after the festival closed for the night—around ten o'clock. In the meantime, they would attend the day's events as planned, maintaining their normal routines to avoid arousing suspicion.

"One more thing," Julie said as they prepared to leave. "Keep an eye out for Edward Thompson today. He's been asking too many questions about the Wilkins journal. I want to know what he's really doing in Meadowgrove."

The downtown area was already packed when they arrived for the parade. Main Street had been blocked off, with spectators lining both sides in anticipation. Children sat on curbs licking ice cream cones, elderly couples had claimed prime viewing spots with folding chairs, and vendors worked the crowd selling festival souvenirs and snacks.

Julie and Eliza made their way to The Yarn Haven, where they'd arranged to watch from the front window. As Julie unlocked the door, she was struck by how normal everything looked in the morning light—no sign of Derek's break-in or their late-night stakeout.

"It all feels surreal," she murmured to Eliza as they entered. "Like we're living in two Meadowgroves simultaneously—the cheerful festival town and this darker place full of secrets and danger."

"Let's focus on the cheerful one for a few hours," Eliza suggested, helping Julie arrange her shawl on a mannequin for transport to the craft competition later. "I think we both need the break."

The parade began at eleven, led by the high school marching band playing an enthusiastic if not entirely in-tune rendition of "Small Town Pride," Meadowgrove's unofficial anthem. They were followed by a procession of floats representing local businesses and organizations—the volunteer fire department on their gleaming engine, the garden club with a flower-covered wagon, the historical society (with Marilyn waving enthusiastically) showcasing artifacts from the town's past.

Mayor Johnson rode in an open convertible, smiling and waving to constituents. Her campaign manager, Thomas Drake, walked alongside, occasionally leaning in to whisper something in her ear. Julie watched the mayor carefully, trying to reconcile the friendly public figure with the woman who might be protecting a dark family legacy of theft and deception.

"There's Thompson," Eliza said suddenly, nudging Julie.

Edward Thompson stood across the street, watching the parade with apparent enjoyment. He wore a tweed jacket despite the warm day and occasionally jotted notes in a small leather-bound notebook. As the mayor's car passed his position, he looked up with particular interest, his expression unreadable.

"I still don't understand his role in all this," Julie said. "He knows about the journal, he's interested in local history, but what's his angle?"

"Academic curiosity?" Eliza suggested. "Not everyone has ulterior motives."

"In Meadowgrove this week? I'm not so sure."

After the parade, they carried Julie's shawl to the community center where the craft competition entries were being displayed. The large room was filled with tables showcasing everything from quilts and knitted items to woodworking, pottery, and preserved foods. Each category had its own section and judging panel.

Julie carefully arranged her shawl on the designated form, adjusting it to best display the intricate cable work. As she stepped back to ensure it looked right, she noticed Edward Thompson again—this time deep in conversation with a man she recognized as the construction foreman from the Wilkins Building renovation project.

"Eliza," she whispered, gesturing discreetly. "Thompson is talking to the Wilkins Building foreman."

"Could be a coincidence," Eliza said, but she sounded uncertain.

"I'm going to try to get closer, hear what they're saying."

Before Eliza could object, Julie moved through the crowd, pretending to admire other entries while edging closer to Thompson and the foreman. Their voices became audible as she paused to examine a delicate lacework tablecloth.

"...definitely unusual structural features," the foreman was saying. "Not on any of the blueprints we were given."

"Fascinating," Thompson replied. "And you say this was in the basement level?"

"Northwest corner. Looks like a sealed room of some kind. We weren't scheduled to renovate that section until next month, but with the mayor pushing up the timeline..."

Their voices faded as they moved away, but Julie had heard enough to set her heart racing. A sealed room in the basement, exactly where the collection might be hidden. And the mayor was accelerating the renovation timeline—why?

Julie returned to Eliza and quietly relayed what she'd overheard.

"This changes things," Eliza admitted. "If they're about to renovate that area of the building..."

"Then we need to get in there tonight," Julie finished. "Before any evidence is destroyed or removed."

The craft judging was scheduled for two o'clock, followed by Mayor Johnson's closing festival address at three. Julie found it increasingly difficult to focus on the competition as the judges made their way around the display tables, examining each entry with serious expressions and making notes on clipboards.

When they reached her shawl, the head judge, an elderly woman who had taught textiles at the community college for decades, spent several minutes examining the cablework, occasionally making appreciative sounds.

"Remarkable tensioning," she commented to her fellow judges. "And the pattern is original?"

"Yes," Julie confirmed. "Inspired by the Meadowgrove forest in autumn twilight."

The judge nodded approvingly and made additional notes before moving on. Under normal circumstances, Julie would have been thrilled by the response. Today, she could barely bring herself to care.

At two-thirty, the judges announced the winners in each category. To Julie's surprise, her shawl took first place in the fiber arts division. She accepted the blue ribbon and small cash prize with a smile that felt mechanical, already thinking ahead to the night's investigation.

Mayor Johnson's speech drew a large crowd to the gazebo in the town square. She stood on the decorated platform, the festival banner hanging behind her, looking every inch the confident small-town leader.

"Friends and neighbors," she began, her voice carrying across the square. "Another successful Harvest Festival comes to a close, but Meadowgrove's future is just beginning to unfold."

Julie listened intently as the mayor spoke about community traditions and progress working hand in hand, about honoring the past while building for the future. Standard political rhetoric, until—

"I'm pleased to announce that the Wilkins Building renovation project is ahead of schedule," Johnson continued. "And I have exciting news to share about its future purpose—news that will put Meadowgrove on the map as a destination for history enthusiasts throughout the region."

Julie and Eliza exchanged glances. This hadn't been mentioned in any previous announcements about the project.

"On Monday morning, I'll be holding a special press conference to reveal plans for the new Meadowgrove Historical Center, which will showcase artifacts and documents celebrating our town's rich heritage." The mayor smiled broadly. "Some of these historical treasures have never before been seen by the public. I can promise you, the reveal will be truly momentous for our community."

A murmur went through the crowd. Julie felt a chill despite the warm afternoon.

"She's going to 'discover' the collection," she whispered to Eliza. "Or some version of it. She's going to use it for political gain—the mayor who restored Meadowgrove's lost heritage."

"Just in time for the election," Eliza agreed, looking troubled. "But that means—"

"The artifacts must still be in the building," Julie finished. "And we need to find them tonight, before she has a chance to manipulate the narrative."

The rest of the afternoon passed in a blur of festival activities and anxious waiting. Julie and Eliza closed The Yarn Haven early, citing festival fatigue, and returned to Julie's apartment to prepare for their nighttime expedition.

Nelly arrived at eight-thirty, carrying a backpack and looking unexpectedly energized. "George says there's likely just one night watchman," she reported. "Standard procedure is to make rounds once an hour, following the same route. The trick is timing your movements around the predictable pattern."

"Did he suspect why you were asking?" Julie inquired.

Nelly snorted. "That man hasn't been curious about anything I do in fifteen years. Just happy to share his expertise." She unzipped the backpack, revealing flashlights, gloves, and what looked like small pry bars. "Basic entry tools, just in case."

"Where did you get those?" Eliza asked, alarmed.

"George kept his work equipment. Said you never know when it might come in handy." Nelly's eyes twinkled. "He was right."

Marilyn arrived last, carrying a folder of historical society documents. "Reference materials," she explained. "In case we need to identify artifacts. And I brought this." She held up a high-resolution camera. "For documentation."

They waited until nearly eleven, when the festival crowds had dispersed and the town had quieted, before setting out. They took Nelly's SUV, parking a block away from the Wilkins Building on a side street with minimal lighting.

The building loomed against the night sky, its windows dark, construction equipment creating strange shadows around its perimeter. A chain-link fence surrounded the site, with a single floodlight illuminating the main entrance gate.

"There," Nelly pointed to a corner of the fence partially obscured by overgrown shrubbery. "That's our entry point. Less visible from the street."

They moved quietly, staying in the shadows. Nelly led the way, demonstrating surprising agility for her age as she held back the fence where a section had been loosened, creating a gap just wide enough to slip through.

"Security guard trick number one," she whispered as they all made it inside the perimeter. "Always check the entire fence line. There's always a weak spot."

They crouched behind a stack of construction materials, getting their bearings. The building's main entrance was locked with a heavy padlock, but Nelly pointed to a basement window that had been partially boarded over.

"Service access," she explained. "Often overlooked in security protocols."

Using one of the pry bars, she carefully removed the loose boards, revealing a window large enough to crawl through. The glass had already been removed for the renovation, making their entry easier.

"I'll go first," Julie said, clicking on a flashlight and shining it into the darkness below. She could make out a concrete floor about six feet down. "Seems clear."

She maneuvered through the opening and dropped lightly to the floor, immediately pressing herself against the wall and scanning the basement. It was cluttered with construction debris and old equipment, but appeared empty of people. She signaled the others to follow.

Once all four women were inside, they took a moment to orient themselves using the map from Derek's phone, which Julie had printed and studied carefully.

"Northwest corner," she whispered, pointing. "That's where the foreman mentioned finding unusual structural features."

They moved through the basement carefully, flashlight beams sweeping over crumbling plaster and exposed beams. Decades of renovations had altered the space, making it difficult to reconcile with the simple hand-drawn map.

"Wait," Marilyn said suddenly, pointing her light at the floor. "Look at the dust pattern."

A faint trail was visible in the thick dust, as if something—or someone—had been dragged through recently.

"Someone's been here," Eliza whispered uneasily.

They followed the dust trail to the northwest corner, where it disappeared at what appeared to be a solid brick wall.

"This doesn't make sense," Julie said, running her hand over the bricks. "The trail ends here, but there's nowhere to go."

Nelly shone her light slowly over the entire wall, then stopped at a section where the mortar pattern changed subtly. "There," she said. "See how these bricks don't quite match the others? Classic false wall construction."

Julie examined the area Nelly indicated. The bricks did look slightly different—newer, perhaps, or at least repointed more recently than the surrounding masonry.

"How do we get through?" she asked.

"In my experience," Nelly replied, "false walls usually have a trigger mechanism. Something that doesn't look like a trigger. A brick that moves, a sconce that turns..."

They began carefully examining the wall and surrounding area. Minutes passed with no success, and Julie was beginning to lose hope when her hand brushed against an oddly shaped protrusion in one of the wooden support beams near the wall.

"There's something here," she said, turning her flashlight on it. Carved into the beam was a small symbol—what looked like intertwined threads forming a knot pattern.

"A weaver's knot," Marilyn breathed. "The Wilkins family were weavers originally, before they expanded into other textiles."

Julie pressed the symbol, but nothing happened. She tried turning it, pulling it, pushing it in different directions.

"Patterns," she muttered, remembering the fragment she'd found in the journal. "Hidden where only those who understand patterns will find it."

She studied the knot symbol more carefully, noting how the threads crossed over and under each other in a specific sequence. Then she looked at the bricks in the false wall, seeing them with new eyes—not as individual bricks, but as part of a pattern.

"I think I understand," she said slowly. "It's not just one trigger. It's a sequence." She pointed to specific bricks that, if connected by imaginary lines, formed the same knot pattern as the symbol. "We need to press these bricks in the right order—following the pattern of the weaver's knot."

Starting at what she believed was the beginning of the sequence, Julie pressed the bricks one by one, following the over-under pattern of the knot. When she pressed the final brick, they heard a faint click, and a section of the wall swung inward a few inches.

"You did it," Eliza whispered, sounding both impressed and terrified.

Julie pulled the concealed door open wider, revealing a hidden room beyond. They entered cautiously, flashlight beams cutting through decades of undisturbed darkness.

The space was smaller than Julie had expected—perhaps fifteen feet square—with no windows and a low ceiling. But what took her breath away were the display cases lining the walls. Glass-fronted cabinets, clearly designed to showcase artifacts, stood in neat rows.

Every one of them was empty.

"We're too late," Eliza said, her voice echoing in the small room. "The collection is gone."

"Wait," Marilyn said, approaching one of the cases. "Look at this." She pointed to the glass surface, which showed clear finger marks in the dust. "These cases were opened recently. Very recently."

Julie examined another case, noticing the same thing—dust disturbed in patterns that suggested careful handling, not decades of abandonment.

"The mayor," she said. "She must have already moved the collection. That's why she's accelerating the timeline and planning a big announcement."

Nelly was examining the floor, where scuff marks indicated something heavy had been dragged toward the entrance. "These marks are fresh," she confirmed. "I'd guess within the last week."

Marilyn had begun photographing the room meticulously—the empty cases, the dust patterns, the hidden entrance mechanism. "Evidence," she explained. "We may not have found the collection, but we've confirmed it existed and was hidden here."

"And recently removed," Julie added, a new realization dawning. "Victoria must have found this place shortly before she died. That's why she was so intent on buying the building—she'd discovered the hidden room but needed legal access to recover the artifacts."

"And if Mayor Johnson found out Victoria knew about the collection..." Eliza let the implication hang in the air.

"It gives her a motive for murder," Nelly finished grimly.

They continued searching the room, looking for any overlooked clues about where the artifacts might have been taken. Julie found a small leather-bound notebook that had fallen behind one of the display cases. Its pages were filled with handwritten inventory lists, dating back to the 1960s.

"The collection manifest," Marilyn said excitedly, examining it. "This proves what was here. Letters from the founding families, jewelry, maps, diaries—including the complete Wilkins journal."

"The complete journal?" Julie echoed. "So the missing pages..."

"Were probably part of what was stolen," Marilyn confirmed. "Pages that might have revealed the Johnson family's role in some historical wrongdoing."

A sudden noise from outside the hidden room made them all freeze—footsteps, moving through the basement toward them.

"The security guard," Nelly whispered. "Must be making his rounds."

They switched off their flashlights immediately, plunging the hidden room into darkness. Julie's heart pounded as the footsteps grew closer, then stopped just outside the false wall.

"I know someone's in there," a man's voice called. "Come out now."

Julie exchanged panicked glances with the others, barely visible in the dim light filtering through the partially open door. They were trapped.

"Should we run for it?" Eliza mouthed.

Before anyone could decide, the hidden door swung open fully, and a flashlight beam swept the room, illuminating their faces one by one.

"Well," said Edward Thompson, lowering the flashlight slightly. "This is an interesting development."

Chapter 17

Double Stitch

Julie awoke to the sound of knocking, sharp and insistent. She blinked groggily, trying to orient herself. After the late-night expedition to the Wilkins Building and the shocking encounter with Edward Thompson, she had collapsed into bed sometime after 2 AM, her mind racing with questions.

The knocking came again, more forceful this time. Glancing at her phone, she saw it was barely 7:30 in the morning. She pulled on a robe and made her way to the door, checking the peephole cautiously.

Sheriff Harris stood in the hallway, flanked by two deputies. His expression was grim.

Julie's heart sank. Had Thompson reported their trespassing? She opened the door, trying to project a calm she didn't feel.

"Sheriff Harris," she said. "This is early for a social call."

The sheriff didn't return her attempt at lightness. "Julie Morgan," he said formally, "I have a warrant for your arrest in connection with the murder of Victoria Winters."

Julie's knees nearly buckled. "What? That's ridiculous!"

One of the deputies stepped forward, handcuffs ready. Sheriff Harris held up a hand, stopping him. "Due to your standing in the community, I'm not going to cuff you unless you give me a reason to. But you need to come with us now."

"This is insane," Julie protested, her mind racing. "I didn't kill Victoria. You know that."

"What I know," Harris replied evenly, "is that we found the murder weapon early this morning, disposed of in your building's trash chute. A heavy decorative paperweight that matches the injuries to Ms. Winters' skull."

Julie felt the blood drain from her face. "That doesn't mean I put it there. Anyone could have accessed that trash chute."

"The weapon was wrapped in a distinctive hand-knit cloth," Harris continued, his eyes never leaving her face. "Blue gradient coloring, intricate cable pattern. From what I understand, it's your signature style."

Julie's mouth went dry. Someone had gone to great lengths to frame her, and they knew enough about her work to make it convincing.

"I need to get dressed," she said finally. "And call a lawyer."

Harris nodded. "You have five minutes to dress. You can call a lawyer from the station."

One of the deputies remained by the door while Julie retreated to her bedroom. With shaking hands, she pulled on jeans and a sweater, her mind racing. Who would go to such lengths to frame her? And why now?

As she gathered her phone and wallet, she sent a quick group text to Eliza, Nelly, and Marilyn: "Being arrested. Murder weapon found. I'm being framed. Call Berenson Law Firm."

When Julie emerged from her bedroom, Sheriff Harris was examining the books on her shelf with apparent interest.

"You have an impressive collection of local history," he commented.

"Is that a crime now too?" Julie asked, unable to keep the bitterness from her voice.

"Just an observation," Harris replied mildly. "Let's go."

They led her through the apartment building to the front entrance. As they emerged onto the street, Julie spotted Dr. David Walker across the road, standing perfectly still, watching the proceedings with an unreadable expression. Their eyes met briefly before Walker turned and walked away.

The short drive to the sheriff's office was conducted in silence. Julie stared out the window at Meadowgrove passing by—the festival decorations still hanging in the square, locals going about their Sunday morning routines, completely unaware that their neighbor was being arrested for murder.

At the station, Julie expected to be processed immediately—fingerprints, mugshot, the humiliating works. Instead, Sheriff Harris led her past the main desk to a small conference room at the back of the building.

"Have a seat, Ms. Morgan," he said, closing the door behind them. They were alone.

Julie remained standing. "I want to call my lawyer now."

"In a moment," Harris said. His tone had changed, the official edge softening. "First, we need to talk—off the record."

Julie frowned, confused by the shift. "I don't understand."

Harris pulled out a chair and sat, gesturing for her to do the same. After a moment's hesitation, Julie complied.

"I had your apartment building under surveillance last night," Harris said without preamble. "We have footage of someone entering around 4 AM, carrying a package that matches the dimensions of the murder weapon we found."

Julie leaned forward. "So you know I didn't put it there?"

"I strongly suspected the evidence was planted," Harris confirmed. "Which is why this arrest is, shall we say, not entirely genuine."

"What are you talking about?"

Harris leaned back, studying her. "Let's be honest with each other, Ms. Morgan. You've been conducting your own investigation into Victoria Winters' death—not very subtly, I might add. You've been asking questions around town, examining old journals, even breaking into construction sites."

Julie tensed. "If you knew about last night—"

"I know a lot of things," Harris interrupted. "Including the fact that your amateur sleuthing has uncovered connections I initially missed. The Meadowgrove Collection, the Johnson family's possible involvement, Victoria's true interest in the Wilkins Building—you've been busy."

"So why am I here?" Julie asked cautiously.

"Because someone is clearly getting nervous about how much you've discovered. Nervous enough to try framing you for murder." Harris leaned forward. "I want to use that nervousness. Your very public arrest this morning will make them think they've succeeded in diverting attention from themselves."

"You're using me as bait," Julie realized.

"I prefer to think of it as a strategic partnership," Harris corrected. "You have information I need. I have the authority to pursue it officially."

Julie considered this unexpected turn. "So I'm not actually being charged?"

"Oh, you're being charged—on paper. We need to make this look completely legitimate. But no, I don't believe you killed Victoria Winters." Harris gave her a wry smile. "I don't think you're the type to bash someone's head in with a paperweight, Ms. Morgan. And even if you were, you're certainly too smart to wrap it in your own distinctive knitting work."

Despite the gravity of the situation, Julie felt a hysterical laugh bubble up. "I don't know whether to be relieved or offended."

"Be practical," Harris suggested. "Tell me everything you know, and let's figure out who's really behind all this."

Julie hesitated, still not entirely convinced she could trust the sheriff. But what choice did she have?

"I need assurances," she said. "My friends—Eliza, Nelly, Marilyn —they need to know I'm okay. And Edward Thompson was at the Wilkins Building last night. He saw us there."

"Taken care of," Harris said, sliding his phone across the table. It showed a text conversation with Deputy Chen, instructing him to visit each of Julie's friends and explain the situation confidentially. "As for Thompson, hc's currently being interviewed in the next room. Been there since six this morning."

"You've been busy," Julie said, impressed despite herself.

"I take murder in my town very seriously, Ms. Morgan." Harris's expression hardened. "Now, I've shown good faith. Your turn."

Julie took a deep breath and began to talk. She explained everything—finding the Wilkins journal, the connection to Victoria's death, Derek's revelation about Victoria's true purpose in Meadowgrove, the discovery of the hidden room in the Wilkins Building, and Mayor Johnson's announcement about unveiling "historical treasures" the next day.

Harris listened without interrupting, occasionally making notes. When Julie finished, he studied his notepad thoughtfully.

"So we have a stolen historical collection, a decades-old family rivalry, a wealthy developer murdered just as she discovers the truth, and a mayor planning to use recovered artifacts for political gain." He shook his head. "It's like something from a novel."

"But it's real," Julie insisted. "And someone is willing to kill to keep it that way."

"The question is who," Harris said. "Let's review what we know for certain."

He stood and moved to a whiteboard mounted on the wall, uncapping a marker. He wrote "VICTORIA WINTERS" at the top, then began listing facts beneath it.

"Victoria came to Meadowgrove ostensibly for property development, but was actually searching for the Meadowgrove Collection, stolen in 1965."

"She found evidence connecting the Johnson family to the theft," Julie added.

Harris nodded, adding this to the board. "She approached Mayor Johnson about it, and according to the letter Derek photographed, Johnson was willing to 'make a deal.'"

"But before that deal could happen, Victoria ended up dead," Julie continued. "Initially staged to look like an accident."

"And now someone is trying to frame you for her murder," Harris finished, writing this down. "Let's move to the Meadowgrove Collection itself."

He started a new column. "Stolen in 1965. Originally blamed on the curator, Harrison Wilkins, but suspicion later fell on the Johnson family, though nothing was proven."

"Hidden in a secret room in the Wilkins Building for decades," Julie added.

"But recently moved," Harris noted. "Around the time of Victoria's death, based on the dust patterns you observed."

"And now Mayor Johnson is planning to 'discover' the collection publicly, probably presenting a carefully edited version that excludes anything incriminating to her family."

Harris tapped the marker against his chin, studying the board. "But there's something off about this narrative. If Mayor Johnson killed Victoria to protect her family's secret, why draw attention to the collection now? Why not keep it hidden?"

Julie frowned, considering this. "Maybe she's trying to get ahead of the story? If she controls how the collection is 'discovered,' she can control the narrative."

"Possibly," Harris conceded. "But it's a risky move. Especially with Victoria's assistant—this Derek—still out there somewhere with evidence."

"Unless she doesn't know about Derek," Julie suggested. "He said he's been hiding since Victoria's death."

Harris turned to face her fully. "What do we know about Derek, really? You said he claimed to be Victoria's nephew and assistant, but have you verified that?"

Julie hesitated. "No. We only have his word."

"And he conveniently left his phone with you—a phone containing photos of documents that implicate Mayor Johnson."

"You think Derek is involved somehow?" Julie asked, beginning to see where Harris was going.

"I think," Harris said carefully, "that we may have been too quick to accept the historical rivalry as the central motive. What if the real motive is more immediate? What if this is about money, not history?"

Julie's mind raced, connecting dots in a new pattern. "Victoria was wealthy. She was planning a major development project."

"A project that would have brought millions of dollars to Meadowgrove," Harris confirmed. "And to whoever was partnering with her."

"Mayor Johnson," Julie said. "She was supporting the development publicly."

"And Dr. Walker admitted to you that Victoria was blackmailing him for his vote on the town council," Harris added, writing this on the board.

A new possibility began to take shape in Julie's mind. "What if someone was using the historical controversy to manipulate both Victoria and Mayor Johnson? Someone who knew about the collection and its significance."

"Someone who stood to benefit financially from Victoria's development plans," Harris suggested.

"Or someone who wanted to prevent those plans," Julie countered.

Harris stepped back from the whiteboard, surveying their work. "We've been assuming the missing artifacts and Victoria's murder are connected because she was searching for them. But what if the connection is more complex?"

"A con," Julie said suddenly, the pieces clicking into place. "What if both Victoria and Mayor Johnson are victims of a sophisticated con? Someone using the collection as leverage for financial gain?"

Harris nodded slowly. "Victoria comes to town looking for the artifacts. Mayor Johnson is willing to negotiate about them. But a third party intervenes, eliminating Victoria and framing both you and potentially the mayor in the process."

"But who would have the historical knowledge to pull this off?" Julie wondered. "The collection has been hidden for decades."

"Someone who'd researched Meadowgrove's history extensively," Harris suggested. "Someone who knew about the hidden room in the Wilkins Building."

A chill ran down Julie's spine. "Edward Thompson. He's supposedly a professor researching local history, but we never verified his credentials. And he was at the Wilkins Building last night, acting as if he belonged there."

"He also asked specifically about the Wilkins journal when you first met him," Harris recalled from Julie's account. "And he was talking to the construction foreman yesterday about the 'unusual structural features' in the basement."

Julie remembered something else. "When we first spoke about Victoria's death, he seemed to know details that weren't public—like the fact that it wasn't a simple accident."

Harris was already heading for the door. "I need to continue that interview with Professor Thompson. In the meantime, you're staying here—for your own protection as much as for appearances."

"Wait," Julie called. "What about Dr. Walker? He was outside my apartment this morning, watching me being arrested."

Harris paused. "Walker is... complicated. He's been cooperative with the investigation, but he's definitely hiding something." He checked his watch. "I need to get back to Thompson before he lawyers up. I'll have Deputy Chen bring you some coffee and something to eat."

As Harris left, Julie sank back in her chair, mind whirling. The narrative was shifting, the pattern rearranging itself into something she hadn't anticipated. If Thompson was behind this elaborate scheme, what was his endgame? And why target her specifically?

She remembered his words from their first meeting: "History has a way of being forgotten when it's convenient. Or selectively remembered." At the time, she'd thought he was speaking generally. Now, it sounded like a confession.

Deputy Chen brought coffee and a muffin from the café across the street, along with reassurances that he'd spoken to Eliza and explained the situation. Julie thanked him, then returned to studying the whiteboard, searching for connections they might have missed.

One question kept nagging at her: if Edward Thompson was their prime suspect, why had someone gone to such lengths to frame her? Was it simply because she was getting too close to the truth, or was there something more personal at play?

The timeline bothered her too. Victoria had died before Julie even found the Wilkins journal. If her murder was part of a con centered around the collection, why kill her before she'd made any progress in recovering the artifacts?

Unless... Victoria had made progress. She'd found the hidden room, perhaps even removed some items before her death. But then why leave the display cases behind?

Julie was still puzzling over these questions when the door opened and Sheriff Harris returned. The grim set of his jaw told her something was wrong.

"Thompson's gone," he said without preamble. "My deputy stepped out to take a call, and when he returned, Thompson had vanished. Left nothing behind except this." He tossed a small object onto the table.

It was a wooden button, intricately carved to look like an oak leaf. Julie recognized it immediately as one of the set Thompson had purchased from her shop during the festival.

"He left it deliberately," she said. "A message."

"Or a taunt," Harris agreed. "I've put out an APB, but he had at least a fifteen-minute head start."

Julie picked up the button, turning it over in her hand. "This is from a local artisan—Tom Blackwood. His woodworking studio is just outside town."

Harris was already reaching for his phone. "We need to check if Thompson went there. Blackwood might have information about him."

As Harris made the call, Julie continued to examine the button. Something about it seemed odd—the weight didn't match the others she remembered from the set. On closer inspection, she realized the back had been hollowed out slightly and fitted with what looked like a tiny SD card.

"Sheriff," she interrupted. "There's something inside this button."

Harris ended his call and took the button from her, extracting the SD card with a pocketknife. "Clever hiding place," he muttered, examining the tiny card. "Let's see what Professor Thompson thought was worth concealing this way."

He left to retrieve a laptop, returning moments later and inserting the card. They huddled together, watching as the screen displayed a folder containing dozens of files—photographs, documents, and video recordings.

"My God," Harris breathed as they began opening the files. "This is..."

"Evidence," Julie finished. "But not what we expected."

The first document was a detailed dossier on Victoria Winters, including financial records showing massive debt hidden behind her wealthy façade. The development project in Meadowgrove wasn't just a business venture—it was a desperate attempt to salvage her crumbling empire.

The next file contained surveillance photos of Victoria meeting with Mayor Johnson at the cabin, weeks before her death. The accompanying audio recording revealed a heated argument about the Meadowgrove Collection and its potential value.

"I want what's rightfully mine," Victoria's voice came through clearly. "My grandmother's journals prove your family stole those artifacts. If you want this development project to revitalize your dying town, you'll give me what I came for."

"Those artifacts don't legally exist," the mayor's voice responded. "They were never found. Never recovered. You have no claim to them."

"Then I'll go public with what I know," Victoria threatened. "How do you think the voters will react to learning your family has been hiding stolen historical treasures for generations? Your reelection chances would vanish overnight."

"And your development permits would vanish with them," Johnson countered. "We both have something to lose here, Victoria. Be smart. There's a way we can both win."

The recording ended there. Julie and Sheriff Harris sat in stunned silence for a moment.

"So Victoria was blackmailing the mayor just like she was blackmailing Dr. Walker," Julie said finally. "Using the collection as leverage to push through her development plans."

"And the mayor was willing to negotiate," Harris added. "Probably planning to 'discover' a portion of the collection, giving Victoria enough to satisfy her while keeping anything truly damaging to the Johnson family hidden."

The next file was even more shocking—a video dated the night of Victoria's death. The quality was poor, clearly taken from a hidden camera, but the content was unmistakable: Derek, Victoria's supposed nephew and assistant, arguing violently with her in the cabin living room.

"You promised me a cut!" Derek shouted. "Fifty percent of everything. That was our deal when I brought you my grandmother's journals."

"Plans change," Victoria replied coldly. "The development project is more complex than anticipated. Your cut is now twenty percent."

"That's not acceptable," Derek snarled. "I'm the one who located the collection. I'm the one who connected it to the Johnson family. Without me, you'd have nothing!"

"Without me, you'd still be a small-time con artist working tourist towns," Victoria shot back. "This is my operation now. Twenty percent or nothing."

The video showed Derek advancing on Victoria, his face contorted with rage. She backed up toward the stairs, reaching for something on a nearby table—a heavy decorative paperweight. But before she could grasp it, Derek lunged forward. There was a struggle, and Victoria fell backward down the stairs. Derek stood frozen for a moment, then descended slowly after her.

The video ended abruptly.

"Derek killed her," Julie whispered. "It was an accident during an argument, but then he staged it to look like she'd simply fallen."

"And Thompson was recording it all," Harris said, opening the next file. "Look at this—documents showing Derek's real identity. Multiple aliases, arrests for fraud in three states. He's no relation to Victoria at all. They were partners in a con."

"A con that went wrong when Victoria tried to cut his share," Julie said, pieces falling rapidly into place. "But where does Thompson fit in? Was he blackmailing Derek?"

The final file answered that question—a series of emails between Thompson and Victoria dating back six months, discussing the Meadowgrove Collection and its potential value. Thompson had been working with Victoria from the beginning, using his academic credentials to research the collection's whereabouts.

"So Thompson, Victoria, and Derek were all working together initially," Harris summarized. "Thompson provided the historical research, Victoria provided the financing and business connections, and Derek... what exactly was Derek's role?"

Julie thought back to what Derek had told them. "He said he brought Victoria his grandmother's journals. What if that was true? What if his grandmother really was from Meadowgrove and had information about the theft?"

"Making him the perfect inside man for their con," Harris agreed. "But then Victoria died, Thompson lost his financial backer, and Derek went into hiding, afraid he'd be blamed for her death."

"Which left Thompson to salvage what he could of the operation," Julie continued. "Including trying to locate the collection on his own."

"And frame you for Victoria's murder to divert attention," Harris added. "But why you specifically?"

Julie stared at the evidence spread across the laptop screen, her mind racing. "Because I found the Wilkins journal. Because I was asking questions about Victoria's death. Because I was getting too close to the truth."

"But the con itself... what was the endgame?" Harris wondered. "Just recovering the collection?"

Julie shook her head slowly. "The collection itself might be valuable to historians, but it's not worth millions. I think the real target was the land—the Wilkins Building and surrounding properties. Victoria's development project would have sent real estate values skyrocketing."

"And Mayor Johnson was supporting it publicly," Harris noted. "Despite knowing Victoria was blackmailing her about the collection."

"Because the development would benefit her too—both politically and financially," Julie concluded. "It was a win-win, once they worked out a deal about the artifacts."

Harris sat back, running a hand through his hair. "So we have a con artist who accidentally killed his partner, another con artist who's trying to salvage the operation by framing you for the murder, and a mayor who's about to publicly 'discover' stolen artifacts that have been hidden for decades—artifacts that are now evidence in a murder investigation."

"When you put it that way," Julie said with a grim smile, "it almost makes our breaking and entering at the Wilkins Building seem reasonable."

"Speaking of which," Harris said, checking his watch, "the mayor's press conference is scheduled for tomorrow morning. If Thompson hasn't skipped town entirely, that's where he'll be. It's his last chance to get something out of this mess."

"So what's our next move?" Julie asked.

Harris closed the laptop and stood. "First, we find Derek. He's our key witness, and according to this evidence, the actual killer—accidental or not. Then we have a conversation with Mayor Johnson about her plans for tomorrow's announcement."

"And me? Am I still under arrest?"

"Officially, yes," Harris said. "Unofficially, I need your help. You know the players in this better than anyone. But," he added firmly, "you follow my lead and take no risks. Clear?"

Julie nodded, relief washing over her. The pattern was finally emerging clearly—not the centuries-old family rivalry she'd initially suspected, but something far more modern and mundane: greed, deception, and the lengths people would go to for money and power.

As Sheriff Harris left to organize the search for Derek, Julie remained in the conference room, studying the wooden button Thompson had left behind. A deliberate clue, but why? Was it merely arrogance, or was there something more to it? Perhaps the professor wasn't quite finished with his game yet.

She picked up the button, running her thumb over the intricate oak leaf carving. Tom Blackwood's craftsmanship was distinctive—a knitter recognized another artisan's patterns instinctively. And as with knitting, sometimes the most revealing aspect of a pattern was not what was shown, but what was deliberately concealed.

Thompson had hidden evidence in the button. What else might he have hidden, and where? The answers, Julie suspected, would be found at the Wilkins Building tomorrow, when Mayor Johnson unveiled her "discovery" to the world. And she intended to be there when it happened, officially under arrest or not.

Chapter 18
Casting Off the Disguise

The late afternoon sun cast long shadows through the blinds of Sheriff Harris's office as he and Julie finalized their plan. After hours of reviewing the evidence on Thompson's SD card, they had a clearer picture of the con, but still needed to catch the perpetrators.

"So we're agreed," Harris said, closing the case file on his desk. "You'll be released, but we'll maintain the fiction that you're still under suspicion. You'll wear this." He handed her a small ankle monitor. "It's not activated—just for show in case anyone's watching."

Julie examined the device with distaste. "And you're sure this is necessary?"

"If Thompson is still in town, he needs to believe his frame job is working," Harris explained. "That gives us room to maneuver while we track him down."

"And Derek?"

"We've got deputies checking all the motels and rental cabins within twenty miles," Harris assured her. "If he's still in the area, we'll find him."

Julie nodded, strapping the fake monitor around her ankle. "What about Mayor Johnson's press conference tomorrow?"

"I'll be there, along with several plainclothes deputies. If Thompson shows up, we'll be ready." Harris leaned back in his chair. "In the meantime, go home, rest, and act normal—well, as normal as someone under suspicion for murder can act. I'll have a deputy watching your apartment discreetly."

"I don't think I can just sit and wait," Julie admitted. "My friends will have questions. And I need to check on The Yarn Haven—tomorrow's a business day."

Harris sighed. "Fine. You can meet with your friends and open your shop. But be careful what you say. We don't know who might be listening."

"Understood." Julie stood, adjusting her pant leg to partially conceal the monitor. "When should I check in?"

"Deputy Chen will come by your shop around closing time. Any developments before then, call my direct line." He handed her a business card with a number scrawled on the back. "And Julie? Don't do anything heroic. You've already had one close call with those brake lines."

The reminder sent a chill through her. "Trust me, I have no desire to be a hero. I just want this to be over."

Harris escorted her through the station, maintaining a stern expression for the benefit of anyone watching. At the front entrance, he spoke loudly enough for the desk sergeant to hear: "Don't leave town, Ms. Morgan. We'll be in touch about your case."

Outside, Julie blinked in the late afternoon sunlight, momentarily disoriented. After the intensity of the past twenty-four hours, the normalcy of Meadowgrove's main street seemed surreal. Festival cleanup was underway, workers dismantling booths and collecting banners that had hung across the street just yesterday.

She checked her phone, finding a flood of texts from Eliza, Nelly, and Marilyn, all expressing concern and confusion. She sent a group message: "I'm OK. Released but still 'under suspicion.' Meeting at my place in one hour?"

The responses came immediately—all affirmative. Julie walked home slowly, aware that she might be under observation. The fake ankle monitor felt uncomfortably real against her skin, a constant reminder of how quickly her life had unraveled.

When she reached her apartment, she was surprised to find her door unlocked. Cautiously pushing it open, she was met by the sight of Eliza, Nelly, and Marilyn already inside, seated around her dining table.

"How did you—" she began.

"Spare key," Eliza explained, rising to embrace her. "Remember when you gave me one last winter during that ice storm? We figured you wouldn't mind, under the circumstances."

"We've been worried sick," Nelly added. "That deputy told us you were safe, but he was remarkably short on details."

"And we've made some discoveries of our own," Marilyn said, gesturing to a stack of printouts on the table.

Julie locked the door behind her and joined them. "I have a lot to tell you, but first—" she lifted her pant leg to reveal the ankle monitor. "This is just for show. Sheriff Harris and I are working together now."

She quickly explained the developments of the day—Thompson's planted evidence, his subsequent disappearance, and the revelation that Derek had accidentally killed Victoria during an argument.

"So it really was a con all along," Eliza said when Julie finished. "Not some historical family rivalry."

"The historical element was just leverage," Julie confirmed. "Victoria and her partners were using the town's secrets to manipulate people and push through the development deal. But when Victoria tried to reduce Derek's cut, things went sideways."

"Speaking of partners," Marilyn said, pushing the stack of printouts toward Julie, "I made a few calls to some colleagues at the historical society conference I attended last spring. Edward Thompson isn't who he claims to be."

Julie picked up the top sheet, which showed a university faculty directory. "What am I looking at?"

"The real Edward Thompson," Marilyn explained. "Professor of American History at Dartmouth College. Currently on sabbatical in Europe, where he's been for the past year."

"So our Thompson is an impostor," Julie breathed, pieces clicking into place.

"It gets better," Nelly added. "Marilyn also looked into Victoria's background."

Marilyn nodded, pulling out another document. "Victoria Winters was married briefly in her twenties to a man named Gregory Thomas—not Thompson. He died two years ago in Florida."

"So that whole story about being her ex-husband..."

"Complete fabrication," Marilyn confirmed. "Designed to give him a plausible reason for being in Meadowgrove asking questions about Victoria and the collection."

Julie sat back, processing this new information. "Sheriff Harris needs to know this. It confirms Thompson isn't just a partner in Victoria's scheme—he's something else entirely."

"A thief," Nelly suggested. "After the collection itself, not the land deal."

"But how did he know about the collection in the first place?" Eliza wondered. "If he's not connected to Victoria or Meadowgrove?"

"That's still the missing piece," Julie admitted. "But we know he's planning something at tomorrow's press conference. The mayor is set to 'discover' artifacts that Thompson likely helped relocate from the hidden room."

"So we need a trap," Nelly said decisively. "Draw him out before he can make his move."

Julie nodded slowly, an idea forming. "What if word got around that I discovered something important before my arrest? Something about where Victoria might have hidden other artifacts."

"Bait," Eliza said, catching on. "Make Thompson think you found something he needs."

"Exactly." Julie turned to Marilyn. "You're still working the historical society booth for the festival wrap-up tomorrow, right? You could casually mention to a few people that I found evidence in the Wilkins journal pointing to a second hiding place."

"I could definitely do that," Marilyn agreed. "People are already gossiping about your arrest. This would spread like wildfire."

"And I'll talk to some of my old bridge club friends," Nelly added. "Those women can distribute information faster than the internet."

"What do we say I found, exactly?" Julie asked.

"It needs to be specific enough to sound legitimate but vague enough that Thompson would need to question you directly to learn more," Eliza mused.

"How about this," Marilyn suggested. "The journal mentioned a 'heart of the treasure' that was kept separately from the main collection. Something particularly valuable that Victoria discovered before her death."

"Perfect," Julie agreed. "And we hint that I know where it is—or at least have discovered clues from the journal."

They spent the next hour refining the details of their story and planning how to spread it through town. As they were finishing, Julie's doorbell rang. Everyone tensed.

"Are you expecting someone?" Eliza whispered.

Julie shook her head, moving cautiously to check the peephole. "It's Dr. Walker," she said, surprised.

"Should we let him in?" Nelly asked dubiously.

Julie hesitated, then nodded. "Yes. I want to hear what he has to say." She opened the door, keeping her expression neutral. "Dr. Walker. This is unexpected."

The doctor stood awkwardly in the hallway, hands thrust into his coat pockets. "I... saw you were released. May I come in? There's something important I need to tell you."

Julie stepped aside, allowing him to enter. Walker nodded politely to the other women, clearly uncomfortable finding them there.

"Perhaps we could speak privately?" he suggested.

"Whatever you have to say, you can say in front of my friends," Julie replied firmly. "We don't have secrets."

Walker sighed, removing his glasses and cleaning them nervously with his handkerchief. "Very well. I've been... less than forthcoming about certain matters. About Edward Thompson specifically."

Everyone straightened, suddenly alert.

"You know him?" Julie asked.

"Not as Thompson, no. But I recognized him the moment I saw him in town." Walker replaced his glasses, his expression grave. "Before I moved to Meadowgrove five years ago, I had a practice in Boston. One of my patients was a man named Richard Ellison—at least, that was the name he used then. He was injured during what police later determined was an attempted theft from a private art collection."

"Thompson is Ellison," Julie said, not a question.

Walker nodded. "He's a notorious art and antiquities thief. Specializes in items with historical significance that can be sold to private collectors who don't ask questions. I treated him for a broken wrist and contusions—nothing that required hospitalization. But I spent enough time with him to remember his face, even years later."

"Why didn't you say something when he first arrived in town?" Eliza demanded.

"Patient confidentiality," Walker replied. "I legally couldn't disclose his identity based solely on recognizing a former patient. And I had no proof he was here for illegitimate purposes. But after your arrest this morning..." He turned to Julie. "I knew something was wrong. You're not a killer."

"So you decided to break confidentiality now?" Julie asked.

"I'm not here as a doctor," Walker said carefully. "I'm here as a concerned citizen reporting a suspicion about a man I've seen around town who resembles someone connected to previous criminal activity. I have no medical records to share, no protected health information to disclose."

Julie understood he was being deliberate with his wording. "A semantic distinction, but I appreciate the risk you're taking." She gestured for him to sit. "What else can you tell us about him?"

Walker took a seat at the table. "Ellison—or Thompson as he's calling himself now—works with a network of specialists. He's not just a thief; he's a meticulous planner who researches his targets extensively before making a move. In Boston, he had infiltrated the victim's social circle months before the attempted theft."

"Like he did here with Victoria," Marilyn noted.

"Exactly," Walker agreed. "He identifies valuable targets and then constructs elaborate schemes to acquire them. Often involving manipulating people against each other."

"Like Victoria and Mayor Johnson," Julie said, pieces continuing to fall into place. "He probably fed information to both sides, playing them against each other."

"That would be consistent with his methods," Walker confirmed. "He's not violent by nature—the Boston incident turned physical only when he was caught by surprise. But he's ruthless about achieving his objectives."

"Did he work with a partner in Boston?" Julie asked, thinking of Derek.

"Not that I'm aware of. He seemed to be operating alone." Walker hesitated. "There's something else you should know. The items he attempted to steal in Boston were historically significant letters connected to the American Revolution. Extremely valuable to certain collectors, but not something casual thieves would target."

"Suggesting he already had a buyer lined up," Nelly concluded.

"Precisely," Walker said. "And I suspect the same is true here. The Meadowgrove Collection may seem like local memorabilia to us, but to the right collector, items connected to early American textile history could be worth millions."

Julie exchanged glances with her friends. "We're setting a trap for him," she explained to Walker. "Spreading word that I discovered information about a particularly valuable piece from the collection—something Victoria found before her death."

Walker nodded slowly. "That could work. He wouldn't be able to resist investigating."

"Will you help us?" Julie asked directly.

Walker seemed surprised by the question. "I... yes. Of course. What do you need me to do?"

"For now, just be another source for our story. Mention it at the clinic tomorrow, say you heard it from a reliable source."

"I can do that," Walker agreed. He stood, looking more resolute than when he'd arrived. "I should go. I have patients early tomorrow."

As Julie walked him to the door, Walker paused. "I'm sorry I didn't come forward sooner. I told myself patient confidentiality was paramount, but truthfully, I was afraid. Afraid of jeopardizing my practice, afraid of being wrong."

"You're here now," Julie said simply. "That's what matters."

After Walker left, the women regrouped around the table.

"Do we believe him?" Eliza asked.

"I do," Julie said after a moment's consideration. "His explanation makes sense, and it fills in gaps about Thompson's background."

"So now we have Thompson's true identity and his likely motive," Marilyn summarized. "He's after the collection to sell to a private buyer."

"Which means he needs to get to the artifacts before they're publicly displayed tomorrow," Julie added. "Once they're officially 'discovered,' they'll be too closely watched."

"So he'll either try to steal them tonight from wherever they're being stored, or he'll make his move during the initial confusion of the press conference tomorrow," Nelly reasoned.

"Either way, we need to inform Sheriff Harris immediately," Julie said, reaching for her phone.

After updating the sheriff with their new information about Thompson's true identity, the plan evolved further. Harris would have deputies watching the Wilkins Building overnight in case Thompson attempted to access the artifacts before the press conference. Meanwhile, Julie and her friends would continue spreading their story about Victoria finding a particularly valuable "heart of the treasure" not included with the main collection.

As evening fell, Eliza, Nelly, and Marilyn departed, each with their role to play in the morning. Julie locked her door, then double-checked the windows, acutely aware of her vulnerability. She tried to focus on practical matters—setting her alarm for early morning, laying out clothes for the next day, preparing a quick dinner—but her mind kept returning to Thompson.

What was the man truly after? If the Meadowgrove Collection was valuable primarily to specialized collectors, how had he learned about it in the first place? And what was his connection to Derek, who had claimed to have his grandmother's journals about the theft?

As Julie picked at her dinner, a new possibility occurred to her. What if Derek's story about his grandmother was true, but his partnership with Victoria was the fabrication? What if he had been working with Thompson all along, using Victoria for her resources and connections?

She called Sheriff Harris again, sharing her theory.

"It's plausible," Harris agreed over the phone. "It would explain why Derek disappeared after Victoria's death instead of coming forward about the accident. If he and Thompson were partners from the beginning, he'd be more concerned about protecting their con than clearing his name in what could be argued as manslaughter rather than murder."

"Have your deputies had any luck finding him?" Julie asked.

"Nothing yet. But if your theory is correct, he might not be hiding alone. He could be with Thompson, preparing for tomorrow."

After hanging up, Julie tried to sleep but found herself too wired. Instead, she pulled out the Wilkins journal again, rereading sections she had previously skimmed. In the clear light of what they now knew, certain passages took on new significance—particularly those describing the most valuable items in the family's collection.

One entry caught her attention: "Grandmother's sampler holds the key to our legacy, though few would recognize its worth. The pattern speaks to those who understand its language."

Julie had initially interpreted this as sentimental value, but now she wondered—what if it was literal? What if there was a key piece to the collection that unlocked something of greater value? Something that Thompson and his partner were really after?

By morning, Julie had barely slept, but adrenaline kept her alert as she prepared for the day ahead. She opened The Yarn Haven at the usual time, making a show of business as usual while wearing the fake ankle monitor visibly enough that customers couldn't help but notice.

Throughout the morning, she heard snippets of conversation—speculation about her arrest, whispers about Victoria's murder, and, most encouragingly, murmurs about a special artifact Julie had supposedly identified from the Wilkins journal. The story was spreading exactly as planned.

Around noon, Eliza arrived with lunch and an update. "It's working," she reported excitedly. "I've heard at least three people talking about the 'heart of the treasure' today. Marilyn says she's had several people approach her at the historical society table asking for details."

"Any sign of Thompson?" Julie asked.

"Not yet. But the press conference isn't until two."

As they ate, Julie shared her theory about the sampler mentioned in the journal. "What if there's something hidden in the pattern? A code or map of some kind?"

"It's possible," Eliza conceded. "Historic samplers often contained coded information—political messages, family secrets, even maps. Women used their needlework as a form of communication when they had few other outlets."

"Which means Thompson might not be after the collection itself, but what it can lead him to," Julie reasoned.

"Something even more valuable," Eliza agreed. "But what?"

Before they could speculate further, the shop door opened. Both women looked up, expecting a customer. Instead, Derek stood in the doorway, looking haggard and desperate.

"I need your help," he said without preamble.

Julie and Eliza froze, exchanging alarmed glances. Derek closed the door behind him, flipping the "Open" sign to "Closed."

"The police are looking for you," Julie said carefully, reaching slowly for her phone.

"I know," Derek replied. "And I'm going to turn myself in. But not until I stop Thompson. He's planning to steal the entire collection during the press conference today."

"Why should we believe anything you say?" Eliza demanded.

Derek ran a hand through his disheveled hair. "Because I'm the only one who knows what he's really after. And contrary to what he's told you, it's not the collection itself."

Julie's pulse quickened. "It's what the collection leads to."

Derek looked surprised. "How did you know?"

"The sampler mentioned in the journal," Julie said. "It contains a pattern that's actually a key or a map."

Derek nodded, something like respect flickering across his face. "My grandmother's journal mentioned it too. The Wilkins family didn't just make textiles—they were shipping magnates. During the Civil War, they transported goods for the Union Army, including gold shipments. One shipment never reached its destination—officially lost in a storm. But according to family legend..."

"They stole it themselves," Julie finished, the pieces finally coming together. "And the sampler contains directions to where it's hidden."

"Exactly," Derek confirmed. "My grandmother was a Wilkins descendant—a distant cousin of the main family line. Her journals contained fragments of the story, passed down through generations. When I learned Victoria was investigating Meadowgrove for development, I approached her with the information."

"And together you concocted a scheme to find the gold," Eliza said coldly.

Derek had the grace to look ashamed. "Initially, yes. But Victoria double-crossed me, bringing in Thompson as a so-called 'historical expert' without telling me his real expertise was in theft."

"So you didn't know Thompson before?" Julie asked skeptically.

"Not until Victoria introduced us. But I figured out what he was pretty quickly." Derek's expression darkened. "By then, Victoria was already cutting me out, reducing my share. We argued, and..." He trailed off.

"We saw the video," Julie said quietly. "From Thompson's hidden camera."

Derek looked stunned. "He was recording us? That son of a—" He broke off, composing himself. "So you know it was an accident. I never meant for her to fall."

"But you still staged it to look like a simple fall and fled the scene," Eliza pointed out.

"I panicked," Derek admitted. "And then when I went back to the cabin the next day, I found it ransacked. Thompson had been looking for my grandmother's journal—which I kept with me—and Victoria's notes. That's when I realized he was planning to cut me out completely."

"So you've been hiding ever since," Julie said.

Derek nodded. "Watching Thompson, trying to figure out his plan. He's manipulated everything—feeding information to both Victoria and Mayor Johnson, playing them against each other while he searched for the collection."

"And now he's planning to steal it during the press conference," Julie repeated. "How exactly?"

"He's created a diversion," Derek explained urgently. "Something to cause chaos during the mayor's announcement. While everyone's distracted, he'll take the key items—including the sampler—and disappear."

"What kind of diversion?" Eliza asked, alarmed.

"I don't know the details," Derek admitted. "But knowing Thompson, it will be elaborate and potentially dangerous."

Julie reached for her phone. "We need to call Sheriff Harris immediately."

"Wait," Derek pleaded. "You need me there. I'm the only one who knows which items Thompson is really after. Without me, he could still succeed."

Julie hesitated, then made her decision. "You're coming with us to the sheriff's office right now. You'll tell him everything you've told us, and then we'll figure out how to stop Thompson together."

Derek looked like he might argue, then his shoulders slumped in defeat. "Fine. Let's go."

As they led Derek out the back door toward Julie's car, she couldn't help but wonder if they were walking into yet another con. But with the press conference less than two hours away and Thompson preparing his move, they had little choice but to take the risk.

The final threads of the pattern were coming together, revealing a design far more complex and valuable than anyone had imagined. A design that had already led to one death and threatened to cause more if they couldn't unravel it in time.

Chapter 19

Weaving the Truth

The early morning light filtered through the windows of Sheriff Harris's office as Julie, Eliza, and Derek finished explaining everything they knew. The sheriff had listened intently, occasionally making notes, his expression growing more serious with each revelation.

"Let me get this straight," he said finally. "Thompson isn't just after the Meadowgrove Collection—he's after what it leads to: a lost Civil War gold shipment worth millions."

"That's what we believe," Julie confirmed. "Based on what Derek has told us and what I found in the Wilkins journal about a sampler containing some kind of encoded information."

Harris turned his attention to Derek, who sat uncomfortably in a chair by the wall, looking exhausted and resigned. "And you're willing to make a formal statement about Victoria Winters' death? Acknowledging your role in it?"

Derek nodded. "Yes. It was an accident—I never meant for her to fall—but I did stage it to look like a simple accident and fled the scene. I'll take responsibility for that."

"And your grandmother's connection to the Wilkins family? That part is true?"

"Yes," Derek insisted. "My grandmother was Margaret Wilkins before she married. A distant cousin of the main family line, but still privy to certain family secrets. Her journals are what started this whole thing."

Harris leaned back in his chair, digesting this information. "Do you have these journals with you now?"

Derek shook his head. "They're hidden in a storage locker outside town. I can take you there after we deal with Thompson."

"Convenient," Harris remarked dryly. "So we have no way to verify your claims about the gold."

"Look, I know how this sounds," Derek said, frustration evident in his voice. "But Thompson is the real threat here. He's planning something at the press conference today, and if we don't stop him, he'll get away with everything."

Harris checked his watch. "The press conference is at two. That gives us just over three hours to prepare." He reached into his desk drawer and pulled out a small black case. Opening it, he revealed what looked like a decorative brooch. "This is a recording device. Small but powerful, with a range of about fifty feet to our receiver."

"You want me to wear it," Julie guessed.

Harris nodded. "You've established yourself as a key player in this drama. Thompson clearly sees you as both a threat and a potential source of information. If he approaches you at the press conference, we'll have everything he says on record."

"And if he doesn't approach me?" Julie asked.

"Then we approach him," Harris said. "Or rather, you do. Your story about finding Victoria's documentation of the 'heart of the treasure' gives you the perfect reason to confront Mayor Johnson publicly—which should draw Thompson out."

Eliza frowned. "That sounds dangerous."

"She'll be surrounded by people, including several plainclothes deputies," Harris assured her. "And we'll have the building secured. Thompson won't be able to make a move without us knowing."

Julie studied the recording device. It was cleverly designed to look like a vintage knitting-themed brooch—a small pair of crossed needles with what appeared to be yarn balls that likely concealed the actual microphone. "It's perfect," she said. "No one would question me wearing something like this."

"What about me?" Derek asked. "What's my role?"

Harris's expression hardened. "You're staying here, under guard. You're still a suspect in Victoria's death, regardless of whether it was accidental or not."

"But I can identify the key artifacts Thompson is after!"

"Write them down," Harris instructed, sliding a pad and pen across the desk. "Every detail you can remember about what they look like and why they're important."

Derek looked like he wanted to argue further but seemed to think better of it. He took the pad and began writing.

"What about Nelly and Marilyn?" Julie asked. "They should be warned about the potential danger."

"I'll have deputies contact them," Harris promised. "Now, we need to go over the plan in detail. Julie, here's what you'll do..."

By one-thirty, the town square was bustling with activity. Though the Harvest Festival had officially ended the previous day, a sizable crowd had gathered for Mayor Johnson's press conference. Local media had set up cameras near the podium erected in front of town hall, and curious citizens milled about, speculating about the nature of the announcement.

Julie stood at the edge of the crowd, the recording brooch pinned prominently to her sweater. She had dressed carefully—professionally but subdued, appropriate for someone under suspicion of murder but determined to clear her name. The fake ankle monitor remained visible beneath her cropped pants, a detail Sheriff Harris had insisted on maintaining.

Eliza had reluctantly agreed to remain at The Yarn Haven, though she had extracted a promise from Julie to text her updates whenever possible. Nelly and Marilyn, briefed by deputies, were positioned strategically in the crowd, each with instructions to observe specific sections for any suspicious activity.

As Julie scanned the gathering, she spotted Dr. Walker near the back, his tall figure easy to distinguish. Their eyes met briefly, and he gave her a small, encouraging nod.

There was still no sign of Thompson, which made Julie increasingly uneasy. If they were right about his plans, he should be here somewhere, preparing for whatever diversion he had orchestrated.

At ten minutes to two, a side door of the town hall opened, and Mayor Johnson emerged, accompanied by her campaign manager,

Thomas Drake, and several staff members. Julie noticed the mayor looked tense, her usual confident smile strained at the edges.

It was now or never. Julie took a deep breath and moved toward the group before they reached the podium. "Mayor Johnson," she called, loud enough to be heard but not so loud as to cause a scene. "May I speak with you for a moment? Privately?"

The mayor turned, surprise quickly morphing into wariness when she recognized Julie. She whispered something to Drake, who frowned but nodded, then stepped toward Julie.

"Ms. Morgan," the mayor said coolly. "I was under the impression you were dealing with legal troubles."

"That's partly why I need to speak with you," Julie replied, keeping her voice low. "It concerns Victoria Winters and the announcement you're about to make."

Mayor Johnson's composure faltered for just a moment. "I don't see how those things are connected."

"They're connected through the Meadowgrove Collection," Julie said. "And what Victoria found before her death."

The mayor glanced around, noting the growing interest from nearby attendees. "Five minutes," she conceded. "In my office."

She led Julie through the side door and down a corridor to a well-appointed office. Once inside, she closed the door firmly and turned to face Julie, all pretense of politeness gone.

"What game are you playing, Ms. Morgan?" she demanded. "First you're arrested for Victoria's murder, now you're approaching me minutes before a major announcement?"

Julie decided to take a direct approach. "I know about your deal with Victoria regarding the Meadowgrove Collection. I found her documentation."

It was a bluff, but one based on the fragments of information they'd pieced together. The mayor's reaction would tell her whether they were on the right track.

Mayor Johnson paled visibly. "What documentation?"

"Notes detailing your arrangement," Julie continued, watching the mayor's face carefully. "How she agreed to help clear your family's name in exchange for something she wanted."

The mayor moved to her desk, gripping the back of her chair as if for support. "Where did you find this?"

"That's not important," Julie said. "What matters is that I know the truth. You're planning to 'discover' the collection today, aren't you? To control the narrative about your family's involvement."

For a long moment, Mayor Johnson was silent, clearly calculating her options. Then, surprisingly, she laughed—a short, bitter sound.

"You have it backward," she said finally. "My family didn't steal the collection. The Wilkins family hid it themselves."

Julie blinked, genuinely caught off guard. "What?"

"It was a publicity stunt gone wrong," the mayor explained, sinking into her chair. "Harrison Wilkins staged the theft to draw attention to the historical society when funding was being cut. He planned to 'find' the items a few months later and be hailed as a hero. But then he had a heart attack and died before he could complete the plan. The collection remained hidden, and without him to defend himself, suspicion fell on my grandmother, who was his political rival."

"So Victoria discovered this truth?" Julie asked, uncertain whether to believe this new version of events.

"Victoria found evidence, yes. Letters between Harrison and his son, planning the fake theft." The mayor's expression hardened. "She threatened to expose the complete story—which would clear my family but would also reveal that the Wilkins family had perpetrated a fraud that shaped town politics for generations."

"So you made a deal," Julie prompted.

"Yes. Victoria agreed to back off her demands about historical preservation of the Wilkins Building, allowing her development to proceed as planned. In exchange, I would quietly recover the collection and arrange for its public display, framing it as having been 'recently discovered' during renovations."

"And the Johnson family would be exonerated without explicitly accusing the Wilkins family of deception," Julie concluded.

"Exactly." The mayor studied Julie. "I met with Victoria the night she died to finalize the arrangements. She had located the hidden room in the Wilkins Building and confirmed the collection was there. We agreed I would handle the recovery discreetly."

"But you didn't kill her," Julie said, not a question.

"Of course not." The mayor looked genuinely affronted. "I left her alive and well at the cabin. Whatever happened afterward had nothing to do with me."

Julie absorbed this information, which aligned with what they now knew about Derek's accidental role in Victoria's death. But something still didn't add up.

"If the collection was just a historical curiosity," she said slowly, "why was Victoria so interested in it? It couldn't have just been leverage for her development project."

A flicker of uncertainty crossed the mayor's face. "She seemed particularly focused on certain items—textiles, primarily. She mentioned something about patterns containing historical significance, but I assumed she was just justifying her interest."

"The sampler," Julie murmured.

"Yes, that was one item she specifically mentioned. An old family sampler with an unusual design." The mayor frowned. "How did you know about that?"

Before Julie could respond, the office door opened. Both women turned, expecting to see Thomas Drake or perhaps Sheriff Harris.

Instead, Edward Thompson stood in the doorway, smiling pleasantly. "Ladies," he said, closing the door behind him. "I hope I'm not interrupting an important conversation."

"Professor Thompson," the mayor said, rising. "This is a private meeting."

"I'm afraid I must insist on joining you," Thompson replied, his pleasant demeanor unchanged as he reached into his jacket and withdrew a small handgun. "Especially since you're discussing items of great interest to me."

Julie felt her heart racing but kept her expression neutral, acutely aware of the recording device pinned to her sweater. "Thompson," she acknowledged. "Or should I call you Richard Ellison?"

Thompson's smile faltered slightly. "You've been doing your homework, Ms. Morgan. Impressive, though ultimately futile." He gestured with the gun. "Please, both of you, sit down. We have a few minutes before the mayor is expected at the podium, and I have some questions that require honest answers."

Mayor Johnson had gone rigid at the sight of the weapon. "What is the meaning of this?"

"It's quite simple," Thompson replied. "I've come for the Meadowgrove Collection—specifically, certain items within it that have value far beyond their historical significance to this charming little town."

"The sampler," Julie said. "And the map to the gold shipment it supposedly contains."

Thompson's eyes widened fractionally—the first genuine reaction she'd seen from him. "My, my. You really have been thorough." He turned to the mayor. "And where exactly is the collection now? Still in the hidden room at the Wilkins Building?"

"No," Mayor Johnson replied, her voice steady despite her obvious fear. "I had it moved after discovering it, as planned."

"Where?" Thompson demanded, his pleasant façade slipping further.

The mayor hesitated, and Thompson stepped closer, the gun now pointed directly at her. "This isn't a negotiation, Mayor Johnson. Where are the artifacts?"

"In the town hall vault," she answered finally. "Downstairs. I was going to reveal them after the press conference, claiming they were discovered during renovation work."

"How convenient," Thompson said. "We're already in the building. You're going to take me there now."

"The vault requires multiple keys and a code," the mayor protested. "I don't have everything we need."

"But you have your key and know the code," Thompson countered. "And I suspect the second key is not far away—perhaps with your campaign manager? We'll collect him on our way."

He turned to Julie. "You'll be joining us, Ms. Morgan. Your knowledge about the sampler makes you temporarily valuable."

"And after that?" Julie asked, though she already knew the answer.

Thompson merely smiled. "Let's focus on the present, shall we? Now, both of you, move toward the door. Slowly."

As they complied, Julie tried to catch Mayor Johnson's eye, hoping to communicate silently that help was nearby. The recording device was transmitting everything to Sheriff Harris and his deputies. They would be mobilizing, preparing to intervene.

"What about your partner?" Julie asked, trying to buy time as they moved into the hallway. "Isn't Derek supposed to be here for this part?"

Thompson's expression darkened. "Derek has outlived his usefulness. His grandmother's journals provided the initial information about the gold, but he lacks the necessary skills for this phase of the operation."

"So you used Victoria to gain access to Meadowgrove and find the collection," Julie continued, "then eliminated her when she became difficult."

"I didn't eliminate anyone," Thompson replied sharply. "Victoria's death was an unfortunate accident—Derek's emotional outburst derailed my carefully laid plans. I merely adapted to the circumstances."

They had reached a staff area behind the main hall. Thompson directed them toward a door marked "Authorized Personnel Only."

"Mr. Drake should be backstage, preparing for the announcement," Mayor Johnson said, her voice tight.

"Excellent. Call him over, but choose your words carefully," Thompson instructed. "Any indication of trouble, and things will become unpleasant very quickly."

The mayor nodded stiffly, then raised her voice. "Thomas? Could you come here for a moment? I need your vault key."

Drake appeared from around a curtained area, looking harried. "Caroline, you're due on stage in less than five minutes. The press is—" He stopped short, noticing Thompson and the partially concealed gun. "What's happening?"

"Your key to the vault, please," Thompson said pleasantly. "No heroics, if you don't mind."

Drake looked to the mayor, who gave a small nod. Slowly, he reached into his pocket and produced a key on a chain around his neck.

"Very good," Thompson said. "Now, lead the way to the vault, Mayor Johnson. Mr. Drake, you'll be joining us."

As they descended a narrow staircase to the basement level, Julie's mind raced. Where were Sheriff Harris and his deputies? Surely they had heard enough to intervene by now. Unless something had gone wrong with the recording device, or Thompson had somehow circumvented their security measures.

The basement of town hall was cooler and dimly lit, with exposed pipes running along the ceiling and concrete walls painted institutional beige. Mayor Johnson led them down a long corridor to a heavy metal door at the end.

"The town vault," she explained unnecessarily. "It was installed in the 1950s for document storage and town valuables."

"Open it," Thompson ordered.

With visible reluctance, Mayor Johnson inserted her key into one lock while Drake did the same with a second lock positioned below the first. Then she entered a code on a keypad mounted beside the door. There was a series of mechanical clicks, and the door swung open.

The vault itself was surprisingly spacious—perhaps fifteen feet square, with metal shelving along three walls. Most shelves held boxes of documents and ledgers, but on a table in the center of the room sat several custom-made display cases, their glass tops revealing the contents within.

"The Meadowgrove Collection," Mayor Johnson said quietly. "Recovered after fifty-eight years."

Thompson smiled, genuine pleasure lighting his face as he approached the display cases. "At last."

Julie followed cautiously, taking in the collection for the first time. There were aged documents in protective sleeves, antique jewelry, small carved figurines, and—prominently displayed in the central case—textiles. A lace collar yellowed with age, embroidered handkerchiefs, and what must be the famous sampler: a rectangular piece of linen with an intricate pattern of stitches forming what appeared to be a landscape scene.

"Beautiful work," Thompson murmured, studying the sampler. "And completely overlooked by most who saw it throughout the years. Few would recognize that this pastoral scene is actually a coded map."

"A map to what?" Drake asked, clearly confused by the situation.

"To approximately four million dollars in gold coins," Thompson replied matter-of-factly. "A Union Army payroll shipment that never reached its destination during the Civil War."

"That's absurd," Drake scoffed. "If such a treasure existed, it would have been found decades ago."

"Not if its location was known only to the family that diverted it," Thompson countered. "The Wilkins family were respected textile manufacturers publicly, but they were also opportunists who saw a chance for wealth during the chaos of war."

He turned to Julie. "You've studied the Wilkins journal. You understand patterns. What do you see when you look at this sampler?"

Julie hesitated, then stepped closer to the display case. The sampler showed what appeared to be a typical country scene—rolling hills, trees, a river winding through the landscape, all rendered in different colored threads and stitch patterns. But as she examined it more carefully, certain elements stood out as unusual.

"The stitching along the river uses an uncommon pattern," she observed. "And these trees aren't decorative—they're markers. The variation in stitches indicates distance." She pointed to a small cluster of stitches that formed what looked like a rock formation. "And this isn't just landscape decoration. It's a specific location."

Thompson nodded approvingly. "Precisely. This sampler doesn't just represent the countryside around Meadowgrove—it's a map to a specific cave system where the gold was hidden."

"And you already have a buyer lined up," Julie guessed.

"Of course. A private collector who has been searching for this particular shipment for years," Thompson confirmed. "The sale is already arranged—all I need is the actual gold."

"Which you won't be getting," came a new voice from the vault entrance.

They all turned to see Sheriff Harris standing in the doorway, his weapon drawn and pointed steadily at Thompson. Behind him, two deputies were visible in the corridor.

"Sheriff," Thompson acknowledged calmly. "I was wondering when you'd make your entrance."

"Drop the gun, Thompson. Or Ellison, or whatever your real name is," Harris ordered. "It's over."

Thompson didn't move, his own weapon still trained on Mayor Johnson. "I think not. I still have three hostages and a clear shot. You won't risk their safety."

"Maybe not," Harris conceded. "But you're surrounded, with no way out. The smart play is to surrender now."

A tense silence fell over the vault as Thompson considered his options, his eyes darting between Harris, the hostages, and the sampler in the display case.

"You know," he said finally, "in my line of work, I've learned to always have a contingency plan." He reached slowly into his jacket pocket with his free hand—

"Don't move!" Harris barked.

"Relax, Sheriff. I'm not reaching for another weapon." Thompson withdrew what looked like a small remote control. "This is simply insurance. There are explosive devices planted throughout the town hall.

Nothing lethal—I'm not a murderer—but enough to cause significant structural damage and the perfect distraction."

Julie felt her blood run cold. "The diversion Derek mentioned."

Thompson smiled thinly. "Derek always did talk too much. But yes, this was meant to be a distraction during the press conference, allowing me to access the vault in the confusion. Now it might serve as my exit strategy."

"You're bluffing," Harris said, though Julie could hear the uncertainty in his voice.

"Am I?" Thompson replied. "Are you willing to risk it? To risk all the people gathered outside for the mayor's announcement?"

Julie watched Thompson carefully, noting the slight tremor in his hand holding the remote—the first sign of genuine stress she'd seen from him. Was he bluffing? Or was the town hall actually rigged with explosives?

Before anyone could decide, a commotion erupted in the hallway. There were sounds of struggle, then Derek appeared in the doorway beside Sheriff Harris, having apparently broken away from the deputies who were supposed to be guarding him.

"Thompson!" he shouted. "It's over! I've told them everything!"

Thompson's expression twisted with fury. "You fool!" He swung his gun toward Derek, and in that moment of distraction, Harris fired.

The shot echoed deafeningly in the confined space of the vault. Thompson staggered backward, the remote flying from his hand as he clutched his shoulder, blood spreading rapidly through his tweed jacket. His gun clattered to the floor.

Deputies rushed forward, securing Thompson and retrieving both the weapon and the remote. Harris approached cautiously, keeping his gun trained on Thompson until he was fully restrained.

"Get the bomb squad in here," he ordered one of the deputies. "We need to determine if his threat was real."

As the chaos subsided, Julie found herself shaking with delayed adrenaline. Mayor Johnson had sunk onto a small stool in the corner of the vault, her face ashen. Drake stood nearby, looking shell-shocked.

"Are you alright?" Harris asked Julie, holstering his weapon.

She nodded, unable to find words immediately. Then, looking at the sampler still displayed in its case, she said, "It was never about the collection itself. It was about what it could lead to."

"A Civil War gold shipment," Harris said, following her gaze. "Worth millions if it exists."

"It exists," Derek said firmly, now in handcuffs but seeming almost relieved. "My grandmother's journals were clear about that. The Wilkins family hid the gold during the war, intending to retrieve it when things settled down. But the family member who knew the exact location died unexpectedly, leaving only the coded sampler as a guide."

Harris studied the textile thoughtfully. "So all of this—Victoria's death, the threats against Julie, the attempted theft—it was all about a treasure that might be nothing more than family legend."

"Not legend," Thompson grunted through his pain as deputies prepared to move him. "I've seen proof. Documentation that confirms the shipment existed and was diverted. The gold is there, waiting. It's always been about the gold."

As Thompson was led away for medical attention before booking, Julie approached the display case again, looking more carefully at the sampler. It seemed so ordinary at first glance—just a piece of needlework created by someone long dead. Yet it had inspired greed, deception, and ultimately violence.

"What happens to the collection now?" she asked Mayor Johnson, who had finally recovered enough to stand.

"It belongs to the town," the mayor replied wearily. "That much hasn't changed. It will be displayed properly in the historical society, where it should have been all along."

"And the press conference?"

Mayor Johnson smoothed her jacket, straightening her shoulders with visible effort. "It will proceed, though with a different announcement than originally planned. The people deserve the truth—about the collection, about how it was hidden, and about how it was recovered."

"The whole truth?" Julie asked pointedly.

The mayor met her gaze steadily. "Yes, Ms. Morgan. The whole truth. It's time Meadowgrove's history was woven correctly, without the gaps and fabrications that have shaped it for too long."

As they made their way back upstairs, Julie found herself thinking about patterns—how they could conceal as well as reveal, how a single missing thread could change the entire design. The Meadowgrove mystery had been like an intricate knitting project, with each stitch building on the last, creating a complex whole that was difficult to discern until you stepped back and viewed it complete.

Now, finally, the pattern was clear. Not the one Thompson had sought in the sampler, but the pattern of truth that had been buried for generations—about the Wilkins family, about the collection, and about the secrets that had shaped their small town in ways no one had fully understood.

Outside, the crowd waited, unaware of the drama that had unfolded beneath them. As Sheriff Harris coordinated with the bomb squad to secure the building, Julie texted Eliza a brief update: "It's over. Thompson arrested. Everyone safe. Will explain everything soon."

The truth was finally emerging, stitch by stitch, into the light of day.

Chapter 20

The Final Row

The heavy vault door swung shut with a decisive clang, followed by the ominous sound of the locking mechanism engaging. Julie lunged forward too late, her fingertips brushing the cold metal as it sealed them inside.

"No!" Mayor Johnson cried, rushing to the door and futilely trying the handle. "Thompson, you can't do this!"

But Edward Thompson—or whatever his real name was—was already gone, taking with him the sampler and several other key artifacts from the collection. His parting words echoed in Julie's mind: "By the time anyone finds you, I'll be long gone with what I came for. Consider this a more merciful end than what I had planned."

Dr. Walker, who had followed Julie to the town hall out of concern after seeing her enter with the mayor, pounded on the metal door. "Help!" he shouted. "Can anyone hear us?"

Julie knew it was useless. The vault was designed to be soundproof and secure—that's why Thompson had chosen it as their prison. She looked around, assessing their situation. The room was approximately fifteen feet square, with metal shelving lining three walls. Most of the display cases that had held the Meadowgrove Collection were now empty, their glass tops left open after Thompson's hasty selection of items.

"How did this happen?" Mayor Johnson demanded, her composure cracking. "Where's Sheriff Harris? He was just here!"

"Thompson must have planned this," Julie said grimly. "The explosives he mentioned—they weren't meant as a diversion for stealing the artifacts. They were to distract the sheriff and his deputies while he dealt with us."

"But there weren't any explosions," Dr. Walker pointed out.

"Maybe the bomb squad found them in time," Julie suggested. "Or maybe there never were any explosives—just another lie to create confusion."

The mayor sank onto the small stool in the corner, her face ashen. "What does it matter now? We're trapped in here, and the vault is only opened twice daily for official business. No one will even think to look for us until tomorrow morning."

"That's not entirely true," Walker said, checking his watch. "I told Eliza I was following you to town hall. When I don't return to the clinic for my afternoon appointments, she'll raise the alarm."

Julie felt a flicker of hope. "And Sheriff Harris knows I was meeting with the mayor. When he doesn't find Thompson—"

"Thompson disabled my recording device," Julie interrupted, touching the brooch on her sweater. "He must have used some kind of signal jammer. That's why Harris didn't hear our conversation or come to stop Thompson from taking us to the vault."

A heavy silence fell as the implications sank in. They were effectively cut off, with no way to communicate with the outside world.

"How much air do we have?" Dr. Walker asked quietly, voicing the question they were all thinking.

"The vault isn't airtight," Mayor Johnson said, though she didn't sound entirely convinced. "There must be some ventilation."

"Even so, three people breathing in a confined space..." Walker didn't finish the sentence.

Julie refused to give in to panic. "Let's think this through. Thompson has the sampler and other artifacts. If we understand his plan correctly, he's heading for the location indicated in the pattern—the cave system where the Civil War gold is supposedly hidden."

"That's assuming the gold is real and not just a family legend," the mayor pointed out.

"Thompson believes it's real," Julie countered. "He's spent months orchestrating this con, manipulating Victoria, Derek, and all of us. He wouldn't go to such lengths on a mere possibility."

Dr. Walker nodded slowly. "You're right. And if he's heading for the caves, he'll need time to locate and extract the gold. That might buy us the hours we need for someone to realize we're missing."

"Unless he already has transportation arranged," the mayor said darkly. "A man this methodical wouldn't leave his escape to chance."

Julie began pacing the vault, studying every inch of the walls and ceiling. There had to be a way out, or at least a way to signal for help. As she moved along the shelving units, she noticed a small metal grate near the ceiling in the far corner—a ventilation duct, just as the mayor had suggested.

"There," she said, pointing. "That must provide air circulation."

Walker followed her gaze. "It's too small for any of us to fit through, even if we could reach it."

"But maybe we could use it to attract attention," Julie suggested. "If we could create enough noise..."

She climbed onto one of the sturdier shelving units, careful not to disturb the boxes of documents stored there, and examined the vent more closely. It was secured with four small screws, the metal aged and slightly rusted around the edges.

"I need something thin and sturdy," she said, searching her pockets. "Like a—"

"Like this?" Dr. Walker held up a metal letter opener he'd found on one of the shelves.

Julie smiled. "Perfect."

Using the letter opener as a makeshift screwdriver, she worked on the vent cover. The screws were stiff with age, but gradually began to turn. As she worked, she decided to keep the conversation going, partly to distract from their predicament and partly because she sensed there was more to the story than they yet understood.

"Mayor Johnson," she called down, "you said earlier that the Wilkins family staged the theft of the collection as a publicity stunt. But Thompson seemed to believe the collection was legitimately connected to the Civil War gold shipment. Which version is true?"

The mayor sighed heavily. "I don't know anymore. The letter I found from Harrison Wilkins mentioned the publicity stunt, but it also referenced 'protecting the family legacy.' I assumed he meant the family's reputation, but perhaps he was referring to the gold."

"And Victoria?" Julie prompted, working on the third screw now. "How did she get involved?"

"She approached me shortly after arriving in town," the mayor explained. "Said she was researching her family history—her grandmother had been a Wilkins before marriage—and had found references to the missing collection. She presented herself as wanting to clear up the historical record."

"But her real interest was the gold," Walker interjected.

"Apparently so," the mayor agreed. "Though I'm not sure she knew about it initially. In our early meetings, she seemed genuinely interested in town history and development. It was only later that she became fixated on specific items from the collection—the textiles, especially."

"After Thompson joined her operation," Julie suggested, working on the final screw. "He must have recognized the potential value of the sampler once he saw her research."

The last screw came loose, and Julie carefully removed the vent cover. Cool air flowed from the opening, bringing immediate relief to the stuffiness of the vault. She peered into the duct, which extended farther than her vision could penetrate in the dimness.

"I can't see where it leads," she reported, "but it's definitely connected to the building's ventilation system."

"Can you make any noise that might be heard outside?" Walker asked.

Julie reached into the duct, tapping the metal sides with the letter opener. The sound echoed faintly, but she doubted it would carry far enough to attract attention.

As she contemplated their next move, Dr. Walker cleared his throat uncomfortably. "There's something I need to tell you both," he said. "About Victoria Winters and what really happened the night she died."

Julie paused, turning to look down at him. "What do you mean?"

Walker's expression was pained. "I wasn't entirely truthful before. I did treat Thompson—or Ellison—years ago in Boston, that part was true.

But I recognized him immediately when he arrived in Meadowgrove, and I should have said something."

"Why didn't you?" the mayor asked.

"Because he approached me first," Walker admitted. "He knew I had recognized him and threatened to expose my financial irregularities—the very ones Victoria was using to blackmail me. He said he only wanted information about Victoria's movements, that he was working with her on a business deal."

"And you believed him?" Julie couldn't keep the disbelief from her voice.

"I wanted to," Walker said miserably. "It was easier than facing the truth. But then Victoria died, and I suspected Thompson was involved somehow. I began watching him, gathering what evidence I could without putting myself at risk."

"Wait," Julie said, a new realization dawning. "If Thompson killed Victoria, not Derek..."

"Then everything we thought we knew is wrong," the mayor finished.

Walker nodded grimly. "The night Victoria died, I saw Thompson leaving her cabin. It was late—after midnight. I was driving home from a house call and took the back road past her property. His car was parked off the main drive, partially hidden by trees."

"And you didn't report this to Sheriff Harris?" the mayor demanded.

"I was a coward," Walker admitted. "Thompson had already threatened me once. And without proof that he had done anything wrong, it would have been my word against his. By the time Victoria's body was discovered the next day, I had convinced myself I might have been mistaken about what I saw."

Julie climbed down from the shelving unit, needing to face Walker directly. "So Derek didn't kill Victoria in an argument? Thompson staged that video?"

"I believe so," Walker confirmed. "When I heard Derek had been apprehended and confessed to accidentally causing Victoria's death, I was conflicted. It seemed plausible, but it didn't match what I'd seen."

"So Thompson killed Victoria deliberately," Julie said, the pieces finally falling into place. "But why? What changed in their partnership?"

"I overheard them arguing at the Harvest Festival," Walker said. "Victoria had discovered Thompson's true identity and his plans to steal rather than study the artifacts. She threatened to expose him to the authorities."

"So he silenced her," the mayor said quietly. "And then manipulated events to keep suspicion circulating among the rest of us."

"Including planting evidence to frame me," Julie added, remembering the murder weapon wrapped in her distinctive knitting work. "But how did he get something I made?"

Walker looked increasingly uncomfortable. "He asked me which local shops sold handmade items. I directed him to The Yarn Haven, not realizing his intentions."

Julie felt a chill that had nothing to do with the vault's temperature. Thompson had been playing them all from the beginning, several steps ahead at every turn.

"We need to get out of here," she said with renewed urgency. "Thompson is getting away with murder and theft."

She returned to the ventilation duct, this time with a new idea. The duct was old, likely part of the building's original construction, which meant it probably connected to a central system that serviced multiple rooms.

"I need something long and flexible," she said, searching around the vault. "Like a—"

Her eyes fell on her purse, which Thompson had allowed her to keep when he locked them in. Inside was a set of bamboo knitting needles she always carried for moments of inspiration or to pass the time.

"Perfect," she murmured, retrieving the longest needle from the set. It was about fourteen inches in length, slender but sturdy.

"What are you doing?" Walker asked as she climbed back up to the vent.

"Testing a theory," Julie replied, inserting the knitting needle into the duct and using it to probe the passageway. After about a foot, she felt resistance—likely a junction or turn in the system.

Carefully maneuvering the needle, she found she could push it around the bend. There was a distant rattling sound, then a faint echoing clang.

"I think this duct connects to another room," she reported. "If I can make enough noise, someone might hear it."

She began using the needle to tap rhythmically against the metal duct, creating a morse-code-like pattern that would stand out from normal building sounds.

Meanwhile, outside the town hall, Marilyn and Nelly had grown concerned when Julie failed to meet them as planned after her conversation with the mayor. They stood on the steps of the building, watching the remnants of the festival crowd disperse after the mayor's non-appearance had been announced due to "an unexpected development."

"Something's wrong," Nelly said firmly. "Julie wouldn't just disappear, especially not after everything that's happened."

"Sheriff Harris said she was helping with the investigation," Marilyn reminded her. "Maybe they're still questioning Thompson."

"Then where is the sheriff? Or his deputies?" Nelly gestured to the noticeable absence of law enforcement around the building. "No, something's not right."

Tessa, Julie's dog who had been staying with Nelly during the investigation, suddenly perked up her ears, sniffing the air intently.

"What is it, girl?" Nelly asked, recognizing the change in the dog's demeanor.

Tessa tugged at her leash, pulling Nelly toward a side entrance of the town hall. The women followed, exchanging worried glances.

"She's picked up Julie's scent," Marilyn realized as the dog led them to a service door that was slightly ajar.

They entered cautiously, finding themselves in a deserted corridor. Most of the town hall staff had left following the cancellation of the press conference. Tessa continued to pull them forward, her nose working overtime, leading them deeper into the building and eventually toward a staircase heading down.

"The basement?" Marilyn whispered. "Why would Julie be down there?"

Before they could speculate further, they heard footsteps coming up the stairs. They ducked into an alcove, Nelly quickly hushing Tessa with a practiced hand on her muzzle.

A moment later, Edward Thompson emerged from the stairwell, carrying a cloth-wrapped bundle that could only be the artifacts from the collection. He moved quickly, glancing around furtively before heading toward the exit.

Nelly waited until he was just past their hiding place, then stepped out. "Going somewhere, Professor?" she asked, her voice steely.

Thompson spun around, his composure momentarily shattered. "What are you—how did you—"

"Julie's dog has quite the nose for trouble," Nelly explained, keeping Tessa firmly by her side. "And you, sir, reek of it."

Thompson's hand moved toward his jacket, but Marilyn had already pulled out her phone. "I wouldn't," she advised. "I've already texted Sheriff Harris. He's on his way."

It was a bluff, but a convincing one. Thompson hesitated, clearly calculating his options.

"Ladies," he said, trying to regain his smooth demeanor, "I think there's been a misunderstanding. I'm simply moving these artifacts to a secure location at the mayor's request."

"Is that why you're sneaking out the back way?" Nelly challenged. "Is that why Julie and the mayor aren't with you?"

A flicker of something dangerous crossed Thompson's face. "I suggest you step aside. You don't understand what you're interfering with."

"On the contrary," came Sheriff Harris's voice from behind him. "I think they understand perfectly."

Thompson turned to find himself facing Harris and two deputies, all with weapons drawn. His shoulders slumped in defeat.

"Where are they?" Harris demanded. "Where's Julie Morgan and Mayor Johnson?"

Thompson's expression turned calculating. "Perhaps we can make a deal, Sheriff. Their location in exchange for leniency."

"Not how this works," Harris said coldly. "Deputies, search him."

As they secured Thompson and retrieved the stolen artifacts, Nelly turned to Tessa. "Find Julie, girl. Find her."

The dog immediately resumed her tracking, leading them back down the staircase and into the basement corridor where she stopped outside the vault door, whining and pawing at the metal.

"They're in there," Marilyn realized with horror. "He locked them in the vault!"

Harris immediately began examining the door. "We need the keys and the combination," he said. "And we need them fast."

Inside the vault, Julie had continued her rhythmic tapping, refusing to give up hope. Dr. Walker had joined her efforts, using a metal paperweight to create deeper, resonating sounds against the vault door itself. Mayor Johnson, meanwhile, was methodically searching through the remaining documents and items for anything that might help their situation.

"Wait," Julie said suddenly, pausing in her tapping. "Did you hear that?"

They all went still, listening intently. At first, there was nothing, then—faintly—the sound of a dog barking.

"Tessa!" Julie exclaimed. "That's my dog!"

New energy surged through them as they began making as much noise as possible—banging on the door, shouting, anything to signal their presence.

Minutes later, they heard the unmistakable sound of the vault mechanism being activated. The door swung open to reveal Sheriff Harris, with Nelly, Marilyn, and a very excited Tessa pushing past him to rush into the room.

"Thank God," Harris said, holstering his weapon. "Thompson refused to give us the combination. We had to call in the previous town treasurer to help override the system."

Julie knelt to embrace Tessa, who was beside herself with joy at finding her person. "How did you know where to look?" she asked Nelly.

"Tessa deserves all the credit," Nelly replied, patting the dog's head. "She tracked your scent right to this door."

"And Thompson?" Dr. Walker asked.

"In custody," Harris confirmed. "Along with the artifacts he was attempting to steal. He won't be going anywhere except prison for a very long time."

As they made their way back upstairs, Julie explained Dr. Walker's revelation about seeing Thompson leaving Victoria's cabin the night of her murder.

"So Derek didn't kill her," Harris mused. "Thompson staged that video to frame him, just as he tried to frame you with the planted evidence."

"And Derek?" Julie asked. "Where is he now?"

"Still in custody, but his story will need to be reevaluated in light of this new information," Harris said. "If Thompson truly murdered

Victoria, Derek's only crime may be obstruction of justice by not coming forward sooner."

Outside the town hall, a small crowd had gathered, word having spread about the dramatic arrest. Mayor Johnson, composing herself admirably after their ordeal, addressed the waiting reporters with a promise of a full statement the following day.

"The Meadowgrove Collection has been recovered," she announced. "And the truth about its disappearance will finally be told—the complete truth, without political spin or historical revision."

In the days that followed, the full story emerged piece by piece. Forensic evidence confirmed that Victoria Winters had been murdered—struck from behind with a blunt object before being pushed down the stairs. The weapon, recovered from Julie's building's trash chute, had Thompson's fingerprints beneath the distinctive knitted cloth he'd used to wrap it.

Derek's grandmother's journals proved to be genuine, containing fragmented family stories about the Civil War gold shipment. But when authorities searched the cave system indicated by the sampler's pattern, they found only a small cache of coins—a sample of the shipment rather than the full treasure Thompson had anticipated.

Most surprising of all was the revelation about the original theft of the Meadowgrove Collection. Neither the Johnson nor the Wilkins family had been responsible. Historical records discovered in the town hall archives revealed that the collection had been temporarily hidden by a caretaker during a fire at the historical society building in 1965. The caretaker had died of a heart attack before he could reveal the collection's location, and in the political climate of the time, suspicion had fallen on both prominent families.

One week after the events at town hall, Julie reopened The Yarn Haven with a small celebration for friends and customers. The shop had been closed during the investigation but was now bustling with activity. Colorful bunting decorated the windows, and a table of refreshments welcomed visitors.

Eliza managed the register while Julie circulated, accepting congratulations and fielding questions about her role in solving the mystery. Nelly and Marilyn had become local celebrities in their own right, their quick thinking having prevented Thompson's escape.

"Quite a turn of events," Dr. Walker remarked, approaching Julie with two glasses of sparkling cider. He had been cleared of any wrongdoing in the case, his testimony against Thompson deemed valuable enough to outweigh his initial silence.

"That's one way of putting it," Julie replied, accepting the glass. "Though I could have done without the near-death experience in the vault."

"Your quick thinking with that knitting needle saved us," Walker said. "Resourceful in a crisis—yet another quality to admire about you."

Julie felt herself blushing slightly. "Knitters are problem-solvers by nature. We see patterns where others might not, find solutions in unexpected places."

"Speaking of unexpected," Walker said, his tone shifting to something more personal, "I was wondering if you might consider having dinner with me sometime. Now that there are no more mysteries or secrets between us."

Julie studied him thoughtfully. A week ago, she would have hesitated, still wary after all the deception she'd encountered. But the experience had also taught her something about trust and second chances.

"I'd like that," she said finally. "Though I should warn you—I might knit through dessert. I have a lot of projects to catch up on."

Walker laughed, a genuine sound that reached his eyes. "I'd expect nothing less."

Across the shop, Mayor Johnson entered, causing a momentary hush in conversations. She made her way directly to Julie, extending her hand.

"Ms. Morgan," she said formally. "I wanted to thank you personally for your role in uncovering the truth. And to apologize for any suspicion I might have harbored toward you."

"Thank you, Mayor," Julie replied, shaking her hand. "I think we all learned something about appearances versus reality these past few weeks."

The mayor nodded. "Indeed. The town council has voted unanimously to establish a permanent home for the Meadowgrove Collection at the historical society, with a special section dedicated to setting the record straight about its disappearance and recovery."

"That seems appropriate," Julie said. "History should be remembered accurately, even when it's uncomfortable."

Crochet Carnage

As the mayor moved on to greet other townspeople, Julie found herself at the center of her small circle of friends. Eliza had closed the register temporarily to join them, bringing Nelly and Marilyn along.

"To Julie," Eliza proposed, raising her glass. "Who noticed the pattern when the rest of us only saw threads."

"To friendship," Julie countered, including them all in her toast. "Without which I'd still be locked in that vault—or worse."

As the celebration continued around her, Julie looked around her beloved shop, at the colorful skeins of yarn arranged by shade and weight, at the samples of finished projects displaying various techniques, at the friends and neighbors who had come together to support her through the darkest days.

Meadowgrove had its share of secrets and shadows, as all communities did. But it also had strength in its connections—the invisible threads that bound one person to another, creating a fabric strong enough to withstand even the most determined efforts to tear it apart.

Tessa lay contentedly at Julie's feet, occasionally accepting gentle pats from passing customers. On a nearby shelf, Julie's latest design was displayed—a shawl inspired by the events of the past weeks, with a pattern that began in chaos but gradually resolved into harmony, each stitch building on the last to create something beautiful and enduring.

Like the town itself, Julie thought, the true pattern only became clear when you stepped back far enough to see the whole. And she was grateful, despite everything, to be woven into its design.

Patti Petrone Miller

Crochet Patterns from the Book:

1. "Harvest Festival Shawl" Pattern
(Inspired by Julie's own autumn design project)
Skill Level: Intermediate
Materials:

- DK weight merino wool in autumn shades (amber, gold, russet)
- Size G/6 (4.0 mm) crochet hook
- Yarn needle for weaving ends

Instructions:
Chain 5, slip stitch into first chain to form a ring.
Round 1: Chain 3 (counts as dc), 2 dc into the ring, *chain 2, 3 dc into ring*, repeat 3 times, slip stitch into top of chain-3.
Round 2: Slip stitch to next chain-2 space, chain 3, 2 dc into chain-2 space, chain 2, 3 dc into same space (corner made), *chain 1, 3 dc, chain 2, 3 dc into next chain-2 space*, repeat around, join.
Continue increasing in this granny-square style, always working (3 dc, ch 2, 3 dc) into each corner and 3 dc clusters between corners.
After 40 rows or when shawl reaches desired size, add a simple picot edge: *sc in next stitch, chain 3, slip stitch into first chain, sc in next 2 stitches*, repeat around.
Weave in ends and block lightly to shape.

2. "Tessa's Cozy Dog Blanket" Pattern

(Inspired by Tessa the dachshund and her cozy shop bed)

Skill Level: Easy
Materials:

- Bulky weight yarn (soft wool blend recommended)
- Size L/11 (8.0 mm) crochet hook
- Yarn needle

Instructions:
Chain 51 (or width desired for small dog blanket).
Row 1: Single crochet (sc) in second chain from hook and across. (50 stitches)
Row 2: Chain 1, turn. *Sc in first stitch, dc in next stitch,* repeat across.
Row 3: Chain 1, turn. *Dc in first stitch, sc in next stitch,* repeat across.
Repeat Rows 2 and 3 until the piece measures about 24 inches or the desired length.
Fasten off and weave in ends.
Optional: Add a simple crab stitch (reverse single crochet) edging around the blanket for a finished look.

3. "Hildi's Window Seat Mat" Pattern

(Inspired by Hildi the cat's sunny perch in Yarn Haven)

Skill Level: Easy to Intermediate
Materials:

- Worsted weight cotton yarn (durable and washable)
- Size H/8 (5.0 mm) crochet hook
- Yarn needle

Instructions:
Chain 40 (adjust for window seat size).
Row 1: Half double crochet (hdc) in second chain from hook and across.
Row 2: Chain 2 (counts as first hdc), turn, hdc in each stitch across.
Repeat Row 2 until mat measures about 16 inches or desired depth.
Border: Single crochet evenly around entire piece, working 3 sc into each corner.
Optional: For extra squish, crochet a second identical panel and slip-stitch them together, stuffing lightly with batting before closing completely.

4. "Meadowgrove Market Bag" Pattern
(Inspired by the local small-town shopping trips and Julie's love of handmade goods)

Skill Level: Intermediate
Materials:

- Worsted weight sturdy cotton yarn
- Size I/9 (5.5 mm) crochet hook
- Yarn needle

Instructions:
Chain 50, slip stitch to form a ring (being careful not to twist).
Round 1: Chain 1, sc in each chain around, slip stitch to join.
Round 2: Chain 4 (counts as dc + ch 1), *skip next stitch, dc in next stitch, chain 1*, repeat around, join.
Round 3: Slip stitch into next chain space, chain 4 (dc + ch 1), dc in next chain space, chain 1, repeat around.
Continue in mesh pattern for 18 inches.
Next Round: Chain 1, sc in each dc and chain space around to tighten the top, join.
Straps: Chain 60, skip 10 stitches, sc into next stitch to form a handle.

Repeat on opposite side.

Single crochet around entire bag including straps for 2 rounds.

Fasten off and weave in ends.

About The Author

Meet Patti, the creative force behind "Where the Magic Happens." More than just an author, Patti brings stories to life as the Executive Producer of an animated TV series based on her heartwarming tale "ELLIOT FINDS A HOME"—the story of a special dog with thumbs and his silent friend who prove that sometimes, actions speak louder than words.

Patti's writing journey has been nothing short of remarkable. A cherished author at Polygon Entertainment, she's danced her way onto the USA TODAY bestseller list and claimed Amazon's #1 spot multiple times. With 7 dozen books spanning from Urban Fantasy to Horror, Patti weaves tales that transport readers to worlds limited only by imagination.

Her life reads like an adventure novel filled with fascinating chapters:

At just 4 years old, she charmed audiences on "Romper Room" She shared memorable moments with Captain Kangaroo and Mr. Green Jeans She once enjoyed a train ride and sandwich with Sidney Poitier She high-fived President Nixon during a circus visit She attended school alongside magician David Copperfield She roller-skated with John Travolta before his rise to fame She warmed her hands and heart sharing cocoa with Abe Vigoda

When she's not crafting bestsellers, Patti embraces life as a teacher, grandmother, and devoted pet parent. Known affectionately as the "Queen of Halloween," this Wiccan High Priestess infuses her spooky stories with authentic magic that keeps readers spellbound.

Patti's books fly off shelves as quickly as they're stocked, so follow her social media to stay connected with this one-of-a-kind storyteller whose magical worlds welcome all who dare to dream.

www.ingramcontent.com/pod-product-compliance
Lightning Source LLC
LaVergne TN
LVHW041659060526
838201LV00043B/493